The Twisted Way

This book is dedicated to my husband Michael, with love and thanks for his encouragement and support.

The Twisted Way

Jean Hill

First published in the United Kingdom in 2009
by Lower Moor Books

The characters and events in this book are fictitious.
Any similarity to real persons living or dead is coincidental and
not intended by the author

ISBN 978-0-9563419-0-7

Produced by
The Choir Press
www.thechoirpress.co.uk

Contents

Chapter 1	London 1940	3
Chapter 2	The Evacuee	17
Chapter 3	First Wedding 1945	24
Chapter 4	John Lacey	42
Chapter 5	The letter 1952	61
Chapter 6	Felicity Brown	68
Chapter 7	The Return of the Evacuee 1995	85
Chapter 8	Primrose House 2004	98
Chapter 9	The Visitor	115
Chapter 10	The Will	128
Chapter 11	Peter Mace 2004	138
Chapter 12	Doctor Alistair Anderson	152
Chapter 13	The Tea Party	164
Chapter 14	Christmas Eve 2004	171
Chapter 15	An Accident March 2005	180
Chapter 16	Enderly Bridge Club	190
Chapter 17	New Friends and a Search	205
Chapter 18	Ronald Brown	216
Chapter 19	A Bridge Evening	221

Chapter 20   Ronald's Second Visit   227
Chapter 21   A Change of Heart   235
Chapter 22   Reconciliations and a Second Wedding 244
Chapter 23   Rosalie   253
Chapter 24   Two Funerals   257
Chapter 25   The Will Reading   263
Chapter 26   The Guest   273
Chapter 27   Settling In   284
Chapter 28   June 2008   294

List of Characters   307

The Twisted Way

The next time Peter visited Primrose House he clambered up the short metal staircase which led to the kitchen from the garden. He sometimes entered the house that way when he thought that Joyce Skillet would be there to let him in, though quite often the door was left unlocked if he was expected. Struggling with the icy conditions he clutched and held on, as well as he was able with bent old hands, to the slippery worn iron handrail in an effort to stop himself from falling, but his arthritic feet and legs were not helpful. On reaching the top he paused for a moment to catch his breath. The door swung open and, to his surprise, an arm shot out and hit him violently in the chest. Losing his grip on the rail he slid backwards. His legs buckled painfully beneath him as he plummeted downwards and landed with a sickening thud that resounded on the frozen earth. Peter struggled to open his eyes and saw someone holding a large stone above his head. He tried to cry out but could make no sound. Something akin to an electric crackle trickled across his brain accompanied by a bizarre and remote feeling of helplessness. Within seconds there was darkness.

Chapter 1

London 1940

Tom Hands quivered with fear and covered his ears in an attempt to shut out the sound of the air-raid siren and penetrating whine from a plane's engine. He was just five years old, and intelligent enough to understand that the home he had known for the whole of his short life was under threat but unaware of the full extent of the danger and the fact that he would soon be thrust into a strange and bewildering future.

'C'mon boy, get a move on, we 'ave to go down to the shelter.' His mother Ruth's voice was high and shrill with anxiety as she tried to prod him into action. 'Those bloomin' benches in the shelter may be 'ard but it's safer there than our beds, wors' luck. Our thick blankets will keep us warm, ducks. Come on luv!' Her voice softened. 'I've got a flask of nice warm tea and some of your favourite biscuits.'

Tom stood rigid and afraid. His muscles felt frozen and moving seemed almost impossible. The last thing he wanted was a mug of tea and sugary biscuits. His stomach churned with rebellion and his hands felt clammy.

His young mother placed her slim arms gently around his shoulders as she urged him forward. 'Down the steps with yer me lad. Grab the torch, luv, 'urry ...' urry ...' He clung to her to gain some comfort and to steady his thin reluctant legs as she dragged him along with her.

Tom's nervousness had intensified as the London Blitz continued night after night without a break. The final months of 1940 developed into a nightmare for both mother and child and this night was as miserable as any they had experienced before. Tom, although not fully aware of the full force of the peril that encircled them, would ask with peevish and bewildered repetition: 'Why, Mum? Why? Wot they doing it for?'

She could not provide any rational reply and tried to comfort him as best she could.

'Don't fret, luv,' she whispered in her distinct soft cockney voice. 'If you can hear those bombs whistlin' down they ain't going to land on you and if you don't hear 'em well ...' We'll not know anything about it anyway, she thought. 'Keep yer pecker up, ducks.' This piece of advice failed to reassure him.

'C-can hear that one, Mum,' he stammered; his legs threatened to fold beneath him and his bottom lip quivered.

'Don't worry my pet, the searchlights will show our gunners where the enemy planes are. You go to sleep now.'

'All clear, Mum,' the boy piped up in his thin childish voice as soon as the unwavering raucous note of the siren blared forth to signal the end of the raid. He had been curled up as usual on one of the thin hard benches with eyes squeezed shut, feigning sleep for what seemed an eternity, but it was only an hour before he heard that shrill continuous sound. He had placed his hands together under his blanket in the way he had been taught by his mother. Please God come on and help us will yer, passed continuously through his mind until the all clear sounded, which was music to his ears.

'That was a short'un, fank goodness that's over,' he uttered and sighed with relief.

Mother and son heard the clanging bells of fire engines, ambulances and police cars rushing to aid injured people, many of whom needed urgent hospital treatment. To Tom the sounds were exciting because he had no understanding of the extent of the carnage.

'Where are they all going, Mum?'

There was no satisfactory reply and Ruth could only shrug and change the subject. The sight of dead and dying being dug from

4

the crumbling ruins of buildings became commonplace but she made a tenacious, almost desperate, effort to protect her son from seeing them. The bloomin' situation was bad enough without foisting memories like those upon the poor little devil, she thought. The smell of burning blowing across the backyard became too frequent for comfort and for her a stark reminder that their turn could be next. Up to now they had been lucky but luck was something in which she had almost no faith. Ruth had not had her fair share of luck during her short life.

Tom recognized the sounds of the different aeroplane engines. 'That's a German bomber, it's got three engines Mum, hear the mmm mmm mmm?' or 'That's an English night fighter,' he would inform her.

'Abs'lutely right,' his mother responded with exaggerated pride. She accepted that the boy was more knowledgeable than she was. She had not excelled in any way at school and accepted that she was not very clever but she believed Tom was exceptional. His teacher had described him as a 'gifted child'. He should go a long way, Ruth told herself, this ghastly war permitting. I'll keep me fingers crossed. But hopes for the rosy future of which she dreamed for her beloved child began to disintegrate. She could see no end to the misery and feared that quite soon they would die in agony in a pile of rubble.

On most evenings they trudged to the damp and unwelcoming Anderson shelter, a monstrosity that had been hastily built in their small backyard from thick grey sheets of ugly corrugated steel bolted together to make a curved roof, set several feet into the ground with one small door in the front. Ruth thought it was an intrusion that overpowered the small backyard but it did look sturdy though a direct hit would be a different matter. Tom loathed the shelter so sometimes, as a special treat, in spite of food shortages, his mother would produce some lemonade and a few sweets in addition to the biscuits and ubiquitous flask of tea. She continued to make light of the situation but the oppressive interior of the shelter frightened the child more than whistling bombs.

An insidious smell of damp and decay pervaded and Tom imagined he was a mouse caught in a trap. He longed to escape from the shelter's claustrophobic musty atmosphere.

'There are rats out there Mum,' he said after seeing one scuttling at the bottom of the backyard one afternoon. 'They are horrible things with dirty feet and greasy tails. Do you fink one could get in the shelter?'

'That's nonsense my pet. We're lucky, it's safe in there,' his mother reassured him whilst she stroked his soft baby-fine fair hair and settled him on his bench for the night. She would cover him with a bright striped woollen blanket that had been his from when he was a baby, a gesture of reassurance, defiance and determination on her part. The blanket had been her first attempt at knitting and displayed bands of garish colours – orange, green and blue, bumpy and uneven – because she had used odd leftover balls of wool given to her by friends and customers at work. An old doubled-up eiderdown filled with goose feathers served as a mattress. Its faded green shot-silk cover was worn and tattered but it was familiar and comfortable. Tom had seen it on his mother's bed and he had always liked it. 'It's pure silk,' she told him with inordinate pride, 'really posh, ducks. 'Twas given to me by a real lady. She used to buy choc'lates in the shop I once worked in.' Tom stroked it and wound the soft frayed edges around his fingers, deriving a vestige of pleasure from the familiar texture.

Ruth was a plucky individual but her fear for the safety of her young son verged upon panic as the nightly raids continued. Since her husband had been drafted into the army she felt an increasing feeling of abandonment. She had waved goodbye to him at the local railway station some months earlier, and the fact that most of her friends and neighbours were in the same position did not provide any comfort. She had lived in the old red brick terraced house following her marriage before the outbreak of war in 1939. The poorly furnished rooms had, until her husband's departure, echoed with laughter, good companionship and a shared pride in their small son. They had been happy. She thought that her Robert was a lovely fellow and this damned war and the wretched Nazis had ruined everything. It wasn't fair.

'Those Jerries won't knock our home down in a hurry. It's built to last,' she told Tom when they heard bombs whistling down around them. Although not religious, she prayed that their home would not be destroyed. The blast from bombs had shaken the walls a few times and blown out two windows which had now been boarded up, and the sound of bricks clattering down and breaking glass nearby was commonplace. A deep uneven crack developed in a wall at the back of the house, a long and invasive tendril that reached from just below an upstairs window to the ground floor. Tom poked small inquisitive fingers into it and surveyed the fine red dust with interest as it crumbled, clung to his hands and crept under his fingernails.

'Mum, I need the lav,' Tom's small voice would prompt her when they were in the shelter and a raid continued for a long time. As tension mounted his need to relieve himself would increase and sleep become elusive.

'Use the bucket, ducks ...' She pointed to the white enamelled bucket in which wet washing was once placed. It now served as an emergency toilet and was covered by a dirty chipped lid.

'I'll wait a bit Mum, I 'ate buckets. Smelly ol' things. That one 'as ruff edges and it's not private eiver,' was his usual reply which made Ruth sigh with frustration although she was sympathetic and felt the same repulsion.

Tom staggered out of the shelter as soon as he could to go to the cold and unwelcoming outside toilet, which was rough bricked and coated with peeling white paint, smelly and neglected, but anything was better than crouching in that Anderson shelter to relieve himself in a bucket. The pipes in the toilet were often frozen, in spite of his mother's stoical efforts to wrap them with old rags, but he was glad the bog, as they called it, was there. He knew the way without a torch, though there was one to hand if they had any batteries.

Their kitchen had a small range that needed regular coating with black lead polish that was applied with stubby brushes. His greatest pleasure was making toast on winter evenings when his mother would open the small door in the front of the range. Tom would sit on a small three-legged stool and hold an old brass toasting fork with a thick slice of bread speared upon it as close as he could manage to the red embers. A large Victorian coal scuttle housed lumps of shiny black coal and a bent iron fender served as his foot rest.

'Take care luv, don't get too close, you could burn yerself,' Ruth would caution him.

'Cors not, I ain't daft,' he would respond. 'Fink I'm silly?'

'There's not much butter with this 'ere rationing but there's some dripping from that scrap of a joint, a bit of salt on that should be good, I think,' his mother said and they savoured the companionship of eating together even if Tom did sometimes singe the toast. Charred edges did not worry them as a good scraping with a kitchen knife was all that was required to make the bread edible and that was part of the enjoyment.

Most days, when he was not in school, Tom would trundle round the rough grey concreted backyard on a rusty old second-hand scooter his mother had bought for the princely sum of three pence from a friend who was glad to get rid of it. With the shelter placed in the centre his route was now limited but he did not care. It was his road and in his imagination he was in a car speeding along. He forgot the horrors of war for a short time as he hooted and tooted or sang to himself.

'Concrete is better for kids to play on,' the landlord had pontificated on the day they that moved in, but did not admit that the maintenance for him would be simpler. Small borders of stiff London clay clung to the edges of the concrete yard. Tom's mother filled these with dahlias, stocks and marigolds in the summer but now that the Anderson shelter had been erected they were overshadowed. The roof of the shelter was covered with earth, ugly and bare, spurned even by weeds. Tom longed for a green lawn, soft and comfortable to play on, and he promised himself he would have one when he was grown up and he had a house of his own. He looked forward to that. Tom grazed his knees on the rough spiky concrete and had numerous pale pink scars as a result.

Robert had built a small rectangular concrete fish pond in a corner of one of the borders in which resided Tom's only pet, a fat shiny goldfish named Cecil, which was chosen with care in a local pet shop and carried home with pride in a jam jar. It was coveted by Tiger, a wily old tabby cat that lived next door, but the fish was a survivor, defying air raids, local cats and the chemicals from the concrete that could have killed him. His gold shiny scales would glint in the hazy sunshine, that is on the days when the rays managed to penetrate the London smog. The only tree, a common purple lilac, small and stunted, occupied a space next to the pond and Tiger would perch precariously on one of the lower branches and watch with feline patience for any activity, his green slanted eyes glittering with animosity and grey striped hunter's body poised for action. His long tail would twitch as he savoured the idea of a delicious fish treat.

'Wretched ol' cat, who does he think he is?' Tom would grumble. 'Clear off you rotten old moggy.' Tiger hissed and sometimes moved up a branch or two but refused to abandon his post. He could wait.

Tom dipped his fingers in the small pond to touch the fish but the swift and slippery body always eluded him. He had planted seeds in the soil that bordered the pond, tipping them out of small paper packets before covering them lovingly with stiff lumps of dark reddish brown London clay. A few of his favourites, tobacco plants and purple and pink stocks, did straggle, thin and weak, along the edge of the pond during the summer months. The conditions were miserable but they lifted bright heads towards the grey sky and basked in any sunshine that penetrated it. Smog from factory chimneys and coal fires was at its most troublesome during the winter months when a swirl of moisture-laden wind bamboozled its way through their clothes and crept with insidious determination into their bones.

'Mum,' Tom urged many times in a begging tone that petered into a whine, 'can my fish go into a bowl and come into the shelter with us? It can't be nice in that dark slimy ol' pond when a raid's on.'

'No ducks, 'e's better off where he is,' his mother retorted. 'No room for blessed fish bowls in that there shelter.'

After further months of heavy raids and whole nights spent in the Anderson shelter Tom emerged one morning to find the small pond littered with pieces of dark grey metal shrapnel. His beloved fish was floating on his back with eyes wide, glazed and lifeless.

'Wot a rotten war,' he cried out, fighting back his tears. 'When I'm grown up I'll be a soldier and fight. I'll pay those Germans back.'

His mother found it difficult to comment on his outburst. The only thing she longed for was peace, not retribution. She heaved a long sigh and subconsciously rubbed the small silver crucifix that hung on a slender chain round her slim neck. She was not a religious woman but wearing the cross gave her some comfort. Her mother had given it to her when she was about five years old. She couldn't remember much about her mother but she did recall her placing the crucifix around her neck, the cool silver links pressing against her skin, and the feel of her mother's soft face as she kissed her cheek. She recalled too looking into gentle deep-set hazel eyes, pools of mottled brown, just like her own. Ruth was orphaned when she was just six years old and until she was fourteen lived in a council care home where she suffered a strict routine, harsh words, tatty cast-off clothing and a complete lack of affection.

'Wot good will trying to pay 'em back do you son? Fink about it,' she said, knowing that he was too young to understand. She found the whole thing bewildering and a five-year-old, well, what hope did he have? She understood that bitterness would not solve the problems of the world or control the ambitions of wicked men. Man was evil enough without her encouraging her child to become antagonistic towards others; in any case revenge and violence only produced the same response.

Ruth's parents had died after contracting tuberculosis at a time when the disease claimed the lives of many young people. Pasteurised milk was not always available and it was often slopped with a ladle into a customer's own jug by a milkman with a lack of personal hygiene who used a horse and cart full of grubby churns. The father she had never got to know was the first to became infected, then her mother. There were no modern wonder drugs or sanatoriums in Switzerland for them. Ruth had been told that she was lucky to be healthy and strong. She did not think that living in a council care home constituted good luck but a natural wit and more intelligence than she gave herself credit for, together with strong memories of a kind mother, ensured that she emerged almost unscathed.

When Ruth left the care home she was just fourteen and shared a miserable one-bedroom flat above a fish and chip shop with another girl she had met in the home. The smell of fish and chips frying in the evening assailed their nostrils and clung to their hair but the rent was low and they were in no position to complain. Ruth felt that she had been lucky to get a poorly paid job in a nearby sweet shop so that she could afford to pay for her share of the food and rent. She served the rich and prosperous members of the local community with boxes of delicious chocolates; the taste of such delicacies she could only dream about. If she was lucky the manager would, when in a generous mood, which was not often, give her a few broken sweets or pieces of chocolate. She had accepted her lot then without resentment, indeed she had known no other way of life, but the wartime restrictions now imposed on her, just when things had seemed so much better, made her angry and frustrated with an almost unbearable depth of feeling.

She met Robert Hands when she was sixteen and they married a year later. Robert, also orphaned, had been luckier than Ruth. He had been brought up by a couple of aunts who adopted him when he was twelve and later apprenticed him to a local baker. Ruth hoped and prayed that Tom, who was born a year after they married and christened Robert Thomas, but called Tom to distinguish him from his father, would never suffer the loneliness and deprivation she had endured as a child. She did not want to leave him as her parents had left her, but that possibility was becoming too real for peace of mind and that terrified her.

The playing field that used to be behind their backyard, where the local boys had enjoyed their Saturday game of football, was now filled with ugly hastily erected factory buildings composed of plain grey concrete block walls and slate-coloured roofs, in order to make shell cases. The poor but proud housewives who had considered it necessary to scrub and whiten their front steps and keep their homes shipshape, no longer cared. There were bigger issues to consider.

A lorry arrived one morning with workmen who removed the ornamental black iron railings from the front of Tom's house.

'They're needed for the war effort,' was the vague explanation. 'They'll soon be melted down to make munitions.'

Uneven stumps of metal were left and with no railings to support it the yellow privet hedge fell forwards onto the crooked paving stones of the path in front of the house.

'What's going to happen to the railings?' Tom asked his mother.

'I'm not sure,' she said. 'They'll probably be made into guns. I'll 'ave to clip that damned hedge now,' she spat out irritably. 'What an 'orrible mess.'

Tom liked the idea that his railings would soon be turned into guns and hoped that they would used against those Jerries. Bang, he thought, another one dead!

At the end of their road there was a small park owned by the local council with lawns and neatly planted ornamental cherry trees whose branches became laden with pink and white blossom in the spring and harboured chirping fat brown sparrows. Tom thought the birds were beautiful. The park was a green oasis in the middle of the dirty dusty streets although a large grey barrage balloon was now positioned on a stretch of grass in the centre. A small tarmac area contained swings and a slide for the children, and beyond that, edging a busy road, several grim-looking factories had been built, their dirty tall chimneys puffing evil smells and smoke over the local neighbourhood, day and night. A sauce factory emitted strong interesting fruity smells that blew into nearby houses, depending on the direction of the wind, and another factory next to it housed printing machinery. Empty barrels that had once contained coloured inks were stacked outside and the hum from the presses could be heard several streets away. Behind the factories there were narrow roads containing small mean terraced houses, labelled 'slums' by Tom's mother, where the factory workers lived.

'They're a ruff ol' crowd, those factory workers,' she used to say in a loud voice before the war started and hurried past them, eyes lowered, as though they were not good enough to mix with her and Tom. 'Ragamuffins, huh, that's what they are. Keep clear of that lot, boy. I'm a housewife and proud to be one. Only the riff-raff work in dirty ol' factories. Scruffy beggars some of 'em are.' Now she was a factory worker herself, having been drafted to the local munitions factory by the local labour exchange, although she called herself a wartime worker. Tom was sure she was enjoying the company of her co-workers, despite her protestations.

'They're a nice crowd I work wiv,' she assured Tom. Tom was confused but thought it best if he did not comment and preferred to play with his tin soldiers.

Ruth had not realized how lonely she had become. It was easy to live in London and not know one's next-door neighbours. She chatted to a few of the other mothers at Tom's school gates but did not have many real friends in their immediate neighbourhood having been born and brought up in the East End. East Enders in her view were great people, salt of the earth, despite the slums. A number of them had been immigrants who could not do much to improve their living conditions during the nineteen thirties. The pearly king and queen embodied a culture of which Ruth was proud. 'It's part of our 'istory,' she never tired of telling Tom, who loved to hear stories about the pearly kings and queens.

'Are they related to King George VI?' he asked.

'Good enough to be,' his mother responded with pride.

'It must have taken a long time to stitch those ol' buttons on,' he said with avid interest. In his bedroom he had a tatty old picture, brown and curling at the edges, of a pearly king and queen and he never tired of looking at it.

Tom's primary school was designated to be evacuated to Russetshire which was assumed to be a safe area for the children and not a target for bombs.

'Tom,' his mother said, after much heartache and worry about whether she was doing the right thing, 'I'm gonna let you go away for a while, to the country, with your school. You'll be going to Russetshire, a country place where there's fields with sheep and cows. You're bound to love it ducks. You'll have your school friends to keep you company, a comfy bed to sleep in and no bloomin' air raids.' At least she hoped not. The shelter was not healthy and she prayed that he would find a billet where he was welcome and could sleep in safety, although nothing was certain. They could be invaded. That did not bear thinking about.

'Mum,' the boy protested, 'I want to be here wiv you.' This was home and he had never heard of Russetshire. What did he want with silly cows and sheep? He had seen pictures of them in a book and that was enough. 'I don't wanna go Mum,' he insisted and his young mother despaired.

Ruth wavered for a while but deep down she knew that to send her son to Russetshire was the right thing to do and Tom was evacuated to the small village of Enderly in Russetshire, a county in the south Midlands. The parting was tearful. The mothers waved a frantic goodbye at the local station. Ruth's hazel eyes looked sunken in their sockets where dark smudges had formed underneath them through lack of sleep. With her head covered in the drab cotton turban most of the factory workers had donned like a proud uniform, she looked much older than someone in her twenties. Tom looked a pathetic little boy; his spindly legs protruded from short grey flannel trousers and knee-high woollen grey socks with a blue stripe round the tops that wrinkled and formed several odd bracelets. The bizarre outfit was topped by a shabby navy-blue serge school coat with shiny worn lapels, purchased in a local second-hand shop. A grey school cap, which was two sizes too large, completed his outfit and the peak protruded half way down his forehead in a way that resembled a bird's beak. A gas mask in a cardboard box was slung across his shoulders and he clutched a small leather case containing a change of clothes, a few small toys and some sandwiches wrapped in crinkled greaseproof paper.

'I'll write, Mum', he said.

'I'll write too,' his mother replied, choked and uncertain. 'I'll send you some pocket money each week, sixpence if I can. Be careful how you spend it.'

'Sixpence Mum, cor ... that ain't 'arf good.' He would be rich. He cheered up.

Tom was learning to read; he was quite advanced for his age, a clever boy who could write his name and understood the meaning of many written words before he went to school, but his mother knew that a long letter from him would be out of the question. Most of the young teachers had joined the forces or were employed in some other war work so there were only retired and elderly teachers in the party to look after the children. It was a motley collection of human beings that left the small London suburb station that day in an old smoke-caked steam train commissioned for the purpose. The dingy black engine puffed into the station billowing a filthy cloud of smoke that swirled around the sad group on the platform as though to envelop them and protect them from what was to come.

'Goodbye,' Tom's mother said, in unison with the other parents, tears brimming in her eyes, as she watched the train crammed with children chug its way out of the station. Small hands, some clutching Union Jacks, were waved out of the windows which were closed by the carers as soon as possible to avoid accidents and to prevent eyes filling with smuts. Mothers and some of the fathers in reserved occupations, including a few firemen and policemen, grouped disconsolately together on the platform and waved back. Some, like Tom's mother, had tears in their eyes whilst others displayed little outward emotion but their faces were, with a few exceptions, stricken and anxious.

Some of the children thought that it was an adventure but homesickness would catch up with them later. Many of them chattered and laughed as the train clattered along although few had been away from home before.

'What fun!' one or two of the bolder children chorused as the more timid shrank back into their seats and tried not to cry. The more fortunate opened their packets of sandwiches and shared them with unaccustomed generosity with those who were not so lucky. Tom carefully unwrapped his. Hmm ... jam without butter.

His mother had said that it was extravagant to have both. He entered into the contagious benevolence and shared his small packet with the other children. Nobody noticed the lack of butter. It was wartime and hunger soon overcame any inhibitions as the group merged together. Middle class, lower class and slum dwellers became for a short time homogeneous.

Chapter 2

The Evacuee

Tom arrived at Everton railway station in the Midlands county of Russetshire with forty other children aged between five and eleven. They were herded onto a rattling old bus and taken to Enderly where they were to be allocated billets with local families. The children sang lustily as they were driven to the village hall which was a small dilapidated building that had been erected in the centre of the village shortly after the First World War. 'Run rabbit run' and 'Hang out the washing on the Siegfried Line' and other popular wartime songs recently learned permeated the air and lifted their flagging spirits, although several of the younger children had begun to cry.

On arrival they were given a glass of lemonade and a plain rich tea biscuit. Official-looking local ladies adorned in obligatory 1930s felt hats sat at a long trestle table with a list of names in front of them and did their best to pair the children up with suitable hosts.

Tom wondered for a few moments if he had been delivered to a cattle market. He had heard somewhere that cattle were sold or chosen by local farmers in such places, though he was not sure what the procedure was. The cold atmosphere increased his discomfort, fingers and feet merging on numbness, and a sad sinking feeling settling like a lump of lead in the pit of his stomach. The rain rattled on the thin corrugated roof of the hall and the rough painted concrete floor was unpleasant underfoot. He thought of his mother and longed to be home once again, to feel her warm young arms around him and toast his feet by the old black range. He was directed, along with several of the other children, to sit on one of the low wooden benches that had been placed round the edge of the main room of the hall. The majority of the evacuees soon became decidedly restless. There was a small kitchen at the back where a young girl of about fourteen was washing up the lemonade glasses in soapy water before wiping them with a scruffy tea towel and placing them in a shabby wooden cupboard above the sink. Tom could just see her and watched her work. Hunger clawed at his insides but apart from the small glass of home-made over-sweet lemonade and broken rich tea biscuit it seemed nothing more was to be offered to the children. At least he could not see any food. His stomach rumbled, his eyes felt heavy and his mind drifted for a while as he waited.

'I want a little girl,' he heard one woman say in a strident tone. He woke up from his reverie with a start. 'I want one who will be company for my Lizzie,' she continued. Nobody it seemed wanted a small timid boy.

Tom sighed. He had started to wet himself, not much but it was getting difficult to hang on. His bladder ached but fear stopped him from asking for a toilet and he pressed himself further into the shadows in one corner of the room.

'Oh, Mum – come and fetch me home,' he mumbled under his breath. 'Perhaps they'll forget all about me. I might escape and catch a train home ... oh Mum.'

Mrs Alicia Merryweather looked with interest at the sad little boy. She had come to help with the refreshments and had decided not, after all, to take in an evacuee because her husband was far from well, although she had earlier arranged to have one when the possibility of having evacuees in the village had first been put forward. One look at Tom's forlorn face convinced her that she would take one after all.

'I'll take that little chap, Madge,' she said to her friend who was officially in charge. Madge was relieved. It looked as though they were going to be short of people to take in all these children. Her head was beginning to spin and ache. She hadn't realised that the villagers would pick and choose and squabble with such ferocity about which children they would allow to share their homes. Poor kids, they were all needy in her opinion.

'Thank goodness,' she said. 'The whole thing is getting me down. I need a couple of aspirin.'

Some of the girls who had still not been allocated billets were crying, their sobs getting louder by the minute, whilst several bold and cheeky older boys ran round the room playing tag until they were cautioned by the village vicar who had arrived with obvious reluctance and fingered his dog collar with nervous jabs for a few moments before attempting to make himself useful.

'Can I help?' his deep voice boomed out after he had composed himself. He was not anxious to become involved but had been coerced into helping by his wife. 'We must do our bit, set an example in the village,' she had insisted but did not herself offer to take in any of the London ragamuffins, as she had labelled them.

'Some of those have dirty habits,' she said with disdain. 'What a scruffy looking lot I saw arriving. They probably never change their underwear or clean their teeth. Ugh, they are not for me. Just say, dear, that we do not have a spare bedroom.' The vicar thought with sadness and shame about the latter remark. The vicarage boasted five bedrooms, all quite well furnished as most of the villagers knew. His two sons had joined the forces. At least they were doing their bit and that salved his conscience. He sighed. His wife was a stubborn self-opinionated woman who made his efforts to follow his vocation very difficult.

Tom put his small cold hand into Alicia's with relief. She gave it a reassuring squeeze and spoke gently.

'Don't worry dear. I've nearly finished here and we can go home, get you a proper meal. The toilet is over there if you want it.' She pointed to a wooden door in the corner of the room and patted his hair, looking with undisguised and sincere interest at his earnest thin little face with the deeply dimpled chin. What a dear little boy. She smiled at him, her warm generous face lighting up, and he began to relax.

Thus began Tom's stay with the Merryweather family, first with Alicia and Will in Honeysuckle Cottage and five years later, when they were no longer able to take care of him, with their daughter Janet and her husband James Anderson in Primrose House on the edge of the village.

Tom's mother was not able to write to him as planned. Before she made her way to the Anderson shelter that evening a bomb hit the house. She lay crushed and mutilated beneath the rubble, covered by the home that she had loved and imagined invincible. Her brief funeral in a local churchyard was attended by Tom's father and his two aunts who were of the opinion that the service would not be suitable for a child. There was too much sadness in London and he would only fret.

'Not right for kids, 'e's better off in that there country place,' Robert's old Aunt Aggie had urged and he had agreed.

Tom's father visited him shortly after his arrival in Enderly.

'Your mother son, she's gone ...' He held his head in his hands and didn't know how to continue.

Tom understood.

'Dad,' he said with a wisdom beyond his years, 'don't fret about me. I'll be all right.'

Tom could not cry. The misery foisted upon him was deep and frightening. He felt lost and alone.

His father handed him a small cardboard box.

'Keep this safe Tom. It was your mother's.'

Tom looked inside the box where his mother's silver cross and chain nestled in some cotton wool; it was the one she had always worn round her neck and once told him had belonged to her mother.

'Course, Dad.' His small face crumpled though his eyes remained dry and expressionless. 'I'll keep it safe.' Reality would confront him later.

When it did Alicia Merryweather tried to console him and he clung to her for comfort and affection. She cradled him in her arms as a vision of his London home invaded his young mind. He pictured the shelter where he slept on a bench near his mother, the fish pond and mean backyard. The nightmare of broken bricks, flames and charred wood that had terrified him then still evoked vivid memories of whistling bombs, the smell of burning buildings, fire engines clanging and ambulances. Black planes like large birds once again droned above him in his imagination, their engine sounds painfully familiar.

'You'll be all right with us, love,' she reassured him. 'You can stay in our cottage as long as we can look after you my lovey.' She was concerned about her own and her husband's health but was determined to do her best for Tom as long as she was able to.

'What a brave little boy,' he heard her say to her husband in her quiet soft country voice. 'Time is a great healer. We'll take care of him.' And they did.

Tom experienced the joys of country life. Red and yellow Pershore plums grew in the Merryweathers' garden and the yellow ones were made into his favourite jam, whilst the others were bottled and stored for the winter. A Worcester Pearmain apple tree provided fresh apples which he was allowed to pick. They were not good keepers and considered unsuitable to store away in the cottage roof with the Coxes and other more durable varieties but he enjoyed their fresh crisp taste. He had accompanied his mother to the local greengrocers in London to buy fruit and vegetables but this was a different experience. The Merryweathers' garden provided them with fresh vegetables most of the year round. Rabbits were given to the family, together with the odd duck or partridge, by fellow farmworkers who were conscious of Will Merryweather's fragile state of health and were anxious to help. Will had suffered for several years with rheumatoid arthritis which was becoming worse.

The friendship of the good-hearted country folk surprised Tom. It was very different to life in south London where many of their neighbours were too busy going about their own business to bother to say good morning let alone be concerned about anybody else's state of health. He began to realize how lucky he was to live with the Merryweathers. The villagers cherished their independence; most of them were not wealthy, but helped the less fortunate with a generous spirit which provoked admiration and awe in the young child. Tom liked to help Mr Merryweather. He fetched his slippers, pipe and paper and tried to make himself generally useful. It was the least he could do. The bombing raids and carnage he had experienced in London were for a while pushed to the back of his mind and he started to relax.

Many of the village cottages were black and white; some were tied to the few big landowners, but all, including the Merry-weathers', lacked modern conveniences, in particular running water, and had a privy at the bottom of the garden. Cooking was done on a paraffin stove in a small kitchen off the main living room. Alicia's father had once owned the cottage and had left it to his daughter so they were fortunate. There was a good deep well in the front garden with a bucket hanging from its slate roof. All their water had to be hoisted up every day, which was hard work. Tom loved the small green lawn at the back of the cottage and the flowers – hollyhocks, pansies, geraniums, roses and marigolds – that provided bright colours during the summer months. He learned their names and how to care for them, planted vegetable seeds for Will and helped him with the weeding and staking of peas and beans; it was knowledge that was to stand him in good stead later on.

Will owned a good-natured collie dog called Gyp, black and white with soft fur and appealing brown eyes who followed him everywhere. Tom enjoyed stroking the dog and the feel of his soft muzzle as he pressed it into his hand. It instilled in the boy a love of dogs which would remain with him for the rest of his life.

Will was proud of his large bushy moustache that reminded Tom of a neat thatched roof as it formed a half circle over his top lip. He was fascinated as he watched him eat his supper of bread and milk every evening and wondered why more of the bread and milk did not stick to those thick whiskers.

'Hush boy,' Will would say in an impatient tone. 'I've got the wireless on now and I want to hear the news.' Tom sat on an old three-legged stool by his feet, the dog curled up between them, and attempted to be as silent as a church mouse. He was happy.

Alicia's hair was long and dark with odd red glints though now exhibiting flecks of grey. A rounded and motherly figure she emitted a feeling of security to Tom. He never heard a grumble or cross word pass her lips. Will too was kind and gentle. Most of his early life had been spent as a shepherd and skilful farmhand working for a local landowner but his illness had forced him to retire. Many fellow workers and local farmers brought him beer or other produce in exchange for a chat and advice about their lambs. Tom listened, entranced, to the tales about the old villagers, the horrors of workhouses and the depression, and to the news about the war and the local boys who were in the forces.

When Tom's father was killed during the D-Day landings Alicia once again consoled the child. Tom vowed that he would never forget her or Will and would always be grateful for their kindness. He promised himself with naive childish resolve that one day he would try to repay Alicia and Will for their generosity. It was a promise that would involve him in some unexpected and difficult situations.

Chapter 3

First Wedding 1945

The church bells rang out loud and clear over the village of Enderly and much of the nearby countryside. Mrs Amelia Grimms the organist played with enthusiasm, though she was aware that the organ was in urgent need of repair after the neglect of the war years. She was not too concerned about a few missing notes. A few odd creaks and groans from the pipes was a small price to pay for the joyous music she produced. The music filled the small Norman church with glorious reverberating sound. It was after all a happy uplifting occasion, the wedding of Janet Merryweather and James Anderson, and there had in her opinion been too few of those in recent years. There had been too many memorial services for young village lads who had been lost in combat.

A group of Enderly villagers waited outside the church with bags bulging with coloured confetti, mostly home-made from small pieces of old Christmas paper decorations chopped into neat pieces. Real confetti was a scarce commodity. Although they were not all close friends of the Merryweather family they looked forward to joining in the festivities. There had been too many drab days during the war; this was a welcome opportunity to celebrate and they were more than ready for it. In any case brides were always worth watching, whoever they might be, especially in a small community like Enderly. They knew that Janet had completed a teacher training course and so was, in their view, a successful young local girl. The Merryweather family had lived in the area for several generations and had earned the respect of the local community.

Janet's dress was made from a creamy white parachute silk remnant given to her by a friend who had worked in a parachute factory during the war and it exuded a shimmering pearl-like sheen. Pieces of old Maltese lace, removed from some handkerchiefs that had been in the family for a long time, had been sewn with care around the cuffs and across the bosom. Her fragile hand-made lace veil was edged with slightly chipped artificial waxy orange blossom, and had been worn by her mother Alicia and her grandmother before that. It was fine and delicate as only such a treasured old piece of material can be.

Tom, now ten years old, presented himself as a shy and reluctant page boy in traditional short grey flannel trousers, pressed neatly with deep creases for the occasion, his starched white shirt for once immaculate. He kept close to Alicia's side, touching her occasionally with a shaky hand for reassurance as she guided him to his place behind the bride. A small blue bow tie adorned his neck. He didn't like it but did not protest because Alicia had made it for him and there was no way he wished to offend her.

'You look really good, son,' she said as she brushed his unruly hair and gave it a lick of Brylcream to keep it in place. 'Fashionable you are, luvvy,' she said, beaming.

Annie, Janet's best friend from her school days, was maid of honour. Annie wore a deep pink crêpe dress refashioned from a pre-war dance dress which had once belonged to an aunt; it was not a good fit despite her best efforts but she was proud of it. It clashed with her bright red hair but that was not important. The austerity of the war years still held them in a vice-like grip; food rationing had not yet been abandoned and things seemed worse than they had been for some time, though hope for a prosperous new era loomed large in the back of all their minds and added to the mounting excitement.

Tom thought Janet looked like an angel in her soft silk dress. It was a memory he believed he would always cherish. Five years with Alicia Merryweather had made him feel part of her family. He thought of Janet as a big sister, someone he could trust and look up to.

*

'I feel like a princess,' Annie had exclaimed earlier that day with unbridled delight as she danced and swirled round the Merryweathers' small sitting room and admired herself in the large old-fashioned mirror that was propped over the mantelpiece. Two pink roses, picked in the garden, were attached to her short bobbed hair and fastened with cheap light-brown Kirby grips. Precious nylon stockings, the seams dark and straight as a die, clung to her legs and she wore her one pair of wobbly high-heeled shoes which she had painted gold.

'I hope it doesn't rain,' she laughed, 'or there might be a trail of gold down the aisle.' She held a small posy that had been wired together by Janet, fashioned from gold leaves rescued from a past Christmas and entwined with soft pink roses and white daisies picked that morning in the Merryweathers' garden.

Janet had laughed at her friend with undisguised affection as she twisted her own brown hair into a coil and pinned it on the top of her head. It's elegant, she thought, and quite sophisticated.

'Dear Annie, this is the happiest day of my life,' she said. Their youthful light-hearted laughter echoed throughout the house.

To complement her dress as she walked down the aisle Janet was to carry a bouquet of pink and white carnations, grown in a neighbour's garden especially for the occasion, and tied with a recycled gold thread ribbon that was a little frayed at the edges, but nobody would notice that.

'Make sure you catch the bouquet Annie', she had told her friend. You will be next.'

Annie had laughed heartily. 'I don't know about that,' she retorted. 'I haven't met Mr Right yet and I'm not likely to in this dump.'

Tom was puzzled. He thought they were all lucky to live in Enderly. It was not a dump. He knew what a dump was and this was not one. It was a pretty village surrounded by green fields and clean fresh air. His home in London could be described by some as a dump but even that had been a happy place when he had his mum and his dad and they had given him love and affection.

*

The small grey stone village church of St Stephen's had been decorated with loving and skilful hands by a couple of elderly spinsters, Ivy and Pat. They had used simple indigenous greenery together with some of their own garden flowers. An abundance of blooms – red, yellow, blue and vibrant orange lifted their heads from dark green leaves and filled the church with a mixture of light floral scents.

A tiny brown bird darted suddenly through the church doorway and it took at least half an hour for the church wardens to drive the frightened creature outside again, but not before the bird made a mess down one of the church columns.

'That's a good luck omen,' said the superstitious Pat, but the verger was not so sure as it would be his job to clean the stone later.

'I could have done without that,' he grouched, looking at the nasty white mark with distaste. 'It spoils the look of the place!'

Nobody in the congregation noticed. They were waiting with unconcealed enthusiasm to get a glimpse of the bride and groom. The old carved pews were soon packed with friends and family ready to follow the wedding service and sing the chosen hymns with gusto. Hymn sheets rustled as heads turned to watch the lovely young bride walk up with aisle with her father. The congregation wore their Sunday-best clothes and listened intently as the vicar pronounced Janet and James husband and wife. A sea of voile hats that had not seen the light of day for several years bobbed up and down like puffs of coloured cotton wool, though a few of them emitted a strong smell of mothballs. There was a hush when the congregation listened to the words 'I do' from each of them, words that would bind them together in holy matrimony. Tom stood close to Janet and felt as though he would burst with pride. He had never been to a wedding before and he thought Janet, his adopted sister, looked perfect, so pretty; he was the luckiest boy alive.

The sun shone through the old leaded paned windows, though the red, green and white glass on which were depicted various religious scenes: Jesus, the shepherd and his sheep, the disciples and other biblical characters, beautifully painted and donated by past village squires and other local benefactors. The church became alive with light and hope.

'What a wonderful service, they are such a lovely couple. It was perfect,' the locals were saying as Janet and James left the church.

James's parents were dead but his sister Anne, her husband Richard Brown, their two small children and several friends, including the best man John, represented the Anderson family. Tom looked at Anne's children, Felicity and Ronald, with interest. He supposed that they were now part of the Merryweather family so in a way part of his family too. The girl Felicity he guessed was about two years old. She had fidgeted and scowled throughout the service. He did not think she looked very nice with her unattractive odd blue eyes and mousy blonde hair. The baby boy of only a few months was pale and quiet. Tom had no idea about the part these children would play in his future.

Alicia and her friend Ada had worked hard. They had scrounged ingredients from various friends to produce a cake and refreshments for the guests to enjoy in the Merryweathers' home after the service. The icing was amateurish, hard and crumbly in places and the bride and groom dolls on the top were oddly dressed but Janet thought it was the best wedding cake she had ever seen and her excitement escalated. Fortunately she, like Tom, had no inkling of the sorrow that was to come. The small cottage and garden were filled with friends and family. Trestle tables and chairs had been borrowed for the guests from the village hall, but nobody minded the lack of space, they were too busy nibbling the cake and refreshments to care. It was a rare treat and they knew it. Tom sank his teeth into a slice of iced cake, the unaccustomed sweetness filled his mouth and he thought he was in heaven. How lucky he was to be billeted with the Merryweather family.

The bride and groom were toasted with wine that had been given to the Merryweathers by their old friend Michael Cross, who had been the proprietor of the local pub, the Green Man, for more years than they could remember. 'It's my contribution to this happy day,' he said. Nobody asked any questions. It was quite old and a good vintage wine; he must have had it secreted away in his cellar for many years. They were thankful to have it.

*

'Darling James,' Janet had said to her handsome fiancé the evening before as he held her close in a passionate embrace and pressed her soft breasts with almost callous firmness against his broad chest.

'I can hardly wait until tomorrow,' he had whispered in her ear, his deep voice sending shivers down her spine as he ran his hands down her back, caressing her slim body and neat rounded buttocks with his large masculine hands.

Sex before marriage was frowned on in the nineteen forties but they would soon be man and wife and James was keen to possess this attractive woman. Janet had not given in to his demands and slept with him as some women had so had kept his attention and respect. 'You'll soon be mine,' he murmured, his breath hot upon her neck, as she leaned against him, subservient and willing.

Janet didn't really know much about James's family but was not concerned; it was James she was marrying, not the Anderson clan although that was something that would rebound on her later. It had been a swift wartime romance and she was very much in love, or imagined she was, with her handsome fiancé. The broad-shouldered man in his glamorous naval uniform had literally swept her off her feet and her usual common sense deserted her. James had made an effort to eliminate his London accent when he joined the navy and his voice was deep and attractive, especially to the young women with whom he worked. He acted the role of the middle-class officer perfectly, although secretly he despised the upper classes.

Janet had been a pupil at the local Everton grammar school and after gaining a Higher Schools Certificate she spent a year with an elderly aunt in Yorkshire before taking a two-year teaching training course in Russhampton, the Russetshire county town. She planned to teach in a local primary school but with war being declared in 1939 she joined the Wrens.

'I must do my bit, Mum,' she said. Her mother was not keen. She had lost two brothers in the trenches during the First World War. Janet remembered her grandmother telling her about them.

One, Edwin, was gassed and the other, Pete, was mutilated and died after a shell exploded by his feet in the trenches. They were not sure where Pete was buried but it was probably in some unnamed grave in France. Edwin died from the damage to his lungs a few years after the war ended. He had been unable to work again or lead the kind of life of which he had once dreamed.

'What a waste of young lives!' said Alicia.

'Times have changed, warfare is now quite different Mummy,' Janet said, with the confidence and brashness of the young.

'Warfare is never different,' her mother retorted. 'It may seem exciting to you but you have a lot to learn, my girl.'

Her mother need not have worried; most of Janet's time in the navy was spent coping with tedious jobs behind an office desk in the south of England, not the adventurous life she had hoped for, but she did meet the handsome naval officer, James Anderson, five years older than she was, who before joining the forces had been a lecturer in a technical college in Bath.

'We're both teachers,' she had told her mother. 'We have a lot in common, we will be happy together.'

'You do not know enough about him,' her mother had retorted.

'Of course I do. We've worked together for the past few years and spent much of our free time together. You don't understand, Mum.'

Her mother understood all right. A wartime romance was in her eyes no better than a holiday fling. She didn't like James Anderson but her protests were not heeded. Despite her mother's reservations Janet and James planned to get married as soon as the war ended and they were demobbed. The idea of living together before marriage was not considered to be an option. 'It is not done,' their families had maintained when they were growing up, and they were expected to get married first. Janet was to think later that perhaps that was a pity. A trial run would have saved them both a lot of heartache.

James was six feet tall and his dark thick hair contrasted with his stunning blue eyes that exuded a permanent cheeky twinkle, which Janet, and many of her fellow Wrens, had found irresistible. She was the lucky one, at least that is what she thought at the time. When their wedding day arrived it seemed like a dream akin to something she had read about in a sloppy romantic novel.

James obtained a post as a lecturer in a college in the small town of Everton, five miles away from Enderly, and Janet accepted a position as a primary school teacher in Enderly village. She was happy they were to live so near her parents.

The village school consisted of an old Victorian building with draughty windows and a small tarmac playground together with a pile of out-of-date equipment but the classrooms were spacious and the number of pupils in each class averaged about fifteen. Many teachers in some parts of the country were struggling with classes containing over fifty pupils.

When Janet first saw Primrose House on the outskirts of Enderly she fell in love with it.

'James,' she wheedled, 'darling it's perfect and we can afford it.'

Primrose House was well placed on the brow of a hill; the one-acre garden was neglected but with careful planning it could be made into something attractive. There was already a vegetable patch, useful in the days of austerity and rationing, and the previous owners had left a chicken run which Janet soon filled with fluffy young chicks.

'Fresh eggs, James,' she said happily, 'we'll grow our own vegetables too.'

'If you say so,' he said. 'As long as you look after the cheeping things and the damn garden. It looks like an overgrown wilderness. I hate gardening. Thank goodness I didn't have to bother with that when I lived in London.'

The four large draughty bedrooms suffered from the whistling wind that crept over the fields from the river and squeezed through the ill-fitting windows. The rest of the accommodation consisted of a big lounge, desperately in need of decoration with peeling wallpaper and a fireplace surrounded with old cracked tiles, a good-sized dining room, a spacious kitchen in need of modernisation and a large bathroom complete with an ancient iron-legged bath under which numerous spiders had woven their webs. The green Aga in the kitchen was old and temperamental but Janet loved its warmth; it gave the impression that it was solid and durable even though it needed some repairs. It was greedy for fuel but Janet considered it was worth keeping.

'We'll buy an electric cooker when we can afford one,' she suggested but James threw her a disgusted look that told her that luxury would have to wait for a long time. His expression suggested to her that she was living in cloud cuckoo land.

The old red quarry-tiled floor had stood the test of time and, though cracked and worn in places, it was comfortable under foot. Janet thought that with some polish it would soon look as good as new. A little elbow grease would make all the difference and she was willing to make the effort.

'What on earth are we going to do for money with this rubbish heap to renovate?' James moaned day after day. 'I shouldn't have agreed to buy it. Why I listened to you, silly woman, I do not know,' but he had to admit the house had potential. 'It could be turned into an attractive home with some spare cash which we do not have,' he added in a grudging tone of voice.

'We will manage,' Janet repeated many times with an optimism she did not feel. 'It's made of solid red brick and the roof is good.'

The latter remark was like red rag to a bull. James snorted with derision and turned his back upon her. He didn't help her, preferring the delights of a pint in the Green Man or one of the Everton pubs, spending money he claimed he did not have. Money that a prudent man would have spent on renewing the rotting window frames or repairing the broken garden fences slipped through his fingers like water. He was not a handyman and he did not want to be one.

She doesn't understand me. We have no interests in common. Why did I let myself get sucked into marrying this woman and ending up in this godforsaken hole? James asked himself. The woman is frigid compared with some I have known. He did not think for a moment that Janet's responses could be anything to do with him. The marriage was turning into a bad dream and was compounded by frustration and misunderstanding.

What is the matter with me? Janet asked herself. She could not understand James's boorish attitude.

Lecturing was not so exciting for James as his life in the navy had been and he found it difficult to settle down. He, like many young men returning from life in the forces hoped for something better than they had experienced before the war. He could be categorized as one of the post-war angry young men. Nothing was right.

'The Government should do more for us,' he whined. 'We have given up some of the best years of our life for England and we are still struggling to improve our lot! The Germans are building better houses than ours and what have we got? At least the stupid class system has been broken down, we don't need that. The ghastly aristocrats should be made to wait on themselves. The Labour Government will be the best thing that has ever happened to the working man. You'll see, we'll have free medical treatment and better schooling. Public schools should be done away with. Thank goodness we have got rid of some of the deference voters and that bloody upstairs downstairs syndrome. Who do those spoilt, arrogant, rich idiots think they are anyway! The middle classes will emerge with greater strength in their ranks; the working man will rise up to join them as better education becomes more widely available and individual merit is recognized.'

Janet tried to ignore his constant grumbling. 'We're lucky James, we have a good solid house, even if it does need a few repairs, we live in beautiful countryside and have survived the ravages of war.'

James did not want to hear that. He tried to ignore her reasoned remarks. 'We are going to be better off under a Labour Government, but class is something so entrenched in the English psyche, which is a pity. Barriers must be broken down,' James would continue like a man demented. It was as though Janet was not there. He did not consider Janet's views were worth listening to and she was relieved when he disappeared, as he often did in the evenings, to the local pub to discuss politics further with a few so-called friends and acquaintances.

There were a number of industrial estates outside Everton and the technical college where James worked provided suitable tuition for the young employees. The classes were full with eager young men but James became demoralized and uninterested in his pupils, which soon became obvious to his employers and reflected in his results in the classroom.

'A lot ot of lazy young clots,' he grumbled. 'They know nothing about life or the hardship of war. At least National Service will do one or two some good. Life in the navy was much more interesting,' he would say bitterly. The expression on his once bland and cheerful face and the mouth that Janet had once found so attractive now looked spiteful and mean.

The mortgage on Primrose House was large but since they were both working it was affordable. Janet felt that it was worth a little scrimping. In her view it was a lovely old family house although there were no children of their own to fill it, she did have Tom with her for a short while. Alicia was struggling to look after her dying husband and because of her own ill health, which later turned out to be cancer, she knew she could no longer look after Tom and asked Janet to look after him for her. She knew that she would soon become too frail to cope with Will and he would have to go into a local care home where he would receive specialist nursing. They had already made arrangements.

Alicia tried to explain to Tom why she had asked Janet to look after him and why she could no longer keep him with her, but without success. A bewildered Tom left for Primrose House after a tearful parting with Will and Alicia.

James was so very anxious to get rid of the boy that she suspected that he did not really like children or young people. His treatment of Tom became unreasonable and harsh.

'He's too much of a responsibility for us at present,' he said. 'We can't afford our own baby, let alone someone else's brat,' and he would tilt his head to one side in an odd way, something he always did when he was angry. James was determined to get rid of Tom.

'You must do what you think is best for Tom dear,' Alicia said sadly when it became obvious that James did not want the boy and Janet had no hope of having any control over the situation.

Her mother had treated the boy like a son and she thought of him as a young brother. James however was so keen to get rid of the child he had even purchased a thin bamboo cane which he placed in the corner of the living room, ready, he declared, 'to keep that little brat in order if need be or to act as a deterrent'.

Tom's world was falling apart once again. He had grown to love Alicia and to think of Janet as a sister. How could Janet abandon him? He knew Alicia and Will would not have done so without a very good reason. Tom was confused. He loved Janet but he longed to escape from the strict and harsh James. If Janet was unable to stand up to the man he certainly had no chance.

After much deliberation and many sleepless nights Janet approached the local authority and Tom was soon placed with foster parents. She would never forget his departure from Primrose House or the look of naked triumph on the face of her husband, ensuring the guilt that she felt when Tom left would stay with her for the rest of her life. Janet thought that she had betrayed him.

'Thank heaven that puerile creature has gone,' James said, 'we do not need kids like him around.'

Janet knew that she was weak but justified her behaviour by telling herself that Tom would be better off with some kind and caring foster parents than suffering James's sharp tongue and threatening behaviour. She felt convinced that sooner or later James would injure the boy and she was right to let him go. She made a nebulous promise to herself that she would try and find him when her marriage was on a more even keel. He was after all not just any evacuee. He was special.

Janet turned her efforts to planting the garden that surrounded Primrose House to fill the gap that the boy had left in her life and erase the guilt she felt. In the summer it became a riot of colourful flowers, bright orange marigolds, pink and red fuchsias, blue delphiniums and sweet-smelling roses. James continued to take no more than a fleeting interest in the house or garden. He hated decorating and do-it-yourself projects and became withdrawn and morose after a short time of what appeared to be wedded harmony after Tom had left. Their sex life, however, continued to be erratic and Janet more often than not was left miserable and unfulfilled.

'Getting to be a right misery, you are, Janet,' James ranted. 'You do not have any confidence, I don't know what is the matter with you.'

He had possessed the woman, savoured her slim body, which had turned out to be no better than a few others he had experienced before, and after that he lost interest.

'I don't find you particularly exciting in bed,' he would tell her in a blunt way. 'I've enjoyed better and more experienced women. You are frigid compared to them and no better than old flat champagne,' he had said on one occasion after they had been married for only a few months and had looked at her with disdain.

'What do you mean?' she had asked, and he had shrugged.

The marriage was failing. She had lost Tom for nothing. She was innately warm and passionate and she could not understand James's behaviour. His sexual advances had been rough and swift. He was not concerned whether she enjoyed herself or responded in any way. In his opinion women were just there to be used and enjoyed by men. If Janet had needs they did not concern him.

James became increasingly restless and irritable as the years slipped by and showed no interest in having the family which Janet longed for.

'I want to travel and see more of the world,' he reiterated with petulance and crass bad humour. A permanent frown had etched itself on to his forehead, growing deeper as time passed.

'There is no room for babies in our life,' he would say with savage intensity. He loved to see the pain in her eyes. 'You probably would not be much of a mother anyway,' he added with spite. 'Snotty nosed and dribbling kids are not for me!'

Janet cringed and believed that he no longer found her attractive. Her once bubbly and lively personality disappeared and she found it increasingly difficult to respond to his rough and brutal lovemaking. It was unfair. She realized that she was not a beauty in the classical sense but possessed luminous clear fair skin, an oval face with high Nordic cheekbones and a neat slim figure which many of her not-so-lucky fellow female teachers coveted. She had let her fine dark hair grow long and wore it in a plait when she was working in the school. Her soft velvety brown eyes fringed with long thick lashes and an intriguing dimple in her left cheek gave her an almost childlike look in contrast to her wide, mature and generous mouth. She was usually vivacious and outgoing, but became listless and was no longer her once exuberant self. In the school she had always commanded the respect of her colleagues because she was an excellent teacher and the young pupils responded to her positively but James's attitude was causing her misery and confusion. She was conscious that one or two of the male teachers looked at her with more than casual interest and would, with very little encouragement, have stepped with eagerness into the boorish James's shoes.

'That man is a piece of shit,' she had overheard one say. She was beginning to believe it. 'He is ruining her life,' was another snippet of conversation that reached her ears.

After four long and tortuous years she had to admit that their relationship had deteriorated into a dismal sham. Janet continued with her efforts to make James happy but he exhibited little interest in her, his job or their home. Leisure time for them as a couple had become non-existent.

'Holidays are too expensive,' James grumbled, 'we're not made of money.' Janet continued working in the garden and decorating the large rooms while James sulked or removed himself to a friend's house to play cards during the school holidays. At least that is what he said he did. Jane, a fellow teacher at the school told her that she had seen him when she had been shopping in Everton. A woman had been clinging to his arm and gazing at him with adoration.

'A redhead,' Jane continued, 'fat and coarse looking, certainly not as attractive as you! A right whore in fact.'

Janet dismissed this as tittle-tattle but felt uneasy and sick at heart.

'It was probably a colleague,' she had responded quickly, irritation creeping into her normally calm voice. There was no doubt in her mind that James was cheating on her, he had made it pretty clear that she was not his ideal woman, but it was not Jane's business and a glance at her face indicated that she was sorry that she had mentioned it.

'I expect you are right,' Jane said with studied diffidence, her mind whirling and stumbling in an attempt to find another less prickly topic.

The autumn term was about to start in their fifth year of marriage and Janet expected that they would be returning to their teaching posts as usual. James announced suddenly and with complete lack of feeling or sensitivity that he was leaving her. He was going to travel the world. He had had as much as he could take of Enderly, Everton and those idiot teenagers.

'You'll be all right old girl,' he stated flatly. 'You can manage to pay the mortgage, it may be somewhat tight but you earn enough and if it becomes too much of a burden ... well, sell the house. It's a rotten old barn anyway. I've always hated it.'

Arrangements for the deeds of Primrose House to be transferred to Janet had unbeknown to her been put in hand.

'I've already signed the necessary papers,' James told her in a dismissive tone. 'Nothing you need to do about it, old fruit. I've withdrawn my savings from Everton Building Society and as we have separate bank accounts there's not much to concern you.'

This was a surprise to Janet.

Unbeknown to her he had already packed his bags ready for a journey.

'My luggage has been stowed in my car boot for some days,' he said. 'I'm only taking the minimum, just three cases containing clothes and a few keepsakes. Anything else you are jolly well welcome to. If you haven't enough money to buy another car you can always get the bus,' he told her callously.

'The meagre bus service permitting,' Janet said softly under her breath, a sarcastic note creeping into her normally pleasant voice. Where did he think she was going to get the cash from to buy another car? The house mortgage was heavy and they had needed two salaries to cope with it. Most of the money they had paid off to date would be interest on the loan.

'The village school is within walking distance even if you do have a load of books to carry,' he said and turned cold belligerent blue eyes towards her, a look she would never forget as long as she lived. 'A young woman like you with strong arms shouldn't have any difficulty,' he expanded in a condescending way. 'I've no idea when I'll return to Enderly, but I'll be in contact as soon as it is convenient.'

Janet reeled with shock. She had realized for a long time that he might leave her but had pushed the idea to the back of her mind. In some ways she had to admit that she welcomed the news but reality was not at that moment palatable.

'Soon as it is convenient' … what on earth did that mean?

The colour drained from her face, her hands shook as her legs turned to jelly and she feared she would fall to the ground. She was a ridiculous weak fool. She had been duped, lost her little brother Tom, had no baby to love and had endured several years of misery with a womanising selfish man.

'We shared that car,' she said in a meek tone. 'I paid for it! Half of it is mine.' Her voice trailed into a quiet whisper.

'My tax and insurance old girl,' he responded with determined swiftness. 'I am the registered owner. Too bad, old chum,' he ended in a dismissive and firm voice. 'You will have the benefit of the money I paid off the mortgage with my salary. Be grateful, woman!'

'Why?' she uttered, after a few moments of empty silence, her voice becoming strained and high pitched.

James shrugged and looked at her coolly, his bright blue eyes icy and expressionless. 'I can't really say old girl. You will be better off without me. I'm just a miserable old chap anyway and no good to you in my present frame of mind. You deserve better.'

This last comment at least rang true although Janet did not appreciate how apt it was at the time. She still had the house she loved, though how on earth she was going to pay the mortgage she did not know. A deep hole of misery appeared to open at her feet ready to swallow her up, though if she was honest with herself, she had been dissatisfied with her marriage and had longed to be free for a long time. She knew that there was only one person James loved and that was himself. The description 'a self-centred egotistical bore' fitted him perfectly. He was a selfish, shallow man. She had let her mother down and lost Tom in a vain effort to keep this rotten husband. What a blind creature she had been. It had been easier that way but she was determined that things would be different in future. If he thought he could crawl back when he was down on his luck he would have to think again. She glared at him, hate distorting her features for a moment as an unaccustomed hardness and resolve surfaced.

James turned abruptly away from her and heaved a noisy sigh of relief. The bloody woman did not show signs of hysteria, thank goodness. The parting was not going to be as difficult as he had anticipated. He opened the car door, lifted his lean body into the driving seat and slammed the door, which emitted a loud clang. He gripped the steering wheel, placed the key in the ignition and started the engine.

'Dull as ditchwater this place,' he shouted over his shoulder as he started to edge the car forward. 'There are a few nice views, pretty in the usual crap Russetshire English way but that's all. I long to savour the vibrant African heat, Australian outback and all the other interesting places I've read about during the past few years!' An old map of Africa had been stowed in his bag and he was determined that North Africa would be his first destination. 'I'll come back if I'm broke and have nowhere else to go,' he continued, 'but I don't know when. Don't worry about me old girl.'

Janet shuddered and gritted her teeth. It was the first she had heard about his plans. What did he mean, don't worry about him? That was something she realized with startling clarity that she would be glad not to do again. Had he really said those dreadful things to her? She had realized that he was restless but had not expected him to depart in such an abrupt manner.

'Goodbye, good riddance dreary teacher wife,' he shouted 'I'm off!'

Janet stood deserted and amazed on the road outside Primrose House and watched as the small red car they had shared disappeared into the distance.

James made his way to Dover where he sold the car to a dealer. He heaved his luggage on to a ferry bound for France and without a backward glance at the white cliffs toasted his freedom with a strong cup of coffee he laced, exhibiting extravagance and greed, with three spoonfuls of fine white sugar.

Chapter 4

John Lacey

J ohn Lacey was the only son of a wealthy merchant and entrepreneur. His father spent thirty years building up a thriving
business near Newbury before he died and John inherited, to
his dismay, a considerable fortune when still only a young
man. Unlike many of his contemporaries and the majority of the
human race he was not interested in money; he would have
exchanged it eagerly for affection and love, something he had
little experience of during his childhood. When he was older he
would appreciate being able to use his wealth to indulge his
hobby of collecting antiques and other beautiful objects he loved,
and buying gifts to please his second wife, but he was a simple
man with simple needs and did not crave luxuries.

John was never able to get to know his mother well and was
left with a vague memory of a quiet young woman with a thin
peaky face and dark brown curly hair that lapped around her
forehead and emphasised her pale grey eyes, who was always ill
and suffered constant headaches. He often observed her reclining
on her bed, pale and wan, whilst her long slender fingers untram-
melled by household chores rested on luxurious silken bed
covers. They were smooth, almost transparent and tipped with
neat manicured nails, a chore untaken daily by her young maid
Betsy who prattled on and on about the weather, her latest
boyfriend or some other useless tittle-tattle which made no
impact upon John or his mother.

'Tiptoe boy, do not disturb your mother,' or 'no noisy toys, take
care,' were constant reminders that his mother was an invalid.

Nobody ever explained to him what her illness was but he guessed that it must have been something serious. There were no motherly chats, walks in the park or birthday parties. He craved attention from this weak and listless woman but it was not forthcoming.

He would creep into her bedroom when he knew that nobody would be watching and became expert at tiptoeing around the room to look at the objects that his mother called her treasures. He was intrigued when he saw the faded old brown photographs depicting grandparents he had never seen and who were dressed in stuffy Victorian clothes. There was one of his mother as a small child nursing her favourite doll and one of himself when he was a baby of only few months. There were a number of elegant china ornaments, figurines and delicate hand-painted vases his mother had collected over the years which were carefully arranged in a small china cabinet. When he thought she was asleep he would open the cabinet doors and run his small, sometimes dirty, fingers over them. He would perhaps collect some himself one day. He liked them and tried to remember some of the names stamped underneath the ornaments although they were not all easy to read. Sometimes he would carefully remove one of the books about antiques and china she kept on a bookshelf by her bed and turn some of the pages so that he could admire the objects portrayed in them.

'Mum,' he sometimes whispered in his small childish voice in the hope of getting some response, even if it was only a pat on his head, a gesture of recognition, but he rarely did.

'Don't worry me, darling,' or 'Run along now, me dear, it is past your bedtime,' or 'Go and play now, Nanny will be looking for you,' she would say in her soft Irish lilt, and that was all would remember about her voice.

Jack Lacey knew nothing about his Irish wife's family and was not interested. His wife had been a disappointment to him. He had wanted someone who would entertain his business associates and provide him with several children to take over his business when he retired. In his view she had let him down. He was left with one quiet academic child who did not, in his opinion and to his regret, exhibit the promising entrepreneurial traits for which he had hoped.

Too often the oppressive smell of the sick room pervaded the young John's nostrils and he had been glad to escape to where the air was fresh. Rough pine stairs led up to a nursery tucked away in the attic, a room devoid of comfortable carpets, where a small camp bed was tucked into one corner in readiness for his afternoon nap and a desk and stool in another in preparation for his studies. It was sparse but his father deemed it good enough. There was one compensation: a small wooden dappled grey rocking horse named Parker that he adored. The horse had soft painted black eyes that were friendly and welcoming and John spent many happy hours rocking himself on the horse. The rocking was soothing and the current nanny, more often than not, was grateful to discover that he was occupied. He could rock himself 'silly' as far as the nannies were concerned so long as he did not get under their feet.

Circumstances ensured that John developed into a quiet introverted child and although he was cared for by a variety of nannies over the years, some young, some old, not one of them was able to provide him with motherly love. He found it impossible to achieve a close and emotional relationship with any of them; his father's choice of carers for his son was abysmal.

'Behave yourself boy, look sharp,' was the ultimate nanny's favourite phrase. He did look sharp or had a quick slap with a large bony hand across his legs. Bedtime had been at the ridiculously early hour of six o'clock until the 'martinet', as he nicknamed her, left for a more lucrative post and his father considered he was too old at eleven years old for more nannies and could be sent to a boarding school about thirty miles away.

John had got into the habit of reading his favourite books under his blankets with the aid of a torch after the martinet had done her final round and disappeared to her sitting room to drink a large glass of sherry or other favourite tipple. Reading in poor light strained his eyesight and as a consequence he was forced to wear thick horn-rimmed glasses. However, he did discover that he did not like alcohol; he helped himself one day to a sip from all the bottles, whisky, vodka and sherry, that were stashed away by the often tipsy and bad-tempered nanny in a cupboard in her sitting room, resulting in violent sickness and stomach-ache, not easily forgotten. If the martinet guessed what had happened she did not mention the incident to his father and managed to show some sympathy with his plight. Shortly afterwards she moved to her new post.

John did not make any close friends at boarding school, he did not know how to, but at last he had some company of his own age and observed their behaviour from the sidelines. He was a loner. Most of the boys just ignored him; one or two tried to be friendly which he appreciated but he was not really concerned about his status. One or two played chess with him and discussed stamp collecting but there the interaction ended. The few that did make friendly overtures left him uneasy and unsure. He felt more comfortable without them.

Before he went away to boarding school he would often slip into the large garden, his father's pride and joy and second only to his business deals, where the gardener, a burly rough fellow with thick red curly hair, was pressed into keeping an eye on 'the child', but actually had no time for small boys.

'Clear off kid,' he would shout. 'Amuse yerself and leave me be – I got work to do. Kids, ugh.' He delighted in giving John a menacing smile exposing large white teeth that reminded the boy of a crocodile he had seen once in the local zoo. His eye teeth were large, sharp and unpleasant. There was a gold filling down the side of one which glinted in the sun. He could be a vampire, John thought, he had read about those. He didn't really believe in such things but the idea sent a shiver down his spine.

John was glad to do leave the man to his work and the further away he could get from those frightful teeth the better. He would make a den in some of the large bushes and act out his childhood fantasies. He could be an Indian, cowboy or whatever he liked. He had an imaginary friend called Roger, who joined him in his games.

'Come on Roger, you can be the Chief Indian, I'll be your best warrior,' he would whisper so that his father or current nanny didn't hear, or 'Come and see my stamp collection,' or 'What would you like for tea? Nanny has promised sticky buns today.' When he went to boarding school Roger was no longer needed and conveniently disappeared.

One of his classmates, Oliver, spent a few weeks during one school holiday with him. Oliver did not really like John but was persuaded by his mother, after a rare invitation from John's father, whose conscience had started to trouble him about the solitary life his son was enduring, to join John in his home, the renowned and luxurious Huxley House. John's father hoped too that a companion would keep him occupied and he would not bother him so much, not that he ever saw very much of him. Oliver's mother had a difficult baby, who seemed to be screaming most of the day and night, as well as a tiresome self-willed toddler so she was delighted at the prospect of a respite from at least one of her children and agreed with undisguised eagerness.

'Do I really have to go?' Oliver had moaned. 'John Lacey is not much fun. He is a really dull fellow,' but on his arrival at John's home his initial reluctance quickly disappeared.

'Lucky chap,' Oliver told John. 'Smashing garden and big house, cook and gardener too. Lovely grub that cook serves up. I live in suburbia in a semi-detached house and would change places with you any day. I could get rid of that pest of a brother who's always breaking my toys. No squawking baby sister either. It's so peaceful here. I love the lake. Have you got a boat? Elizabethan house, isn't it?'

He was going to enjoy himself after all. He looked with envy at the moat filled with murky brown water that surrounded the house. It conjured up pictures in his boyish mind about the films he had seen depicting Robin Hood – fighting, drawbridges and moats in which the actors fell and died dreadful deaths, arrows often protruding from their backs. A narrow stone bridge now linked the house with the rest of the large garden, drawbridges being a thing of the medieval past, but Oliver thought it was wonderful. He fancied himself as a modern day Robin Hood. His thick fair hair surrounded his head like a halo and he was convinced his vivid blue eyes were a legacy from some prestigious Saxon ancestor. The old ice house intrigued him. He had visions of illicit carcasses of deer being stashed there. The antiques and pictures of men and women in Edwardian clothes that adorned the wall above the large oak staircase in the hall interested him. He had never seen anything like them before. He loved history and was surrounded by objects in a house and grounds that stirred his vivid imagination.

John could not reply. He nodded mutely and turned away. He couldn't answer his questions or tell him what a barren and miserable place he thought he lived in. Oliver would not understand. Nobody had told him who the stuffy looking men and women in Edwardian clothes were and he did not care about them or the history of his home. John longed to change places with Oliver. He had a mother and father as well as a small brother and baby sister, although he did not seem to love them, especially the brother. He, on the other hand, would appreciate them. It was not fair. His own house and his opulent surroundings oozed money but what good was that without love? He could not understand why pieces of paper and filthy coins should be allowed to determine people's lives. Having money and a large opulent house did not make a person feel good inside.

There were no other relatives to spoil John, doting aunts or uncles, and he turned to his studies for solace and mental sustenance. He learned to play a number of card games and complicated chess moves; he quite liked solitaire, too. It was not, he discovered, necessary to depend on others for his hobbies and he soon learned how to be independent and rely on himself for amusement. Many indulgent hours were spent arranging his collection of foreign stamps in books. Any attempt to interest his father in his efforts fell upon stony ground. 'Look at these Dad,' he would say to his father, 'aren't they interesting?' or 'Are those worth much? Are they a bargain? Have I spent my pocket money wisely?' He thought the latter at least would impress his father. After all making money was his father's chief interest.

'Will you play chess with me Dad? Please.'

'That's a silly game,' his father would reply. He really had no idea how to play chess and he did not have the time to learn such a tedious hobby. Stamp collecting, what rot. Business games, in his opinion, would do more to improve John's mind. The boy would be better employed reading about the business world, stocks and shares, as soon as he was able to appreciate such things.

Jack Lacey rarely held any lengthy conversation with his son. He considered him to be too young to be a decent companion. In his opinion a grunt or two was all the boy merited. Jack had a habit of wiping his face with his hands as though brushing away cobwebs and John felt he was being brushed away, too. Jack's once pretty and promising young wife was dead and with her his hopes of a happy life. In his view children should be seen occasionally but never heard. He wanted control, total control, over the situation.

'Mrs Osman,' or the name of the latest nanny, John's father would shout out in the days before John was banished to boarding school, when he was tired of the boy in the evening, which was more often than not. 'Time this lad went to bed,' and John would often find himself sent to the nursery or to his bedroom on the floor below, out of the way, at six o'clock so that his father could work on his business papers in peace. Jack Lacey was relieved to get rid of both the nanny and the child when John went to school. He convinced himself the boy was well cared for physically but apart from that he had no interest in him. What more could the little brat want? He had done his duty.

When Jack died suddenly of heart failure in his fifties John could not grieve. He tried to cry but could not and felt guilty. John had never really known him. He was his father, his features and genes declared that, but his cold and undemonstrative attitude had left John with no deep affection or feelings akin to love for the man; it was as though he was in some ways already dead and never a significant part of his life.

'What is the matter with me that I cannot grieve for my own father?' he asked himself many times when a feeling of guilt threatened to overcome him.

He trailed behind his coffin when he was buried but the funeral service was meaningless.

'My father,' he had said when urged to do so during the service,

'Jack Lacey, a good man ... he always took care of me. An astute businessman ...' What was he saying? He stumbled on in an attempt to deliver the eulogy that was expected of him. Numb and detached, he endured the burial in the local churchyard and the funeral lunch afterwards where he was joined by his father's business colleagues and associates, large strong tough men with sly fox-like faces who were anxious to keep on the right side of him, just in case he stepped into his father's shoes and became their boss or business associate. They need not have worried. John had no interest in his father's business ventures and sold them as soon as he could. He was an academic, that was his world, he was not a businessman and in no sense considered himself to be a wheeler or a dealer. Lacking confidence, he feared that he would be crushed like an ant underfoot in the business world so it was fortunate that he wanted to teach after completing a university course and obtaining a first class honours degree. He was thrifty which was a trait he had inherited from his father, and invested his father's fortune with care in what he considered were safe options. Unlike his father and many of his associates he was not a risk taker. He had studied and learned more about investing on the stock market and safe savings accounts than he ever admitted to his father and was more sensible than many when investing in the 1930s. Jack had, however been smart enough to avoid huge losses during the Wall Street crash and, unlike some who were not so astute, survived with most of his fortune intact. Several of his business associates became bankrupt after making a number of bad decisions but the majority had followed Jack's lead. They did not have the same faith in his son and would have been surprised to discover what a shrewd young man he had developed into.

John did not crave flashy cars or fast women, a small economical Ford car suited him. He was content. He had a theory that if one looked affluent, greedy and unscrupulous people would attempt to take advantage and he would have difficulty in coping, being soft and gentle at heart. Whether they would succeed was a different matter. With greater confidence in his own abilities he would have dealt with them with ease. His father had been fond of pontificating in a scathing tone when he spoke about his son,

'That boy will be eaten alive by the sharks if he enters the business world,' but John's gentle appearance disguised a firm resolve his father failed to recognize. 'He was born that way,' his father said many times, 'just a wimp, how on earth could I have spawned a child like that! He is far too shy and introverted to ever be a successful businessman.'

The fact that he did not help the boy to socialise or understand how to interact with other people did not occur to him. He thought it was not his fault that his son was so shy. He had done his best. 'I have provided the little brat with good nannies and plenty of pocket money,' he never tired of telling his friends. 'Useless though. He will never amount to much.'

The real problem, John was intelligent enough to understand, was that he, John, was alive and well and his mother had died and left his father with a child he did not want to complicate his life. Jack was an entrepreneur and a child was something his wife should have been able to look after. A man with his brilliant business aptitude should not have been burdened with a small boy.

After boarding school John went to Oxford University where he met Pamela, a quiet studious girl who wore her thick horn-rimmed glasses with flair. The lenses made her fine blue eyes look larger than they actually were and her eyes were her main asset. She loved to look like a bookworm. Her unruly thick mousy hair was cut short in a fashionable bob with an uneven fringe she had a habit of flipping back carelessly in the middle of a conversation. It hung down her forehead like a curtain, stopping just short of the top of her eyes and her short straight nose.

Pamela was too plump for her short stature, and lack of exercise and a head more often than not hovering over a book during her early years had not done her any favours. She was described by a friend as 'cuddly' and her cheap poorly cut tweedy clothes and uninteresting flat laced shoes emphasised her dumpy shape. She didn't at that time see any reason to waste money on expensive clothes she didn't need.

Pamela made the first advances.

'John Lacey,' she said, sidling up to him one day after a lecture, 'can you help me with my assignment? I really am stuck and would appreciate it.' She moved towards him and placed a small chubby hand over one of his. He jumped away as though stung by a bee. The warmth of her touch lingered for a few moments, strange and unfamiliar. It was an unusual experience for him to be touched in such an intimate way by any other human being. She moved her hand slowly up his arm.

'Come and have a coffee with me in my digs,' she wheedled and he found himself agreeing. The warmth of her soft and neatly manicured hand crept through his thin shirt. Feelings for the opposite sex that he did not fully understand and had until that moment denied, flooded through his body.

She was akin to a magnet he could not resist and she pursued him with determination in an effort to win his affection. She stirred feelings within him that he had never been fully aware that he possessed, except perhaps in the odd dream. She longed to get married but had not attracted many boyfriends; her dumpy and studious looks disguised the passionate and loving woman that lurked behind the shapeless clothes and hid her curvaceous body. John, though pitifully inexperienced with the opposite sex, knew he was lucky. He worshipped her; indeed he had never got to know any other girl very well so comparison was not relevant. Pamela gave him the affection he had craved all his young life. She had obtained a scholarship to allow her to attend Oxford and her background was very different from John's, money always being in short supply, but in his eyes that made her more desirable. She did not appear to be interested in the demon money which was God to his unfeeling father and that for him was a big plus. John was convinced that she had what he considered to be good principles and appreciated the affection and good companionship she offered him. All that glitters is not gold, he told himself, and he soon appreciated that Pam, under the dull exterior, was pure gold, and he eventually plucked up enough courage to ask her to marry him after they had completed their teaching training courses together in Bristol. They got engaged following a reluctant blessing from her parents, who thought John was a skinflint or perhaps really did not have enough money to keep their beloved daughter in reasonable comfort, though they would have been agreeably surprised, indeed amazed, if they had discovered the extent of his fortune. They never did.

'No fuss,' Pam had said. 'I don't want a flashy engagement ring or a white wedding, complete waste of money,' a sentiment that pleased the introverted John. They purchased a modest second-hand solitaire diamond engagement ring from a small backstreet shop. A blue imitation silk suit, flat black patent court shoes and a small spray of yellow carnations were her choice when they got married in the local register office.

'Lovely ring, darling John,' Pam had said. 'Reasonable too.'

'Cheapskate,' her mother muttered under her breath when she set eyes on the ubiquitous ring. 'What is the matter with the man? It looks worn and jaded.'

'It's antique, Mummy,' Pam had said with pride when she showed it to her parents.

'I should jolly well think it is,' her mother responded with sarcasm and struggled to swallow her irritation in order to spare her daughter's feelings.

'Darling Pammy,' John had called her; in his eyes she was perfect. Love and affection were, at long last, his to enjoy.

'Darling,' she would reply and fuss around him. She was warm and loving and that was an ingredient of which he had been starved for a very long time. He could not receive enough of her attentions.

Pam's parents were disappointed that they were not able to invite all their relatives to the wedding. A couple of college friends who were witnesses and Pam's mother and father were the only guests.

'You are letting us all down,' her mother declared in a fierce high-pitched voice but her ranting fell on deaf ears. 'The miserable buffet and wedding cake were a disgrace. We would have arranged something much better if you had let us. Uncle Bob and Auntie May will be most upset when they realise that they were not invited and they won't be the only ones.'

Shortly after John obtained a post in Everton Grammar School Pamela became pregnant. They purchased a rambling old cottage in need of renovation on the outskirts of Everton and looked forward eagerly to the arrival of their baby. A large garden and lawns surrounded the cottage on three sides. It was well fenced and private. 'Ideal for children to play in, perfect,' Pam declared.

'There will be plenty of room for our family,' John said. 'We'll have three or four, I expect. I've always wanted to be part of a large family.'

Pamela was like a clucky hen; she bought a wicker cradle, lined it with pink and blue gingham, decorated the small spare bedroom in cream (suitable for a boy or a girl) knitted various baby garments and planned with avid enthusiasm for the future of their baby. She would stand in front of a long mirror that hung in their hall for at least half an hour almost every day gawping at her expanding shape. It was fascinating John thought, though he likened it to the swelling belly of a fish in a local pond but was sensible enough to keep that idea to himself.

'I'm sure he or she will go to Oxford, John,' she said. 'Our child is sure to be academic just like we are.'

She looked at him through her thick pebbled glasses and pressed her soft expanding body against him for comfort and love. John was ecstatic. Pam and the baby she was expecting were all he needed.

'I wonder if it will be a boy or a girl?' she often said to him. 'It's kicking, darling, feel it, the doctor told me it is a good healthy child,' and she would press his hand to her stomach.

'A fluttering, just like a tiny bird,' he would marvel and looked forward to holding their first child in his arms. A child that would be part of him, his own flesh and blood. He would never treat it like his father had treated him. Their baby would be loved and cherished.

Two months before the baby was due Pamela slipped on ice on an old patch of cobbles that formed a short path from the kitchen to the dustbins at the back of the cottage. Nobody could see her or hear her when she cried out for help though she called out many times as loudly as she could manage.

'Somebody help me, please, somebody ... oh, help me,' she called until her voice grew faint and weak.

Tears trickled down her face and cramping pains determined to assail increased in strength as her womb reacted with strengthening contractions in an effort to abort the baby. Her voice became weaker as the minutes passed. She tried to cry for help but soon found it impossible to make any sound. Her mouth felt dry and her skin cold and clammy.

'My baby,' she mouthed. Have I damaged my back? Oh God, she thought. Someone help me. Her legs had begun to feel strangely numb. She tried to drag herself a few inches, holding on to the branch of an old plum tree that grew nearby. The sharp flinty stones that were interspersed in the cobbles dug into her legs, tore her fine silk stockings and inflicted deep scratches but she could hardly feel them. Dampness crept deep into her bones and she lifted her right hand to button the top of her cardigan to keep out the cold wind that licked her neck without mercy. The branches of the large trees at the bottom of the garden rustled and creaked as the wind found its way through her clothes. 'My right arm,' she groaned. 'It's difficult to move it. Have I broken it?' The mounting shock threatened to overcome her. She could feel the warmth of what she thought was liquid creeping down her legs. Perhaps her waters had broken, or was it blood? Her hips started to shake uncontrollably as fear gripped her. How could her bones keep jogging about like that?

'Pray God, stop the dreadful jerking, the awful pain!'

She turned her head and looked at the large white snowdrops nodding their heads under the trees. Purple and yellow crocus too were evident, their buds shut firmly as though objecting to the harsh frosty weather. The daffodils and tulips had yet to burst through the cold ground. Her attention momentarily shifted towards them.

'They'll be lovely in the spring, Pam,' she recalled John saying when they planted them together in the autumn. 'They'll give us pleasure for many years. They'll form part of our future together.'

Was there a future now? That thought became uppermost in her mind as her body foisted painful spasms upon her.

She managed with fresh resolve to cry out once again in a voice now reduced to a faint quivering whisper, tempered by the shaking that her body was enduring. Nobody answered. It was futile.

The back door she had painted with zeal a bright deep blue shortly after they had first moved into the cottage now beckoned her. If only I could open that door and feel the warmth of my small kitchen, she thought. Tears trickled again down her cheeks. A vision of the new units they had installed recently passed through her mind. She was proud of them and had filled some of the shelves with goods that would be useful when the baby arrived. She thought too about the small white wool jackets she had recently knitted, booties and hats stowed carefully away in the small bedroom that they had equipped as a nursery.

'Oh, thank heavens, the pain is going and the shaking is stopping, perhaps I will have some bones left,' she told herself with relief. She heaved a sigh, deep and languid, and watched her breath, misty and white, float away from her. As her strength ebbed and she almost lost the struggle to keep her eyes open she instinctively placed her hands across her swollen stomach in an effort to protect her baby.

'My baby ... darling ...' she whispered. 'I can't feel you kicking ...'

Their neighbours were working in Everton and an uncomfortable silence cloaked the cold damp mist that later started to form as the wind dropped. It was her only companion. Pam felt the insistent cold and dampness sink deeper into her bones and the blood from the haemorrhage trickle from her body. What could she do about it? She must be able to do something, though exactly what now eluded her. From the corners of her eyes she saw some of her rich red blood filtering along the edges of the stones where she lay, outlining them with resolute force.

She mouthed. 'John, oh my love, where are you?'

The bright blue door was the last thing she saw before she slipped into unconsciousness.

John found her cold and lifeless in the pool of frozen blood when he returned from his teaching post that evening. Their baby had died within her. He never knew whether they would have had the pleasure of a son or daughter, but that no longer mattered. He did not want to know. With Pam gone and the baby gone he retreated once more into his lonely self, unloved and unwanted, a state with which he was familiar. He found the idea of having any more children in the future abhorrent and vowed he never would. Pam had been his hope for a happy life and now that had been snatched away from him. He knew he was being illogical but a huge barrier rose up; a barrier that would be very difficult to remove.

He called out to her in his sleep night after night, 'Pam, my Pam, come back to me. I need you,' and cried like a child, the kind of free-flowing tears he had never been able to shed when he was young. She had released his inhibitions and liberated his emotions but she had gone and the fear that he was destined never to have any children became entrenched in his mind, indeed he no longer wanted them.

His health suffered and life become bleak once again for the introverted lonely John whose one taste of genuine affection had evaporated. He found concentration difficult and his work unsatisfying. The outbreak of war in 1939 became his salvation. He joined the army in 1940 and spent the war in army intelligence. He did not see much active service though he did spend six months in Egypt in connection with his duties at headquarters.

After the war the lost and bewildered man returned to teaching. He did some supply work in junior schools and found to his surprise that he enjoyed working with younger pupils; their eagerness and candid behaviour lifted him out of his introverted shell, so that he eventually applied for the post of headmaster at Enderly Junior School, a post he obtained with unexpected ease. Experienced teachers of John's calibre were hard to find and the Government were offering short courses to returning servicemen in the hope of filling the shortage of trained teachers. He sold his cottage, there were too many unhappy memories there, and purchased a small terraced house near the school. 'It's good enough for a widower like me,' he told himself. The fact that he was a wealthy young man and could have bought something more prestigious did not even occur to him.

'What a nice chap,' his neighbours proclaimed. 'Not at all stuffy and stuck up, probably hasn't got much money, like us.' He found himself, to his embarrassment, plied with home-made cakes and pies from his neighbours who were themselves still suffering from the effects of food rationing.

'He's a returning solider, he's done his bit,' and 'Poor fellow, he needs fattening up,' were remarks that he heard passed around in broad Russetshire accents. They were pleased to have their new headmaster and accepted him into the community with open arms. He was happy, at least as happy as he could be without Pam. He fitted into village life and respected the villagers' needs. He became a pillar of strength for many parents who had difficult children, and they appreciated him. It was good to feel wanted.

Pam and her unborn baby had been buried in a churchyard in Everton in an unobtrusive grave with a small headstone of which she would have approved. Almost every week he took a bunch of her favourite yellow roses to place on her grave and would sit for a while and talk to her if there was no one else nearby in the cemetery to hear him, and it made him feel less lonely. He would tell her little snippets about school life.

'Darling Pam, there is a little girl in my class, just about the same age as our child would have been at the end of the war. She even looks like you, she has the same colouring … and there's a very naughty boy …'

He replaced the small headstone after a few years with a suitably engraved one made of marble and embellished with a cupid, a symbol of his undying love. He anticipated that he would join her there one day, his bones rotting above Pam's and those of the child they had made together, something precious, worth more than any amount of his damned hoard of money. The larger stone had room for his name to be added when he died. John told himself that he would end up in this life a crusty old man with a dog or cat for company. It was his destiny.

John worked hard, the school became his life, and he appreciated the dedicated staff he had inherited, particularly Janet

Anderson, who appeared to be as hardworking as he was. A charming woman, he thought many times, although her husband was a right misery. He found himself feeling very concerned for Janet who was obviously distraught and fighting hard to hide her unhappiness. He had not liked her husband when he met him at a school function which James had apparently condescended to attend. What a selfish beggar, he's not good enough for Janet, he had thought and was surprised by the emotion that coursed through him. The wretched man is bound to let her down sooner or later.

After the war the infant and junior schools in the village had been amalgamated for the sake of economy. A new post-war estate of shoddy modern houses had been built in haste just outside the village and with the returning servicemen there had been an inevitable baby boom which John anticipated would ensure the future of his school and eventually compensate for some time for the dwindling numbers of children in the village. The post of deputy head in the school became vacant shortly after James Anderson left Janet and John hoped, with more than professional feeling stirring in his loins, that Janet might apply for the position. He decided to approach her.

'Janet, could you come to my study in the lunch hour, say 12.30?' he asked. 'I have something to discuss with you.'

Janet arrived looking sober and miserable. Tears welled in her eyes all too often lately and she tried to concern herself with the school children in her care, not the fickle and unreliable James.

'As you know, the post of deputy head has become vacant,' John said. He brushed his fine thinning hair back from his forehead with his hand that had to his surprise developed a slight tremor. 'You are a good teacher,' he continued, trying to get a grip on his emotions, 'have you thought of applying? We would work well together. Of course, the post will have to be advertised and suitable applicants interviewed so there is no guarantee you will be offered the position.'

'I have considered applying for the post but I am not sure I am able to at present. My husband, you know …'

'Yes, I understand he has left you and I am sorry.' He was not, good riddance to the man, indeed his spirits had soared when he heard the brute had left. 'But ... er ...' he continued after a short pause, 'that is all the more reason for applying isn't it?'

To his chagrin he felt his normally pale slim face colour slightly. He felt hot under the collar, a feeling he was not used to. He got out his handkerchief and mopped a slight sweat off his forehead that threatened to trickle down his face. What on earth was the matter with him? He usually handled his staff well and was naturally aloof which stood him in good stead. He prided himself in not displaying his personal emotions in public.

Janet glanced at him. He was such a nice man but not easy to approach or talk to. He was, however, a good headmaster and she admired him.

'Well, yes. I will need an increase in salary to help me pay my mortgage. I could sell my home but I'd prefer not to.'

She looked perplexed which provoked a further nervous reaction in John. He was startled. She was the one who should be quaking in her shoes, though he realised that she was not a timid woman. I am in charge here, he told himself, and stretched to his full height, looked down at Janet and made an effort to compose himself. He was suddenly very happy with the idea of working with her. He looked into her large sad eyes and felt an unexpected surge of emotion. He caught his breath and his arms tingled. He longed to hold her and comfort her. What was happening to him? He was a professional man and she was a married woman. Since his wife died John had not considered having a personal relationship with any other woman. A door closed on that side of his life and although many young women tried to flirt with him in the army he had turned away from them with cold disdain. Scathing remarks from his fellow officers like 'must be a pansy,' and 'queer chap,' had flown around but the memory of his dead wife and baby had stayed with him like a lead weight that until now could not be shifted.

A disconcerted Janet watched the flush on his cheeks and the pink creeping around his neck. She thought he was a virile and handsome man who had kept his feelings in check for a long time; quite the opposite from flippant and fickle James. She looked at him as a man for the first time. He had dark hair which was now receding slightly and a pale lean face which was strong and did not display emotions easily. Wide set grey eyes fringed with stubby lashes looked at her with an interest and thoughtfulness she had not imagined possible. He was over six feet tall and his broad shoulders exuded strength. His imposing presence was an effective asset when controlling unruly pupils and dealing with cantankerous parents, something his staff appreciated.

He felt emotions that he had not felt since Pam had died and knew that he was in danger of falling in love with this woman, and that knowledge frightened him. I really must keep my feelings in check, he told himself. I am behaving like a silly schoolboy.

'I will apply,' Janet stuttered, surprising herself. She was mesmerised for a few seconds by his attractive mouth which she found it difficult to take her eyes off, he noticed.

'Good, I'm glad,' he answered and treated her to one of his rare smiles which, to her amazement, lit up his normally self-contained features like a beacon. He turned away from her with unusual abruptness as though dismissing her and she returned to her classroom with her spirits rising and a lightness of step. Perhaps life had something to offer her after all. The challenge of a new post was just what she needed; John was right. Despite her sadness after James's departure, if she was honest with herself she was relieved that the wretched man had gone away.

That ungrateful oafish James doesn't want Janet but I'll appreciate her working here with me, John thought. His loss is my gain. He noticed that Janet had looked happier once she had made the decision to apply for the job and he felt more content than he had for a long time, although knew it would be wise to keep his new-found feelings for her under tight control. After all, they were colleagues.

Chapter 5

The Letter 1952

J anet obtained the post of deputy head and worked well with John Lacey as they had known they would. They developed a friendship which they would not have considered possible when they first met. Almost a year after James had left John suggested that they might go to a concert in Everton together.

'We're both on our own,' he said in his deep, strong voice, a voice Janet was beginning to find increasingly disturbing. 'We're professional people but there's no reason why we shouldn't spend some time together as good friends.'

Janet agreed. The memory of James and his unexpected, almost brutal, departure was fading and she was enjoying her job. She liked working with John Lacey and not only in a professional capacity. She must try and be sensible, she told herself. John could only view her as a friend and colleague.

'I'd like that,' she replied, her face lighting up in pleasure and anticipation. That was the first of many relaxing evenings they spent together when work was not too pressing and they could spare the time. Some of the other teachers in the school had observed their growing closeness and there was the inevitable staffroom chat. Janet was popular and her friends hoped that she would not be hurt again.

'He's a cold fish, that man,' and 'I thought he wasn't interested in women,' were some of the comments that flew around the staffroom. 'He's a bit of a loner, our headmaster. Quite dishy though, and he seems to like Janet,' some of the women gossiped. One or two thought they would not mind stepping into her shoes.

Janet had overheard and agreed with some of their comments. Feelings crept through her body that she knew would be best ignored. A warm glow spread over her, and into her intimate parts when she thought about his tall masculine form. She longed to feel his strong arms around her, feel his broad shoulders, stroke his hair, and smell his aftershave. This line of thought would not do. She would have to stop daydreaming about him; she was lonely, that was the explanation. Her husband had not long left her and could return at any time. She was just a silly and vulnerable woman but she wondered, painfully aware of her heightened senses, what it would be like to have his fine long fingers stroke her body. If only she had been able to form a relationship with him years ago instead of the diabolical James.

Almost eighteen months after James had walked out of her life a letter with a South African stamp and an airmail sticker fluttered down onto her hall mat. The crinkled white envelope was smudged at the edges with dirt and looked as though someone had kept it in his or her pocket for some time before posting it. The writing in pale purple ink was unfamiliar and erratic. Large loops imposed on some of the consonants. Curiosity prompted Janet to open it but it was difficult to dispel a feeling of dread and her hands shook as she slid the single sheet of writing paper out of the envelope. Although she did not recognise the writing she thought immediately of James. She often wondered where he was and if he would ever return to Enderly. The thought of his return had hung over her like a dark cloud since his departure and whenever she thought about the possibility she experienced a sense of mounting panic which was difficult to overcome. She did not want him back, and the fear that he might soon be back in Enderly took her breath away.

'It's so unfair,' she said out loud. 'Why now? Oh why?' I've moved on ... '

The marriage had been a horrible mistake and she had been a fool to put up with him for so long. She knew too that what she was now feeling for John Lacey was far from platonic or just empathy for an admired headmaster. She loved him passionately in a way that she had not experienced before. She had been infatuated with James but that was all. She thought too, or more accurately hoped, that John was fond of her and was beginning to look upon her as more than just a friend and colleague. He was a good honest man unlike her wretched husband who was nothing less than a cad and a cheat.

Her heart lurched and she felt sick as she began to read the letter. Salty teardrops trickled down her face and landed like a small pool on the unwanted letter, blurring the strange purple ink.

The signature at the bottom of the letter, Judith, was a name she could not associate with anyone that she knew. Judith wrote that she had been a close companion of James for the past year after they had met in Tunisia and travelled together to Cape Town, where her family lived. James lived with her at her family's home for a short time before becoming ill and later dying from a fever in a local hospital. He had been cremated, that was his wish, and there was, she stressed, no need for Janet to fly out to South Africa. His ashes had been scattered in her garden. She loved him and was happy to have them near her. He had told her about his failed marriage. She would, she continued, be returning a few of his personal possessions, including a wedding ring that he had worn on a chain around his neck, as soon as she could afford the postage. There was also a letter James had addressed to Janet which she claimed she had already forwarded. Judith did not include an address or contact number.

The letter from James did not arrive, nor did the parcel containing James's effects. Months passed and Janet was no nearer to solving the mystery. She consulted her solicitor Peter Mace and he promised to help her in any way he could.

She was grateful to her old friend Peter whom she had known since she was a child. He was fond of Janet and considered her to be one of his best friends. Janet knew that Peter was disappointed when she married James but, although she was fond of him, she did not want anything more than friendship. She was relieved when he married Alice a year later, another old friend, a middle-class girl his family approved of. Peter and Alice had a son called

Jeremy, a precocious, lively and intelligent boy they hoped would one day join the family firm of solicitors. Janet felt guilty when she thought about Peter. He had told her when they were teenagers that he would always love her but there was no way now she could return his affections. For her that teenage romance was well and truly buried in the past. It had been a disaster. Their family backgrounds were different and Peter's family made clear at the time that there could be no future for them. She noticed that he too often glanced at her with the kind of interest that he should be reserving for his wife Alice but ignored his overtures with firmness. She was happy to be his friend but that was all.

'I'll make some enquiries for you, but don't be too optimistic,' Peter told her now. 'His death may be difficult to prove and we have no idea who this Judith woman is. We have no address or surname to help us.'

Janet hoped that there was no mistake about James's demise. If James was dead she would be free. Free, that was a word that sounded wonderful when she said it out loud.

'Free, free ...' She felt guilty but elated. If only she had not married the man, a sentiment echoed many times in the mind of Peter Mace.

Peter contacted the appropriate authorities in South Africa as he had promised and also the police but no trace could be found of a James Anderson or Judith in Cape Town, though there was a Thomas Mason who had a daughter Judith and he had once owned a small hotel in the area not far from the hospital, but that line of enquiry petered out – a mistake, as was to be proved later. It was as though James had been rubbed out like the writing on her blackboard at the end of a lesson, an analogy she found interesting. She would, however, have to wait a long time before she could file a petition to have him declared dead. Was she a widow? She was embroiled in painful limbo. Janet longed to get on with her life, perhaps get married again, though there was only one man she was interested in, and maybe have the child she had yearned to have for so long.

She wanted to be with John Lacey but knew that unless she could obtain an annulment of her marriage she was not free to pursue this relationship. She dreamt about him and woke up each morning with his name upon her lips. She was lonely and longed to feel his body close to her own. She wondered as the months passed if John felt the same about her and suspected that he did. She had noticed how he looked at her on occasions with a smouldering warmth in those appealing wide grey eyes and with what she thought was definite longing, but convinced herself that she was being foolish and imagining it. They could live in sin – had John considered that possibility? She ached to know. It would be a scandal that would be frowned on by some of the village residents and the school authorities but she started to dream about a future with John. The nineteen fifties were still bound in many ways by old-fashioned Victorian values. They could meet secretly, she fantasized. She longed to have his children who would be beautiful, and knew she wanted to be with this wonderful man for the rest of her life. She became obsessed with the idea. She lost weight and looked wan. Their behaviour in the school and on their frequent outings to local concerts continued as before and the physical closeness of working with him was becoming unbearable. She decided the only answer to the problem was to apply for a job elsewhere, sell Primrose House and move far away from Russetshire.

John had developed deep feelings for her too but was not in a hurry to get married again. When he considered the possibility he would creep back into his inner self, like a snail retreating into a shell, for safety. However, he could not imagine life without Janet and had begun to depend upon her for company as well as support in his job. Feelings of guilt and the knowledge that he was being selfish assailed him. She may want a family, something he no longer wanted; the possibility terrified him, and he would have to make that clear to her if it was proved that James was dead and she was free to marry him. Procrastination was his only option.

'I am applying for a post in Yorkshire,' Janet announced one day three years after James had left Enderly, when they were alone in John's study at the end of a busy day. 'I have a few friends and relatives there still, though the aunt I stayed with and was particularly close to when I was a girl is now dead.

'I can't stay here any longer John. I'm becoming too fond of you and it isn't professional or fair. I'm foolish, and I'm sorry ...' Tears welled up in her eyes and her breath caught in her throat. She emitted a loud sob. 'I enjoy my job here with you and can't imagine living anywhere else but it's the only way forward.'

John was shaken, his normally confident voice deserted him and his cheeks became flushed. He stretched out a hand and gripped a chair in order to steady himself, then he opened his mouth to speak but could only produce a hoarse whisper.

'Don't leave me Janet. I need you.'

'Need is not enough,' she responded with inordinate swiftness. Her usual placid features became puckered and twisted in an attempt not to break down. She moved away from him. Her heart thudded and thumped with rapid strokes in her chest and her breath deteriorated into short gasps.

'Don't go, Janet. There must be a way. James has left you and the letter you received indicated that he died in Cape Town. He was not right for you anyway. File for a divorce or a petition to have him declared dead as soon as you can. I love you Janet. I want to marry you one day when you're free, that is if you will have me. We can wait, it will be worth it.'

He surprised himself with his offer of marriage but he now knew without any doubt that was what he wanted. He was a fool to deny himself the physical comfort and joy Janet could bring him and he longed for that, though he had tried to convince himself that he did not. His greatest fear was that she would want children and he didn't think he could cope with the idea of Janet having a child and perhaps losing it. He knew it was stupid and something that may never happen. He told himself that perhap he could overcome his fear in time but the memory of Pam and her unborn child still haunted him.

Janet was overwhelmed and moved towards John. He placed his arms firmly around her waist and pulled her to him. They kissed.

'I can't wait for years, John; I want to be with you now, to share our lives.'

'Hush, Janet. We can continue our shared social life, and sleep together. It's the fifties and things are more relaxed now. There are still a few old-fashioned strait-laced people in the village but the younger generation are seeking freedom from old Victorian constraints. We'll have to be discreet but we can manage that.'

He undid her plait and stroked her dark hair with tender fingers. He touched the intriguing dimple on her face and ran his hands enthusiastically over her body, something that he had longed to do for so long, and was fired with feverish desire to possess her, urged on by the warm response he was receiving.

Thus began the regular routine of finishing their day's work in either Primrose House or John's home. More often than not they would go to Primrose House where Janet would cook them supper and they would spend an hour or two indulging in passionate sex in the large spare bedroom at the top of the house. Janet would make up the double bed ready for them with her best lavender-scented sheets. Her daily help did not go into that room; she assumed as it was kept locked it was only used for storage. It became their retreat until the day when Janet's petition to have James declared dead became reality. After all, even in the days when sex outside marriage was still frowned upon by the older generation, and some of the younger strait-laced parents of their pupils, they had the excuse that they had work they needed to do together. They would lie entwined, naked and sated with their lovemaking, and plan their future.

Seven years after James departed from Enderly Janet and John were married in Everton Registry Office. James had been officially declared dead. It was common knowledge in the school, despite their efforts to keep their personal life secret, that they were lovers. Janet was popular with the staff and John, in spite of his aloof manner, was an admired and respected headmaster. Everybody wished them well.

Life for Janet was wonderful. She had made a few silly mistakes with her relationships in the past but this was not one of them. John had told her that he was not keen to have children but she hoped that he would change his mind. She longed for a baby but John's happiness was the most important thing.

Chapter 6

Felicity Brown

Felicity's mother Anne Anderson was younger than her brother James. She was an insidious individual as a child but blossomed into an attractive teenager. She wasn't very academic but when she was just fourteen she obtained a job as a trainee typist in a local accountant's office near her home in South London.

'It's boring work,' Anne complained bitterly to her parents. 'The money's not half bad though. One pound ten bob a week for typing a few letters and hanging about doing a bit of filing. I can't complain, I suppose.' She gave a pound to her father every pay day for her keep and enjoyed spending the rest on herself. It was pure luxury.

The 'gang' as they liked to refer to themselves, a group of her old school pals, met once a week in a local pub, some pretending they were older than they were, where they would order sherry or beer and boast about how much they could drink without feeling tipsy. Fortunately they were restricted by their lack of ready cash. A few illicit fags were also passed around. 'We must be sociable, everybody smokes,' was their excuse to justify the cheap Woodbines they coveted. All the film stars they watched in the small local ABC smoked and the cinema was always full of choking tobacco fumes. There were no objections or health warnings to deter them. It was the accepted norm.

'Come on, have a puff, be sociable,' was a favourite phrase.

The outbreak of war with Germany in 1939 put an end to their innocent existence. Several of the boys who were eighteen rushed with a patriotic fervour to join the forces as soon as they could and one or two of the girls followed suit. They imagined it would be better than the dull life they endured at home. The rigid class system had kept many of them in their place for many years and this was an opportunity to break some of those unwelcome bonds. Service in big houses or working long hours as shop assistants were not things they wanted any more. Freedom, although dangerous, beckoned them and they were keen to taste it.

Anne was directed to work in a factory that made parachutes. 'I must do my bit,' she said but she found the work very dull. She was pleased to be able to make her underwear out of a few remnants of the silk but that was the only bonus.

'It's worse than office work,' she told her father. 'I wish I was old enough to join the forces. Another year and I will.'

'Be thankful you are not old enough my girl,' her father retorted. He had been a young conscript in the First World War, and was gassed before being invalided out of the army. That experience had dented any patriotic enthusiasm he once possessed. Shortly after the outbreak of the Second World War he contracted pneumonia which, because of the damage inflicted on his lungs earlier by mustard gas, ensured a swift demise. He had been an intelligent man who had attended the local county grammar school but his war-time injuries meant that he could only work part-time in a simple clerical job for most of his life and money was always in short supply.

James joined the navy as soon as he could in 1939 and Anne and their mother Jane rarely received any letters from him. He was intelligent like his father and had completed a degree course in History at London University, an achievement of which he was proud. He was going to make sure he obtained a better job than any his poor old dad had obtained.

'I've been accepted for officer training,' he told his parents with pride the last time she saw him and received the admiration and pat on the back for which he had hoped.

Anne coveted a job as a clippie on the London buses. There were plenty of vacancies now that the men had joined the forces, and, although too young, she lied about her age and was accepted for training. She had several boyfriends, one of whom was Richard Brown, a local boy she had met whilst still attending school in Putney, in South London.

On his first leave before being posted to France Richard made amorous advances towards Anne.

'Sleep with me, Anne,' he begged. 'We may not get another chance – I'll probably be killed in France like my uncles in the First World War. I don't want to die a virgin.'

Anne considered that reasonable enough despite the warnings of her mother over the years.

'Keep yourself for your husband, girl, nobody wants soiled goods! Dirty behaviour never pays.'

Silly old-fashioned ideas they were, Anne told herself, out of date and complete rubbish. She was jolly well going to please herself now and she did. Richard and Anne made love wherever they could when Richard was home on leave from his barracks only twenty miles away. After the death of his parents Richard lived with an elderly uncle whose greatest pleasure was to drink with his mates in the local pub, the Pig and Whistle, and they often had his uncle's house to themselves in the evenings. German bombing raids and nights spent in uncle's damp old Anderson shelter were not ideal but so long as they could indulge their passion they didn't care. This arrangement came to an abrupt end when Richard was posted to France.

'We'll get married after the war, Anne,' he promised.

'I'll keep you to that.' She laughed and hugged him. She thought that she might marry him but was in no hurry to be tied down. She was far too young. Now, that young Canadian billeted with her father's old aunt Gladys, he really was something. Oh well, as long as they were careful she thought she would not have any unwanted kids, and it would give her a chance to test the waters elsewhere.

The same arrangement of sleeping with a boyfriend was transferred to the young Canadian, Johnny. Old Aunt Gladys was often out visiting friends or sleeping in a neighbour's Morrison shelter, which was convenient. In fact, Anne preferred Johnny in some ways, he was better in bed, and surprisingly handsome despite his plump build. He often seemed restless and unpredictable but she dismissed his behaviour as normal for a young man away from home and faced with the horrors of war. He was killed after a few months when his plane was shot down during the Battle of Britain.

A few weeks later Anne found she was pregnant and she knew that an illegal abortion would be a risky undertaking. She didn't want some old backstreet crone helping her out for a few pounds. There was another way.

The next time Richard came home on leave she decided to tell him about the baby. 'Richard, I'm pregnant,' she said. 'It's your baby and it must have happened last time you came home on leave. I'm sorry, but you did say we would get married one day ... it will just be earlier than we had planned.'

'Of course,' he said. 'We'll get married straight away, it's not the best of times but we don't want too much gossip, and whatever happens we will have done the honourable thing and won't give the local old righteous busybodies too much to talk about over their garden fences. Our baby will be born in wedlock.'

The baby, Felicity, was born a few weeks later than expected but nobody in the family was any the wiser.

'First babies are sometimes late,' Anne said, assuming an innocent expression, and Richard believed her.

'Looks like her dad,' Anne lied. 'Just the same shaped face, she will be a pretty little girl.'

Felicity looked very much like her mother, the same odd pale flecked blue eyes and fine curly fair hair. She was a problem child but Anne was convinced that if Felicity had not been so restless she could have been a high flyer instead.

Richard became suspicious but usually kept his doubts to himself.

'I can't believe I've spawned a child like Felicity,' he said in an unguarded moment. 'She's an unsettled little girl, nobody in our family is like that.'

'Nor in mine,' Anne retorted. 'It's just one of those unlucky things. Of course she's your daughter, there was nobody else. She must be a throwback, it does happen. Maggie who lives in the next street married a white American soldier last year and her baby is black. Her husband's family traced the baby's genes back three generations to when a great granddad had married a coloured girl.'

Anne's heart beat furiously and she prayed that Richard would believe her. She thought sometimes about Johnny. He too had been 'restless' and it occurred to her that it might be hereditary, though she had never heard or read about such a condition.

Richard did not answer, at least their son who had been born the following year must be his; he had the same shaped ears as Richard, though both children had Anne's tapir nose and odd blue eyes. He did not trust his wife, a feeling that grew and festered within him.

Felicity continued to be a difficult child. Anne was not lenient but became exhausted in her efforts to control her. In a later decade Felicity might have been diagnosed as hyperactive and suffering from an attention deficiency disorder and she would be offered medication or counselling. The theory that her condition could be hereditary would have been considered and her family helped to discover the best way to cope with their difficult daughter. Anne did not have the benefit of accurate assessment, helpful drugs, counselling or internet information to fall back on to help her child. She felt responsible, guilty and inadequate and often drank a swig of whisky or gin when she could afford it to drown her feelings of incompetence. Felicity continued to cause her parents much grief and her younger brother Ronald had a difficult time dealing with his sister's behaviour. He was too young to understand, indeed nobody understood her behaviour and Felicity knew it. She could not control her mood swings and erratic actions but craved reassurance, love and help.

When Felicity was six years old Anne and her mother were killed in a car crash. Felicity and her younger brother Ronald were sent to live with Richard's Aunt Dolly in Northumberland. Janet and James were asked if they would have one or other of the children occasionally to give Aunt Dolly a break. Janet was not really keen.

'I will have them for a week or two during the school summer holidays Richard, but we are both working and can't have them here for long.'

A week would be more than long enough, she decided. Richard was too eager to ditch his responsibilities.

'Well,' James had retorted when she told him about Richard's request, 'they may be my niece and nephew but as far as I am concerned they are a dead loss. You can entertain them, I'm not going to stay around and put up with that silly Felicity. Ugh, kids … Richard is too keen to get rid of the little brats. He should have made more effort to stop his wife from drinking, especially when driving that old car. She was unhappy. It was probably his fault anyway.'

Janet agreed and regretted her generosity.

Richard soon obtained a job which entailed working abroad for an oil company.

'I won't be able to get home as often as I would like to see the children,' he had bleated at the time but Janet knew he really did not want to see them.

There were no grandparents to help and Richard's aunt and uncle in Northumberland, though really too elderly to take on two children, were the only relatives who had, though with some reluctance, agreed to help. Richard had jumped at their initial tentative offer to take the youngsters off his hands.

'Poor little children,' his soft-hearted aunt had said at the time. A statement she was later to regret.

In no time Richard had a string of girlfriends who were far more interesting than his children. He didn't want to get married again and enjoyed his freedom. He continued to doubt whether they were really his children anyway. Ronald might be but he was not a child he felt pleased to call his own. The boy was intelligent but had no spirit and was weak and useless, and probably wouldn't amount to much anyway.

The first holiday the children spent with Janet and James was a disaster. It was one year before James decided to leave Enderly and he was morose and miserable most of the time. Felicity at just seven years old was pining for her mother and hated living with her great aunt in Northumberland.

'Can't I live with you and Uncle James?' she would ask every day.

'Not possible dear,' Janet had replied quickly. She knew that James would be livid if he thought he was stuck with 'those children' as he labelled them and for once she agreed with him.

Ronald was quiet and subdued and he hardly uttered a word during the time he stayed in Primrose House. Janet was concerned for the boy and did her best to make him welcome. She feared he was afraid to speak and would benefit from speech training which could help him release his inhibitions but James thought that would be silly and Janet's efforts to obtain a teacher for him were quickly squashed.

Felicity was spiteful and jealous of any attention Janet paid her brother. James disappeared to the Green Man Pub most evenings to enjoy a pint of local ale in peace, leaving Janet on her own to put the children to bed and attempt to read to them. She tried playing cards, various games she had played as a child like snap and sevens. She introduced them to Snakes and Ladders and got out her old Monopoly set. Ronald tried to concentrate on the games but Felicity made sure he could not succeed or win anything. Her lack of concentration became contagious.

'Silly boy,' she would chant, 'can't play any games properly, just a Dumbo.' Ronald burnt his arm on the Aga twice and managed to injure himself however carefully Janet tried to avoid accidents, and that worried her. Felicity was agitated, restless and unpredictable and appeared determined to ensure Ronald could not think clearly about anything he was doing for long. Janet heaved a sigh of relief when their father appeared at the end of their stay, having flown home from the Middle East, to take them back to Northumberland.

'They need help, Richard,' she stressed. 'Felicity is like a jack in the box most of the time and Ronald's withdrawn and miserable. The poor lad can't concentrate and is accident prone.'

'Oh, they will be all right,' Richard had answered cheerily with a flippant wave of his hand and with what appeared to Janet to be an appalling lack of concern. 'Aunt Dolly and Uncle Bert will keep them in order.'

Janet thought the best thing would be for Richard to meet some nice homely woman who could be a mother to his children, although she would feel sorry for any person who had the bad luck to cope with Felicity.

Richard was daydreaming about the luscious dark girl he had met at work the week before, not the marrying or motherly type but fair game for a while and no strings attached, which suited him. He had not been happy with Anne and their daughter Felicity was nothing less than a nightmare. His son lacked backbone and his affection for his children was fast diminishing.

The children came twice more to stay with Janet after James had left her. Janet coped with them with mounting dismay. Things did not improve.

'I can't have your children again,' she told Richard after a gruelling few days with them in the first school holiday after James had left her. 'I have a large house and garden to look after and a new post as deputy head. I need to do a lot more preparation and paperwork for the school. James isn't here to help and life is difficult. You are responsible for them, Richard.'

The children were an unwelcome burden. She thought with burning resentment that James had done enough to ruin her life and she needed to move on. She certainly did not need his unpredictable niece and her young brother in her life. The only person she wanted now was John Lacey.

Richard's Aunt Dolly too was finding Felicity increasingly difficult.

'Bert,' she would grumble to her husband day after day, 'I'm getting too old to cope with a kid like Felicity. I just can't do with it now.' She would sigh and groan. 'Richard will have to make other arrangements. Ronald isn't too bad, the poor little devil would be better on his own.'

Richard despaired. It would cost him hard-earned money but he agreed to send Felicity to a boarding school in a small village outside Bristol. He hoped it would be worthwhile. At least it would give him and Aunt Dolly some breathing space. He looked forward to concentrating on his latest girlfriend, a young busty blonde who had just joined his work team; a relationship that was promising and had even prompted him to think about marrying again one day.

The boarding school classes were small and the atmosphere friendly but Felicity made no attempt at first to befriend other girls or learn. This was her father's way of getting rid of her and separating her from her brother. A deep resentment almost consumed her and twisted her thinking. She endured the lessons and cheeked the staff as often as she could. The majority of the teachers became exasperated with her but her fees were paid on time and that was the Head's chief concern, at least at first.

The school boasted a small commercial department, consisting of a tiny room with four typewriters, and an inexperienced young woman, Miss Badley, who had little teaching experience, in charge. When she was fourteen Felicity opted for the commercial course. It must be better than French she told herself, and the French mistress Miss Lamont cheered when she realised that the disruptive Felicity would no longer be a member of her class. Felicity had spattered ink over the textbooks, spat in other pupils' faces and made herself objectionable during the time Miss Lamont had tried to teach her. Letters of complaint to the Head from parents and a string of detentions and threats of expulsion made no impression upon Felicity. She would have been delighted to have been thrown out of the wretched school, especially that boring French class.

'Come on Felicity, you could become an excellent secretary one day,' the pretty, young and somewhat naive Miss Badley told her. 'You have a natural aptitude for commercial subjects.' She was unaware of Miss Lamont's unusual jollity and pats on the back from other colleagues in the staffroom. In fact, Miss Lamont produced a bottle of good French wine to share with her colleagues when Miss Badley was not around, something she had never done before. Until she met Felicity she considered that she was an excellent disciplinarian.

'That girl is really something,' she declared with passion to her fellow teachers. It was a sentiment they all endorsed.

Felicity thought Miss Badley was a soft touch and liked the attention she received. The woman was in her opinion a tad dopey but she would go along with the commercial course for a while. To her amazement she discovered something she liked doing. Her fingers flew over the typewriter keys and she even managed to pass three examinations and reach an advanced standard. She was too busy and intrigued to be a nuisance. Her English skills were weak but she managed with the help of a dictionary to improve her spelling and achieve a reasonable command of punctuation and grammar. She made a conscientious effort to write shorthand but that proved difficult for her, though she boasted later on when filling in job applications: 'I have almost achieved verbatim standard.' She actually had difficulty in deciphering any of her so-called shorthand notes and more often than not resorted to writing quickly in longhand and hoping that her translations were acceptable. Miss Badley, as she had anticipated, didn't notice, or pretended she didn't. Felicity relaxed and her behaviour improved.

Simple accounts were no obstacle. At least she understood the difference between debtors and creditors and the necessity to make accounts balance. The dream of obtaining a secretarial post with a handsome wealthy boss who would want to marry her sustained her interest in her studies. A secretarial post could be her passport to riches in the future.

She fantasized. He would be rich and handsome and she would walk down the aisle in a white satin dress. They would live in a large mansion in the country. She looked forward to the day when she could live in perfect luxury. She longed to have money but so far she had very little experience of possessing much or the security and pleasures in life that she imagined it could bring. Many of the girls in the school had wealthy parents, snobs she labelled them, and on occasions envy shot through her, twisting further her already muddled thinking.

Some of the teenage girls were quite worldly and they chatted at length about their sexual experiences and life abroad during the school holidays, and bragged about their affairs to the innocent Felicity.

'When I return to Africa with my parents in the holidays I have sex with several men,' Betty Smart boasted frequently when the lights had been turned out in the dormitory at night and the girls chatted quietly so that Matron would not hear them. Her voice would quiver with excitement. 'I am going to marry one of them when I leave school. He owns a big farm and is a rich and handsome fellow and has promised to buy me a big diamond engagement ring.'

Hmm … Felicity thought. It's probably all lies, he only wants to sleep with her.

Felicity's bed was next to Betty's in the dormitory they shared with three other girls. Betty would describe her experiences to the other girls in minute detail.

'Come on Betty, what is it like?' they would ask and the answers always provoked many oohs and aaahs. Felicity was convinced that she was missing something wonderful and the sooner she was able to leave school and indulge herself the better.

When she was just sixteen Felicity persuaded her father that she was ready for the big wide world.

'I'm not going to learn any more here,' she urged. Richard, after a chat with the Headmistress, was inclined to agree. The Head made it quite clear that she would like to see the back of the unpredictable Felicity and the sooner the better. Nothing it seemed could subdue the girl's restlessness and often unpleasant behaviour. There had been too many occasions when ink had been splashed on the back of the blouses of other girls and broken pencils hurled with force across a classroom when Felicity had failed to understand some minor point in a lesson. Without the commercial course to fall back on she would have got rid of her long ago whatever the consequences for her father, who was a weak character in the Head's opinion and should have taken that girl in hand long ago.

'It may be sensible,' she told Richard, 'for Felicity to be assessed by a child psychologist.' Heaven knows the girl needs that, she thought.

'There is no point in having an assessment,' Richard insisted. 'I don't want my daughter to be labelled mentally deficient by some quack. She is just high spirited.'

Richard was far from weak, he was just uninterested and was convinced that Felicity was not his daughter. The sooner she stood on her own feet, preferably a long way away from him, the happier he would feel. That day could not come fast enough for him.

With Richard's help Felicity obtained a job in London as a typist in a Government Office, and a place to stay in a hostel for girls. She was lucky. So was Richard, at least he thought so. She did not stay long, however, there were too many rules and regulations.

'Be in by ten, keep your room tidy, make your bed. It's like a damned prison,' Felicity fumed. She was not very well organised and tended to put off tidying up her things, to the annoyance of two other girls with whom she shared a room. She couldn't see any hope of getting out of the tedious typing pool so that she could enjoy bright lights, sex and true independence. She was not in any case earning enough money. The wizened old bat who supervised the typing pool was far from the handsome boss she had dreamed about marrying one day. She would leave. Richard despaired.

Felicity moved erratically from one job to another, insurance offices, solicitors, stockbrokers, estate agents and others, only staying a few months in each one until she went to Canada to work for a friend of her father's when she was twenty.

'He's a good chap, my friend Bob,' Richard told her. 'He's doing us a favour by taking you on. It will be a wonderful experience for you. Canada is a lovely country.'

It was Richard's last desperate attempt to do something to rid himself of his difficult and trying daughter.

Bob had told Richard that he needed some secretarial help in his lumber business and he agreed to employ Felicity to repay a favour he owed Richard.

'Any good, is she?' Bob had asked.

'Marvellous', Richard had replied. 'She's a really good typist.' That at least was true. 'She takes shorthand and can handle all your accounts,' he continued, with his tongue in his cheek.

Arrangements were made for Felicity to travel to Canada and Richard heaved a sigh of relief. It was worth every penny he had paid for her air fare.

After writing her a pleading letter, Felicity paid a brief visit to Janet a few days before she went to Canada and noted with interest that

Aunt Janet's new husband John was quite a spunk. Rich, too, she discovered and hoped that some of the wealth he had inherited would one day be passed down to her. Money was her greatest interest; she longed to possess it but so far it had eluded her. They have no kids, after all, she thought. I'll keep an eye on this situation just in case I don't meet my millionaire. She did not correspond often with Aunt Janet but needed a contact in the area to report to her from time to time what was going on at Primrose House. She had met a girl when walking along the river bank and they became friendly in quite a short time, which was unusual for Felicity.

'I'm staying with my rich aunt in Primrose House,' she said. 'I'm off to Canada soon to work but would like to know how things are here, would you write to me? It could be in your interest too one day. I would love to have some news about Enderly.'

She had chosen her contact well. The girl, Pattie, who was about the same age as Felicity, was interested to hear about the residents of Primrose House and liked the idea of having a penfriend in Canada. Pattie was not very well educated and her family had worked on the land around Enderly for several generations. It suited both girls to correspond and they wrote to each other regularly over the coming years.

Pattie worked for a while as a hairdresser in Brinton, a small town about five miles away, before marrying a local boy who worked in the fields for a wealthy landowner, as his parents had done before him. They had one daughter Helen who when she grew up worked in the Everton office of Janet's financial adviser. The fact that Felicity had said that Janet was rich was interesting to both mother and daughter. Helen, who should have been bound by the ethics surrounding client confidentiality, was in a position to observe Janet's investments and was so impressed by their size she passed this information to her mother who was delighted to pass the latest figures on to Felicity.

Richard wrote to his friend shortly after Felicity had started work in Bob's office in Canada and asked how she was settling in. He was pleased to receive a satisfactory reply. 'A nice, girl, helpful and willing,' Bob wrote. He did not comment on her lack of prowess as a secretary or her inability to make friends with the other members of his staff. Richard smiled with satisfaction. She is probably sleeping with him, hot little tart, he thought wryly, but what could he expect with a mother like Anne? His doubts about Anne and the parentage of their first-born had grown and festered like a rotting apple. The wretched woman died and left me with a demon in skirts. Felicity resembles Anne but not my family in any way, he thought. She could be a throwback as Anne had once suggested but he thought it was unlikely. Ronald was his but he would not mind if he wasn't. The boy still lacked spirit and showed no sign of improvement the last time he set eyes upon him. 'Useless, huh ...' he would mutter when he thought about his son, which was not often.

Felicity married a lumberjack but that marriage didn't last long. Very few worthwhile things lasted long in her chaotic life. She had considered her husband to be handsome and virile at first but soon decided that he was a silly and uncouth man who always dressed in checked shirts and thick twill trousers. All he thinks about is drinking with his mates and chopping wood. I will never be rich if I stay with him, she thought.

She was tired of the outdoor type and ghastly cold weather in the north of Canada. 'All bears, wolves, snow, frostbite and ugly thick clothes,' she remembered shouting at him. 'I'm off!' At least the marriage had given her a chance to get away from the lecherous Bob and she was thankful for that. Bob was fun at first but too demanding and rough for her taste.

She obtained a divorce as quickly as she could, claiming untruthfully that he had slept with several bimbos in the lumber camp, and moved to Vancouver where she found a job as a cook in a restaurant. She once again took her maiden name of Brown which she preferred to her married name, Griffiths. Felicity became an efficient cook, she loved the work; it was, like the typing at school, one of the few things that interested her. It was fun for a while and not too mentally demanding. She moved from one job to another, never staying more than a few years, and lived with several doubtful men until she moved in with an Italian immigrant Roberto who was six years older than she was.

Roberto was a steady and reliable man who had a calming influence on the nervous and anxious Felicity. He had a poorly paid job in a department store but did earn a steady income and that was better than nothing. They rented a small flat and had little money to spare but Felicity was as happy as she could be without the cash she longed to have. She dreamt about buying jewels and smart clothes but her wardrobe remained sparse.

He's a lovely Latin type, she would tell herself in an attempt to convince herself that she should stay with him and that things could be worse. He's a good lover but it's a pity he hasn't got a better job.

She wrote to Ronald when she felt like it, which was not often, and she would, if she was lucky, receive a reply from him in the form of one or two paragraphs on cheap white paper, which she considered were as dull as ditchwater.

'He was always a boring quiet child. What a miserable tyke of a brother to have,' she would grumble to herself. He did not send her any photographs of his daughter as a baby which she would have liked and had asked him for several times, after all she was her niece, or of his wife whom she had been curious about, but just one small snap when his daughter was about eighteen years old sitting on a bench with her mother under a strange exotic tree in his garden. His wife and daughter appeared to be as uninteresting as he was. 'Ugly bossy-looking bitches, like a couple of hippos!' she exclaimed as her temper flared and she tore it up. 'He's welcome to them. No wonder he has not sent any photographs before.' She did wonder, however, if he had any money and if it would be worthwhile sending him a hard-luck letter. She understood he had a successful dental practice and should be ripe for a penny or two, but doubted if he would oblige. He had always been mean and careful with money.

'OK, here. We are doing well, real Aussies now ...' was repeated with monotonous regularity on postcards depicting kangaroos, koala bears or some obscure surfing beach. Even his Christmas cards had an Australian theme and bored her stiff. If they had been accompanied by a few dollars they would have been much more interesting.

She had considered visiting him for a cheap holiday but never had enough spare money to pay the air fare and he didn't offer to help her. She realised that he probably would not welcome her with open arms and it would be a complete waste of time.

When Felicity reached her early sixties Roberto died suddenly from a heart attack. She had few friends, those she had made found her too difficult for any length of time, and her thoughts returned to dear Auntie Janet. She decided to write to her. She had made sure that she kept in contact with her at Christmas and it was now time for that long-delayed visit. She was getting too old to start another more lucrative career and had lost interest in men. Also money was tight.

She sat down at a rickety old cheap pine desk, rough and fit for not much more than firewood, that she had bought with Roberto in a sale a few years before, and found an old and slightly crumpled piece of cream paper tucked away in one of the drawers.

'Dear Aunt Janet,' she began. 'I suppose I still call her that,' she muttered to herself. I wonder what the old hag is like now. She was not very welcoming last time I saw her, she thought. Hmmm, she must be about eighty-six or -seven now. 'I find myself alone,' she continued to write, 'my dear partner Roberto having died recently and I would love to return to England and visit some of my old friends.' She could not for the life of her think of the names of any old acquaintances, except Pattie Moore, who had proved useful as a spy over the years. 'I have booked a flight next month and wonder if you would let me stay with you for a while? I would really love to talk about old times and catch up with all your news dear Auntie. I should be arriving in London on the 18th October and could be with you on the 19th. I am so looking forward to seeing you once again. Your loving niece Felicity.'

Hopefully, she tried to convince herself, the old girl will want to see me after all this time, though she doubted it. Primrose House and luxury for a while seemed a good proposition and she sighed with pleasurable anticipation. If nothing else it could prove to be a free holiday and a holiday she needed.

She sold the meagre furniture that she had purchased with

Roberto over the past few years, together with her mother's diamond ring. Her father had given the ring to her just before she left for Canada when he waved her off at the airport. 'It's a fine stone and should be worth a bit,' he said. It had been a last-minute gesture from a man with a conscience that had started to trouble him.

'Thanks Dad,' she had muttered and gave him an unexpected kiss. Richard cringed but she did not notice. He had given her something valuable and for that she was grateful. The fact that it had belonged to her mother was unimportant. She was not sentimental.

Felicity wore it for a while, showed it off to her colleagues at work, then thought better of that and placed it in a safe and secret place for a rainy day. She had not told Roberto, her husband or any of her other men friends about it. It was her nest egg for emergencies and it had now come into its own. She hoped fervently that it would lead her to a better life. A sprat to catch a mackerel, she thought and smiled. I'm over sixty now and have nothing much to show for my years of hard work in hot kitchens and typing pools or the useless men I've had the misfortune to shack up with. Now I'm going to collect my inheritance. Uncle James would approve of that if he was still alive, God rest his soul!

She purchased a few new clothes – she didn't want to look like the poor relation she was – had her hair trimmed and dyed, and packed her few belongings into an old battered suitcase that had belonged to Roberto. It's quite good quality, she thought, after giving it a much needed lick of cheap furniture polish. It doesn't look too bad, she convinced herself in a desperate effort to boost her self-confidence. There are a few scratches and dents but I will look well travelled and will soon be in England. Her spirits lifted.

Chapter 7

The Return of the Evacuee 1995

Rejection by Janet and James Anderson was a bitter pill for the young Tom Hands to swallow but he was fortunate. He was fostered out with a solicitor and his wife, a charming and kind couple, who lived in a large rambling old house on the outskirts of Everton not many miles from Enderly. He attended Everton Grammar School for a short while then, after he had been formally adopted, a private school of his new parents' choice in Russhampton so that he lost touch with any previous acquaintances from Enderly. His adoptive parents were a middle-class couple with inherited capital and were in a position to give Tom a comfortable and happy existence quite different from any he had known before. Tom took their surname of Barker and was known by his first name of Robert, or Robbie, to his new family and friends. Fulfilling his earlier promise, he won a scholarship to Oxford University.

'He is a clever lad,' his parents said, 'we will be proud of him.' And they were.

'We were lucky when you came to live with us,' they never tired of telling him. He thought he was the lucky one, although a corner of his heart would always remain with Alicia Merryweather.

Robbie matured into an attractive man and it would have been difficult for Janet to recognise him if she had passed him in the streets of Everton or Brinton. He did not look for her; he had no desire to meet the obnoxious James who had rejected him, something he found difficult to accept as well as what he considered was betrayal by Janet, try as he might to understand her point of view. As he was growing up he did wonder if Janet ever looked for him. He hoped she did but doubted if he would ever find out. He owed some loyalty to his adoptive parents. They were kind and gave him affection when he needed it and he swore that he would not set foot in Enderly whilst they were alive.

His adoptive parents died within a short time of each other when he was only forty years old but left him their large old house on the outskirts of Everton and a reasonable amount of capital. He was the son they had always wanted and he had brought joy and pleasure into their lives, something that they had not thought possible after they had lost their only son as a baby and discovered that they could not have any more children of their own.

Robbie married a girl he met at college but they divorced after a few unhappy years, after which he decided to remain single. When he retired at the age of sixty he considered visiting Enderly once again to see Alicia's daughter Janet, if she was still alive, though he had no desire to see James. He knew Alicia and Will were dead, he had read about their funerals in a local paper shortly after he had been adopted. He had not forgotten his childish vow to repay their kindness one day but how he might do that he had no idea. He had no family and only a handful of friends in Oxford so that there was no reason for him to stay there. In any case he was now interested in going back to see Enderly and the surrounding area again. It had been a haven when he was only five years old and perhaps it would be again in retirement. He did not think any old school acquaintances, if there were still any about, would recognize him after so long – at least he hoped not.

Robbie looked forward to visiting a few old haunts near Enderly and Everton, the area he had loved when he was young, and thought longingly of the vista provided by the vast orchards filled with plum, apple and pear trees whose gorgeous blossom attracted many visitors in the spring. The Vale of Everton boasted a mild climate, indeed it was sheltered compared to many areas in the country. He remembered too the vast fields of cabbages and spring onions that were grown just outside Enderly. The smell of rotting cabbages had filled his nostrils in an unpleasant way when he was a child but the industry had provided employment for many of the local boys and a number of gypsies who visited the area in the growing season to look for temporary work.

Robbie had no idea that Janet had searched for him after James had left, and although he harboured a vestige of affection for her he did not quite forgive her for abandoning him. Time, despite his fondness for his generous adoptive parents, had not yet healed the wounds inflicted on him by the odious James.

When Robbie returned to Enderly Janet was seventy-seven years old. Although he had been reluctant to set foot in Enderly after James had rejected him he now looked round the village with surprising and unexpected interest. He parked his new silver car at the edge of a small triangle of grass that served as a mini village green and set out on foot to explore. Excitement caught up with him. He felt he had come home again, a feeling that strengthened as he wandered down the main village street flanked with old cottages, the pub, shop and the old church at the end next to the village school. A sprawling housing estate built just after the war near the school appeared vast and dilapidated. Paint was peeling from windows, front gardens were neglected and littered with broken toys, but otherwise things seemed very much like he remembered. Memories flooded back. The old grey stone church, the row of cottages, at one time occupied by agricultural workers when local landowners farmed most of the land around Enderly, and Honeysuckle Cottage where he had stayed with Alicia Merryweather and her ailing husband for five years looked much as he remembered them. Pink, red and yellow roses clambered over the doors as they had done when he was a child White and purple wisteria drooped from walls and the gardens were bursting with cottage-garden flowers. The scent of the flowers filled the air. Some of the large old trees, including the pretty white lilac that he remembered once had pride of place in the Merryweathers' front garden, had been chopped down. A few of the window frames had been renewed together with the once dilapidated thatch. There was still one honeysuckle straggling over a metal arch that spanned a small brick path at the side of the cottage but most of the plants that had given the cottage its name had disappeared, at least he couldn't see any from the front gate.

The well was still in the front garden but was now home to baskets of flowers that had been placed below the small tiled roof. There was a pump attached underneath the roof and a yellow hose on a hook so Robbie guessed that the well water was only used for watering the garden. The houses now had piped water and no doubt modern bathrooms. A small car stood on the sparse grassed verge in front of the cottage, a testament to progress.

He stopped to speak to a bent and wizened old man who was working in the garden.

'I lived here near here for a while as a child,' he said, after a slight hesitation, as the old man continued to prune bright yellow roses near the gate. The man sighed and did not turn round immediately. He rubbed his right ear with a gnarled and dirty hand as if he needed time to consider before he replied. The silence was heavy. Robbie was anxious not to give too much away. 'I'm sorry to trouble you,' he continued with caution, 'but ... er ... could you tell me what happened to the Merryweather family? I believe they once lived in this cottage.'

The old man turned towards Robbie and leaned on the gate. He tipped his old brown cap back on his head and his deep-set blue eyes lit up with a vestige of a smile. His face was wrinkled and weatherbeaten from many hours spent in the sun and wind. However, he appeared almost pleased to talk to the stranger, which was a relief.

'Dead long ago,' he said slowly in his broad Russetshire accent and clipped tones. 'Janet, their daughter, is still around though and living in Primrose House. She was a teacher for a long time. I can't tell you much more.'

He turned away from Robbie and continued with his pruning. He had done his bit.

Robbie thanked him and the old man grunted and cleared his throat.

Well, he had found out something useful, Janet was still alive and living in the village, but would have to try elsewhere for more information.

The vast fields of cabbages and the unpleasant smell of rotting leaves wafting in the breeze round the edge of the village had disappeared. That was an improvement he thought. There were still some plum and apple orchards, their short stubby stumps and branches promising good crops. Enderly now looked like many other Russetshire villages. Some executive-style houses had been built by a large well-known firm – he had seen some similar in style in Oxford – and some retirement bungalows, small and box like, had mushroomed a short distance from the housing estate. Several new prefabricated classrooms had been erected in the old Victorian school's playground. Newcomers had renovated cottages, many just for holidays, and smart expensive cars, Porsches, BMWs and four-by-fours of various makes, were parked outside on verges: the age of the commuter had invaded this once sleepy and quiet village. The community had it seemed expanded but there were, he estimated, still only about 200 dwellings.

The black and white village shop no longer had a thatched roof but one of grey slate that fitted in reasonably well with the village scene, but otherwise was much the same as he remembered it. The well-trodden step and green painted door, at odds with the rest of the building, were still the same. If anything the green paint was brighter than the one he could remember seeing as a child. There was not much room inside and the layout was much as it had been when he was an evacuee. A Post Office counter, small and cramped, had been fitted into one corner, but the shop shelves were well stocked with essentials for the villagers who needed the odd item they had forgotten when they did their weekly shop in the local supermarkets. As well as the usual groceries like biscuits, jam, milk and bread there was a rack full of greetings cards, post-cards and an assortment of envelopes and writing paper. Local eggs, ham and cakes were on display together with a few vege-tables and some fruit. There was a small freezer with some ready meals and cartons of ice creams. The elderly couple running the shop seemed pleased when Robbie went in to buy a local news-paper. The woman, whose thick white hair was sprayed with so much lacquer that it stood up in a stiff quiff several inches above her head, chatted voraciously in an attempt to find out about the newcomer who she hoped was not just another visitor but a potential regular customer. Astute grey eyes fixed themselves on Robbie who was in his turn having difficulty in making an effort not to stare at her almost beehive hairstyle that contrasted incongruously with her small wrinkled face.

'Er, four ounces of those sweets please,' he said pointing to a jar on the shelf behind her.

'Just visiting are you?' she asked, tipping mint humbugs into a bag and weighing them in ounces, as their predecessors had done for several generations. To Robbie's amazement, several large jars filled with old-fashioned sweets similar to those he remembered seeing as a child stood on a shelf behind the counter.

'Well ... sort of. Re-visiting you could say.'

'Oh, been here before then?'

'Yes.' It was cool in the shop and he was grateful for the respite. Robbie rummaged in his pockets for some change to pay for the mints and his newspaper and turned away from her penetrating gaze, stepping out of the door with haste into the scorching midday sun. He mopped the perspiration from his forehead with a handkerchief and strolled down the road to the local pub, the Green Man, where he hoped to obtain a decent lunch. The pub had a well-cared-for look and seemed promising. The landlord was young with a mop of red hair, tall and muscular with a wide chest and shoulders, almost as broad as those possessed by a town club bouncer that Robbie once knew, and he greeted Robbie warmly as he walked through the open door. A smell of beer and midday cooking reached his nostrils and he felt pangs of hunger. The area near the bar was dim, old slate floors and horse brasses provided atmosphere and there were some good oak trestle tables covered with check cloths, a welcome sight. His stomach rumbled; he had not realised how thirsty and hungry he had become.

'What can I do for you sir?' the landlord called in an accent that sounded Cornish and reminded Tom of a bull bellowing for his favourite heifer.

'Pint of best bitter, please and some lunch.' He walked towards the bar. 'Can I have a menu?'

'Of course,' the landlord answered in a deep resonant voice and passed a bar menu to Tom. 'There's a nice table for one there by the window, make yourself comfortable and Mary here will bring your drink over.'

Mary was a luscious-looking barmaid; her short skirt revealed long legs and a skimpy T-shirt exposed a generous portion of a large low-slung bosom. Robbie made a determined effort to keep his eyes on the menu.

A few of the locals glanced at Robbie under lowered lashes as they sipped their pints and toyed with ham, eggs and chips, obviously the favourite meal of the day. A stocky lad in white overalls ventured to ask if Robbie was just visiting.

'Well, yes, I am. I used to live near here years ago.'

The lad held out his hand. 'Welcome, then. I was born here and my mum and grandma were too. My grandma was a post-war baby. When were you here?'

'Oh, in the nineteen fifties or thereabouts.'

'Gosh, yes,' the boy said. 'There's a picture of some of the evacuees in the other bar, you should have a look. You might recognize some of them. They were here just before your time I should imagine but a few stayed on in the village, mums and dads killed and no one else to look after them, that sort of thing you know. There are one or two more photos in the roof, I believe, but the landlord is not very interested in them which is a pity.'

Tom, or Robbie as he was now called, remembered that picture well; it was taken in front of the village hall before he was rescued by Alicia Merryweather. He had stood in the centre of the front row, a small and miserable figure. When he looked at it later he found that it had faded, and was so brown and misty that it was difficult to recognise anybody. That was a relief. He wondered what happened to the other evacuees who had stayed in the village. He hoped they would not recognize him if they were still around and doubted that they would. He had lost his cockney accent, grown a beard which covered the deep dimple in his chin and had developed a portly figure during the last few years.

'Do you know a Mrs Janet Anderson?' he asked, a cautious tone surfacing in his voice.

'I can't say I do,' the lad replied, 'but old Pat over there might,' he pointed to a man of about seventy sitting on his own at a corner table, 'best ask him – he knows most folks around here.'

'Thanks, I'll do that,' Robbie replied gratefully.

Robbie looked with interest at Pat. He did not remember him but he probably had been around when he was a child. He was a thin bony old man with a large bulbous nose and a dark mole on his chin. His old tweedy trousers were tied with string a short way above the ankles in the manner that many old countrymen who worked on the land did earlier. He had been working on his allotment and did not want to dirty his turn-ups. Pat gave him a brief nod and managed an apology for a smile, displaying uneven and yellowing teeth.

'I knows her,' he volunteered, his slightly high-pitched voice emerging clearly from the corner of the room. 'She used to teach in this here village. She's now Mrs Janet Lacey. James Anderson, her first husband, disappeared years ago, rotten devil he was.'

Robbie agreed with that. A slight frown appeared on his forehead but he said nothing.

'She married the headmaster of the junior school, dead now poor fellow, but nice chap. She still lives in Primrose House. Are you a friend?'

'Well, not really, I knew some of her family many years ago,' Robbie said, wondering if he had given too much away.

'She's not well now,' Pat continued. 'I used to help her in the garden but my knee is playing up too much these days, I had to give it up. Don't want a job do yer?'

Robbie smiled. 'Not really.'

'No, you's too much of a toff,' Pat said in a resigned tone as he noted Robbie's distinct upper-class Oxford accent. 'She could do with some help, lovely lady. Her second husband died a long time ago now. The advert is in the local shop.'

Robbie considered his remarks. Husband dead. Hmmm ... interesting. Robbie loved gardening and was an excellent handyman. He had enjoyed doing jobs round his house in Oxford and woodwork had been a hobby he had indulged in over the years as a relaxation from his academic career. The money was not important but it might be interesting to take a job as a handyman and gardener for a while so that he could get to know Janet once again incognito. She would not recognise him now, at least he hoped not. He was no longer skinny as he had been as a child and his once thick thatch of brown hair was almost white with a receding hairline. The skin around his deep-set hazel eyes had crinkled and his thick pebbled glasses would not make it easy for anyone to compare his eyes with those of young Tom Hands.

Perhaps he could buy a little cottage nearby to stay in and still go home to his own rather large and up-market house outside Oxford when he wanted to. The idea began to take hold and he felt more excited about the idea of moving back to Russetshire, especially Enderly, than he had thought possible. Now that he had revisited the area he had become quite enamoured with the prospect. Although he had avoided setting foot in Enderly for so long he had an unexpected and inexplicable feeling that this village was his destiny. He looked forward to seeing Janet and if he could help her now it could be a way of repaying some of the kindness shown to him by Alicia and Will. He told himself he was being fanciful and perhaps foolish, but it did seem worth looking into.

There was no doubt that his housekeeper could keep an eye on things in Oxford for him while he made up his mind. It could be fun. Most of his academic colleagues were busy with their families and he knew stuffy old Robbie would not be missed greatly, if at all. He would go and look at advertisements for cottages after lunch. He smiled to himself and felt a surge of interest and antici-pation that he had not felt for years. It could be an exciting adven-ture and certainly a new way of life. He had travelled all over the world during his vacations after his brief marriage failed so he had no interest in that now. He had not wanted to get married again or return to London where he was born. But village life, that could suit him very well, in retirement. A satisfied smile lit up his face. If Janet did not need him … well, he would enjoy living in Enderly anyway.

After a filling lunch of steak pie and chips, followed by local apple pie, he looked round Enderly for a suitable property. A small black and white cottage had just been put on the market and was about the right size. It was quite near the pub, too. Osborne Smith Estate Agents, Everton. He remembered them, they had had a very good reputation in the area; he would contact them that afternoon. He booked into the Green Man for the night and arranged to meet the estate agent at the property early the next day.

The young estate agent arrived promptly, keen and brimming with enthusiasm. He need not have bothered, Robbie was already smitten. There were three bedrooms, one quite large, the others rather small but he could turn one into a study and the other one would be a guest room suitable for occasional visits from any of his friends, though his best friend had now moved to Scotland and the rest were busy family men. The bathroom was old fashioned but that could soon be remedied and he would install a shower room in the old pantry on the ground floor and another in the large bedroom. The lounge was spacious and the beams sturdy and well maintained. The last owner had knocked two small rooms into one and added a conservatory at the back. If he liked life well enough in Enderly he would definitely consider staying and might even sell his large house in Oxford. It was a beautiful house and he had worked hard to keep it in good order but he would not miss it. It was empty, no wife or children, just full of dusty books and one man rattling around in it on his own. He would play things by ear.

Robbie spent several weekends in Enderly, booking into the Green Man, during the time he was buying his cottage. That gave him time to chat to the locals and stroll round the familiar lanes reminiscing. One or two vaguely familiar faces appeared in the pub when he stayed there but there was not a hint of recognition by any of them which was gratifying. The Green Man was a comfortable old place and Robbie enjoyed reading the history of the pub and the surrounding area. He thought he might do some research in his spare time and even write a booklet about it.

One weekend he plucked up courage to wander up to Primrose House and look over the old rickety garden fence. It appeared to be in need of repair and a good handyman could soon do that. An elderly lady sat in a striped deckchair under a large umbrella by the side of the house, which was covered with a straggly pink climbing rose also in need of attention. He knew immediately that it was Janet. She had a sturdy wooden stick by her side and looked frail. Her once pretty dark hair was now a pepper-and-salt grey but her brown eyes were still large and kindly which was what he remembered from the time when he first met her. Emotions and memories, many he thought he had forgotten, almost overpowered him. He would like to take care of her now, as she and her mother had taken care of him so many years ago, or at least watch over her. A surge of affection rose up in his breast. Robbie had no family to care for and he decided that it could now be his mission in retirement to watch over his earlier benefactor's daughter, help her in her house and garden in any way he could. He needed first of all to consider how to get to know her once again without being recognised.

Two months later Robbie moved into his cottage. He had attended the local sales and found some sturdy oak furniture which he enjoyed renovating. A local builder, Mr Jones from Brinton, installed the new shower rooms and modernized the kitchen. He thought Mr Jones was a fat greedy man but he had done a good job. The cottage would be easy to care for and he would no longer need a housekeeper, just a woman from the village to do a little cleaning and dusting. Robbie was enjoying the solitude and to his surprise did not miss academic life at all. He installed numerous bookshelves in the lounge and dining room and looked forward to reading the books that he had acquired over the years. Robbie ate most of his evening meals in the Green Man which avoided too much cooking, something of which he was not fond, and chatted a great deal with old Pat.

'Have you thought any more about that gardening job?' Pat asked, smiling slyly, and not really thinking that Robbie would be interested.

'Well, yes but I thought the position would have been filled by now,' Robbie said anxiously.

'My nephew Jack has been doing a bit of work for her but he is off to Australia soon to a good job. Not many people round here want a job gardening. She's a lovely lady, nice to work for, good pay for gardening and handyman work too, although I should think the pay doesn't bother you,' he continued in his strong local accent.

He looked at Robbie's smart cord trousers and Saville Row shirts. An undulating grin lingered round the corner of his mouth.

'I might be interested,' Robbie said, his Oxford accent distinct and clear. 'I've a lot of time on my hands, or will have when the cottage has been fitted out to my liking. Yes, I might be.' His hazel eyes lit up in anticipation. Would Janet recognise him? He hoped not. 'Does she mind dogs?' he asked.

'Dogs?' Pat spluttered.

'Well yes, I've arranged to adopt a collie called Nap from the Everton Collie Rescue Centre. Intelligent animal, gave up working for some reason. Only four years old. I wouldn't want to leave it all day.'

'She loves dogs,' Pat said quickly. 'I don't doubt you could take it with you. She's got a small Jack Russell puppy, about nine months old, snappy little thing but I should think you could handle him.'

Pat really had no idea about Janet's views on other people's dogs but if this chap would like to work for her he was all for it. Odd, though, that accent. It could be interesting if he took the job. He liked the man, well educated but not too toffee-nosed.

Pat took Robbie to see Janet the next week. He was right, she did not recognize him. She would have been overwhelmed with joy if she had known that her mother's young evacuee had returned. He agreed to work in her garden two mornings a week and to drive her to the shops in her large old Rover once or twice a week, or as required, and do other odd jobs as a handyman when asked.

'Feel free to bring your dog when you're working in the garden,' Janet said, 'but I don't think it would be wise to take him in the car. Jack stays at home when I go shopping. My house-keeper would be happy to look after him for you or he could stay in the garden when the weather is good.'

They discussed terms and a bargain was struck. It suited them both.

Janet was surprised that such a well-educated man was willing to work for so little pay. However, she looked forward to enjoying his company when he was not busy. She was lonely now and her heart lifted at the thought of having such a pleasant and intelligent man around to talk to sometimes. She felt she had a known him all her life but could not think why. His dog too was a gentle creature and would sit by her side while Robbie tended the flowers or the few vegetables that were now grown in the Primrose House kitchen garden. Jack liked the dog too and they romped around the lawn together. That was surprising, Jack did not like many other dogs, especially if he thought they were invading his territory. Janet was happier than she had been for a some time as she watched him work. Where had she met him before? Her memory was starting to play tricks upon her, it really was disconcerting. She wondered if her brain was shrinking. There was definitely something familiar about the man but she failed to draw any conclusions about what it was that she recognized in his character or where she might have seen him before.

Robbie enjoyed walking with his dog and exploring the many footpaths and the river bank round Enderly. He had forgotten how pleasant the countryside was. He frequented the local shop and chatted with other villagers who owned dogs. He was lucky. The dog had been well trained and was obedient to a fault. Poor thing, he thought, he is just like I was when I was that evacuee so long ago. He needs love and affection and he will get it now. Although he was a working dog and was not used to much kindness he soon attached himself to Robbie. The dog was adaptable and intelligent as are many of this breed. He looked very like Will Merryweather's collie, with a white streak down his forehead, white blob at the end of his tail, neat white ruff and soft black border collie fur that brought back more good memories for Robbie who was happier than he had been for a long time. He had come home.

Chapter 8

Primrose House 2004

J anet Lacey shifted uncomfortably in her armchair, groaning as severe pain shot through limbs riddled with rheumatism. Her wrinkled face appeared perplexed as she looked round the lounge with weary eyes. She tried to imagine a way to escape from the room that was closing in on her but felt entangled and she could see no way out. Dreams had become her only means of escape, they were a way of seeing people she had once loved or hated. She made a strenuous effort to grasp her loved ones with outstretched hands but they had an unfortunate habit of slipping away just when they seemed within reach.

She looked out of the window and watched her gardener Robbie who turned round as though he sensed her gaze and waved before continuing with some pruning. He had been working for her for some years but she still did not know much about him. She knew that he was well educated, kind and considerate but although she had tried to find out more she had been unsuccessful and after a while she gave up trying. He was reluctant to discuss anything about his past but the feeling that he was familiar and that she had known him a long time ago remained with her.

A raucous 'Cuckoo, cuckoo ...' from the landing clock interrupted her thoughts. It jarred and irritated her as the strident screech pirouetted painfully through her aching head. Once it had been a welcome chirpy and pleasant sound. She must tell Joyce to send it to the local charity shop as soon as possible. It had become a ghastly thing with its gaudy painted red and blue bird that flew in and out of a small brown painted wooden door exactly on the hour, every damn hour, for too many years. Why had she put up with that awful sound for so long? Time was in any case running out for her like sand trickling through an hourglass ensuring hours, days and minutes became almost meaningless. The clock reminded her that she was a fragile human being and that it could make a terrible noise long after she was gone.

She heard her housekeeper's light footsteps in the hallway. Joyce Skillet put her head round the door.

'Are you all right, Mrs Lacey?'

'Yes Joyce. I was just thinking. Can you get rid of that horrid cuckoo clock? Get Robbie to take it to the charity shop in Brinton next time he goes, you know … the one that supports the local hospice.'

'Of course,' Joyce answered. An axe might be more appropriate she thought but she was more than happy to oblige. 'I'll pack it up into a bag right now.' Hurrah, the damned thing had annoyed her for years.

Janet gazed with unease at the exquisite pictures: a valuable collection of remarkable oil paintings and delicate watercolours arranged and displayed with infinite care against the pale antique white walls. There were some first-class paintings – a couple of Dutch and several French Impressionists that glowed with light and glorious colours. Hand-crafted ceramic vases and fine orna-ments were displayed in an artistic manner on wooden shelving. Worcester porcelain had been her favourite, but the pieces that had once thrilled her with their aesthetic qualities no longer inter-ested her. The sooner some of that junk, as she now thought of it, was sent to a sale room the better. Acquiring antiques and valu-able china had been a hobby shared with her late husband John and these once coveted and eagerly sought after acquisitions had become nothing better than tiresome dust traps.

'I like the Staffordshire dog in spite of it having been repaired with a false collar,' she recalled John saying at the end of a busy and exhilarating day they had spent searching in local antiques shops. 'Beautiful old Worcestershire pot too. Look at those colours, darling.'

'Marvellous, sweetheart,' she had replied, enjoying the feeling of his strong arms round her and the excitement and pleasure derived from their purchases.

She would happily smash them now and stretched out an arm to reach one of her walking sticks. The stick did not reach the mantelpiece or she would have swept some of them off on to the tiles below. She felt irritable and knew she was behaving in an irrational manner but no longer cared.

John and Janet had studied numerous books about antiques, now languishing in the bookcase in the lounge and ignored by Janet for the last twenty years. She would get rid of those too, she decided. Some poor fool may enjoy them.

They had attended many stuffy auctions to bid for items they liked. When they bought something John dug deep into his pockets to please his wife although he was in other ways careful with money, a trait that had been instilled since childhood. Money, he insisted, was no more than a necessary evil; love and affection were much more important. She now agreed with that sentiment with all her heart. He was right.

She caught a vague movement in her peripheral vision and felt her old dog press his cold damp nose against her arm. She experienced a moment of deep gratitude for the hound which had for many years been her faithful companion.

Janet again surveyed the clumsy settee and armchairs. What on earth was the point keeping that ghastly old furniture? The thick wooden legs made it heavy and difficult to move so that sooner or later Joyce, or the girl who came to help her some days, would strain her back trying to shift the damned things, all for the sake of a sprinkling of dust. Money and possessions were no longer of interest but as she sank back into the luxurious new armchair with the elaborate lifting gear that Joyce had recently acquired she had to admit that the comfort it afforded did give her some pleasure. It was nice to be miserable in comfort.

'I can't take John's fortune with me when I die,' she said out loud, and a worried frown deepened the already sculptured furrow on her forehead. That disquieting fact had often intruded on her thoughts in the last year or two. She and John did not have any children who would have wanted these worldly possessions and in any case, she thought, the furniture is far too old fashioned for today's tastes. John had justified the extravagant expenditure by calling it 'investment'. Investment indeed, how foolish they were. What was the value of such silly investment now!

Janet had longed for a baby, especially one that looked like John, to cradle in her arms, but John hadn't wanted any children. He made many excuses and in the end she gave up. She loved him and that would have to be enough. What a weak fool I was, she chided herself. Both John and the wretched James Anderson denied me the family I longed for. It's my own fault and I deserve to be lonely.

She shifted her position to see the other side of the lounge where a tall Tiffany standard lamp was crammed into a corner. The shiny polished brass stalk topped with a heavy red and green shade of hand-crafted bumpy glass encased in metal culminated in red dragonflies with odd torsos that crawled down the sides. Small clear glass pebbles formed a pattern at its edge like rain-drops dancing and flickering in the light. She gave the lamp a derogatory glance. With a sudden flash of memory she recalled buying it in a second-hand shop many years ago. She had consid-ered it a wonderful bargain but could no longer find any joy in it. It was as if her appreciation of such objects had died with John.

'What an ugly, boring lamp,' she mumbled, 'just black iron and thick glass that looks like pieces of old broken bottles, quite useless. It should be melted down.'

She raised bumpy arthritic fingers, sighed as she touched her once flawless skin and cupped her chin, which sagged into her hand like a soggy old cloth reminding her of an elephant's hide. Depression gripped her. Oh heavens, I must be a pitiful old hag now but it's stupid to feel so sorry for myself.

'My beautiful wife, such lovely skin and that dimple ...' she recalled John saying. Dear John, always complimentary. Oh heavens, what on earth would he think if he could see me now, she thought, thank goodness he can't.

John had enjoyed running his fingers through her long soft dark hair flecked with golden red hues, but had not lived long enough to see the thin grey and unruly mess that now cloaked her scalp, with bare patches of pink skin that were becoming more difficult to disguise as the days passed. She brushed her remaining hair over them with little hope of success.

A wig, she thought, I'll get Joyce to buy me one in Everton; no that would be stupid but the idea did please her. She laughed out loud. A lovely thick wig, it could be grey of course ... or silver.

Her once full mouth had made her face interesting but now stretched into a thin unpleasant line when she attempted to smile.

There were some good memories left in the house. The most important, of course, were of her second husband, a gentle, kind man so very different from her first husband James, but, however hard she tried to hang on to those memories, they would disappear as though anxious to float away like the fragile blue bubbles she had once blown from a white clay pipe when she was a small child. They would dance upwards towards the sky to burst and be gone.

I'm a foolish old woman to feel so sorry for myself, she chided herself. I must make the best of the last few months, or perhaps even a year, that I have left. She realised with mounting fear and inner panic, that threatened all too often now to spiral out of control, that her frail eighty-six year old crumbling body would soon let her down. Her feet ached, the soles hot and pulsing, and she could not bear the thought of the effort she must make in order to reach the bathroom to relieve herself. She sometimes waited until her housekeeper came to assist her, though she could manage with the help of her sturdy rubber-ended walking sticks, her props she called them, to shuffle painfully towards the bathroom. At least she could still remember where it was. To get there was a triumph.

Visions of old ladies in nursing homes sitting like zombies in circles, smelling of urine which their leaky aching bladders allowed to trickle into padded pants or down their legs, too often invaded her mind with surprising clarity, further disturbing her peace of mind.

'Oh God,' she sighed and shuddered. Was that going to be her fate?

The heavy dark oak chest of drawers with its beautiful shiny antique handles looked more or less the same as it had sixty years ago. It stood where it had for so long next to the door that opened into the hallway and its surface gleamed in the shaft of sunlight that crept through the partly drawn curtains. The mollycoddled thing had been indulged by numerous willing hands, including hers and her housekeepers', over many years. The smell of the latest layer of oversweet beeswax polish invaded her nostrils but sparked no joy, indeed the damn smell gave her the jitters and made her feel sick. She tried not to heave. So many masking smells had invaded her house puffing and blowing from the plastic packets her housekeeper favoured, so that good old-fashioned smells like lavender had been lost, polluted and distorted, swallowed by a maze of synthetic whiffs.

She listened, as well as she could, to the clatter of cups in the kitchen. Joyce was busy preparing tea and the supper she would leave for Janet to enjoy later. Janet's mouth felt dry and she longed for a cup of her precious Earl Grey tea laced with a slice of bitter lemon. For a few strange moments she found herself counting sheep and wondering why. What was the point? She could not remember. Time slipped by and turned into an eternity as she waited. She shivered, twitching and uncomfortable, as she pulled her expensive soft pale green cashmere cardigan closer to her neck. The smooth material soothed her and she felt less irritable.

Janet's attention turned with renewed interest to the furniture she had chosen as a young bride and which she had had reupholstered many times in the modern materials that she had read about in house and home style magazines. Their solid, elaborately carved mahogany frames had stood the test of time in spite of the numerous clumsy tacks left by various upholsterers. Where would the wretched things end up? Some house clearance shop more likely than not, to be pounced on and pawed by some ignorant ingrate who would use them for firewood. She visualised their thick curly carved legs lifting heavenwards, licked fiercely by vivid red flames and issuing grey smoke. She uttered a loud and satisfied chuckle. Good riddance.

She leaned forward to obtain a better view of the Afghan rugs. Their backgrounds of pale brick-red and brown were littered with strange fawn characters she could not understand. The rugs were placed strategically on the uneven old oak parquet floor. She pushed her walking stick forward to trace some of the patterns and pictured young dark-skinned boys, their glossy heads bent low, weaving the intricate patterns in thick wool. Well, at least they may have enjoyed weaving them, she thought, in spite of the hard work.

'What on earth do you want those for?' she recalled John saying.

Janet had purchased them defiantly using her own wages. Why on earth did John have to be such a skinflint when it came to things she liked and he didn't?

Expensive foibles they may have been but they had worn well, though one of the fringes stuck up stiff, awkward and bristly, evoking memories of her old ginger tom cat, long dead, who had sometimes amused himself by biting it when he was bored. His long ginger coat had been splattered with bright brown zigzags that resembled flashes of lightning and moved as he chewed. A sad smile flickered briefly over her strained old face as her limited attention span once again caused her thoughts to change direction.

Many of her friends had died, or no longer called because good conversation with the old woman had become too trying for most of them. Joyce Skillet said, 'They are fly by nights and good riddance to them if they can't stick by an old friend who is having a few blips with her memory. They're not worth knowing.' Now her main companion was her faithful Jack Russell, often sitting next to her in companionable silence. Jack's rough and ragged white coat, which was never very clean, enveloped him like an old moth-eaten rug; his legs, long and delicate for his breed, still carried him with speed to his bowl in the kitchen when he antici- pated that food would be forthcoming. His muzzle, soft and light brown in his youth in contrast to the black patch over one ear, had become, like an old man's drooping moustache, grizzled and grey. Janet still loved to feel his soft nose pressed against her legs. He, like his mistress, felt his age and as the days passed they bonded even closer.

'Well, Jack,' she would repeat, 'it is only the two of us now.' He would lie on his back, completely shameless, showing his genitals, with legs stretched out as if to say, 'Rub my chest,' and he was usually rewarded by receiving the attention he craved.

The dog's aged eyes had cataracts causing him to bump into unexpected obstacles. He no longer needed long walks but would limp along for a short distance by the river bank with Janet's gardener or housekeeper when they could spare the time, although the garden was large enough for him to amble round. He displayed a good mouthful of sharp yellowing teeth when he felt it necessary to warn off strangers who might threaten his beloved mistress. In contrast to Janet's, his mind remained active and his hearing acute. Despite his ancient appearance, he surprised a few unwanted guests with a deep warning growl causing the more timid who valued the shape of their ankles to move with nimble steps out of his way.

A clatter of cups from the kitchen and the tapping of Joyce's heels on the hard floor broke into her thoughts. Her mouth watered and she looked forward to her food hoping that tea would soon be ready. 'Come on Joyce, hurry up,' she grumbled. She often felt irritable these days, which threatened to destroy her normally pleasant and even temperament. Her nostrils twitched in anticipation. She could smell egg sandwiches which were her favourites; tomato and cucumber too with a good splash of mayonnaise no doubt.

The only children who had jumped on the springs of that clumsy furniture had been her niece and nephew, Felicity and Ronald, the unfortunate legacies from her first marriage, and for a short while her mother's young evacuee Tom, though he was such a quiet child he did little more than sit like a meek little mouse. Felicity, thank goodness, had emigrated to Canada when she was twenty years old and her younger brother to Australia, after he qualified as a dentist. Janet had a vague idea that their mother Anne had died when only thirty. Was it a car crash? Yes, that was it. She remembered now. Anne was, as usual, drunk at the wheel. Her useless husband Richard obtained a job in the Middle East almost immediately after the accident, skipping neatly out of his responsibilities, and sent the children to Northumberland to live with his elderly aunt and uncle. That was something she did remember.

'Bloody kids, fretting and fussing, they will forget their troubles there,' Richard had said. 'Good countryside and my old aunt running after them, what more could they want?'

'Out of sight and out of mind' Janet had commented with a bitter edge to her voice. 'What a feckless man! All talk and no trousers. Somebody will pay for that neglect.' She feared that it might one day be her but hoped not. Her first husband James, Anne's brother, had shown no interest in the children.

The odd tatty cheap Christmas card or birthday card fluttered down on to Janet's doormat when Felicity and Ronald managed to remember that she was still alive but those were easy to deal with, being put straight into her waste bin.

She was in some inexplicable and illogical way sorry for them. 'Let us hope,' she recalled saying to her second husband John, 'that they will be happy in their new countries,' but refrained from saying, 'and stay there!'

Felicity had been selfish and spiteful, particularly to her younger brother Ronald. Janet recalled, as if it was yesterday, Felicity enjoying herself running her bicycle wheel over his hand when they were playing in the garden. She had been overjoyed to hurt him, the black, blue and red marks left on the back of his hand were a testament to her prowess and the lack of remorse was quite chilling.

'Silly stupid boy,' she had shrieked at Janet, 'always getting in my way, he deserved that!'

Ronald, mute and distraught, held out his small wounded hands.

'Poor child, poor child ...'

'Aunt Janet, hold me.' Then silence. No sobbing. Janet felt angry, helpless and unsure of how to deal with the dreadful girl.

She had a fleeting memory of a painfully thin and unhappy Felicity aged about twenty. She came to stay in Primrose House for a few days before departing for Canada where she had been offered an office job by a friend of her father's who ran a lumber business. Was she anorexic? Whatever she was Janet was very glad to see the back of her.

'It will be a new start, Aunt Janet,' she had announced with a boastful arrogance. 'I will do well there you know.' Janet did not think she would do well anywhere but thought better of commenting on the proposed arrangements. She just heaved a sigh of relief.

She must be about sixty-four now, Janet mused with vague interest stirring in her chest. She had no idea how life had treated Felicity and did not really care. She hoped that she would not see her again.

'Cup of tea ma'am!' Joyce Skillet's voice, sharp and local, rang out like a tinkling bell, disturbing her reverie.

'Thank you dear,' Janet murmured as she brushed a lock of grey hair out of her eyes. Her housekeeper carefully placed the tray in front of her on a small antique oak table. She had set the tray in the way Janet liked. It was covered with a small blue and white embroidered cloth and two delicious home-made scones thickly buttered were placed side by side on a fine bone china plate. Joyce really is a treasure, Janet thought and uttered an appreciative sigh. The linen cloth Janet had embroidered many years ago had stood the test of time well. She ran her crooked fingers over the edge of it, feeling soft pure silk blue stitches. It was a little worn but still attractive.

'I don't know what I would do without you Joyce,' Janet murmured.

'I'll be here as long as you need me,' Joyce replied with affection and touched the old woman's arm gently in an effort to reassure her. 'It seems cold in here, I'll light the gas fire. You don't want to catch a chill.'

'Is there any post today, Joyce?' Janet asked without much enthusiasm in her quiet, clear and modulated voice, a voice of authority that remained with her after many years of teaching.

'Oh, a letter from Canada and the usual junk mail. Those stupid advertisements really do waste a lot of paper! Green planet ... huh!'

There was one person Janet wished she could hear from but

knew she never would, a girl she remembered still despite her memory lapses, someone she had known when she was young and whose sweet face she had thought of so many times over the years. She had not received any news about her for some time but prayed that she was well and happy. There was little else she could do. Her hands were tied.

Joyce passed the letters to Janet. Janet looked at them with a sigh and opened the one from Canada with her silver tea knife. A single sheet of cream paper emerged from the envelope. She glanced at the signature and saw the words 'I have booked a flight ... I am so looking forward to seeing you once again. Your loving niece Felicity.' She groaned.

Joyce looked at Janet's face but did not comment. She hoped the letter did not contain bad news but feared it did. She did not wait to find out but scurried back to her chores in the large old-fashioned kitchen at the back of the house. Some of the worn pine units had been modernized but the ancient tiles that were on the floor when Janet came to the house as a young bride were still in place, patched and repaired but twinkling and glistening following numerous coats of polish. Joyce was quite proud of her efforts. The old Aga too still chugged along emitting steady and comforting warmth.

Joyce was anxious to finish her work because she was looking forward to enjoying a meal in the Green Man that evening where she would be celebrating her husband's birthday with him and a few of their close friends. She didn't want to be late getting home and was looking forward to wearing the purple dress and imitation pearl necklace she had purchased for the occasion. Fred would be surprised and she knew that he would be wondering first and foremost how much the dress had cost. 'Meanie!' she thought uncharitably and chuckled. That was something he was not going to find out. But she knew that he would be pleased that she had made an effort on his behalf and would soon forgive her extravagance. She glanced at her newly tinted hair in the old cracked pine-edged kitchen mirror and beamed with satisfaction. A few dark roots still showed and irritated her but the carefully applied blonde highlights were quite becoming, after all she was only fifty and deserved to pamper herself sometimes. What was it called? Retail therapy, yes that was what it was. Jolly good it was too. It always worked for her.

Young Lily Jones, gormless and spotty faced, who hailed from the Vicarage, had offered, or rather been coerced by her father, to keep Janet company during the evening, assisting her to undress, though Janet preferred to do that herself, and helping her get into the bed that was made up by Joyce with the crisp fresh lavender-scented sheets that she enjoyed. Spotty-faced girls of Lily's ilk Janet did not want or like but Joyce had persuaded her that she would be good company though she had stressed that she did not need her.

'You must learn to help the less fortunate,' Lily's father lectured her earlier that day, stretching to his full height and fingering his stiff white dog collar. 'Gadding about with those layabout friends is not good for the soul!' He cleared his throat and waited for her response, which was not forthcoming.

'Silly old man!' Lily scoffed behind his back as soon as she got out of his hearing range but knew that, for the time being at least, she had must make an effort to keep on the right side of her pompous and pious father. One day she would be free of his ridiculous religious ranting and that day could not come fast enough for her. No one believes that rubbish these days, she'd told herself when quite a small girl and she had not wavered from that opinion for one moment since that time. She was far too intelligent to be deceived by that all that stuff. She chuckled to herself when she thought how, together with several of her friends, she had refused to sing a hymn in assembly the week before. The headmaster's face had turned beetroot red with frustration and Lily had giggled with delight. The detention she had received was a mild punishment and in no way dented her joy.

Nevertheless she turned up at Primrose House promptly at five o'clock as arranged, neat and meek, a stance in which she revelled. She wore a plain cheap cotton skirt and simple home-made blouse, which were both sober and innocuous. She didn't have anything very pretty; most of her clothes were purchased in the local charity shop by her mother to ensure her humility. There was little chance of looking like the Jezebel-type girls in the village that she admired but she played the part of the innocent little vicar's daughter well; something that had stood her in good stead on many occasions, which was some kind of compensation. Her long dull blonde hair which fell down her back reached almost to her waist and was cut into a wispy ragged fringe above her forehead. One day she would dye it orange or deep red and buy clothes that would enhance her figure, which she considered was quite good.

A substantial supper of salad, cold chicken, fresh fruit and cold white Chardonnay had been left in the fridge for Janet and Lily had been instructed to serve that up on a tray, using one of the best fine wine glasses, the ones etched with a grape-like pattern which were Mrs Lacey's favourites, at about seven in the evening.

'I'll pop back at about half past ten to see all is well, it's only a couple of minutes' walk from my cottage,' Joyce said to the reluctant and subdued Lily. 'What a kind girl you are to offer to sit with Mrs Lacey, she doesn't have much company in the evenings. You could go home once she is tucked up in bed. She usually goes to bed at about nine. She'll be all right, no need to worry about her, she has a cord round her neck with an emergency button she can press if she needs help when she's on her own. There's plenty of milk for you to drink, or fruit juice, if you want it, dear,' Joyce continued. 'Help yourself to biscuits or cake. Don't worry about Mrs Lacey. Her memory is getting worse, she has started to suffer from Alzheimer's disease you know, it's not too bad yet but she keeps talking in her sleep about her schooldays and someone called James. At least she still has her dreams. Just humour her, Lily. She's quite harmless. The dreams are probably not doing her much good but that can't be helped. I'm afraid even those will disappear soon, poor soul.'

Lily smiled sweetly and exposed a row of small and even white teeth between pale lips that had never, at least in public, been smeared with lipstick ('something only whores wear,' her father impressed upon her), but her eyes remained bleak and expressionless.

'It's OK,' she said smoothly, 'we will be fine, I'm happy to stay here until you come back. Doubtless Mrs Lacey will enjoy a little company.'

She glanced at Joyce with innocent round pale blue eyes fringed with pale yellow lashes, which looked like enormous empty blank blobs in her young bland face. She thought with avarice about the ten-pound note she had been promised for her trouble, it would be worth waiting around for that, and she looked forward to watching the large new television in the lounge. Her do-gooder father had pressed her into helping Joyce but had not been informed about the cash incentive. She smiled at the thought, though it would be more fun if she could go out with her teenage friends and just 'chill out'. It was a nuisance being a vicar's daughter because the expectations pressed upon her to be helpful and kind to others were onerous and she looked forward with increasing fervour to the glorious day when she would achieve freedom from that pressure. With any luck she could leave home the following year and attend a college course some way away, the further the better. However, she expected the supper left for her and Janet in Primrose House would, as usual, be delicious. Lily was always hungry and her mouth began to water. The old woman probably would not notice if she helped herself to an extra slice of cold chicken and a sip or two of wine. Drinking wine, except the odd quick drop of communion wine, was taboo at home and she looked forward to tasting the crisp white liquid. She would have something to boast about to her friends when they next met. The evening she had been so reluctant to participate in was not going to be so bad after all. The ghastly old-fashioned red armchairs in the lounge looked comfortable. The wretched dog Jack was a smelly and growly old thing but she liked dogs and she would get round him again with a biscuit or two or a succulent piece of chicken.

Janet did notice that there was not so much chicken as usual on her supper plate and she only had a half glass of wine. It was unfortunate that she could no longer struggle up the stairs to her bedroom to get away from that gawping girl. Perhaps she should not have been so stubborn and agreed to have had that stairlift installed.

'They are dreadful clumsy new-fangled things,' Janet had said to Joyce when the idea of installing one had been suggested by her old solicitor friend Peter Mace. 'Peter is too keen to spend my money!'

If only she could be independent and not have to rely on daft girls like Lily for the odd snatch of company.

Joyce left Jack his tea in the kitchen but the smell of cold sliced chicken was enticing, better than boring tinned dog meat and dry biscuit. He sniffed the air expectantly and remained alert, keeping a beady eye out for the supper tray. His efforts were rewarded when he obtained a nice chunk of chicken breast from Janet when Lily was not looking.

A new single bed, graced with a modern memory foam mattress, had been strategically placed under the dining-room window, which was on the side of the house that faced the river so that Janet could enjoy the view. A modern walk-in wet shower room and low toilet with rails had been installed nearby which cost more than any stairlift but that was her choice and she was, despite the memory lapses, still determined to remain in her own home, on her own terms, for long as possible.

Janet loved the large sweeping green fields dotted with old oak trees that adjoined her garden. She could see them clearly where they joined a large orchard that swept down to the winding river in the distance to provide a stunning vista. The trees in the local orchards were covered with pink and white blossom in the spring, which attracted many visitors to the area and was aptly called the Blossom Trail. The River Brinton could only just be seen from her window but at times when it burst its banks after a period of heavy rain it would creep nearer to form a large untidy lake. She loved to watch the ducks and swans but was not sure she liked the Canada geese. Flocks of the noisy creatures flapped over Primrose House on most days, and their wretched loud cackling voices invariably disturbed her afternoon nap. 'Tough as old boots some of those,' a neighbouring farmer hold told her, 'they are inedible, at least the old ones are, and the numbers of the wretched things are increasing.'

Lily cleared away the supper things and Janet leaned back in her chair and started to dream. Confused snatches of happenings from her past often merged together like pieces of a jigsaw puzzle, difficult to decipher and often forgotten immediately she woke up. Her mother and father, their evacuee Tom, friends whose faces were becoming strange blanks, would intrude for a moment then disappear. She could hold on to the distant past with greater ease than recent events but she moved slowly in her dreams, much slower than she had in real life, and she was often left with a disturbing sensation that made little sense to her.

Janet stirred as she was propelled back into time. 'James,' she said.

'I wish she'd shut up,' Lily muttered under her breath. 'She's spoiling my television programme.' She reached out and turned up the volume.

Janet slept on. She had promised her mother to look after her evacuee Tom when her parents were no longer able to. Eleven years old, he was a quiet and timid boy, though very intelligent. Tom's face often came to mind when she was dreaming, thin and peaky with a dimple in his chin, deep-set hazel eyes, winsome and appealing.

Janet stirred. She could hear James shouting, the shouting became louder, she fidgeted and her heart beat faster. She turned in her chair.

'He's a child of very little value, certainly not worthy of being treated as my son,' he grumbled. 'He should be made to work and pay his way. Burnt crusts and leftovers are good enough for that brat.'

The nightmare continued as it had so often, coming back to haunt her although it was becoming less vivid. Her deteriorating mind made sure of that.

She woke up with a start and remembered how earnestly Tom had expressed an interest in learning to play a musical instrument. His school had provided him with a violin and offered tuition for a reasonable fee but James would have none of that.

'Awful noise, I cannot stand that caterwauling. Screech, screech, screech scratch. Whoever invented that ghastly instrument should be shot!'

Janet had tried many years later to trace Tom. What a weak idiot she had been. She did discover that an older couple had adopted him and after that the trail ran frustratingly cold. All she could do was hope that he had been treated with kindness and was happy. Where was he now? It was a question she had asked herself many times over the years although now, like her personal possessions, Tom's whereabouts were becoming less important. She no longer felt the cold hand that had gripped the pit of her stomach the day he left clutching his small battered brown suit-case, which held all his worldly belongings. She no longer despised herself for being so feeble and giving into her husband's wishes though the boy's departure had caused her considerable pain at the time. It was entrenched in a past that was fading.

She dozed fitfully again in her chair. 'James,' she said again out loud several times as Joyce had said she might. Lily took no notice and returned to the kitchen to see if she could find a few more dregs of wine in the bottle. 'Silly old woman, dreaming. It will be a good thing when she gets into bed, it's nearly nine, thank goodness!' she said out loud. 'I might, with luck, be able to watch the next programme without her daft mutterings spoiling it! At least she didn't drink all the wine, though I'll tell Mrs Skillet that she did.' She grinned.

Chapter 9

The Visitor

It was a cold and damp autumn day when Felicity arrived in Enderly. 'Heaven help me,' she muttered, 'Enderly village looks as uninteresting as ever.'

There were a few new box-like houses with minuscule gardens that formed a small estate just where the road from Everton entered the village and the old dull grey stone Victorian school nearby had been expanded; some decent prefabricated class-rooms had been erected and a well-designed playing field added at the back. No wonder Uncle James made himself scarce all those years ago, she thought. Ugh, it still looks a boring dump. A mist rose up from the grey streak in the distance that was just recognizable as a river and she had a dread of the cold dampness it exuded creeping into her bones when she reached her destination. The same tatty little village shop and post office in the centre of the small main street, same dingy window display too. She grimaced and gave it a surreptitious glance as she was driven past on her way to Primrose House, which was about half a mile out of the village on the other side. There was a SPAR notice in the door of the shop which she estimated meant some progress had been made. Separated from the shop by three old terraced cottages that had been renovated with care, stood the Green Man pub; the black and white façade had recently been painted and two large oak flower tubs, planted with a collection of bright winter pansies, had been positioned either side of the old oak door. That is one place that may be worth a visit, she told herself with a flicker of genuine interest.

She looked with increasing anticipation at the Enderly scene from the windows of the taxi. The driver had looked at her with disdain when she had flagged him down outside the Everton railway station twenty minutes earlier and merely grunted as he opened the door for her to get in. Felicity was determined to arrive in style but was reluctant to spend her money. A few days before leaving Canada she had purchased what had been described as a 'fairly new' camel wool coat from a second-hand shop. The coat would have been expensive but had seen better days; the cuffs were somewhat faded and worn and it had been necessary to repair a couple of small holes near the hem. To appear poor and impoverished was not an impression she wished to convey when she arrived. Her feet ached. She had crammed them into her best leather shoes that were a size too small because she could not bring herself to splash out on a new pair, despite the fact that they pinched her feet without mercy.

She heaved a sigh of relief when they arrived outside Primrose House and leaned forward from the back seat to give the taxi driver a meagre tip together with the fare. He responded with a scathing look, causing her to scowl.

'Sorry the tip is not more, I'm short of change,' she said in a belligerent tone, as she opened the door nearest to her and got out. She pulled her case out on to the ground, slung her cheap plastic handbag over her shoulder and wondered why the oaf of a driver had not made any effort to assist her.

'You OK with that bag?' the driver asked in a broad Russetshire accent. It appeared to her to be a miserable afterthought.

'Yeah, nice of you to ask! It's a bit late to think of it.' A peevish tone crept into her voice.

It was quite out of character for, the driver not to get out of the car to open the door for her. The gravel drive was quite short and from that a pitted and uneven brick path led to the front door. The gates had been left open so he had no need to get out of the car to open them. The man usually prided himself on his polite manner but something about this woman caused him to be rude. His usual courteous behaviour deserted him although he normally assisted his passengers without question. For some inexplicable reason he could not force himself to be polite. He knew Janet quite well and thought the new arrival looked like trouble. The strange Canadian accent tinged with some odd northern English tones irritated him. She has only one fairly small bag, he noted, and decided that she could darn well keep it on the seat next to her and carry the bloody thing herself. She looked brawny enough although she was no doubt getting on a bit. He guessed that she was a spiky tough old bird and quite spirited and that he did admire, but not enough to assist her.

He returned to Everton Station without a backward glance in the hope that a more lucrative and agreeable fare would present itself. What a lousy tip she had given him!

Felicity struggled up to the front door with Roberto's battered leather case and stood for a few moments looking around. The view of the River Brinton stirred memories of walks along the reedy banks when she was young. The mist was deepening and threatened to cover the surrounding fields with long damp fluffy fingers. It was possible to make out the outlines of the old willow trees, still in need of pollarding, as they bent their droopy branches over the low banks. Orchards of apple and plum trees were just visible, the trees arranged in neat rows like regimented crooked fence posts. Their dark twisted branches were now mostly bare, but there was still unpicked fruit amongst the yellowing leaves. Beyond them the narrow grassy fields which once contained plump Herefordshire beef cattle swept down to the edge of the river. The mist was now becoming thicker and would soon hide the fields from view. She remembered that a public footpath straggled from Primrose House to the river bank and then turned along the edge of the river until it reached the other end of Enderly village. It was difficult to see through the mist in the fading light and she wondered if it was still there.

'What a bleak old place this house is,' she muttered under her breath, 'but it must be worth a penny or two now.' Her spirits rose. Money was her god, to obtain it was her greatest aim in life, and there could be some here if she played her cards with care. Her excitement mounted. The windows, she noted, had been replaced with double-glazed units. Well that is interesting, she thought. The old draughty sash windows were neck stiffeners when one had to sleep near them as she had soon found out as a small child. The trees had grown. Good heavens, huge birches and firs had sprung up, tall and imposing, and large branches creaked in the slight wind, stirring a vague memory of a young Aunt Janet planting small wispy saplings and bushes. The old oak front door was the same, grainy and scratched, but boasted a proud new black iron knocker in the shape of a lion's head and an electronic bell at the side with a notice above it – PRESS HARD. Felicity sighed audibly and pressed the bell. The journey to Enderly from Canada had been long and she was tired. Her back ached and her neck was stiff following her efforts to sleep in an awkward position during the long flight.

She heard some brisk steps approaching the door which was opened with caution by a thin sharp-looking woman who did not look more than fifty. The housekeeper or maid, Felicity surmised. What a miserable looking biddy, she thought. Gracious, what a rotten welcome after all the years I have been away.

'What do you want?' asked the woman, her tone exuding suspicion as her glance swept over the stranger with obvious dislike. 'If you are selling something ...'

Felicity bridled. 'I'm Felicity Brown and I've come to stay with Mrs Lacey. I'm her niece. Aren't you expecting me?' The wretched woman's face would crack if she smiled, Felicity thought.

The woman's nose wrinkled with disapproval.

'Of course, madam,' Joyce Skillet responded with difficulty and almost choked on on her words. 'Come in, I'll tell Mrs Lacey you are here.'

Joyce ushered Felicity into the spacious hallway.

'Leave your case in the hall, we can see to it later.' She gave it a derisory glance and emitted a loud disapproving sniff.

What a mean old cat, Felicity thought. It's not as though my case will make a mess anywhere.

The woodwork, painted a wishy-washy eggshell blue, just as it had been when Felicity was a child, looked faded. The wallpaper with the strange gooseberry pattern had been removed and the walls covered with a pale blue emulsion to match the woodwork.

The floor was covered with a good imitation wood patterned vinyl and an expensive looking Persian rug had been deposited with aplomb in the centre. A large elegant crystal chandelier hung from the centre of the ceiling.

Huh, Felicity thought. I don't think much of the decor. With all her money, too! The only decent thing is that rug, though the chandelier is not bad, it was probably expensive. I'll get rid of that dreadful blue if the house is mine one day, and it could be with some luck. A good oak floor would be much better than that vinyl. Her mind started to race as she considered the possibilities.

'Mrs Lacey will see you now,' cut across her thoughts and Joyce led her into the large dining room at the back of the house where Janet had her bed installed under an imposing double-glazed picture window. Janet sat in an armchair supported by well-stuffed soft velvet cushions. Her grey hair was twisted into a bun at the back of her head and she was dressed in a fine pink cashmere twin-set and well-cut black trousers. A heavy expensive-looking gold necklace hung round her thin neck and the imposing large links caught Felicity's eye. The thick gold necklace glinted and for a moment Felicity was mesmerized.

Janet took pride in her appearance and liked to look chic and smart, even if she was over eighty years old. She could afford to look elegant although she could not always remember the time of day or what happened yesterday. Joyce would help her dress and make up her face with expensive cosmetics, including the soft pale Italian lipstick she liked, purchased in her favourite chemists in Brinton. Good well applied make-up was a habit she had developed and maintained over the years.

Her old dog Jack sat at her feet. His hackles rose when he saw Felicity and a low rumbling sound emerged from the back of his throat.

Felicity was surprised. She thought that old Auntie did not look too bad and probably she had got a year or two of life in her yet, though that might be remedied if need be without too much effort.

Felicity stepped forward quickly and gave Janet a warm hug but avoided kissing her. She shuddered when she saw the deep wrinkles on her face and a couple of large hairy moles on her chin.

She made a determined effort to ignore the low growling and showing of Jack's unhygienic yellow teeth. I would like to give you a swift kick, she thought, but it might upset Aunt Janet. That would not be an auspicious start. What a dreadful dog you are!

'So lovely to see you Auntie,' she gushed. 'It's been too long but I'm here now and I'd like to stay a week or two if it's all right with you?'

She felt Jack's muzzle brush dangerously close to her leg and cringed.

Janet looked at her niece, or rather, James's niece, with some misgiving. She hardly recognised her after so long. She looked at the short plump woman with unattractive pepper and salt hair and made an effort not to shudder. Felicity had crows' feet, reminding Janet of the blue veins in gorgonzola cheese, that radiated from flecked blue-grey cold emotionless eyes. The once attractive mouth that Janet remembered was now thin and stringy and drooped at the corners. A bumpy roll of fat circled her waistline and bulged over her ample hips and thighs. Janet thought for a moment about Anne, and wondered what she might have looked like at sixty if she had lived that long, though she could only recall her as being tall and slim. Felicity did not look a happy individual, and although she had been pretty in her youth, she was no longer attractive.

Janet struggled to think back to the days when Felicity had stayed with her when she was twenty, a disturbed young woman who had been difficult to understand. The same restlessness showed on her face and she feared that it could be just as uncontrolled, but with any luck she may have mellowed. She hoped so. Although Janet was getting old and forgetful she could still understand that. Felicity smiled and for a moment Janet saw an unwelcome resemblance to her first husband James. She had the same cold expression in her eyes that James had in his when he left Primrose House. Shivers flickered along her back and she made an effort to cover up her disquiet.

'Of course, you must stay dear,' she said too quickly. 'Joyce has prepared the blue room for you. It's at the back of the house and there are lovely views of the river from the windows. Please make yourself at home. There is a bathroom next to the bedroom you can have for your own use. It is so lovely to see you after all these years. We have a lot of catching up to do. I look forward to that.'

Felicity heaved a sigh of relief. Getting her feet under the table here was going to be easier than she had anticipated. The old girl was obviously becoming gaga and suffering from arthritis. It must be bad if she has to sleep downstairs. I should be able to wheedle my way in here easily enough, she thought in her cold and devious way. I could offer to keep her company in the evenings when her housekeeper is not here. She had heard from her old acquaintance Pattie in the village that the housekeeper did not live in. I'll make myself useful and hopefully indispensable. She suddenly felt more cheerful than she had for months. She was sick of poverty and with any luck if she could inveigle her way in she would one day inherit her aunt's fortune. She must find out who the beneficiaries were in her aunt's will, assuming she had made one, and her calculating mind ran this idea over with pleasurable anticipation.

'I am so looking forward to getting to know you again, Auntie, and talking about old times.' She smiled in the most ingratiating way she could manage. She stepped forward once again and this time, with eyes shut, kissed Janet on the cheek. Janet was startled and managed to avoid showing her distaste. Her skin prickled and shivers ran down her spine once again. The feeling was mutual.

'You were so kind to me when I was a child,' Felicity continued, oblivious to Janet's trepidation.

'Joyce will show you to your room. I hope you will be comfortable,' Janet said.

'I'm sure I will Auntie.' She turned. Joyce was hovering in the doorway, her face set and grim. She was not going to worry about her. She was only a servant.

Joyce carried her suitcase up to the blue room and turned down the luxurious cream silk bedspread.

'You should be comfortable here, madam,' she said formally. 'The bathroom next door has fresh towels for you. You will no doubt want to freshen up after your long journey and when you are ready I will serve tea in the lounge. The radiator under the window has been turned on. It is easily controlled by the knob at the side, turn it down if you are too hot. There's plenty of room in the wardrobe if you want to hang up any clothes and there are some empty drawers in the dressing table. I cleared several at the top for your use earlier today.'

She gave Felicity's small case a disparaging glance. Not much of value in that, she calculated.

Joyce turned abruptly away. She had disliked Felicity on sight and, like the taxi driver, knew trouble when she saw it and she told herself that this woman was not to be trusted. She hoped that she would not stay too long. It would in her view take more than a hot radiator to thaw her.

Felicity looked out of the large bedroom windows. Some of the trees in the garden were still a glorious colour but a foggy haze now almost completely obscured the river. The normally attractive view was cold and unwelcoming. Slivers of a dull setting sun cut faintly through the mist and penetrated a gap in the heavy velvet curtains illuminating in an eerie way one wall of the room. The pale blue paint almost glowed and Felicity groaned. What a beastly colour, so cold and unfeeling, she thought. I much prefer green.

A man, not young, who she thought may be about the same age as herself or slightly older, was raking up leaves and placing them in a wheelbarrow. He looked vaguely familiar but she could not think why. She was convinced that she had seen him somewhere before, perhaps in a photograph. Strands of wiry grey hair protruded from an old woollen hat that he had pulled over his ears in an effort to keep warm. He had a small pointed beard and was quite small and wiry. He is probably an old age pensioner in need of a pound or two, she thought, though his jeans and thick fleece jacket looked as though they were very good quality garments. Oh well, he would not bother her. As she stared at him he glanced up towards her window and she noticed his piercing hazel eyes. She turned away. She felt disturbed and fancied that in some strange way he was looking right through her.

After hanging her few clothes in the big old-fashioned

wardrobe she placed her cheap pink plastic-backed hair brushes on the elegant glass-topped dressing table, moving to one side the heavy silver-backed brushes that occupied it. She had come home and was certainly not going to depart from Primrose House in a hurry. Washing quickly she tried to make herself as presentable as she could with her cheap tacky make-up. Exhaustion and jet lag began to set in with a vengeance but she looked forward to a good cup of English tea. 'Now for that food,' she muttered to herself. 'Hopefully there will be some decent cake and biscuits.'

As she ambled slowly down the stairs, her sharp sly eyes noticed with avarice the excellent collection of watercolours and oils that Janet and John had collected over the years and hung with pride above the wide staircase. They are worth a bit, she gauged. She strolled into the dining room where Joyce Skillet had set a tray, on which stood a delicate blue and white china teapot and dainty porcelain cups and plates, on a small antique dining table. On another table nearby there was a jug of milk, some dainty scones, iced cakes and small sandwiches. Pretty floral-handled tea knives and stiff starched napkins rested on the plates. Auntie certainly lives in style here, I could get used to this, she thought, and I will! She made an effort to exhibit a confident air, which she did not feel, as though she was already the mistress of the house. The idea pleased her and boosted her flagging spirits. She made an effort to play the part.

'Shall I pour, Auntie?' she asked in as sweet a voice as she could muster, though it came out as a rather unpleasant rasping husky tone.

'Yes please dear,' Janet said.

Felicity passed Janet her tea and offered her the scones and cakes as though she did that every day. Janet had a small swivel table by the side of her chair which she could pull closer to her in order to make dining easier. Felicity sat on a fine antique dining chair at the side of the dining table where she could eat and be near enough to her aunt be able to chat. She began to relax and was almost enjoying herself.

Janet too was almost enjoying having some company but could

not overcome the uneasy gut feeling she had about this woman. She was not sure why she disliked her but knew it was due to something that had happened in the past. Janet felt mean and uncomfortable. She should be welcoming this niece, even if she was only an in-law, and because of the unaccustomed guilt she dropped her habitual guard and gave her a warm, though somewhat vacant, smile.

They sipped their Earl Grey tea laced with fresh lemon slices. Both women were stiff and wary as though they were partaking in an uneasy truce as they nibbled the cakes and scones, or rather Janet nibbled hers and Felicity ate hers with greedy abandon. She was hungry and had not considered it wise to spend her limited cash on a snack when she travelled to Everton Station from Heathrow but she was jolly well going to make up for lost time. Like James, many years earlier, she laced her tea with three heaped teaspoonfuls of sugar; anything less and the tea would taste insipid. She preferred milk to lemon slices and was determined she would make that clear next time. She also liked Indian tea. Earl Grey tea had a rotten habit of going right through her. What a foul taste it had. Felicity looked forward to making the most of her time with dear Aunt Janet and her thoughts raced. The old bird would probably not live long, not long at all if she had anything to do with it, and she hoped that she would one day be able to inherit some, if not all, of her money if she played her cards right, and she had every intention of doing that. In the meantime, well, she would see.

Felicity shivered and rubbed her hands together vigorously in an effort to dispel the coldness that had started to make her fingers feel stiff. Her cheap thin clothes were not helpful. They were her best summer garments and not suitable for a chilly month like October. She had been a fool not to pack one or two of her old knitted jumpers even if they had been worn, darned and only fit for the dustbin. She shifted in her chair. Her legs and back ached. It had been a long day and she longed for a good hot bath and early night.

'It is rather cold in here auntie,' she said in a petulant tone. 'My clothes are a bit thin for the English climate. I didn't pack enough warm things. It was silly of me. Are there any good clothes shops near here?'

'Oh, quite a few,' her aunt replied. She thought back carefully with an effort to the shop in Brinton which sold good quality clothes. This woman could certainly improve her style, she thought, though she probably does not have much money. She sighed and looked closely at the shabby niece. Vancouver could be fairly cold too. The woman was obviously trying it on. She was without doubt as poor as a church mouse, as her mother used to say.

'Robbie, my handyman, will take you in the car to buy a few new clothes if you would like that. A pair of warm trousers, a jumper or two and a thick duffel coat would help, wouldn't they my dear? You could go in the morning. I'd like to buy them for you if you will let me. Robbie has a few errands to do for me in Brinton tomorrow.'

She had an uncomfortable feeling Felicity would jump at her offer. Well, she had plenty of spare cash and no children around to spend it on, and the least she could do was to see that this woman had some warm clothes, though quite why she should feel like that she didn't understand. The earlier feeling that she didn't want this visitor returned. Hopefully Felicity wouldn't stay long, after all an old lady with a failing memory would not be very good company for her.

'Sure, Auntie,' Felicity answered quickly, her Canadian accent coming to the fore. 'I haven't any spare cash though and don't want to be a burden or sponge on you.' Janet felt distinctly that was just what she did want to be but she would enjoy some company for a while even if it was James's niece, though she would have to pay the price for it. She had no illusions about that. Anything or anybody connected with James would be trouble in some form or other.

'That's all right dear, I'll treat you. I've not bought you any birthday presents for years; just think of a few clothes as gifts to make up for my past lapses. You can charge what you want to my account there. Mrs Betty Bumble the shopkeeper knows me well and will help you. She is rather a fussy old thing but she has good taste. I'll ask Joyce to telephone her to let her know you're coming and Robbie will go with you to the door of the shop to let Mrs Bumble know who you are. He can wait for you in the car when he has finished his business in Brinton while you shop in peace. Would eleven o'clock be all right?'

Felicity smiled to herself. This was going to be a piece of cake! 'Thank you dear Aunt Janet, you don't know how much I appreciate your kindness.'

Felicity thought that a few new warm dresses, tights, trousers, jumpers and some soft comfortable shoes too would not go amiss. The old girl could obviously afford them and would not miss the money. She hoped Mrs Betty Bumble stocked something decent and that her forgetful aunt would remember to ask Joyce to phone the shop in the morning as promised. She would remind her anyway. She felt a sense of relief and excitement that she had not felt for years. She was determined that she would stay as long as she could in Primrose House and ingratiate herself to Auntie. She congratulated herself on making such a good start.

Felicity decided that the first thing she must do after buying new clothes was to search for a copy of the old girl's latest will. She no doubt kept a copy somewhere. There probably was not a safe, not the sort of thing her aunt would bother with she guessed, but she had noticed a locked bureau in a corner of the lounge which looked a likely place to store documents. She would find out how much the old bag was worth now. Pattie's daughter still worked in her aunt's financial adviser's office in Everton. With luck Helen could find out even if it meant breaching confidentiality. She would probably have an eye to obtaining a good reward one day even if the financial adviser was tied by the Financial Services Authority rules. She struggled to repress a bubbling up of glee and greed which threatened to overwhelm her. Her face lit up in a veiled anticipation which Janet mistook for pleasure at the thought of buying some new clothes.

Janet was pleased to think that she could make this strange woman happy, though was not sure why. She suspected correctly, with an astuteness that her ailing mind had not yet wholly eliminated, that Felicity had endured a lifetime of poverty and unhappy relationships. She could at least offer her a little kindness now; indeed she would make an effort to do that. She vaguely realised that she was getting soft in her old age and a possible target for the unscrupulous but could not worry about it. She was just glad to be able to help and have a member of the family for company even if Felicity was not too delightful or a close blood relation. She could not be held responsible for her horrid uncle James. Thank goodness she did not resemble the beastly man in too many ways.

Felicity hovered round Janet and plumped up her pillows. Janet flushed with pleasure. Felicity decided that she would make herself indispensable as a companion, if only for a short while. She could just about stand that and if that smelly dog proved too much of a problem, well, that could easily be dealt with, she thought with malicious intent. A little something in his food would do the trick. As though he read her thoughts Jack made a lunge once or twice for her ankles. His teeth scratched her skin but she made light of his efforts. She would get round him with a biscuit or two, at least until she was well settled into her new home.

'It is so nice ... to have ... some company,' Janet stammered. Her niece may not be too bad after all and she could perhaps tolerate the woman for a short time. Well ... she hoped she could. Did she know her well? For a moment she could not remember.

Chapter 10

The Will

Felicity bought two finely woven woollen trouser suits, several blouses and jumpers, cardigans and a stunning dress with an Irish label. Astronomically expensive but that was not her problem. Fortunately, Betty Bumble had a few pairs of smart leather shoes in stock, not a style Felicity really liked, but good quality, and a selection of fine lacy underwear, which she decided was her style though she had never possessed anything so delicate before. She ran her hands over the intricate lace and sighed with pleasure.

'These clothes look lovely on you,' the old woman cackled as she surveyed Felicity with her sly slanted grey eyes through ugly dark red-rimmed glasses.

She fussed and fluttered around Felicity who was not used to so much attention. She did enjoy the pampering although she considered Mrs Bumble to be a silly old woman who was too keen to sell her over-priced clothes. She was an ugly old bird, must be at least seventy-five Felicity thought; ghastly bottle-red hair, with long and spiky finger nails painted to match. They reminded Felicity of a chicken's talons, though she had to admit that the woman's clothes were smart and so well cut that they were able to hide some of the obvious lumps round her expanding middle which were making a strenuous effort to protrude, like heaps of stodgy blancmange, through the expensive material.

Mrs Bumble understood that Mrs Lacey would be paying for the goods. Felicity had her credit card and Joyce had phoned earlier in the day to say that this was in order. No limit with regard to the total cost of the goods had been mentioned.

'Beautiful quality,' 'Lovely on you,' and 'Best I have,' were words trotted out. 'That really suits you dear,' and so on. Mrs Lacey could afford the best and the best she would produce for her niece. Felicity was not concerned with the prices on the goods. She did not give the tags a single glance. She was in seventh heaven. She tried on an endless number of garments and thoroughly enjoyed herself.

'I have a good handbag selection here, do have a look. This Italian leather bag would match your shoes and suits beautifully,' Mrs Bumble pressed. Felicity agreed to have the bag without hesitation.

'Quite nice leather,' she said in a tone that indicated she was used to buying the best and Mrs Bumble's bags were just about acceptable.

The bill was larger than Felicity had anticipated but she hoped dear Aunt Janet would not be concerned about that. She would offer to help with her aunt's accounts to ensure there were no difficulties encountered through her lavish expenditure. She was quite adept when it came to fixing accounts. She understood from the chatty Mrs Bumble that Janet had difficulty when writing cheques these days and preferred to use a credit card when doing her shopping.

Whilst chatting with her aunt the previous evening Felicity had discovered that Janet's old friend Peter's son Jeremy Mace was now her solicitor as his father had been before him. If he did not interfere too much, she could perhaps get away with a lot. The credit card and pin numbers were all she needed. Jeremy had offered to pay bills for Janet and it seemed that he did so on occasions when Janet seemed more confused than usual. She understood he had set up a direct debit so that the credit card bills were paid automatically at the end of each month. She vowed to deal with Jeremy and his so-called good intentions as soon as possible.

The first thing she needed to do when she got back to Primrose House was to find out if Auntie had an up-to-date will and what was in it. That would be her next task. Her mind started to wander, as it so often did, and she imagined what her life could be like if she owned Primrose House and her pockets were full of money. No more scrimping and scrounging, that would be wonderful. She had already endured years of living on the bread-line. The lure of a better life was sweet and a mounting excitement threatened to overcome her. This was one opportunity she did not intend to let slip through her fingers. The morning's shopping had whetted her appetite.

The goods purchased in Mrs Bumble's shop were packed in large paper holdalls topped with elegant pink string handles. Robbie was startled when he arrived outside the shop to collect Felicity and looked with surprise at the number of bags on the pavement.

'Put my shopping in the boot,' Felicity said in an imperious tone and waved her hand with a gesture that would have done credit to the Queen in order to indicate where her goods were stacked, though the pile was obvious, and with uncharacteristic swiftness settled herself in the back of the car whilst Robbie struggled to load her purchases into the car boot. She observed that his face turned a deep pink with annoyance and his hazel eyes glittered but she did not care.

'Hurry up man,' Felicity shouted and smirked with satisfaction as he stumbled under the weight of her goods.

Mrs Bumble hovered anxiously and struggled to hide the smug smile that threatened to contort her thin lips.

'Do come again soon Mrs Brown,' she croaked as she twisted and rubbed her bony hands together. What a good morning's sales, she told herself. With any luck that niece will be staying for some time.

Several days passed and Felicity was feeling more comfortable. She was enjoying herself. Joyce disliked her more each day and showed it rather too openly.

'How long is that woman staying?' Joyce asked her employer several times.

Janet took very little notice and Joyce's veiled and somewhat derisive mutterings behind Felicity's back made little impact upon her. Felicity, however, quietly vowed to remove the insolent Joyce as soon as she was able. She would have to put up with her for some time yet but her day of retribution would come. She would make sure of that.

She did not like the gardener and general help, Robbie, either though she conceded that he was quite useful. She felt he was watching her too often for comfort. Robbie did indeed keep a beady eye on the usurper. Felicity wondered why he was showing so much interest in her, after all he was only an employee.

'How long are you staying, miss?' he asked politely when he drove her to Brinton once again to do her shopping a few days after she had arrived.

'Oh, I am not sure yet. I will probably stay a week or two longer.'

The conversation lapsed and apart from the arrangements for the return journey they did not say another word to each other, a silence maintained when he struggled to stow her mountain of parcels in the boot, which took him a good five minutes. Robbie had an uneasy memory of an unpleasant little girl who had attended Janet's wedding years before when he was a page boy. Time had not improved her manners.

'Strange fellow, Robbie,' Felicity said to her aunt later that evening. 'Have you known him long?'

Her aunt smiled and thought for some time before replying.

'I'm not sure. He has been here a while I think,' she responded in a quiet voice, almost a whisper. She seemed slightly bewildered and the subject was dropped.

Old girl does not seem to know, Felicity thought. That man is far too inquisitive but he is quite useful. It was a conclusion she had an uncomfortable feeling that she may regret later.

Janet had an afternoon nap, usually for about two hours, each day and Felicity would sit in the lounge and attempt to read though her concentration would only allow her to peruse a chapter or two at a time. To her chagrin Joyce Skillet kept a beady eye upon her but on Thursday afternoons Joyce usually went home early and Lily from the vicarage came to help. Dopey looking creature, Felicity thought, but I will have to tolerate her I suppose.

On the second Thursday of Felicity's visit Lily was sick.

'Lily has a really bad cold,' her mother had telephoned and

informed Joyce Skillet that morning. 'She cannot possibly come. Really streaming, I would not like her to pass the cold to Mrs Lacey. It would be very unfair.'

'I wanted to get away early,' Joyce moaned. 'Always the way ...'

'Don't worry,' Felicity said in a patronizing voice. 'I can look after Auntie.'

Joyce looked doubtful but Felicity insisted. 'We really do not need that girl anyway now that I'm here. Daft creature anyway.'

'Well ...' Joyce agreed dubiously, 'I'll leave the supper ready and you can help Mrs Lacey to get into bed I'm sure.' The slightly sarcastic edge to her voice was not lost upon Felicity.

Felicity had been looking forward to the chance to rummage for the will and an opportunity had at last presented itself. She had found out from her friend that Auntie was worth a couple of million at least. She must make sure that some, or preferably most of it, came her way. Felicity's eyes shone and her body tingled with anticipation. It should not take her long to go through a few drawers. She would start on that likely-looking oak bureau in the lounge where she had earlier considered that important documents might be kept. Felicity was expert at undoing locks if she could not find the keys. It was something she had learned from a boyfriend she had lived with for a while after leaving her husband. He had been a cat burglar and fairly successful for a while. He had shown her how to pick locks and had been amazed at her aptitude. Unfortunately for him he been caught stealing from a warehouse about a year after they had met and had been sentenced to five years in prison. Felicity had thought that a good point in time to move on and until she met Roberto she lived with several petty thieves and sometimes violent criminals. When she found out they did not have any money stashed away she moved on quickly, until she met Roberto who was simple but honest. Roberto had been a conven-ient prop just when she needed one. She liked and to some extent admired the man but never loved him. He was in her opinion too weak and that was something she did not respect. In any case, what real love for a man entailed was a complete mystery to her. Men had satisfied her lust and provided her with some security when she needed it but that was all. She took but did not give.

When supper was over and Janet soundly asleep with the aid of a couple of sleeping pills Felicity began her eagerly awaited search for the will.

The old oak bureau indeed proved to be the hiding place for a number of documents including a copy of the last will and testament of Janet Lacey which had been made shortly after her husband John died in 1980. The will was, after a few very small bequests and £5000 to Thomas Hands, divided into three parts: one part to Janet's trusted friend the solicitor Peter Mace or if he did not survive her, his children; the second part to herself Felicity Griffiths, her married name; and the third to her brother Ronald.

It was better than she had expected. She beamed and sank her ample bottom into the large plush lounge sofa to dream about a luxurious future when Auntie had gone. It would be even better if she could eliminate some of the other beneficiaries before Auntie popped it. If she was a sole beneficiary she could also be mistress of Primrose House. She started to plan and scheme how that might be achieved and in what colours she would redecorate the rooms. Ronald she was not too concerned about, after all he was her own flesh and blood and she convinced herself that he would not wish to leave Australia. He was too far away to do anything about anyway. She had a small lingering feeling of affection for her little brother. He surely would not want to turn her out of Primrose House, although it might have to be sold if he wanted his share of the estate immediately. That solicitor, Peter Mace, and his family, hmm, she would check how many of them were still alive. Who on earth was Thomas Hands? The name was familiar. She needed to do some research. She ached with excitement. She told herself that she would have no hesitation in disposing of any of them if the opportunity arose. She had knifed one difficult and bullying boyfriend who had threatened to kill her when she first moved to Vancouver and disposed of his body in a lake with little compunction. She had decided he was of little value and her conscience was in no way troubled. After all, she was entitled to defend herself. The local police had not suspected her as far as she knew, though they had questioned her and taken her fingerprints.

Her ego had been boosted by the fact that she had, as she thought of it, got away with murder. Not many women are capable of that, she reminisced with considerable pride.

Huh … she looked more closely at the small bequests: one thousand pounds to her financial adviser. She would see about that: the FSA Ethics Committee would find that interesting. That would be fun, she would like that.

Her thoughts turned back to Primrose House. It would be dreadful if it had to be sold but she realized that would most likely be the case; it was after all part of the estate. She wondered once again if there was some way round that. Her turbulent restless mind flitted from one idea to another. She was anxious to use any means available to her in order to increase her share of her aunt's fortune. The way may prove to be twisted, but Felicity was determined to overcome any obstacles in order to achieve her all-important goal, money.

It was imperative to check first of all if the will was the last one her aunt had written. She could perhaps pretend that she needed to write a will and discuss the pros and cons with her aunt. That at least could be a starting point and so she did this at the next opportunity when they were having their afternoon tea alone in the lounge.

'Do you think it is a good idea Auntie if I make a will? I have not much to leave to anybody except perhaps my brother Ronald's daughter in Australia, but it could save a lot of trouble, couldn't it?'

Felicity did not look as though she had much to leave anyone but Janet remembered vaguely that she had made a will herself in the past and Jeremy had said it was a good idea.

'It's certainly a good thing to do, Felicity,' she said after a few minutes of struggling to gather her thoughts together. 'I'll give you the address of my solicitor; Jeremy will help you, though you could possibly ask him when he visits Primrose House next. I made a will, think it was in the nineteen eighties but I'm not really sure. I can't really remember what was in it but I know one should always make one, it does save others a lot of trouble.'

Janet wondered for a brief moment what was in her will, but

she couldn't remember, so she stretched her hand out for one of Joyce's newly iced fairy cakes, her mouth watering slightly. It no longer seemed important. She was tired and looked forward to a nap. Her eyes felt heavy and she sighed audibly. The saliva dribbled with invidious determination from the corners of her mouth and ran down her chin. Cake crumbs tumbled on to the floor to be snapped up with rapacious eagerness by the odious Jack.

Felicity made a strenuous effort to hide her repugnance. Ugh, revolting old woman, passed through her mind, but I won't have to put up with her too long, or that fleabag dog. Auntie is not going to live much longer, she looks so frail. It would be easy to doctor Jack's supper with a little poison but she could wait until a more appropriate time to do that. A feeling of pleasure rushed over her when she thought about it. She considered him to be a horrid stinking animal. It would give her great pleasure to see the back of him.

Felicity shifted in her chair and Jack growled with ominous intensity. He would have enjoyed savaging her ankles but was smart enough to know it would not be in his best interest. She had already given him a swift kick when she thought his mistress was not looking. He could wait, his time would come. His eyes glittered with animosity.

Felicity was reasonably satisfied that the will was the latest, but she would try and check again later if the will was the last one Janet had signed. She did not want any nasty surprises when her aunt had been buried in the local churchyard. In the meantime she would make some further enquiries about the other beneficiaries and think carefully about removing a few of them if practicable. She thought it would be, indeed she would enjoy the challenge and she experienced a welcome rush of adrenalin. She found herself daydreaming for a few moments about the possibilities. The will and Janet's money filled her thoughts on most days and she often dreamt at night about a life of pleasure and comfort in a beautifully decorated and transformed Primrose House; a house decorated in the way she admired and not a beastly blue wall to be seen.

Felicity was enjoying the luxury her aunt afforded her more

each day. Janet had foolishly arranged for Felicity to have the joint use of a credit card and given her some signed cheques in order that she could buy goods for the household and any other small items of clothing or make-up that she needed when she went into Brinton to shop. Janet's current account balance was substantial and she had stubbornly ignored suggestions from her bank and financial adviser that she should transfer excess funds to more lucrative accounts. She had a good pension and income from her large fortune which was paid into the account on a regular basis.

'Never know when I might like to spend some of it,' she had responded to their sensible suggestions and now she could indulge her poverty-stricken niece, though she was unaware of the full extent of her generosity.

Whenever she went into the lounge Felicity took pleasure from patting her newly trimmed hair and glancing quickly at her reflection in the expensive-looking bronze-edged mirror that dominated the old, but elaborate blue-and-white tiled Dutch fire-place. It became a habit. She delighted in her new image. She made a point of wearing pretty mohair cardigans under which matching silk blouse collars peeped out. She had bought several cardigans and blouses in various soft colours though green was her favourite. Her woollen trousers were the best the old woman in the shop in Brinton could produce. The cut of these trousers was better than any others Felicity had owned before and her figure, she decided, really looked quite trim, or at least her slightly dumpy waist did not seem so prominent. Her attractive soft leather Italian shoes moulded themselves to her feet and complemented the trousers. They fitted perfectly and she no longer needed to hobble. She had been stupid in the past to buy shoes that were too small just because they had been reduced. She hoped auntie would not mind too much, that is if she ever found out how expensive the purchases were. She did not appear to mind, indeed she had noticed that her aunt sometimes looked at her smart image with approval and had a satisfied smile that would linger around her mouth for a while when Felicity appeared in one of her new outfits. It had been wonderful to treat herself to some good French make-up, Janet had given her enough spare cash for that, and had obtained some excellent advice from some of the staff in the one rather up-market chemist's shop. Quite a find that shop she decided; she had not expected to come upon such good products in a tip like Brinton.

Janet was not concerned. It was only money and her niece looked happier. She was not sure now what arrangement they had come to about paying for the goods, she could not remember, but it did not really matter. It had been interesting to watch her emerge from a cheap-looking tart into a smart woman who now dressed with good taste.

Joyce Skillet however had noticed with some disquiet that Felicity looked so much more presentable. She was suspicious and resentful of this usurper who seemed to be creeping and grovelling around her aunt. She did not like her any better as the days passed and wondered who she could ask for advice about the unwelcome newcomer to Primrose House. She decided eventually to talk to Robbie. He seemed to her to be a genuine man who cared in his way for Mrs Lacey. In that assumption she was right but he didn't have any idea what they could do about the unwelcome visitor; their only option was to commiserate and wait.

Chapter 11

Peter Mace 2004

P eter felt his age. His back often felt stiff and his knees ached. Pains radiated down his arms from his shoulders and settled in his wrists, making many every-day tasks uncomfortable and difficult. He was born in the same year as Janet and had been her solicitor and closest adviser for many years. He'd sympathised with her when James Anderson had departed so abruptly although he had been glad to see the back of the man, and comforted her when her second husband John Lacey died from cancer in his early sixties. Janet was devastated and he had been there to give her as much support as he could, which he was more than happy to do. Peter had promised John Lacey that he would look after Janet, something he agreed to with alacrity; he did not find that prospect onerous. Janet had always held a corner of his heart and he had loved her since they were pupils in the local primary school, far more than any other woman he had known, including his wife.

'Don't worry, John,' he had said. 'I'll help Janet,' and he did. It was not an arduous task and he took pleasure in it. He was intrigued to discover that John had left Janet a very wealthy widow. He helped her to obtain a financial adviser, a friend he strongly recommended. He was anxious to make himself indispensable and, with luck, persuade her to leave a little something to his family. She could afford to do that. He had no conscience about encouraging her to leave a legacy to his son and grandson.

Peter had helped Janet when she made her will in 1980 but when Peter retired in his mid sixties his son Jeremy had taken over the reins of the business, following in his father's footsteps. His grandson Matthew, who had also studied law, was now in charge of the business. Whether Jeremy or Matthew had updated Janet's will since he had retired he could not remember. They had probably mentioned it to him and he thought Jeremy had possibly made another will for Janet in 1990 but he was getting almost as forgetful as Janet. He had a vague idea that Janet had left some money to the Mace family together with some of her better pieces of furniture. He would have no hesitation in accepting anything she wanted his family to have. They had looked after her well over the years. The financial adviser he had recommended had no doubt kept a sharp eye on her affairs and increased her fortune through good investment.

Peter's wife Alice had died ten years previously which had left him lonely, and he valued Janet's friendship. Janet did not have any children and depended on him and a few other close friends for company. He was lucky to have his son Jeremy and grandson Matthew.

Peter climbed the road to Primrose House one afternoon almost every week to visit and talk about old times with a dog treat tucked in his pocket for Jack, who would nuzzle and press against his legs until he produced it. He thought that he was a smelly old dog, a bath would not go amiss, but he did not care to express that feeling to Janet and upset her in any way. Janet was becoming very forgetful and Peter was concerned about her state of mind. He would struggle up the slight hill to see her, stopping every few yards to catch his breath and lean on his trusty walking stick.

Approximately one week after Felicity arrived he paid one of his usual visits. The October damp crept into his bones insidiously as he made his way to Primrose House that day. His nose had turned a deep pink, purple veins cloaked his cheeks and his feet felt numb with the cold. Joyce showed him into the lounge and disappeared with haste into the kitchen to produce the afternoon tea of egg sandwiches and the sugar-splattered Eccles cakes she knew he liked.

'Poor old man,' she muttered to herself. 'He's still a good friend though and Mrs Lacey could do with a few of those.'

He warmed himself for a few minutes by a radiator before sitting down gratefully in an armchair. He expected that Janet would join him as usual, making her way to the lounge with her walking sticks, independent as ever, and not allowing him to assist her.

He heard footsteps, quicker than he had expected, and adjusted his old metal-rimmed glasses which had a habit of slipping down his nose. He turned his head as Felicity entered the room. For a moment he was startled. A stiff and somewhat false smile was glued to Felicity's countenance and she gave him a derogatory look.

'Who are you?' he stammered rudely, which was unusual for this mild-mannered man.

'I am Felicity Brown. Mrs Lacey's niece. I've come to stay with Auntie, and who are you?' she retorted sharply, a scowl creeping over her face which emphasised a spiteful hard expression which was impossible to disguise. Peter cringed.

'I'm your aunt's very old friend. We were at school together. I used to be her solicitor many years ago. We have tea together most weeks. Haven't we met before?'

Felicity looked at Peter with a brief flicker of interest in her cold eyes. Huh, she thought. He is the one named in the will but he does not look as though he is going to last long. She expelled an audible sigh of relief. She wondered what his son was like and how many of the wretched Mace family still lived and were waiting ready to grab a share of her aunt's fortune. She made an effort to compose her face into a pleasant and innocuous countenance and sat down on a chair next to him.

'We probably met when I stayed with Auntie as a child,' she responded in as pleasant a tone as she could muster. Her expression lost some of its suspicious edge.

What is the ghastly woman planning? Peter wondered. She is a typical leech and without doubt only interested in her aunt's money. He was for a second or two quite dismayed and dumfounded as this realization sunk in.

'How long are you staying with your aunt?' he managed to say after a slight pause.

'Oh, a month or two if Auntie will have me,' was the swift and confident reply.

'Well, then, we will probably see quite a lot of each other.'

Felicity hoped not but she looked forward to finding out more about the will she had found in the drawer. The wretched man may be able to help her.

Joyce's head appeared at the door.

'Tea will be served in the dining room today sir,' she said, ignoring Felicity. 'I've made a few of your favourite egg and cress sandwiches.'

Felicity quivered. Ugh, egg. What a silly old man. We could have had smoked salmon if he had not come, but still her mouth watered. She was always hungry. She should watch her waistline which was threatening to expand and spoil the sleek lines of her new clothes but she was enjoying the luxury of the free food in Primrose House. There would be chocolate cake with cream filling, she thought and cheered up. The sight of the sugary looking Eccles cakes was not welcome. They would sit like lumps of lead in her stomach and that she did not want. She hoped her face was not turning green. They sat with mounting unease around a small table in the dining room. Janet had struggled to move from her usual comfortable armchair with her stiff and unyielding limbs in an effort to sit between Peter and Felicity like a good hostess should. Felicity looked at Peter with small sly eyes. She must pump him about that will sometime. To do it without raising suspicion in the old fart's mind would probably take some guile but she would think of something.

'I think we definitely did meet when I was a child,' she proffered in her strange Canadian accent, breaking the charged silence and looking at Peter with the most innocent expression she could muster as she fluttered her short stubby eyelashes. 'I remember now.'

'Yes,' Peter replied. 'I remember too; it was a long time ago.'

He remembered all right. A vile child, malicious and cruel, he had considered at the time though disturbed was a more apt description. She did not look much more agreeable now.

'How is your brother Ronald?' he asked after a short pregnant pause. Poor little fellow. He was unlucky having to put up with a sister who behaved like she did.

'Oh, OK, sure,' Felicity replied in a flippant tone. 'He is a dentist now and married with one kid. They live in Melbourne, Australia and are doing all right I think. We don't correspond much.' She turned her head to look at her aunt and gave her a warm smile, the subject of Ronald neatly closed.

Janet nodded and passed the rather gooey egg sandwiches to Peter. They were soft and oozing with mayonnaise with flecks of wilted green cress hanging out of the sides. There was a vacant look in her fading brown eyes as her mind wandered.

Felicity sniffed and wriggled in her chair. Peter took his fifth sandwich, mayonnaise dripping down his fingers, and an odd silence engulfed them for several minutes. In Felicity's eyes he was just a greedy old twit. He held a torch for auntie years ago she reflected and almost laughed out loud. Good old Uncle James got there first and they did not have any brats to complicate matters. Thank goodness for that.

Felicity poured the tea from a large elegant fine china teapot into the matching cups that Joyce Skillet had set out earlier. Peter was surprised. He always did that for Janet when they had tea together. The wretched niece was playing at being hostess and usurping him. She was unnerving him and forcing him to make an effort to stop his hands from shaking.

Peter looked with avarice at the antique dining chairs, a look that was not lost on Felicity. The six chairs were elegant and no doubt worth a penny or two, Felicity turned over in her mind. Peter caressed the soft striped velvet chair covers with his arthritic fingers and smiled with satisfaction. Jeremy had taken the chairs to be repaired and re-covered in a traditional style only a few years ago, having made the excuse that they were getting wobbly and unsafe for visitors to use. They cost Janet a lot to repair but were, he was sure, valuable antiques and Janet had promised to leave them to the Mace family in her will.

'Another sandwich, Felicity?' her aunt said interrupting her reverie and making an effort to take over the role of hostess.

'No thank you Auntie dear,' Felicity responded in a gushing

tone. She observed the fine Minton plate. Nothing but the best it seemed for old Peter Mace. A feeling of nausea was threatening to overtake her. She swallowed several of what she considered to be the tasteless soggy old sandwiches. There was no added salt in them because Peter had said he did not like that. It was bad for his blood pressure.

'Would you like another one Peter … er Mr Mace?' she drawled, smiling in as charming a manner as she could manage, and took the plate from her aunt in order to pass it to him. Scraps of egg already clung in an unsavoury way round the edge of his mouth and Felicity groped for a napkin and made a desperate effort not to retch. Her face blanched but both Peter and her aunt with their failing eyesight did not notice.

Peter Mace continued his visits as usual during the month of November. He liked to look round the garden at Primrose House before taking tea with Janet. He had a habit of wandering round to the kitchen garden at the back where there was a small greenhouse which contained many of Janet's garden plants that needed shelter at that time of the year. Robbie was a wonderful asset to his friend, he had concluded. Peter never failed to be impressed. There was a large potting shed next to the greenhouse where Robbie kept the garden tools, which were all well oiled and cared for, and an old table and chair he used when he took his morning coffee or ate his lunchtime sandwiches if he stayed that long.

The next time Peter visited Primrose House he clambered up the short metal staircase which led to the kitchen from the garden. He sometimes entered the house that way when he thought that Joyce Skillet would be there to let him in, though quite often the door was left unlocked if he was expected. Struggling with the icy conditions he clutched and hung on, as well as he was able with bent old hands, to the slippery and worn iron handrail in an effort to stop himself from falling, but his arthritic feet and legs were not helpful. On reaching the top he paused for a moment to catch his breath. The door swung open and, to his surprise, an arm shot out and hit him violently in the chest. Losing his grip on the slippery rail he slid backwards. His legs buckled painfully beneath him as he plummeted downwards and landed with a sickening thud that resounded on the frozen earth. Peter struggled to open his eyes and saw someone holding a large stone above his head. He tried to cry out but could make no sound. Something akin to an electric crackle trickled across his brain accompanied by a bizarre and remote feeling of helplessness. Within seconds there was darkness.

Joyce Skillet had gone to visit her elderly mother in the cottage hospital in Brinton and Felicity had been left in charge of making the egg sandwiches for Peter. She had prepared them with a heavy heart, vile things, especially if they did not have salt in. She set the small table in the dining room as usual and Janet and Felicity waited for the guest. The clock in the hall struck half past four but there was no sign of the old man.

Janet became anxious.

'I can't understand it Felicity, he rarely forgets to come,' she repeated many times until Felicity's patience began to run out.

'Don't worry Auntie, something unexpected has probably come up and he has forgotten to let us know.' She smiled smugly as she poured two cups of the foul-tasting Earl Grey tea which she made using an electric kettle in the dining room, and handed her aunt an egg sandwich. She helped herself to a slice of soft chocolate cake and one of Joyce's delicious home-made iced sponge fingers. She spread one of the dainty Japanese napkins that her aunt liked across her lap to catch any unwanted crumbs and tucked into her tea with relish.

Felicity looked out of the windows at the white puffs of cloud that had begun to drift across the sky as the north-easterly wind strengthened. 'It is probably too cold for him today,' she said in a dismissive tone. 'The sky is a nasty colour and it looks as though it may snow soon.'

Peter's body was found the next day by the milkman when he delivered the milk, eggs and Janet's favourite fruit yoghurts. Felicity, like many of the villagers, preferred the Everton supermarkets. She thought the milkman's goods were too expensive but had to admit to herself that it was a relief that he had arrived early to find the body and for that she was thankful.

'I am so sorry Auntie,' she said to Janet. 'Peter was such a good friend.' She smiled inwardly and the thought that there was one less Mace to benefit from Auntie's will was satisfying.

The police were called, enquiries made, and it was concluded that his death was an unfortunate accident. Detective Inspector Holmes from Brinton who had been assigned the case did not think it was an accident but no evidence could be found at that time to support his suspicions. He had placed the bloodstained stone that had been found lying a short distance from the body into a plastic bag and sent it to the local Police Forensic Science Laboratory but he was not optimistic about obtaining a positive and useful result. There was one smudged fingerprint which would not be easy to identify.

Peter Mace was buried in Enderly churchyard next to his wife Alice. A sprightly lady curate conducted the service. The church was filled to capacity with curious villagers, a few old clients and the small Mace family consisting of Jeremy and his son Matthew. Jeremy's wife Betty had died three years earlier and Matthew, who was now in his late thirties, had so far shown no interest in getting married, though he did have a few girlfriends when he was in his teens. He was an attractive bachelor and Felicity was pleased to discover that he was not married; it would make things easier for her if she did not have too many of the Mace family to deal with.

Robbie drove Janet to the church and helped her with care into a pew at the back. She looked sad and bereft following the loss of her old friend and Robbie determined that he would try and discover what happened that fateful day. Like DI Holmes he found it difficult to accept the accident theory but without witnesses or some concrete evidence he knew that murder would be difficult to prove. Robbie had vowed to repay Janet and her mother's kindness to him when he was a child and he was now very anxious and fearful with regard to Janet's safety. He was a clever man, far more intelligent than Felicity realized at that time, though she appreciated that he was no fool. The fact that he intu-itively suspected that she might have been involved in Peter's demise was something of which she was blissfully unaware.

Janet had dressed for the funeral with conventional respect in her best black suit and thick woollen overcoat. She was not sure why but had been prompted by Joyce to wear black. She stumbled as she entered the church, though she was leaning heavily on Robbie's arm, and looked with unease down the short aisle where she could see Peter's coffin. There were white lilies draped over the lid and their sickly smell wafted towards her. A cheap coffin she thought, and wondered if the family were short of money. For a moment she forgot whose body was inside that horrid pine-coloured box, then she remembered and groaned. The sea of faces, a mixture of the firm's clients and villagers, were almost all strangers to her. Many of the people she had known well in the past were dead or had moved away. She was convinced for a few moments that she had drifted into some alien world. Had she been in this church before? She was unsure. The cold grey stone walls and pretty stained-glass windows looked familiar.

The organist played Handel's *Largo* as the mourners took their seats. When the service started the congregation reached for their Order of Service and their voices became subdued. There were only two short hymns which had been Peter's wish though Janet thought that the service continued for an eternity. She longed to get away from the musty damp smell coming up from the floor below the pews that reminded her of rotting bones. She had made the effort to say goodbye to her old friend but there was no way she could stand for more than a few minutes on her weak and wobbly legs to join in the singing. The curate's sermon and some-what tedious readings by Jeremy and Matthew drifted over her head without real meaning or understanding. Jeremy was slightly tipsy and his speech was slurred and muddled. Janet dreaded having to follow the family to the graveside and was glad of the support of Robbie's strong arm to prevent her frail body from falling.

'It's all right Mrs Lacey,' Robbie assured her. 'I've borrowed a wheelchair to take you to the graveside.'

Janet was relieved but insisted on standing up, stiff and miser-able, to watch when the coffin of her friend was lowered into the cold earth. The weather was raw and a bitter wind whipped round her thin legs. She uttered a pitiful sob and Felicity patted her arm with feigned sympathy. Felicity's blue flecked eyes looked calm and expressionless. Robbie supported Janet as well as he could and Matthew also offered her an arm.

Felicity turned her attention to the other mourners with somewhat muted interest and then her thoughts wandered to what lunch in the Maces' home would be like. She was hungry and her mouth, as usual, threatened to water. Felicity had scarcely noticed Janet's obvious distress or her need to be supported by Robbie and Matthew. She was too busy wallowing in pleasure as she clutched her new thick black cashmere coat closer and tightened the pretty black fake-fur scarf around her neck in an attempt to avoid the effects of the cold whistling wind. Thank goodness she had purchased some new long fur-lined boots and a fur hat to match the scarf. She glanced down at her lovely leather boots and ran her hand down the front of the immaculate soft and voluminous handbag she had purchased to match. Quite perfect, hmm ... quite perfect.

Matthew and Jeremy threw a sprinkling of fine black Enderly earth onto the coffin lid and as it pattered down Janet thought for a moment that her heart would break. She removed a faded pressed rose from her handbag and watched as it fluttered down onto the coffin lid. It was a flower she had saved with care. She had kept it pressed between the pages of her Bible after Peter had given it to her when they were schoolchildren and there it had stayed until now. Peter dead! Janet tried to get her head around that concept. It was defeating her. Glimpses of the boy he had been at school and the friend who had supported her tirelessly over so many years passed through her mind then drifted away again like snowflakes melting on desolate ground. A fleeting memory of him as a small child in school, perhaps only about ten or eleven, came to mind. She had a hazy idea that they had been sweethearts for a while in their early teens, but she knew that she had never really loved him with any passion or thought of him as being more than a friend. She recalled with difficulty that his eyes had been grey-blue with flecks of brown, more flecks in the left eye than the right, and had fine arched eyebrows which he told her many times with pride were inherited from some revered aristocratic ancestor, a lord somebody or other. Ridiculous, she had always maintained. Why should anyone care about something so trivial?

Janet's short-term memory had become so poor that she soon forgot the funeral as she was helped by Matthew and Robbie to the wheelchair and taken to her car so that Robbie could drive her the short distance down the road to Jasmine Cottage. A spread of cold meats and salad and a selection of sweets were waiting together with wine to toast Matthew's grandfather's memory in a way that he would have wished. Janet was confused and forgot after a while why she was there but was enjoying the unaccustomed company. Robbie helped her to the dining room where she was able to sit on a firm high-backed chair next to a small table.

'It is a lovely day,' she said to Felicity as a blank and worried expression appeared on her pale, lined face. 'It has made quite a change. I not sure who all these people are dear.'

Felicity's thin mouth crinkled into a sardonic smile.

Felicity gave the impression to many people that she was cold hearted, lacking in conscience and very intelligent. The latter was far from the truth but she was, for the majority of people, a difficult person to understand.

Felicity's thoughts wandered when she entered Jasmine Cottage. She looked forward with increasing fervour to the lunch that had been promised but she found herself repressing a shudder when she looked at the dining room walls painted with dull beige emulsion paint that had seen better days and the thin, almost threadbare, faded, beige curtains chosen to match many years earlier by the late Alice Mace. She estimated that the curtains would benefit from a jolly good wash though they could fall to pieces if they were not handled with care. She considered that would be an appropriate end for the dreadful things. Two clumsy home-made wooden chandeliers hung at precarious angles from the ceiling, their skimpy imitation candle bulbs coated with thick dust which served to reinforce her initial feeling of disgust. The carpet below her feet was matted with wear and displayed numerous marks where blobs of food had splattered down over many years to penetrate the surface and had not been cleaned. She looked with disdain at the cheap prints that hung on the walls and then considered for a few moments how satisfactory and enjoyable it would be to be able to dispose of Jeremy and Matthew. That was more interesting to her than the tatty old furniture and fittings. One down and two to go . . . She would certainly welcome their absence from her life. The aroma of cooked meats reached her nostrils and her thoughts switched to the food set out on a large dining table covered with a crisp white linen cloth. She moved forward as soon as it was announced by Jeremy that the guests should help themselves to the funeral lunch, and piled a plate high with meats, salads, new potatoes, quiche, three crisp brown rolls and several pats of butter. She continued to daydream whilst she tucked heartily into her meal. Hmm . . . no more tasteless egg sandwiches or Eccles cakes now that the old man was out of her life. Hurrah! She was for a few moments almost as restless as she had been as a child although her turbulent nature was now hidden with cunning skill from those closest to her. Lavender-scented spray polish muffled the smell of cheap whisky that followed in Jeremy's wake as he staggered round in a weak attempt to mingle with his guests. Felicity felt nauseous for a few moments when he passed by but she soon recovered her appetite and served herself with a slice of fruit cake and a portion of cheesecake. She had forgotten about Janet and when she remembered her just before she finished her sweet she was relieved to see that she was eating some lunch and was being waited upon by Robbie. For one moment she almost felt a tremor of regret for her thoughtless behaviour but soon dismissed any feeling of guilt. The old bird had enough people to run round her. No harm had been done.

Robbie however was uncomfortable. He saw Felicity as a disturbed and tormented woman and he wondered why. Perhaps something had happened during her childhood to twist her mind. Like most people he could not understand her but he would watch and wait. What a gluttonous woman she was. There was no real proof that she was involved in Peter's untimely death. However, if she was, she would slip up sooner or later and he would be waiting to pounce. That thought cheered him.

Janet glanced round in a vague way with little interest but, like Felicity, did observe that the furniture in Jasmine House was cheap and old which surprised her. Most of it looked as though it had come from a second-hand shop. The dining-room chairs in particular were worn and scuffed and parts of the carpet, between matted patches, almost threadbare. She was puzzled. The Mace family had a good business, or did they? They were a typical middle-class family. It did not make sense.

Janet dismissed the poor surroundings as being of little consequence, indeed they would, at least for her, soon be forgotten, but Felicity continued to smirk with a cruel and satisfying feeling as she looked at the faded furniture, sagging settee springs and worn old rugs. No wonder they are after Aunt Janet's money, she thought. They will not be lucky if I have anything to do with it. Greedy creatures! She drifted once again into her own private world and considered how she could eliminate the rest of the Mace family if she got the chance. She would enjoy that. Her mind raced and her heart beat faster as she mulled over the possibilities. The old grandfather clock in the hall struck a tremulous three and she stopped daydreaming about the demise of the Mace family and attempted to make some stilted conversation with a few of the uninteresting-looking mourners who were drifting around the room with bored expressions. They consisted mainly of a few of Peter's very old friends from the village and some of his past clients. What a dull lot she thought and as for the wine … ugh, cheap and nasty. After making an effort to take a few sips during the few minutes after Jeremy made a sad speech about his father and glasses were raised by the guests, she disposed of the wine that remained in her glass in a handy plant pot when she thought that nobody was looking. Ghastly stuff. Ugh, she told herself. I wonder where they purchased that rubbish! The food was not bad but she understood that had been provided by the Green Man and they had a good reputation. It was a pity they had not provided the wine. She knew that they had a good cellar and did not stock any junk. She was surprised that the Mace family could afford such a good spread if the contents of the cottage were a true measure of wealth but the meal, together with her new outfit, had made an otherwise miserable day worthwhile.

The disposal of the contents of her wine glass was seen by Robbie who looked at her with increasing interest as she moved with stealth round the dining room and later the lounge into which a number of the guests had drifted. She glanced at him for a moment and he gave her a polite innocuous nod. There was something lurking under the surface that was dangerous: misdirected rage or was it bitterness? He was unsure. Cold bitch, he almost said out loud. She does know something about Peter's death. His suspicions deepened and as he felt an unpleasant nagging settle in his chest he exhaled deep and long. Who would be next?

Chapter 12

Doctor Alistair Anderson

The boy sobbed quietly. His stepfather John Peters had banned him to his bedroom once again for some trivial misdemeanour, although he expected that his mother would intervene and he would soon be released from captivity. Alistair was only five when John Peters had come to live with them. He had never known his real father but had been a happy child living in the hotel his mother Judith had inherited from her parents when he was just two that had been his only home since he had been born. The boy was doted on by the young African maid who assisted his mother to make the beds, dust and clean the small Cape Town hotel's eight bedrooms. He was spoilt too by the large motherly woman who undertook the cooking and who kept a tin of small treats ready for his visits to her kitchen. It was a world in which he had been content until local accountant John Peters had married his mother. John, a conscientious man and self-professed disciplinarian did, Alistair understood in his childish way, love his mother and tried to be a good father to him, but did not show him any love. It was Judith's first marriage and Alistair, although young, knew she was thankful to have a husband who helped her in the hotel and could remove some of the burden of the day-to-day organisation from her shoulders but he couldn't help himself wishing that she had married someone nicer than John Peters.

'Mum,' he asked many times, 'tell me how you met my real dad.' The answer became more important now that John Peters had entered their lives.

Judith would oblige, usually at bedtime after she had read him a story and tucked him in for the night. A few minutes expanding on the life of James Anderson became part of their routine. The story of the strong tall James she had met whilst on holiday in Tunisia was embellished and expanded into a romantic tale.

'We met on a silken sandy beach, gold and clean, where the blue sea lapped continuously,' she would say and told him about the Tunisian souks, houses, Roman ruins and camels, embroidering the truth in an effort to provide a romantic backdrop. She did not mention the poverty they had witnessed.

'We travelled to Cape Town together, across the sandy desert, and we fell in love.'

'What did he look like?' Alistair liked to ask.

'Oh, handsome, tall, an adventurer ...' she continued in an effort to embellish the story in a way that she thought would please the child she adored. 'He had thick dark hair and stunning blue eyes, just like your eyes. Lovely deep voice ...'

'Why did he die?'

'Your father became ill darling. He caught malaria, there was nothing that could be done for him. The poor man died before you were born but if he had seen you he would have loved you as much as I do. We wanted to get married but he already had a wife in England. He no longer loved her as much as he loved me ... and would have loved you too.'

It was what he wanted to hear but his mother knew that Alistair was astute and suspected that her memories were not accurate. A young imagination had, however, been fired. As he grew older he became ambitious and anxious to remove himself from the clutches of the pedantic John Peters and his desire to pursue knowledge about his biological father took second place. He attended medical school and when he qualified he changed his name from Peters, the name he had taken after his mother's marriage, to Anderson. Doctor Alistair James Anderson. It felt right. His real father would have been proud of him.

Unlike the invidious James, Alistair was kind and loved children and animals but his blue eyes and deep voice stamped him as James's son, the baby he had told Judith he did not want and had he lived would have abandoned in the same way that he had abandoned Janet.

When James died Judith arranged his funeral. She had promised James to send Janet his wedding ring together with a letter he had written to her but in her grief this was overlooked. She did not consider Janet was important but after a few months her conscience troubled her and she decided she should write to her. After all, it was only fair that she should know that she was now a widow.

'Dear Mrs Anderson,' she wrote. 'You must be concerned about the whereabouts of your husband James. I am so sorry to tell you that he died a few weeks ago in Cape Town, South Africa, after suffering a bout of malaria. He has been cremated.' How much she should tell this woman, this stranger, his wife he had claimed he no longer loved, she did not know. She decided to describe herself as a friend he had met on his travels and wrote that there was no point in Janet travelling to South Africa. She signed the letter 'Judith' but did not enclose the letter James had written to Janet, her own address or the wedding ring he had worn around his neck which would have given Janet the closure and proof that her disastrous marriage had ended. Judith was pregnant, grieving and struggling to come to terms with the death of her lover. Her parents were frail and she was involved in running the small hotel, which would soon be her own, and that was enough.

Alistair obtained a prestigious job in a large clinic. He never felt John Peters was a real father to him and John Peters had made it clear over the years that he only tolerated the boy for the sake of his mother. Alistair thought that the man was welcome to the money he gained from the sale of the hotel after Judith's death; after all, he had worked hard at his mother's side for a good number of years. Alistair told him that he only wanted a few of his mother's possessions, which included a watch that had belonged to his biological father, some brief notes his mother had written about James's funeral, James's death certificate, the letter his father had written to Janet and the wedding ring. John had found them tucked away at the back of a dressing-table drawer after

Judith's death and felt honour bound to tell Alistair about them.

'They are no use to me,' he told Alistair. 'They would only end up in a dustbin. What she ever saw in that philanderer I cannot imagine.'

Alistair smiled. He wondered what on earth she had seen in John Peters. John was described as a charming and considerate man by many of the hotel guests. On the surface he was but he never showed Alistair any of that charm or consideration. Alistair became convinced when he was growing up that James would have been different. He was after all his own flesh and blood.

'He would have loved you,' his mother had lied many times. How could she tell her beloved child anything else? She did not possess any photographs of James but described him as a good man to Alistair, who was thirsty for knowledge about the father he would never meet. 'He was once a handsome officer in the British Navy and loved adventure,' she repeated with conviction. 'He loved to travel. That's the reason we met on our journey across Africa.' Thus the character of the self-centred selfish James became changed in order to placate the young child who would secretly dream about going to England one day to trace his roots.

John Peters tried to warn Alistair that his dreams about James Anderson could crumble. A more honest side of the story had been relayed to him by Judith.

'I tried to be a good husband to your mother. I could not bring the excitement into her life that she experienced during the short time she was with your father. She did not get to know him really well. I hope that if you pursue your search for your father's family roots you will not be disappointed.'

Alistair looked at John Peters with some empathy for the first time. The thought that he had misjudged him occurred to him. The man seemed cold and introverted, but, Alistair had to acknowledge, had supported and encouraged him during his student years. He owed him something but although he did feel a stab of pity for the frail and bent old man with white hair who was still anxious to do the right thing for Judith and her son, he doubted if he would visit him again though his conscience told him that he should if only to clarify a few misunderstandings between them.

Alistair noted Janet's address – Primrose House, Enderly. He wondered if she was still alive. After making some enquiries he discovered that she was, and still living in Enderly. He packed the letter and ring in a case as he anticipated making a trip to England and he hoped Janet would want them and would receive him courteously. That was the most he could expect.

Alistair had married when he was thirty and had two daughters, Jenny and Alice. By the time he was in his early fifties, his wife had a responsible job as a journalist and his daughters were attending a good private school. He was comfortable and successful. He turned his attention once again to discovering his parental roots and perhaps visiting Janet if she was still alive.

'Daddy, find out all you can,' his daughters chorused when he booked a visit to England a few months later. Their faces were framed with thick blonde hair just like Alistair and Judith which was a legacy from their Boer ancestry. They were eager to find out more about their English ancestors, just as he was, but had exams to sit so it had been agreed that Doctor Alistair James Anderson would set out on his travels around the Russetshire countryside on his own.

A few weeks before he left South Africa for England he attended a party held by one of his wife's friends in a large house on the outskirts of Cape Town. He chatted for some time with a man called George Berry who apparently knew Russetshire well. George suggested that he should stay in the Red Rooster public house in Little Brinton before visiting Enderly.

'It will give you time to look round the area before looking up your father's wife. Little Brinton is an interesting place,' he had uttered smiling mysteriously. 'I lived there for a while. There is a thriving bridge club in the village,' he smirked and continued to outline some of the delights of the place. 'There is a good village shop worth a visit. The old girl Mrs Blunt that ran it was an interesting character – a bit of a battleaxe.' He laughed as he remembered the woman and her forceful behaviour, not that she ever got the better of him. 'I'm going to travel across the Kalahari Desert to Botswana next week but I'm not sure where I will go after that. I like Botswana and worked there for a short while years ago. There are some good game reserves and I'm handy with a gun. My new young wife is African you know, who likes to travel.'

He looked at Alistair with cold blue eyes and Alistair struggled to repress a shudder. There was something untenable and odd about this man. He unnerved Alistair but he could not, despite all his medical training, think why.

'I'll certainly look round there,' he said quickly and stuttered slightly. 'I – I'll look forward to it. Good idea – going to Little Brinton first. It will enable me to make a few discreet enquiries and check the lie of the land. Thank you.'

Alistair arrived at Heathrow on a dull November day not long after Peter's funeral. He shivered and wished he had worn some thicker clothes. He should have waited until the warmer weather but was anxious to complete his mission and visit Janet, once he had made the decision to travel to England. He hoped she was still fit and able and that she would be willing to meet him. In any case, it would enable him to make some enquiries about his father who had lived and taught in the area for a while. He would be home again at Christmas with his family and perhaps have some interesting news to tell them.

He collected his hired car at the airport and drove leisurely to Russetshire, looking with interest at the small towns and villages as he neared his destination. He stepped gingerly through the door of the Red Rooster public house in Little Brinton. The pub faced an attractive village green which was not looking at its best at that time of year but the old black and white cottages and village shop on the other side of it looked inviting. Typically English, Alistair thought and his mouth curved with satisfaction. The landlord stepped forward quickly and spoke in a gruff and grouchy voice.

'Can I help, sir?' His eyes were speculative but his face creased into a forced smile displaying several gold fillings that glinted. His naturally curly hair had been brushed back to expose a receding hairline and emphasized dark bushy eyebrows. Astute deep brown eyes looked at Alistair with undisguised interest. He placed a neatly folded clean cloth on the bar and tried to give Alistair his undivided, though somewhat forced, attention.

'Oh, yes please,' Alistair stammered after a slight hesitation. For a few moments he had felt mesmerised by the eccentric-looking landlord.

'I'm taking a holiday in Russetshire, visiting old family haunts, and would like to stay a day or two if you have any vacancies?'

'Certainly sir,' the landlord responded with alacrity. 'I have a good room with ensuite, recently refurbished, which has a lovely view of the hills at the back. Would you care to have breakfast too?'

'Oh yes,' Alistair answered with a feeling of relief. He was tired and weary after his long journey and hoped there was plenty of hot water for a refreshing shower. 'How much will that cost?'

'Only twenty-five pounds a night including a good cooked breakfast, or continental if you prefer. You can choose. Just let me know in the morning. Stay as long as you like. It's quiet at this time of the year. There are a few locals in the evenings and some of the village bridge club members come in for a drink on Thursday evenings after their game. We have some good bar meals too if you are interested?'

'Great,' said Alistair. 'I would like to stay at least two nights if that is all right?'

'Perfect,' the landlord, known locally as Grouchy Tim, said with enthusiasm and rubbed his hands together with satisfaction. Looks good for a quid or two he thought. He is a big fellow and will probably tuck into a hearty bar meal.

'I met a man in Cape Town just before I came to England,' Alistair said in an attempt to make polite conversation. 'He told me about Little Brinton and thought I should start my holiday here. I plan to go to Enderly later.'

'Oh,' said Tim as cordially as he could manage. 'What was his name?'

'George Berry.'

Tim's face paled.

'I hope that's a coincidence.' His voice became hoarse and he felt a shiver down his spine. 'A George Berry murdered a chap here in 2000. He went back to Africa where he had lived for many years but framed his brother-in-law for the crime. He got away scot-free and made fools of the local police.'

'I shouldn't think it's the same man,' Alistair said, almost too quickly. 'He seemed a nice enough fellow.'

A nasty suspicion was forming in his mind. He vaguely remembered reading something in a local paper about a South African jockey who was murdered in Russetshire.

'He told me he lived in Lilac Cottage.'

'That's him all right,' Tim said.

Alistair's face too had now blanched. He was momentarily stunned.

'Oh, he seemed such a, well, nice man. He had recently married an African girl and was planning to move to Botswana, at least – that's what he said but he could be anywhere in Africa now of course .'

'Tell the local police,' Tim urged. 'DI Peter Holmes was involved in the case, he will be most interested to hear what you have to say about the man.'

Alistair was not anxious to become involved.

'I'll think about it,' he said, procrastinating, as he brushed his hair away from his forehead and tried to erase a deepening frown. It may be better to forget the whole conversation, though he did not think the landlord would let the matter rest.

He enjoyed an excellent meal in the bar that evening and learned a little more about the events that surrounded the death of the jockey Karl Davies at the hands of George Berry. Several locals and one or two of the bridge club members were delighted to tell him. It had caused quite a stir in the quiet Russetshire community.

'Our local bridge club was badly affected,' one elderly man told him. 'The chairman and founder of the club, Jack Headley, was framed by George Berry for the murder of Karl Davies. He was clever, of course and left clues that implicated Jack Headley. George Berry was the brother of Jack Headley's first wife Belle and blamed Jack for Belle's ill health and the cot death of their only child. It was not true, of course, Jack was innocent but George Berry was hell bent on revenge and he got it. Jack Headley went to gaol for a while for a murder he did not commit.'

Alistair was intrigued and wished to learn more. He did not have to wait long.

'George wrote a letter to DI Holmes, who was in charge of the case,' said another man who had been listening and was anxious to tell Alistair about his recollections of the case. 'George Berry confessed that he was the murderer and Jack Headley was pardoned. He moved away though to be near his sister in Scotland. His name was blackened here of course. Someone would be bound to think he might have done it despite the evidence.'

Alistair decided he might contact DI Holmes after all. He didn't think there was much hope of finding George Berry in Botswana or wherever he had gone.

Alistair explored the village the next day. He visited the lovely old Saxon church and looked with renewed interest at the outside of Lilac Cottage. It was the one that George had described to him, Alistair had no doubt about that. He wandered into the village shop and bought some local postcards from Mrs Blunt the proprietor. She was direct and businesslike. George had described her as an old battleaxe but Alistair discovered she was quite friendly. She must have mellowed, he mused and wondered why.

After much heart searching and reflection he decided to visit DI Holmes in Everton. He could not tell him much about George Berry but the detective was interested. Alistair gave him his address in South Africa and promised to let him know if he met George again, but he doubted that he would.

DI Peter Holmes, however, was keen to make up for his past mistake in not following his original hunches about the psychopath George Berry. An innocent man had been sent to prison, his life disrupted, and it was his fault. He contacted the police in South Africa and after being informed about a possible sighting in Botswana decided to fly out himself to investigate. An arrest looked promising. It appeared that George Berry was also wanted in South Africa for the killing of several local people when he had stayed in a small house he had rented in Cape Town. He had tried to cover his tracks well with his usual guile but had become over confident and had been recognised by several residents who were convinced that it was Berry who had strangled his victims and disposed of their bodies. They had been thieves and George had always considered that eliminating such people was just. However, these thieves had families and friends who wanted retribution and were willing to come forward. One way or another DI Holmes was determined that this time George Berry would pay for his previous crimes. Alistair's chance meeting with George was the break that the detective had been waiting for.

After a couple of days in Little Brinton Alistair booked into the Green Man in Enderly. He was anxious to meet Janet but wondered how she would react to seeing the unopened letter addressed to her from his father James. It could be a shock. She would be at least eighty-five and possibly frail.

His stepfather had told him that James had treated his wife badly. He was an adventurer and would not have stayed in Cape Town very long. Alistair did not want to hear anything unpleasant about his father but had to admit that he did appear fickle.

Alistair enjoyed the local ales and pub atmosphere. The punters in the Green Man were friendly. He chatted to old Pat and soon discovered that Janet was fairly fit, though her memory was troubling her, and still lived in Primrose House, the house she had bought with James Anderson. She had married again and was now Janet Lacey but there were no children. Old Pat, with a wry smile, suggested that Alistair should talk to her handyman, Robbie. A son of James Anderson could be quite a shock for the elderly lady and Robbie was a knowing fellow who would handle things tactfully and could be helpful.

Robbie was surprised when Alistair introduced himself but did not doubt that he was James's son. One look at those almost sky-blue eyes convinced him of that. His voice too shot through him like an echo from the past causing him to shudder. It was deep and strong, just like James's voice had been so many years ago. He instinctively knew this man had a very different character but found it difficult to bury his antagonism. Robbie's usually pleasant face hardened and his smile was tight. He had difficulty in controlling his irritation. Damn the man. What did he want to come here for stirring up the past? The only consolation was that Janet's memory was fading and she would probably not remember him for long.

'Can you take me to see her?' Alistair almost begged. His charming manner infiltrated Robbie's growing resentment and he found himself, against his better judgment, agreeing to arrange a meeting.

'I'll sound her out first,' he said. 'We don't want to give her too much of a shock. Leave it to me; I'll let you know how she reacts to the news. She's very fragile and has only recently lost one of her oldest friends following a tragic accident.'

Alistair agreed. His shoulders, which had been feeling stiff, slumped slightly as he started to relax. He told Robbie about the ring and the letter. 'She deserves closure,' he continued with determination and Robbie, with an obvious lack of enthusiasm and mounting resentment, felt obliged to agree.

'I'll tell her when I go to Primrose House tomorrow morning. I am not sure how she'll react. I can't promise anything. She's so forgetful and weak now.'

Alistair wondered why such an intelligent and obviously well-heeled man needed to work as a handyman. Oh well, he was clearly very fond of Janet Lacey and just the man to approach her. If anyone could pave the way for an amicable visit this man could manage it.

Alistair had worked for some time with the mentally ill before taking up his present post. He knew quite a lot about memory loss in the elderly and he assured Robbie he would be tactful and careful when he told Janet about the ring. The letter was another matter. He did not know its contents.

The next day Robbie asked Janet if she would like to meet Alistair and perhaps ask him to afternoon tea.

'The man claims he is your first husband's son,' he said. 'He is a very nice man, a doctor from South Africa – it may be worth meeting him to find out if there is any truth in his allegation. His mother's name was Judith.'

'Judith,' Janet said with deliberation. 'Yes, a Judith did write to me to inform me of James's death and also that she would be sending James's wedding ring and a letter quite soon but I didn't hear any more from her.' She looked at Robbie anxiously who was surprised that she could recall so much. 'Do you think I should meet him?'

'Well, yes if you feel up to it. It could answer a few questions for you. Would you like me to stay too?'

'Yes. It would be a great comfort to me, we will all have tea together, a tea party.'

She giggled like a very young child who knew no better, a strange almost gurgling sound that burst out of her chest. Robbie, though not a religious man, found himself praying that the visit would not be a mistake. Janet was behaving as though she was in her second childhood, which in some ways she was, but the ring and letter might give her satisfactory closure with James and that could be worth the effort, although he was doubtful if anything could obliterate the pain that man had inflicted upon her.

'Tomorrow at four o'clock,' she suddenly said pertly. 'I'll tell Joyce to set out the best china teaset in the dining room.' She smiled foolishly after which a look of odd wonderment returned to her face. 'An afternoon tea party, what fun! Oh lovely.' Her eyes sparkled like a child's. She was looking forward to meeting James's son. Robbie was relieved but at the same time dismayed. Perhaps she couldn't remember what a dreadful man James had been. He thought it was cruel and unnecessary of Judith not to send the ring and letter to her before. All could be resolved now, though it was rather late in the day, and that idea consoled him. He would hope for the best.

Chapter 13

The Tea Party

J oyce Skillet placed a beautifully embroidered lace cloth on the
dining-room table as her mistress had instructed in one of her
more lucid moments. She washed and dried with care the best
Worcester china painted with elegant rosebuds, before setting it
on the table together with fine lace napkins that had not been
used for years, and heavy silver tea knives that, with much
cursing, she had polished for the occasion. 'Tea party indeed, I
expect this Anderson man is a fraud,' she muttered crossly to
herself. Joyce, with Felicity's assistance, made a selection of
dainty sandwiches and small iced fairy cakes to tempt the guest.

Felicity scoffed and moaned to Joyce. 'I have never heard of any
son of Uncle James before. He is undoubtedly some ghastly
impostor. Huh! Fancy Aunt Janet inviting the handyman to tea
too!'

For once Joyce and Felicity were in agreement.

The grandfather clock in the hall struck a sonorous four notes
and this was followed promptly by a knock on the front door.

Joyce led Alistair and Robbie into the dining room. What next?
she thought irritably. Bloody handyman, much as I like him, and
some charlatan coming to tea. He's bound to be a con man at best
although he is not bad looking and has a pleasant manner. To her
dismay Joyce felt herself warming towards Alistair, but she was
still convinced that no good would come of this meeting.

Janet remained sitting when Robbie introduced Alistair. Felicity
scowled, stood up with obvious reluctance and stretched out a
limp hand to take that of the stranger.

'I'm Felicity,' she drawled, 'Mrs Lacey's niece. My aunt's first husband was my Uncle James, my mother's brother, so I suppose we must be related if he was your father.'

She hoped not, but if he was Uncle James's son she would have to make the best of things. A cousin, goodness what a fag. He did not look short of a penny or two and with any luck would not be hanging around Primrose House too long. Her mood lightened.

They sat down at the dining-room table and Joyce brought in the tea on a large silver tray with the aid of an old wooden trolley that bumped precariously over the thick rugs.

'Are you going to be mum and pour?' she screeched at Felicity who jumped but for once did not argue. She was far too busy gawping at Alistair. There was something familiar about those piercing blue eyes.

Janet leaned forward to take a better look at the newcomer. She scanned the thatch of blond hair then her eyes travelled down to his eyes. She was startled. They were, as Felicity had realized, familiar.

'I am so glad you agreed to meet me Mrs Lacey,' Alistair said in his deep resonant voice.

For a moment Janet could not speak. She had heard that voice before. Slowly the memories crept back. It was James's voice and this man had James's eyes. Her face grew white for a few moments but the colour crept back and settled in two odd rose-coloured patches upon her cheeks, making her look like a painted doll. To Robbie's surprise her mouth trembled then broke into a odd wide and eager grin. He cringed. What on earth was she thinking about? She was so unpredictable.

Felicity poured the tea and made the usual murmurs, 'Sugar? Milk?', while keeping her sly eyes fixed firmly on the guest. She too had recognised the familiar sounding voice. It provoked a mixture of emotions. Uncle James's disparaging attitude towards herself and Ronald came to mind. He had not been kind and welcoming when they had stayed at Primrose House.

'Three teaspoonfuls of sugar please,' Alistair said.

'Three … well yes, of course, just like Uncle James,' Felicity said out loud.

She passed the sandwiches and cakes round and they helped themselves with exaggerated politeness. There was a strange reluctance to make conversation interspersed with a few odd, almost inane-sounding, giggles from Janet who seemed to find the situation quite amusing. Eventually Alistair broke the silence.

'I'm so pleased to meet you at last. It must be difficult for you. My mother told me a little about you. I never actually met my father and I was brought up by a stepfather. However, I took my biological father's surname when I qualified as a doctor. My stepfather never really wanted me and I felt happier with the name Anderson.'

Janet looked at him with a blank expression in her eyes.

'Really,' she uttered in a quiet voice but showed no visible emotion. It was as though she accepted his situation as quite normal and it was nothing to do with her.

Hmmm . . . Robbie thought, the wretched James would not have wanted you any more than your stepfather did but you are better off without that knowledge.

'I understand my mother wrote to you to tell you that my father had died of malaria but forgot to send you a letter addressed to you and his wedding ring as promised. It was an unfortunate oversight on her part but when she died my stepfather found them and gave them to me. I thought I should at least try to set the record straight.'

Alistair looked at Janet with anxious concern etched on his face. She seemed very frail and he doubted if she really understood what was going on. He hoped he was doing the right thing and not stirring up too many unhappy memories for the poor woman but, to his relief, she did not look too worried.

Janet no longer had any feelings for James, she had pushed any thoughts about him to the back of her mind long ago, but there was no doubt about the fact that this was James's son. Memories of his voice and build, things she thought she had forgotten, came back. The sight of Alistair had acted as a trigger. A nice man, she thought, honest and kind. He must get those traits from his mother; he certainly did not inherit them from his father. She managed to conjure up a picture in her mind of the unpleasant husband who had deserted her so long ago.

'Thank you,' she said without flinching. She looked at the pale suggestion of blond stubble on his chin. His face was lean with high cheekbones and a firm well shaped mouth. Her eyes softened. She felt almost calm and gave the impression of being quite lucid as she observed him with studied coolness.

'We will sit in the lounge after tea and you may give them to me,' she said in a voice as commanding and direct as she had used in the classroom years ago. He was certainly Felicity's relative too, she thought, quite amusing really. She relaxed further. They were so very different and that she found interesting.

Joyce cleared away the tea things and with the aid of Felicity and Robbie and her trusty walking sticks Janet led the party into the lounge.

'Sit by me on the settee Alistair,' she commanded.

Felicity looked startled. The old bird has perked up a bit, she cogitated.

Alistair produced the ring and letter from his pocket and passed them to Janet.

'Oh,' Janet said swiftly. 'Pass me my glasses, Felicity.'

Felicity, always anxious to butter up Auntie, obliged. Janet's face became pinched and anxious.

'Yes, it is definitely James's ring. The inscription J and J and the heart on the inside of the ring are unique I imagine. Can you see the letters?'

The memory of their vows taken in Enderly church drifted back to her. She had a vague recollection of placing the ring on James's finger and colour crept with greater depth into her cheeks.

'Yes, the letters are definitely J and J and there is a heart engraved between the letters.'

She turned her attention to the letter. It was in a blue faded and creased envelope clearly addressed to her in James's all-too-familiar untidy handwriting.

'Open it Auntie!' Felicity urged.

'It is personal Felicity,' her aunt retorted tartly.

She slowly opened it with care, after donning her old steel-rimmed glasses, and squinted at the faded writing. She sighed audibly. 'It is just to tell me how sorry he was for leaving' she said then folded the letter and placed it in her skirt pocket. That there was nothing more to say became clear to Alistair, Robbie and Felicity. The subject was closed.

'Thank you Alistair,' she said. 'So lovely to meet you,' and with an odd gesture of her wrinkled and knobbly hand dismissed him. Definite closure, she thought. I can at last rest in peace.

'Have you any photographs of my father?' Alistair asked with some trepidation after a few moments of poignant silence. He realised that Janet's first marriage could not have been happy but he had not travelled so far to be fobbed off now. He wanted some information about his father. 'I never knew him,' he continued. 'He died before I was born and my mother and stepfather brought me up.'

'There are a few in a trunk in the roof, I think,' Janet responded in a hushed voice. 'Robbie can get them for you. He can handle the roof ladder.'

She turned to Robbie. 'They are in an old brown travelling trunk quite near the trapdoor. There are only three or four, most of them I tore up and threw away years ago. I thought that best.'

Robbie thought so too.

'I'll get them,' he uttered pensively and thought he did not really want to set eyes on the wretched James again. There was little doubt in his mind that Janet did not want to either, which was satisfying.

He returned ten minutes later with an old brown envelope containing a number of faded and slightly creased photographs.

'These must be the ones you want,' he said and passed the envelope to Janet.

Janet opened it and three photographs of James fell out on to her lap. The first was of a handsome naval officer, the second depicted James in the garden of Primrose House just after they married, young and smiling, and the third, faded and rather brown, of James as a boy of about fifteen in school uniform. Why on earth she had kept that one she could not imagine. Callow youth, good looking even then, but a face lacking in strength of character which did not improve, though she had not been perceptive enough to know that when she first met him.

'Please take them Alistair. They are of no further interest to me but your family may wish to see them.'

Robbie was relieved. Unlike Felicity, who was craning her neck forward in an attempt to peak at them, he did not want to see the photographs but Alistair's face lit up with pleasure and he thought that the unwelcome tea party was perhaps worthwhile after all.

'Thank you,' Alistair said. 'I know this meeting has been difficult for you but I do appreciate your kindness. My daughters will love to see them.' He was startled to find that his youngest daughter's face looked uncannily like James. His family would be pleased to see the photographs but he sensed that James was not such a nice person as he had imagined. That was something he would keep to himself.

Janet looked at Alistair and smiled. She would not have thought it possible that James could have given life to such a charming and sincere man but here he was, living proof that some good could come out of 'evil', which is how she had come to think of James over the years.

Alistair and Robbie met again that evening to discuss the situation. They enjoyed a steak, salad and chips and glass of ale in the Green Man.

'Well, I've met Janet and done my best to make up for my mother's lapse', Alistair said. 'I did intend to travel to Hampshire for a couple of days before returning to Africa – I believe my father's family came from a small village there before they moved to London – but I don't know of any living relatives to contact. It could perhaps be an interesting project for the future when I can bring my wife and daughters with me. Felicity may be able to tell me about her mother sometime but I understand that she was very young when her mother died, she did tell me that much, and that her brother is living in Australia. I was left with the feeling, however, that she's reluctant to pursue any future contact. She's an odd character, I must say.'

Robbie told him about Felicity's erratic behaviour since she had arrived at Primrose House. He had warmed to Alistair but the blue eyes and voice evoked too many unpleasant memories of James Anderson.

'I knew your father,' he said. 'Janet does not know and I don't want her to. It must be our secret.'

He told Alistair briefly about his life after leaving Enderly as a child and his reasons for returning when he retired. He continued, 'James treated Janet badly and was unkind to me when I stayed with them for a while. I'm sorry to tell you that he made my life hell. You haven't inherited any of his vile ways. Be thankful you are like your mother. I am glad I have met you Alistair, though I'm not so sure about your relative Felicity, I think she's a dark horse.'

'Me too,' Alistair retorted quickly, 'my sentiments exactly. You've answered a few of the questions that had been forming in my mind about you Robbie; a really intelligent and educated man, who need not work as a handyman, but who is concerned and anxious to do his best for Janet Lacey.' He smiled with a glimmer of affection at Robbie. 'We probably won't meet again,' he continued, 'but keep an eye on Felicity Brown. I've worked with mentally ill people and a few psychopaths over the years. It sounds as though she's not to be trusted though her main problem could be hyperactivity, perhaps Attention Deficit Disorder. It's a condition that's difficult to understand although considerable research has been carried out in recent years. Professional assessment is, of course, essential to be sure. It's a pity that she did not have counselling when she was younger, from which she may have benefited.'

'You have just voiced my worst fears,' Robbie responded. 'I certainly intend to watch her!'

Alistair left Enderly early the next morning after promising Robbie that he would keep in touch but they both knew, as they shook hands, that another meeting was unlikely.

Robbie was left with an feeling of unease. What, he wondered, would that unsavoury Felicity do next? He would need to keep his wits about him. Hyperactivity … hmm. He would read about that sometime. It may help him to understand her and deal with her more in a more effective way in the future.

Chapter 14

Christmas Eve 2004

Felicity became more agitated as the days passed. She had still not discovered if the will she had found was the last one that her aunt had made. Matthew Mace had now taken over the solicitors' business which had been run by his father and grandfather. The loss of Peter had left Jeremy shaken and so morose that he decided to take early retirement from the Mace firm. Drinking a great deal of alcohol and gambling still constituted an important part of his life, it was not easy to change his long-established habits however destructive they had been to the family business, but he did plan to take a holiday in the New Year, in order to 'recharge his batteries'. A holiday would assist him to reorganize his life and he might then be able to address his addictions and even overcome them. Jeremy hoped that Matthew would marry soon and produce a grandchild who might one day carry on the family business but at present that did not seem likely. He was disappointed that Matthew had not brought any girlfriends home for a long time and was only interested in work.

'I have no time for dolly birds, Dad,' Matthew would say. 'I might get married one day but not just yet. The business demands my full attention. We are barely solvent.'

Janet invited Jeremy and Matthew for drinks and supper on Christmas Eve as she had done for many years. Peter would be sadly missed but she appreciated in her more lucid moments all the help with her affairs that Jeremy and Matthew had given her in the past and it was her way of rewarding them. A sadness overcame her when she thought about her old friend Peter who had died so recently in her garden. She could not now remember with any accuracy how it had happened. She had some idea that they were going to get married in the near future, or was that some dream that lingered from the past?

Felicity entered into the spirit of things. She purchased a small freshly cut Christmas tree from a local nursery and decorated it with the bright baubles and tinsel she found in the roof. She placed the tree with care in the hall and was proud of her efforts. It cheers up that dowdy area, she thought. It's a load of rubbish and a waste of money really but it will please Auntie. Jack liked the smell of the tree and christened it neatly with a quick squirt of urine when she turned her back. It saved him a trip to the garden. To help Felicity Robbie cut some branches of holly and bought some mistletoe in a local market. Felicity took pride in decorating Primrose House with the holly and some gold-painted twigs that Auntie produced from a bag that was tucked under the stairs and had shared a space with the Hoover for many years. The mistletoe she hung up over the lounge doorway. 'Never know my luck,' she whispered to herself. 'I might get a kiss from that hunk Matthew,' and that could make the whole evening worthwhile. The thought cheered her. Primrose House she hoped would be her own one day then she could arrange things as she liked and entertain her friends.

She looked out of the dining room window to watch Robbie in the garden where he was cutting some more holly for her. The way he stood and placed his hand on his right hip reminded her of a photograph Auntie had at one time, which she could no longer find, of the evacuee Tom Hands. The wretched Mace family had occupied her thoughts in recent weeks and she had pushed any interest she retained in Tom Hands to one side. She wondered now with renewed interest where he went after leaving Enderly. It would be necessary to deal with him after the Mace family problem had been solved. It was unfortunate that his name still appeared in the will. She would make some enquiries soon but the local authorities may, she realised, not be willing to help her, though tracing one's biological parents after adoption was no longer so problematic as it had been in the past. She might be lucky. He might even be dead by now – that would save her a lot of trouble.

Robbie came into the dining room bearing a further load of holly for the animated Felicity. Janet sat in her chair with a strained expression on her face. She too had been thinking of Tom Hands and had noticed that the way Robbie had stood with his hand on his hip in the garden was so like Tom. Tears filled her eyes. Felicity was too busy to notice and would not have cared if she had.

'Can I help, Mrs Lacey?' Robbie asked quietly.

'No, I was just thinking of someone I knew in the past, an evacuee I think.'

He turned his sharp hazel eyes towards her. She still cares, he thought, but he would never reveal that he was the evacuee she cherished so long ago. A stubbornness gripped him and he made an abrupt and swift turn away from her. She had let him go and although he vowed to protect her now and had watched over her for about ten years in order to repay her, and her mother's, earlier kindness, that was as far as he was willing to take the relationship. It did work both ways, of course, he loved his job in the garden and enjoyed helping as a handyman in the house. It was an incredible contrast to his academic career but he was happy. If she had to go into a home then he would take a well-earned retirement in the village he had come to love.

'I'll be off then Mrs Lacey. I hope you have a happy Christmas Eve with your friends. There should be enough holly to decorate the whole house now! I'm having Christmas lunch with an old friend from Oxford tomorrow but if you need me I'll be in my cottage in the morning.'

His face felt strained and he turned away from the sight of the feeble old woman. He was looking forward to meeting Pat and two of his other friends in the Green Man that evening. They were going to play bridge, a game in which they had asked Robbie to join them recently and he thought that when he had improved his skill he would apply to become a member of the nearby Little Brinton Bridge Club. He had played rubber bridge for a short time when he was young with a colleague in Oxford so he had not been completely new to the game when Pat had suggested that he played with them. He studied a few books and learned with little effort so that he was now in a position to look forward to playing duplicate bridge in the club with his friends as they had recently suggested. It would be a challenge and he needed mental stimulus. Old Pat never tired of telling him that bridge is a good exercise for the elderly brain. Well, he would see.

Felicity supervised the drinks and nibbles for the Maces who were arriving at seven that evening. A cold supper, to be preceded by hot onion soup, had been set out in the dining room by Joyce. Felicity was annoyed because she had been instructed not to let the soup boil and she considered herself to be a good cook. The dining room was looking slightly like Father Christmas's grotto, laden with red-berried holly and silver tinsel but Felicity was pleased with her efforts.

Joyce was almost glad that Felicity had come to stay with her aunt. For the past few years she had been worried about Janet staying on her own in Primrose House during the Christmas break except for the supper on Christmas Eve with the Mace family. Joyce always prepared food for Christmas Day and Boxing Day for Janet to cook and the kitchen fridge and freezer were always well stocked, but Janet was now finding that arrangement difficult and Joyce knew it would not be long before her employer would have to go into a nursing home. In the past Robbie had also agreed to call and see if Janet was all right over the holiday and hadn't gone to see old friends in Oxford, which he would have enjoyed. Joyce had returned to Primrose House each day to wash up dishes and see that all was well and she had to admit that she was now looking forward to spending Christmas with her family and not having to worry about Janet, although she could not quite dispel the feeling of unease she had about Felicity. She still did not like the woman. Janet had spent Christmas with her school colleagues for a few years after John Lacey died but the majority were now occupied with their families, including numerous grandchildren or great grandchildren, or were too old to bother any more.

Felicity lit the candles in the dining room a few minutes before the guests arrived. She ran her hands down her new ruby-coloured velvet dress with pleasure and checked the clasp on her shimmering fine pearl necklace – the real thing, no imitation pearls for Felicity. Cost an arm and a leg she chuckled to herself but old Auntie's credit card had proved useful once again. She had permission from Auntie and the bank now to sign cheques for her.

'It will make things easier, Auntie,' she had wheedled until the arrangement had been agreed.

Janet's financial adviser had called to see her one day a few weeks before Christmas and had expressed some unease about the plan but his fears had been dismissed by Janet who said she was grateful for the help her niece was giving her.

'It's only money after all,' she said. 'It makes her happy to pay the bills and I am happy that she is able to buy a few baubles for herself at the same time.'

'A few baubles . . .' the financial adviser mumbled. 'Is that what they are? It's more like fraud.'

The doorbell rang and Felicity put on a pleasant countenance, at least as pleasant as she could manage, to welcome the guests. She greeted Jeremy and Matthew with an almost grudging expression in spite of her efforts, led them into the lounge and poured them a glass of Auntie's best sherry. This could be her chance to pump them about Auntie's will. She had a good supply of red and white wine to hand, obtained from Janet's wine store in the garage, together with a variety of strong liquors to follow. She assumed that they would walk home to Jasmine Cottage where they lived in the centre of the village, in any case she had not heard their car arrive. Her plan was to make them tipsy so that they would talk rashly about Auntie's affairs.

Jeremy was a good-looking man for his sixty years. His hair was almost white but quite thick and his blue-grey oddly flecked eyes were still alert. His greatest weakness was that, although he still possessed a good and clever brain, he was a lazy man and too fond of his 'booze' as he put it, whisky and vodka being his favourites. He often cut corners which had backfired on him a few times during his career. He had spent money without enough thought and amassed some large and needless gambling debts. Matthew was working hard in an effort to put things in order but a legacy from Janet would be appreciated. Jeremy could not remember for a moment whether the Mace family had been included in her latest will. He believed so, yes of course they had, but he would press for a codicil to be added in their favour and to ensure their share was increased before she became completely gaga. He would talk to Matthew about that some time but he was pretty certain that they had been left a reasonable amount of money. She was a wealthy woman and a little more cash for the Mace family would not go amiss. The chairs she had promised them would not go far towards paying off the firm's creditors, valuable as they might prove to be in an auction. Despite his grief following the death of his father and his absence this year from the usual Christmas festivities, he looked forward to one of Joyce Skillet's excellent suppers and hoped it would be as delicious as it had been in the past.

Matthew was an attractive man in his late thirties and consequently a great asset to the family business. Women adored him, though he was adept at keeping them at a distance, and many looked upon him as a possible future husband. He appeared to be not only an eligible bachelor but efficient and astute in the office. Matthew was suspicious about Felicity's role in her aunt's life but he was careful not to let her know that. He had a deep rumbling voice. Hmm, Felicity thought, he is not a bad looking man and has a lovely deep voice like a bull trying to attract a mate. What a pity he is in my way. He is far too young for me, a veritable toyboy, but I would not mind getting him between my sheets before I am forced to dispose of him. Prickles crept down her plump wrinkled arms.

Matthew would have been horrified if he had been able to read her thoughts. He looked at Felicity with extreme distaste. Her face reminded him of a tapir, her nose curved slightly downwards and he thought that even vinegar would not scorch her mouth. She was an ugly looking old bird and looked just like a gaudy old pheasant in that velvet dress. Mutton dressed up as lamb seemed an appropriate phrase to describe her.

They enjoyed the meal and the excellent Australian red and white wines Felicity had found for the occasion. She filled her guests' glasses to the brim as often as she could but although Jeremy drank his at disgusting speed, gulping and spluttering, stamping himself as the alcoholic he was, to her annoyance Matthew only sipped his. He was determined to keep a clear head. Concerned that her plan to get him drunk was not working she pushed her thin lips into a pout and gripped her wineglass with a fierceness that caused her knuckles to look like white knobs. The well-devised plan was failing and even her appetite diminished.

Jeremy, like Peter before him, ran thin well-manicured fingers down the sides of the velvet dining chairs. Charming, elegant pieces he thought. They will soon be ours. They have such skilfully carved legs ... quite unusual.

The gesture was not lost upon Felicity.

'You seem to like those chairs,' she said, her Canadian drawl coming to the fore.

'Um, nice pieces,' Jeremy said with feigned disinterest and they finished the rest of the meal in thoughtful silence.

The party moved to the lounge to enjoy the liquors and chocolates placed there by Felicity in an obvious and tempting way. Auntie nodded in her chair and was soon fast asleep. She had drunk too much wine.

'Has my aunt left those chairs to anyone in her will?' Felicity asked, opening her eyes wider as she assumed an innocent expression. 'I guess she has made a will, I do not ask her about such things, of course.'

'I have no idea,' Matthew and Jeremy chorused.

They are guilty, Felicity thought, they are too evasive.

'There is a will, of course,' Jeremy continued in a slurred voice. The good wine and cherry brandy was taking over his weakened body. 'The original is kept in our safe room in the office though Mrs Lacey will have a copy somewhere I believe. It is a confidential matter, we cannot discuss it, Felicity.'

He had gulped the wine and brandy down during the meal as though he had a raging thirst, which he had, eyes sparkling and mouth slobbering with alcoholic greed.

'Of course,' said Felicity brightly. She was getting nowhere. She would have to try a different way to find out if the will she had found was the latest.

'I seem to remember a will was made in the nineteen eighties,' Matthew said with a calmness he did not feel. 'That's all I can tell you. You must ask your Aunt Janet about it. As I have already made clear, we cannot disclose confidential matters.' His voice had become abrupt and hard.

He knew that Janet would not remember much about any wills and that he could play games with the avaricious niece. Indeed he was quite enjoying himself. Greedy objectionable old hag, he turned over in his mind, but the woman is not a bad hostess he had to admit. He took his third chocolate mint, chewed it with obvious pleasure, sipped his cup of good percolated coffee and wiped his mouth with a napkin from which Father Christmas, who was weighed down with a sack of toys on his back, leered through a straggly white beard. Felicity had bought the garish napkins in Brinton in what she called the 'cheap shop' where nothing cost more than one pound. Good enough for them, she had told herself at the time.

Janet stirred in her sleep and sighed deep and long.

'Time for bed dear,' Felicity said. 'It's almost ten o'clock. Amy will be here soon to help you get undressed and tuck you in.' Amy, a rather stocky young woman from the village, was due to appear at any moment to help Janet undress. Amy was paid well for her services and had for the past few months or so been pleased to help out when asked. Felicity decided that she was much more proficient than the dippy Lily.

'Can't you help her get into bed?' said Jeremy, who was the worse for drink, indeed his head felt quite muzzy. 'Does she really need Amy? It's a waste of money,' he continued in a foolish and rash tone.

Felicity's eyes flashed. They appeared wild and stormy, awash with grey waves, almost manic. She turned a calculated and spiteful gaze on Jeremy but he was past caring. Matthew, however, stiffened. She was dangerous and reminded him of a wounded tigress. They would have to be careful when dealing with this woman. She found him attractive, that much was clear to him, and perhaps he could use that to his advantage though he certainly did not want to get close to her, or indeed any woman. He preferred the male sex but had not come out. It would upset his father and some of his female clients and it would achieve very little. He could wait.

'Of course,' Matthew said quickly, in an attempt to smooth the troubled waters, 'you need help with your aunt. It must be very difficult for you. She is so lucky to have you here now. We really must go home. My father is overtired and has had too much to drink. It was a lovely supper.'

He glanced at her provocatively under his long pale blond lashes and she, as he had intended, softened.

'Is there anything we can do to help?' he asked in patronizing tones, hoping that there was not.

'No,' Felicity said in a sharp high-pitched voice. 'I can manage!' and the Maces left after a feeble attempt to say goodnight to Janet who was by that time exhausted and confused. She was uttering odd snoring snorts and snuffles and Felicity felt sick.

Matthew said he would call the next day to see if Janet was all right. Felicity hoped he would not, despite the physical attraction she felt for him, but thanked him for his concern. They wished each other a happy Christmas in a stiff and forced manner. Felicity shut the front door after they had gone and heaved a sigh of relief. That is one family that will not be coming here when I am mistress she vowed. She hoped and prayed that the good Amy would arrive soon and remove the slumbering and slobbering Janet from her sight.

A plan was forming swiftly in her twisted corkscrew mind though whether she would have the courage to follow it through she did not know.

'One down, two to go,' she chanted softly to herself, as she clenched her fists.

Chapter 15

An Accident March 2005

Christmas faded into the past and life in Primrose House settled down into a familiar and comfortable routine though Joyce Skillet watched Felicity like a hawk. Her dislike for Felicity grew as the days passed but she acknowledged the fact that the woman was in many ways a good companion for her aunt. 'The creature', as Joyce had dubbed Felicity, had apparently endeared herself to Janet who now liked having the woman around her, a fact which amazed both Joyce and Robbie.

Felicity was still in contact with her old friend in the village whom she would invite for morning coffee on at least one day a week. Muffled conversation filtered through the lounge door when the friend came but Joyce found it difficult to interpret what they were saying though she tried. She sometimes pressed an ear against the wooden panels in the hope of hearing something of interest but was always disappointed. She had an idea that the friend had a daughter who worked in Mrs Lacey's financial adviser's office and that bothered her. She thought that it was not a healthy situation.

Jeremy took a holiday in France early in January and returned refreshed, at least he said he felt better for the break, though he was without doubt still drinking too much. He had spent far too much money as usual and admitted that he had consumed a lot of cheap French wine, some of which he brought home with him, so that his once pale face now began to exhibit red and blotchy patches and his beer belly protruded in an unpleasant manner which made Felicity think that he looked about nine months pregnant.

'Old fool,' she muttered behind his back, but almost cheered when she thought about the possible damage the man was doing to his liver.

Matthew hired a new young male solicitor to help him in the office.

'The load is too much for one person Dad. Timothy is worth every penny I pay him.'

Jeremy thought the new boy looked as though he was a 'pansy', a word he used to label men with homosexual tendencies. He felt a definite repugnance when he was near him, cold and deep in his gut, but it was Matthew's business now and he could not interfere.

'Queer chap, literally, that one,' he commented to Matthew one morning over breakfast whilst piling a bowl high with cornflakes and fruit and patting the silver flask of brandy he kept in his inner jacket pocket. The anticipation of taking a sip of the contents as soon as Matthew left the room was more interesting than Timothy. The craving for his morning fix of alcohol was growing.

Matthew smiled.

'He's a good worker Dad, that's the most important thing,' he said and quickly changed the subject. He thought about Timothy and his heart raced. They were growing closer. It was only a matter of time. He is a lovely young man, he mused, so slim and lively with a mop of curly reddish-brown hair and stunning green eyes framed with long reddish-blond lashes. There was no doubt he was receptive to Matthew's charms. They had brushed hands a few times and he had noted the heightened colour on Tim's face. It would be sensible to wait a while, not too long though, and invite Timothy to spend a weekend with him in London, or some other place where they would not be recognised. It was imperative to fool his father and the locals about their relationship which was a pity but he knew that Jeremy would be horrified if he knew the truth about his potential liaison with Timothy and no doubt some of his best clients would take their business elsewhere. The latter he certainly did not want to happen. The firm could not afford that. He knew that he would have to exercise caution for some time yet where this possible relationship was concerned but a relationship he determined it should be. The firm's mounting debts were going to be difficult to resolve, thanks to Jeremy's careless habits, and he needed to improve their financial prospects before he took any chances.

Matthew and Tim had, however, started to walk by the river bank together most days during their lunch hour.

'It will do us good to have a breath of fresh air,' Matthew said to Tim. 'It will blow away the cobwebs before we're stifled by the central heating in the office during the afternoon.'

One day during one of their walks they stopped at a fisherman's platform which was low and protruded into the river. It was not easy to be observed there by passers-by and in any case at that time of year there were very few walkers venturing along the muddy path next to the river. The river was swollen and fierce and the current quite fast which was a contrast to the lazy pace it maintained during the summer. Huge willows dipped their branches down towards the water's edge and provided some, though limited, screening for the two friends. They chatted amicably as usual and were conscious that their relationship and feelings for each other were strengthening. The wind whistled through the branches of the trees above their heads and it was not easy to talk in a quiet tone.

'Will you join me for a weekend break in Devon next week Tim?' Matthew at last plucked up courage at to ask. 'The hotel is comfortable and is situated in a lovely spot. The views are excellent, food good and it's quiet there. The change will do us good since we have been working hard and deserve a rest. I would appreciate your company Tim.' He glanced at his companion and smiled warmly. 'We can travel separately, nobody should be the wiser.'

He stretched out a tentative arm to touch Tim. His heart beat so strongly he felt as though it might burst out of his chest. Tim moved closer, put his arms round his friend and kissed him upon the lips. They clung together in ecstatic joy for a few moments and savoured the idea of future delights.

'I'll look forward to it my darling,' Tim answered, 'but we mustn't be seen embracing by the villagers. I have to deliver some papers to old Mrs Brownlow who lives near the pub. She's expecting me and I'd better get going but I'll see you back in the office in about half an hour.'

He had not officially 'come out' either and was fearful of prejudice which could harm his career and offend his family. Matthew was more concerned that a liaison with Tim could hurt the Mace family firm and its struggle to keep its head above water and any scandal he realized could be disastrous. It was imperative to exercise caution, a least for the time being. Dear Tim. He sighed with pleasure.

Tim turned away, a satisfied smile lingering at the corners of his mouth, and walked swiftly towards the far end of the village which could, shortly after leaving the river bank, be reached by a narrow footpath across a field about three minutes' walk away. They had reached their meeting place after walking up the road that passed by Primrose House and Matthew planned to return that way, unobserved, he hoped by any nosy old village busybodies and he considered that there were plenty of those around. The village was full of oldies who liked to stroll with their dogs along the river bank most days then chat about what they had seen in the local shop. The bad weather had that day deterred the majority of them, a fact which he thought was fortunate.

Matthew stood still and gazed at the brown and murky water for a moment. Happiness welled up in his chest. He had found a companion of his own choice at last, a beautiful young man too. He was overjoyed.

Felicity too had decided to take a breath of fresh air that day. She longed to get away from Auntie and Joyce Skillet's prying eyes if only for a short time. She donned her new expensive green Barbour mackintosh and wellington boots, grabbed a stout walking stick from the hall stand, and set off on the path from Primrose House to the river. As she neared a large clump of willow trees she set eyes on Matthew. He was not alone. There was a young man she did not recognize, fair and effeminate, with his arms twined around Matthew and, horror of horrors, they were kissing. She felt violently sick. Nausea passed through her body in unrelenting waves. 'A homo, oh heavens!' she muttered to herself. What a fool she had been to fancy him. What a waste of an attractive man. She stood still for a moment and watched.

Tim moved away and after a loving glance at Matthew and what she construed as a sickly smile he walked along the towpath towards the far end of the village.

A clandestine meeting indeed Felicity, thought. We will see about that.

She approached the unsuspecting Matthew quietly, her wellington boots making no sound in the long soft wet grass. She tapped him on the shoulder with her walking stick. Matthew was startled and jumped.

'Meeting a lover?' Felicity spat out and hissed like a cat about to pounce.

'You don't know what you are talking about,' he retorted. 'Tim is a colleague. We were discussing business and he has gone ahead to deliver some papers to a client. I really don't know what it has got to do with you anyway!'

He scowled at Felicity, his lips curling down at the corners with disdain. What a ghastly woman, trust her to turn up like this.

'A few people would like to know about it,' said Felicity, thinking quickly in her usual devious way. 'It will cost you something for me to keep quiet.'

'What do you mean?' Matthew retorted scathingly. 'You are going to blackmail me?'

'I want to know if Auntie has made another will since the nineteen eighties. Tell me the truth and I will forget about your vile liaison.'

Matthew stepped backwards further on to the wooden fisherman's perch and smiled, a malicious expression spreading over his face. What a ghastly woman, who did she think she was? She was not going to get the better of him.

Felicity took a step towards him.

'Keep back!' he uttered in a warning tone and lifted an arm as if to strike her.

Felicity smiled with a feral look upon her face that reminded him of a wild mountain cat.

The next moment Matthew's feet slipped on a patch of the thick oozing mud that coated the surface of the fisherman's platform and he slid backwards into the swift and swollen river. It was almost freezing and he cried out in fear.

'Help ... help me.' Long arms flailed wildly. He was a poor swimmer and his thick woollen coat soaked up the water like blotting paper and the dirty river water trickled with surprising speed into his strong leather boots, threatening to force him with alarming swiftness into its murky depths. The only sound he could hear was the roaring of the water in his ears. Gasping for air he flung his arms upwards once again in a desperate bid for help. Help was not forthcoming. The water was deep, and drowning – his worst dread since he had been forced to endure swimming lessons when he was a schoolboy – threatened to become reality. As he gasped for air his mouth filled with foul dirty liquid, gritty spiteful stuff that scratched and made its way down the back of his throat. He tried to speak but could make no sound. There was no doubt now in his mind that he was going to drown and a feeling of sheer panic engulfed him.

Felicity laughed like a banshee and ran along the bank waving her stick. This was fun and in her view Matthew deserved a cold ducking. He was a nasty arrogant man.

'Grab this,' she shrieked holding out her stick but he could not reach it. She did not think he could and that suited her. If they had been observed she could always say she had tried to save him. She knew that she should report the accident but did not want to become involved in any rescue attempts or be asked any awkward questions.

Matthew's body was flung by the force of the water towards the nearest bank as the river curved slightly downstream. His muscles flexed and he stretched out to clutch a long spindly branch of a willow tree but the current swung him round viciously and he felt a sharp pain which travelled down his arms as his fingers slid off the slippery wet branch. Vicious cold wind whipped the surface of the water which sprayed like coarse sand on to his face. Almost immediately another much thicker tree trunk collided with his head. As Matthew slipped into unconsciousness his last thought was that the evil and ugly Felicity had won.

Felicity's only concern was that she had lost her chance to find out the information she wanted about the will but didn't think that she could do anything to save Matthew even if she wanted to. She could no longer see any sign of him, or anybody else. She glanced round furtively, all clear, not a soul in sight. She turned away from the river and returned to Primrose House with a spring in her step. She looked forward to smoked salmon sandwiches and chocolate cake. It was nearly time for afternoon tea and that thought took precedence. If Matthew was rescued, and that was a big if, she was sure he would not want her to tell anyone about their meeting. There was no point in worrying about him, after all she could do nothing to help the man and his drowning was not going to trouble her conscience.

At the time of the accident Timothy had vaguely heard some voices as he made his way along the path and ducked under the branches of another willow tree surrounded by hawthorns for a few moments. His heart started to beat fiercely. He prayed that they had not been seen. A strong gust of wind whistled swiftly through the branches above his head for a few minutes then everything seemed eerily quiet until the wind rose again. His face blanched as he thought about the possibility that that someone had seen them kissing. A woman appeared and stopped in front of him. She too was strolling along the path towards Enderly and Primrose House from the other end of the village where he was heading.

'Are you all right?' she asked anxiously.

'Fine,' he said quickly. 'I'm just catching my breath, this wind is vicious.'

The woman, though not convinced, turned away to continue her walk along the path that would eventually take her back to the village past Primrose House. 'It's busy today,' she muttered. 'I thought I saw a woman ahead of me just now in a green Barbour but I must have imagined it. There is nobody around now.' She turned once again to Timothy. 'Did you see her?'

Timothy replied, 'No, I haven't seen anyone else today.' His voice sounded strained and threatened to spiral upwards and end almost in a shriek. That was a close shave, he thought. We must be more careful. A drop of sweat trickled down his back despite the cold and the muscles in his shoulders knotted.

Felicity felt smug. I wonder if Matthew got out of that icy water, she thought whilst sitting in Janet's warm lounge and tucking into a large piece of chocolate cake. She smiled and struggled to stop herself laughing out loud. The Mace family had now been nicely diminished. She had been pleased to note that Jeremy was still drinking heavily and although he called at Primrose House some afternoons to see Janet, as his father had done before him, Felicity was satisfied that he would not live too long which would save her the trouble of pushing him down any steps or having to think up any other way to get rid of him. Jeremy's face was now an overall beetroot red and purple veins stood out with startling clarity at the base of his temples whilst small puffy bags hung in a revolting manner from beneath his watery blue flecked eyes and odd arched eyebrows. He was suffering from vague chest pains and, although he had been warned by his doctor to take care, he liked his wine and cigars and he would not give those up in a hurry even if they did lessen his expectation of living to a ripe old age. There could soon be another funeral, or perhaps two, to attend, Felicity ruminated with interest. What a pity the Mace family offer such poor quality wine at their wakes!

An elderly resident from the village found Matthew's corpse the next morning when she took her small Yorkie dog for its constitutional. The body had been washed to the Enderly village side of the river and was wedged between two drooping willow branches. She felt her stomach turn over and almost fainted with shock. 'My angina,' she croaked in a low husky voice, shaky and full of fear that the familiar chest pains would rear up and over-come her. 'I could do without this,' she moaned. The pain did not come and after a few seconds she managed to reach into her handbag for her mobile phone. Steeling herself she raised the alarm.

The local police were soon at the scene. Matthew was stiff and cold, streaky brown river weeds clung to his once attractive pale yellow hair and a purple bruise showed clearly on one side of his forehead. His face was ashen but mud had splattered across his high cheekbones and clung to the edges of his once attractive mouth. His body was removed to the local morgue after careful inspection at the scene by DI Peter Holmes and his assistants who combed the river bank for clues without success.

DI Holmes was convinced that Matthew's death was not the result of a simple accident but there was no proof of foul play. He thought that Timothy and Felicity knew more about the incident than they had admitted. The autopsy too indicated that there were no injuries to the body other than those that could be inflicted following drowning and bruising as a result of being buffeted by trees and other obstacles encountered in a swiftly flowing river.

Matthew, like his grandfather, was buried in Enderly church-yard. Janet did not feel well enough to attend the funeral so Felicity acted as her representative. It was a quiet affair compared to Peter's. Hardly anybody had been invited. Jeremy had mumbled a few words about his son in the church, between deep sobs. She had labelled Timothy Carter 'the fairy boy' and was interested to note that he attended the funeral service but to her amusement crouched at the back of the church like a frightened animal. The meal that had been arranged in the Maces' cottage later Felicity thought was dreadful, and the wine was in her opinion even worse than the rubbish she had tasted at Peter Mace's wake. She made an excuse to leave early. Jeremy consumed at least three bottles of the putrid wine and had to retire to bed before all the guests had left.

After Matthew's accident the Mace business was taken over by rival local firm Wilkins and Partners and Janet's will was stored in their vault. Felicity was interested to discover that the Mace business had, until Matthew took over, not been in a healthy financial state. She learned too through listening to local gossip that Jeremy had drunk and gambled away the profits over many years, but had already guessed that might be the case.

A young woman from the new firm appeared one day to have a chat with Janet but became concerned about her mental condition and to Felicity's relief decided to leave things as they were.

'Mrs Lacey's last will, though slightly old, was adequate,' she said. 'There is no point in worrying her about making any changes.' Felicity was now convinced that she had seen the latest will and her spirits rose.

Felicity decided to turn her attention to Tom Hands. She would make some enquiries about him now. She was pleased to have something like that to do.

Chapter 16

Enderly Bridge Club

Robbie enjoyed his game of bridge each week in the Green Man. He had been unwell recently, though so far he had kept it to himself, and he needed a change. A good duplicate club could perhaps offer a chance to take his mind off things. It was a good game and he hoped it would help him to keep his mind active; at least that was a theory he had read somewhere – it was beneficial for the elderly. He gave some thought to joining Little Brinton Bridge Club which was only about four miles away where his old friend Pat Field and another villager, John Elk, were already members. Pat was feeling his age and did not really enjoy club bridge so much as he had in the past.

'Robbie,' he urged, 'you would be doing me a big favour if you would partner John Elk. I'm getting too tired at the end of an evening's bridge. John is a shy chap and would not like to play with a stranger. He would play with you, he knows you well and has played with you in the pub. You'd enjoy Little Brinton Club and the standard of play is quite high.'

'I would like to Pat, but are you sure? You've been a member there since the club started in 1995.'

'Quite sure.'

John Elk was pleased too. 'I'll look forward to playing with you Robbie, we know each other's game.'

Pat was getting forgetful and their results were not so good as they had been in the past. Pat found it difficult to learn any new conventions and John was anxious to improve.

Robbie phoned the Secretary, Patsy Croft.

'You would be welcome to come as a guest next week,' she told him in a brisk tone. 'We can probably find you a partner if you do not have one.'

'I have arranged to play with John Elk,' Robbie said in a tentative voice.

Patsy's tone changed on hearing the name John Elk; her reply was soft and almost pleasant.

'Oh that's good. Well then, we'll look forward to meeting you on Thursday. Play begins promptly at seven. You know where we are, in any case I expect you could get a lift with John.'

Robbie was intrigued when he met Patsy. She was skinny, angular and almost anorexic in appearance, with a sharp commanding voice. He had pictured her in his mind after his telephone conversation as being older and even more shrew-like than she was. Her straight hair was a dull mousy colour which she twisted into a small bun on the top of her head giving her a stern matron-like appearance. Tiny blue eyes sheltered behind thick metal-framed glasses that balanced on the bridge of a small straight nose. She pressed her wide but well sculptured and full-lipped mouth together in a stiff and rather unnatural way but if she had relaxed, rather than assuming the role of a martinet, Robbie thought that she would be quite pretty and underneath that stiff exterior he guessed that she was quite soft hearted. He thought she could only be at most in her early forties though he was not very good at guessing the ages of women. Patsy greeted him with a thin and slightly waspish smile on her narrow face but introduced him to several of the other members and made him welcome, or as welcome as she could manage. She was an odd young woman, efficient but somewhat antagonistic towards the male sex. The vibes reached him.

Robbie shrugged. It would not worry him. He was too old to care and he looked forward to playing duplicate bridge in a well-established club. Robbie found the majority of the members helpful and he began to enjoy himself. Many of the players were his age or about ten years younger but there were a few bright and eager young people who had recently joined who had previously been members of a much larger club in Everton but enjoyed the friendlier atmosphere found in the club in Little Brinton. They thought the standard could have been better but they might have a reasonable game. One or two were in Robbie's opinion quite competitive but it would not hurt to play against them, indeed he might even improve his own game.

'Have you played much bridge?' one conceited young man asked him, looking Robbie over as though he was something the cat had brought in.

'Quite a lot,' Robbie answered swiftly and was rewarded by the man's face dropping an inch or two. Silly young puppy, a good smack on the bottom would not be amiss. He, without doubt, thought he was God's gift to bridge. Robbie looked forward to the challenge he presented. Yes, he was going to have a rewarding time in this club.

The chairman, Ned, was an odd fellow. He had an East End London accent which he tried to hide. Ned Windsor was quite a regal name, Robbie thought with interest.

Ned stepped forward to greet the newcomer.

'Welcome,' he said, and gave Robbie a lopsided smile that at best made Robbie feel ill at ease. There was something he did not trust about the man but he was, as far as he could tell, running the club well. He could be an ex-con Robbie thought. He certainly looks like one. He wondered how he came to be chairman of the club.

A few of the members had dubbed Ned appropriately 'King of the Bridge Club'. He had been the club chairman now for a year and, although efficient, he was considered by many of the members to be a rather a rough diamond. He had a mocking look in his watery eyes as though he found the whole bridge scene amusing. He was, a member was pleased to tell Robbie later, an excellent card player and had played for many years when he was in the Merchant Navy.

'Our first chairman, Jack Headley, you know,' one elderly lady insisted on telling Robbie, 'was framed for murder by his brother-in-law George Berry. It was a dreadful business. He was sent to prison for a while but his name was cleared and he is now living in Scotland near his sister.'

'Really,' Robbie replied feigning interest.

'Oh yes,' the woman continued with relentless determination, 'Jack was a nice man, helpful to the old people in the village but he had an eye for the ladies. His wife was killed in a car accident in Germany where Jack had been working for a good number of years – they had been just about to buy a retirement bungalow in Little Brinton too. It was very sad.'

Robbie vaguely remembered reading something about the Little Brinton murder in a newspaper. A well-known jockey from South Africa had been strangled in June 2000. It was obviously still a talking point in the club and had put Little Brinton on the map for a while.

Tea and good quality chocolate biscuits were served in the interval by Emily, a pretty young girl from the village. The previous lady had given up the job, Robbie was told, after an altercation with the Ned who thought she was too nosy and a spy for the Village Hall Committee.

'Nonsense, of course', old Mrs Noakes told Robbie, 'she was a nice woman, very helpful and much better than young girls when it comes to making tea and coffee. Emily does nothing but listen to pop music with earphones strapped to her head and dream of boys. She spilt tea on Mrs Brooker's feet a few weeks ago. Luckily they were not badly burned.'

Robbie smiled. Old Ned was running a tight ship and enjoying himself.

There were about twelve tables in the club and the overall atmosphere seemed quite pleasant. Robbie was relieved. He had heard some disturbing tales about competitive duplicate bridge players in the past that were not encouraging.

John Elk was painfully shy. He had a mop of curly red hair about which he had been teased at school. His large slightly bulging grey-green eyes were heavily lidded and fringed with short stubby lashes though his face was strong and masculine. He was a keen, astute bridge player who was quite popular. He, like Patsy, was slim and angular with narrow shoulders and long gangly arms that were tipped with slim artistic fingers. He could not be described as a handsome and outgoing man but Robbie liked him. He found him intelligent and a good, if somewhat terse, conversationalist. He lived in a small terraced house in Enderly that he had recently purchased, in fact the same one that John Lacey had bought when he first moved into the village.

That John Elk liked Patsy Croft was obvious to Robbie. They were approximately the same age. He must have been one of the few men in the club who did really like her, Robbie thought, and he found it difficult to know what the attraction was. Her slim face was shrew-like and she made little effort to improve her looks though she could be quite pretty with care. A number of the members made a point of telling him what he had already surmised about her dislike of the male sex. She had been secretary for a year when Robbie first played with John Elk and like John Elk Patsy was highly intelligent, he thought. He was soon informed by one of the chatty elderly members that she held a good managerial post in a firm in Everton after studying Economics and Mathematics in Everton Technical College and had a flair for organisation, which was appreciated by her employers. He was told too that she was one of the founder members and a much-respected local girl and, despite her uncharitable attitude towards the opposite sex, she had quite a few friends. He detected admiration and pride by a number of the members for the prowess of their somewhat prickly secretary.

'Patsy,' John ventured one evening shortly after Robbie had joined the club, 'would you like to go to a classical concert with me in Everton next week? I belong to the music club there and the Jubilate quartet, a good local group, will be playing some Mozart.'

There was a stunned silence. Several of the bridge members turned their heads with eager anticipation. They expected that Patsy would send him packing in her usual scathing sharp voice. This could prove to be entertaining. After a breathtaking few moments Patsy replied in a voice that sounded unusually meek and controlled. There were a few audible sighs of relief. She glanced at John Elk through her modern shallow glasses, purchased earlier that day, that she hoped improved her small eyes. As she peered at him her heart unexpectedly missed a beat. He has a nice face, he's skinny like me, not too much of a hunk, she thought. He probably will not be much of a threat and I have actually got to like him over the past year. That thought surprised her. In fact she had to admit to a slow-growing affection for the man. She would enjoy going to a concert with him she thought, and Mozart was her favourite composer. How on earth did he know she liked classical music? A strange affinity had begun to draw them together.

'Hmm ... well yes, I would love to, thank you.'

By that time the whole room of bridge players had been alerted to the conversation. Patsy Croft going out with a man, my goodness that was unheard of! What a gracious reply she had made too; some of the members looked as though they would swoon in their seats. A few surprised mumblings could be heard echoing around the room: 'Patsy is going out with a man,' and 'That's a turn up for the books ...'

Patsy and John appeared oblivious to the mutterings. They were busy looking at each other with mirrored surprise. Patsy could not believe that she found a man so interesting and shy John found it difficult to believe that he had summoned the courage to ask her out on a date. He was elated now that she had accepted his invitation.

Patsy and John Elk started to go out on a regular basis as a couple and soon became close friends, something they had not anticipated. Neither of them seemed anxious, at least on the surface, for a physical relationship. John had had one or two girlfriends when he was at school but no serious relationships. He had worked long hours in a local accountants' office in recent years and, although he had thought about the possibility of obtaining some female company he had not done anything about it and as a result his social life had been limited. Something about Patsy had allowed him to overcome the barrier he had formed between himself and the opposite sex.

John did not mind Patsy's pinched and anxious-looking face, though she was gradually relaxing and looked much more attractive. She bought some make-up: some good quality face creams, powder and a soft pink lipstick. She had her hair cut in a becoming style and coloured a light brown shade with blonde highlights in the best hairdressing salon in Everton.

John Elk worked in Everton with another man from Little Brinton, Peter Saunders, who had encouraged him to join the bridge club. John was seen as a confirmed and rather dull bachelor by his colleagues so that the courtship of Patsy was an interesting move on his part and his bridge club acquaintances were keen to see how things developed.

Tongues wagged in the Little Brinton village shop. Mrs Blunt the proprietor and local know-it-all was, together with many of her customers, quite intrigued. However, nobody was as pleased as Patsy's father. He hoped Patsy would marry John Elk and get out of his hair for good but admitted to himself that might be wishful thinking. She had been far too antagonistic towards men since she went on a trip to Germany with the school band as a young teenager. Whatever happened in the past had certainly succeeded in making her dislike the opposite sex. He patted his young black Labrador puppy.

'We may get a chance to have a peaceful old age after all Bruce my boy,' he said out loud, looking at his young canine companion with pleasure. 'A grandchild too perhaps though it's probably too late. Never knows yer luck. If her mum had still been alive she may have got married years ago.' He scratched his head, utterly perplexed as always when he thought about his daughter. She needed a woman to talk to; it could have made all the difference.

He was right but it was unlikely that Patsy would have confided in anyone about her experience on that holiday. She kept it close to her chest and did not utter a word to even her best friends, and certainly not her crotchety old dad.

Robbie was intrigued to hear about the history of Little Brinton Bridge Club. He wondered if Jack Headley, the founder, would ever visit the club. He hoped so. It would be interesting to discuss the setting up of a new club with him. He discovered that one of the main reasons Jack had started the club in 1995 was to find a new lady companion after the death of his wife. One or two of the older members were happy to tell him in depth about the murder of the South African jockey Karl Davies who had lived in the village and how Jack Headley had loved Karl's wife Kitty.

'Silly man,' one of the ladies said. 'Kitty was gay, as they call it these days, and went to live in France with a woman, another of our bridge club members, believe it or not! Jack did not possess much sense when it came to choosing lady friends. He even had a fling with a local shop girl. Stupid man. He has gone to Scotland now to live near his family. He probably won't want to come back here, there are too many unpleasant memories.'

Hmm, Robbie thought to himself. That is a pity. This bridge club has certainly changed village life, mainly for the better, for a good many people. He had started to think seriously about forming a small duplicate club in Enderly. Janet loved to play bridge years ago he was told but would no longer have the concentration required, which was a shame. He wondered about Felicity Brown. She had settled in to Primrose House rather too well. Perhaps she would be interested in playing bridge; she had mentioned to him one day that she enjoyed the game and had played in a club in Canada. She had boasted that she was considered to be a good player, though Robbie considered that too many bridge players had an inflated opinion about their skill. He decided that he would mention the possible new club to her and hoped she would take the bait. He was perhaps playing with fire but it would be one way to keep a better eye on the woman. Robbie still considered that she was a very shady character who had wheedled her way into her aunt's life and would not be easy to dislodge though the latter was something he would really enjoy doing if the opportunity ever presented itself.

He consulted some of the rubber bridge players in the Green Man who seemed quite enthusiastic. There were enough people to make up a few tables though whether they could meet in the Green Man or the old dilapidated village hall they were not sure. It would depend on numbers. Like Jack Headley had done in Little Brinton in 1995 when he had started the bridge club there, he placed notices around the village in an attempt to attract players to join a small club in Enderly. He placed one in the local shop and another on a notice board on the edge of a small triangle of unkempt grass known locally as the village green. He also inserted a small advertisement in the *Everton News* and another notice in the Green Man. If they could meet in the Green Man there would be enough parking space at the back of the pub for the locals and a few of the bridge players that might come from outside the village.

Roderick, the red-headed publican, threw his head back and laughed heartily when he read the notice.

'That club idea won't come to much, only a few customers bother playing cards in this pub. Duplicate bridge, heck,' he spluttered. 'Not many of my punters will care to play that form of bridge. They like playing rubber bridge for money – friendly like. Only a penny a hundred or some similar small amount I believe.'

He was about to proclaim it a daft idea but thought with interest about the small room at the back of the pub which could be let out for a lucrative sum and a bridge club, however stupid he might consider the idea to be, would be one way of obtaining a regular income from the room. He certainly could do with it. He had got married recently and his new young wife was expecting a baby and he would soon have an extra mouth to feed, apart from the baby clothes, toys and prams. There were suitably sized tables and chairs already in the back room. The chairs were a little the worse for wear and the tables slightly scratched but they could be used, especially if some good bridge cloths were purchased by the bridge players and the bumpy old surfaces hidden. There would be a break and one of his barmaids could make coffee, or better still serve the members with beer or spirits. A little more profit could perhaps be made in that way, he calculated. The thought of the money brought a smug smile to his face when Robbie approached him about a possible room in the pub in which to hold a meeting of would-be bridge club members.

'We have a good room at the back you could rent for a reasonable sum,' he proffered. 'It would be really cheap and there are already some tables there. It would be better than that draughty old village hall venue. The Village Hall Committee should apply for a grant to renovate that hall in the same way that the Little Brinton Committee did. They now have a lovely hall which has replaced the old tin hut that sufficed for many years.'

Their loss and my gain he thought as a comfortable greedy feeling settled upon his slightly bulging stomach.

Twelve people turned up to Robbie's meeting in the pub. They were keen and included, as he had hoped, the unpleasant Felicity Brown. When he had mentioned the new club to her she had been scathing in her remarks.

'I'll think about it,' she said. 'I'm not sure that it will be up to my standard but it may be worth trying.'

Felicity was bored with auntie's wandering mind and limited company. Conversation was becoming tedious. An evening playing bridge was attractive. She was, at least in her opinion, an accomplished player and would enjoy it. It could give her the chance, she hoped, to find out some information about Tom Hands. She was convinced that someone would remember something about him sooner or later. She also understood that there had been a photograph of the evacuees hanging up in the pub and if it was still there it may help to refresh her memory.

John Elk and Patsy Croft offered to help and Robbie accepted their offer with alacrity. They came to the meeting that Robbie had arranged in order to meet the prospective members and to consider joining the committee, after all they were experienced in bridge club affairs. There were several elderly ladies, at least seventy or eighty years old, and two young women who taught in the local junior school who claimed that they were competent bridge players. John Elk offered to be treasurer and Patsy said she would act as secretary for one year only, after which perhaps one of the other members would take over the post. Robbie hoped that the new women could play bridge reasonably well but was willing to help anyone who needed some tuition and he thought a few might. Pat said he would play with Robbie so that John and Patsy could play together if they wanted to, though he was not really keen to play duplicate bridge now.

'You play with John,' Patsy had said generously to Robbie, 'I can play with Margaret Jones, she needs a partner and I know her from Little Brinton.'

This was agreed, but Robbie knew that John and Patsy would really prefer to play together in the new club and he would soon have to find another partner.

Felicity was quiet during the initial meeting. There was no way she was going to be coerced on to the committee, it would be too much trouble and a tie, there were after all several other things to occupy her time and thoughts like disposing of the remaining member of the Mace family and checking up on Tom Hands, but she did offer to help. She would make the tablecloths. Auntie had a sewing machine she could use and she was quite experienced with a needle and thread.

'I'll buy the material in Everton,' she said taking the stance of a generous benefactor and thought how useful Auntie's credit card was proving to be. 'Robbie will drive me in tomorrow. The club can pay me back when it is able to.'

She looked at Robbie with a mistress-to-servant look and smiled with magnanimous delight. Robbie flinched but decided that he would ignore her unpleasant attitude. She was a revolting woman, but if she would make the cloths he would be grateful and not look a gift horse in the mouth, even if he had to rely on the unpalatable Felicity for that gift.

It was agreed that he should act as chairman and Patsy approached Roderick the pub landlord to discuss details of the rent. Terms were agreed and the group decided to meet the next week for a trial evening. John Elk said that there were some old cards and boards they could borrow from Little Brinton until they had enough cash to buy their own. Members would pay a yearly subscription of five pounds and one pound fifty pence each evening they played; this would be used to pay the rent and eventually pay for new cards and the tablecloths. There was space in the room for at least eight tables and hopefully they would be able to attract a few more members later on. One man offered to do the scoring on his computer and direct if they wished him to do so. He was about eighty-five but had experience of directing and scoring when he lived in Everton about five years ago.

'I will be delighted to help, until you can get someone younger to take over,' he said a slow smile spreading over his lined face. 'I won't want to do it for long but someone will be sure to be able to do the job later. It's nice to be wanted and feel useful.'

Robbie thanked him. It certainly would be helpful.

Felicity found some suitable thick green velvet material in a shop in Brinton and made the bridge cloths as promised. She gave the bill to John Elk. The cash in hand would be useful when the club could afford to pay her back. It did not occur to her to give the cash to Janet.

It had been agreed that the new Enderly Club should meet every Tuesday evening, which was the day that the members found most convenient. Roderick did not mind which evening it was as long as they paid up and consumed a few drinks during their break. He found a few old pictures in the attic and hung them on the dull old walls in the 'bridge room'. One of these was another old photograph, taken in Enderly village hall, of a group of the evacuees.

'It will cheer the place up,' he quipped with his tongue in his cheek.

Felicity was intrigued and peered closely at it. The photograph had faded, like the other one already hanging in the pub, so that it was difficult to recognise anyone who could be Tom Hands, though she tried. She was determined to find out what had happened to him. 'Dead with any luck,' she said to herself.

Marianne Fright (dubbed frightful Marianne locally), an old Enderly resident, decided she would like to join the club, or rather as she put it 'give it a go'. Marianne was a scratchy and bad-tempered woman in her seventies. Life had not treated her well in the past two decades and she had been short of money since her husband died twenty years ago. Her only son was working in Australia and had only visited her once in the last fifteen years and that visit had been brief. Not too surprising, some of her neighbours had gossiped; miserable old bat that woman. She had played bridge on and off over the past thirty years with friends and considered herself to be a reasonable player. She was lonely and looked forward to some company and a local bridge club would suit her very well. She could walk to the pub in less than five minutes though she did not really approve of beer drinking and some of those, in her opinion, local louts who frequented the bar.

'I'll need a partner,' she announced in an abrasive tone. 'Someone who can play, not a rabbit.'

It was decided after some discussion by Robbie and Patsy that she could partner Felicity if they both were happy with that arrangement. A good pair Robbie thought, it should be interesting. They were both difficult women and would suit each other well.

'I hope you are some good,' Marianne had spat out with rude abandon when she first set eyes on Felicity. She did not like the look of the woman but would put up with her if she could obtain a reasonable game of bridge.

Felicity bridled.

'Of course,' she retorted. 'I hope you are too!'

They glared at each other and attempted to sum each other up.

Robbie smiled and struggled to smother a grin. Well, that is a promising partnership, he told himself. They are a couple of right old battleaxes.

Felicity agreed to meet in Marianne's cottage the next day to discuss bridge tactics, a meeting that proved more interesting than Felicity had thought possible. Marianne Fright, nee Bridgman, had been an evacuee and remembered Tom Hands quite well. She even produced some old photographs she had taken as a child with her precious Brownie camera. There was one of Tom holding Janet Merryweather's hand on her wedding day. It was not very clear but she could make out some of his features, including the deep dimple in his chin. Felicity was riveted. She held the photograph up to the light and studied it carefully.

Marianne was a strange woman. To Felicity's surprise she looked presentable in her wedding photograph which had been placed in a good solid silver frame that took pride of place on the top of an old mahogany upright piano at one end of the lounge. The woodwork was in need of a dab of good beeswax polish and some effective treatment for woodworm but was a good-looking piece of furniture. Marianne had been slim and waiflike on her wedding day, almost pretty with thick dark hair that tumbled around her shoulders. She was wearing a suit tailored in the 'new look' style so fashionable just after the war with a flounce on the short jacket which circled her then neat waist. The skirt was flared and reached to her ankles. Her shoes were neat with high heels and sported pale ribbon bows. The photograph was black and white so that the finer details that would have been enhanced through colour were lost which Felicity thought was a pity. Marianne's husband she decided looked a real country yokel. He was small and wiry and had the air of a man who was out of place in his dark suit and neat tie. He would not have interested me, ugh, she thought. Marianne was welcome to him.

Marianne's hair was now thin and white, and her shiny pink scalp glistened through thin strands of hair in the front. She had brushed it upwards and sprayed it with some thickening agent which had made little impression upon it. A wig would not be amiss, Felicity thought. Marianne's once pretty green eyes were faded too, her eyebrows and eyelashes were almost non-existent and she wore incongruous horrid thick brown rimmed glasses which Felicity guessed were cheap. It was hard to equate this grumpy old woman with the young girl in the photograph. Her old red woollen jumper was faded and badly felted in places and she had an unpleasant habit of running her fingers over the ruffed up areas and picking off the bumps of wool, which she dropped with careless abandon on to the already dusty floor.

They sipped good Indian tea, a brand Felicity approved, and ate elegant chocolate thins which she was amazed Marianne could afford. Marianne told Felicity that she had as an evacuee been billeted with the local butcher, a shop long since gone, forced out by the arrival of the supermarkets in Everton. After her parents were killed in the Blitz she had stayed on in Enderly as nobody else in her family had wanted her. She worked for a while in the shop before marrying a local farm labourer, Bert Fright, in her teens.

'He was a rough old farm chap, really, but kind hearted and I needed someone to take care of me. I didn't love him, at least not at first but I missed him when he died.'

Felicity proved to be a good listener and Marianne enjoyed telling her about her past in her high pitched and slightly cracked old voice.

And what a 'fright' she looks now, Felicity thought spitefully and smiled to herself at the pun.

They agreed on their bridge conventions and Felicity realized she had quite enjoyed herself talking to Marianne. She had liked even more finding out something about Tom Hands. It was a starting point anyway.

'Tom Hands, oh yes I remember now,' Marianne had said just before Felicity returned to Primrose House to partake of a second cup of tea and the usual sandwiches with Janet.

'He lived with your aunt's mother and then briefly with your aunt and her first husband James but James Anderson did not want him. He was quite nasty to the boy by all accounts. Tom left suddenly and I heard he was adopted by a couple in Brinton but I'm not sure what happened to him after that. I believe Janet Lacey did try and find him some years later, or so a friend who worked for her in the house at that time told me. She did not have any luck.'

This was a good snippet of information and Felicity rubbed her hands together with glee, bade her new friend 'Goodbye, see you next Tuesday,' and returned to Primrose House with a distinct spring in her step. Things were looking up. It would not be long now before she found Tom Hands, if he was still alive, and then she would see.

The next Tuesday found an enthusiastic group of bridge players in the small back room of the Green Man. Enderly Club had been launched and Robbie thought the outlook was promising. He hoped that Felicity would not be too much of a thorn in his side and that he would be luckier than the hapless Jack Headley. Time alone would tell.

Chapter 17

New Friends and a Search

Felicity was delighted to discover that Tom Hands had been adopted. She decided to approach the local authorities first in order to try and trace him, but she didn't think they would be helpful because they would need Tom Hands' permission before they were able to tell anyone his whereabouts. She felt an increasing and urgent desire to trace this usurper and possible heir to some of her aunt's fortune, albeit a small part. If necessary she would hire a private detective to help her, that might be the best way. She could use Aunt Janet's credit card. There had been no queries so far about her illicit expenditure. A direct debit arrangement to pay the monthly bills was in hand and Janet's current account balance had so far proved to be adequate. Felicity kept a close eye on the bank statements. She laughed out loud and an almost demonic screech issued from her mouth as she considered the situation. That little piece of plastic and its easy-to-remember pin number, following the introduction of chip and pin, had certainly changed her life. The post was easy to divert to her hands when it arrived; 'We must not worry poor Auntie,' she had said to Joyce, and dear Auntie had willingly signed any cheques: she assumed they were for food and household bills. It was difficult now for her to check the figures; she became confused and so long as there were not any serious problems she was happy for her niece to help her pay the bills. So far so good Felicity told herself. She hoped that nosy financial adviser would not interfere. He was making a fortune out of Auntie's investments anyway so she thought he wouldn't want to lose such a lucrative account by rocking the boat and complaining about the now too helpful niece. At least she hoped not.

Felicity had noticed a small detective agency in Brinton and the next time that Robbie took her to do her aunt's shopping she planned to visit them in order to make some enquiries about their fees and perhaps make an appointment. She was sure that there must be some records somewhere and the sooner she got her hands on those the happier she would be. If Tom Hands was alive she could track him down. She would be glad to devise a plan to get rid of him and her skewed mind whirled with anticipation and pleasure. The pursuit to increase her share of Janet's will had turned into an enjoyable pastime. She may not be able to get rid of some of the contenders but she would do her best to ensure her share of the money was substantial.

In the meantime she was enjoying playing bridge with Marianne. Patsy Croft and John Elk only had eyes for each other and Felicity hoped that there would soon be a wedding to which she would be invited, along with some of the other bridge club members. She appreciated the sense of companionship that the bridge club afforded her, something that had not interested her in the past. A wedding would be another welcome diversion to enliven her dreary existence in Primrose House. There would more likely than not be a good spread of food as well as interesting company. Her mouth watered as usual when she thought about good food. She could use her aunt's credit card to buy something nice for them. She would enjoy that. New friends and a bridge club, hmmm, things were improving and she was feeling happier than she had for many years. Making friends and being accepted into a group without antagonism was a new experience for her. She had mellowed and was a less aggressive individual than she had been when she played in the bridge club in Canada and that was, she had begun to understand, the key to her current success.

Patsy and John continued to grow closer; Robbie and John were enjoying a good partnership and Patsy was happy to play with Margaret Jones, a pleasant woman in her early fifties. She liked her but unfortunately Margaret did remind her of the teacher who had accompanied the Brinton Comprehensive School Band party to Germany when she was a teenager. Her experience on that holiday of a liaison with one of the young German band members had left her scarred mentally and physically and she was only just, after so many years and thanks to John Elk, recovering from the trauma that had been inflicted upon her by the young German boy who had raped her. It had been her own silly fault. In her innocence she had been willing to participate in a sexual experience, But with a swift and brutal act he had forced her out of her girlish romantic dreams into the harsh reality of a liaison with a violent insensitive boy. He had delighted in her degradation, enjoyed her humiliation, laughed about her with his friends, and almost destroyed her capacity to love or enjoy sex with any man. Time was mellowing her perception of the incident but there was still some way to go before she could put the whole scenario into a reasonable perspective. She was developing feelings for John of which she had not realised that she was now capable. She had tried for too long to bury any attraction that she might have developed for any members of the opposite sex. They were all, in her opinion, disgusting. It was the easiest way to forget the shame and dismay that had been foisted on her. There was still a slight barrier to overcome but perhaps she would manage that soon. She was experiencing an exhilarating longing for John's gangly arms to hold her close to his thin and angular frame that was so very like her own.

Robbie kept a close eye on Felicity. He was interested to hear her chat to Marianne one evening about someone she was trying to trace. It was impossible to make sense of all of the conversation but he was suspicious that she was searching for him. He heard the name Tom and something about a detective agency in Brinton. Why she would want to trace him after all this time he could not imagine. He wondered if his name was mentioned in Janet's will and Felicity had found a copy. That could be the only feasible explanation. He was not interested in inheriting any of Janet's money; he was comfortable and had more than enough to live on through his investments, but greedy Felicity might be anxious to remove him from the frame. Emitting a deep sigh he thought about money, something that was without doubt the root of so much evil, and Felicity was evil incarnate. The lust for money could rip families apart and provide a motive for murder. Janet would not leave him more than a very small legacy, if anything, but if his name had been mentioned in her will he would need to watch his back.

Felicity approached the local authority in order to trace Tom Hands. As anticipated her efforts fell on stony ground.

'I cannot possibly give you any information without tracing and asking the permission of the gentleman in question,' she was told firmly and sharply by a woman at Everton Town Hall where the records were kept. 'After all this time it could be difficult to find him, he could be dead,' she continued unhelpfully. The woman, Mrs Crabb, looked at Felicity suspiciously over the top of pale pink half moon spectacles. What she saw she did not like. 'Why are you anxious to trace this man anyway?' she asked in an antagonistic tone.

'Well', Felicity lied, 'I have reason to believe he is a long-lost relative and I am anxious to discover if he is still alive.'

Pull the other one, Mrs Crabb's sceptical expression indicated.

'Sorry, can't help,' she said shortly, which was quite uncharacteristic of her, and she dismissed the irate Felicity with a swift wave of a chubby arm.

Pompous old bag, Felicity thought. She would be within her rights to insist that the woman was more helpful, or at least pleasant, when dealing with the public, but it was not worth making a fuss. Instead she made her way diffidently to Richard West's Private Detective Agency in a small back street in Brinton. It would cost her money, or rather it would cost Aunt Janet some money, but she may get a swifter result than messing about with the local authority staff if that Mrs Crabb was typical of the type of person they employed.

Richard West's office was small and dingy. A thin young girl with a strong Russetshire accent sat behind a scratched and battered old desk filing the tips of long bright red painted finger-nails. Her ragged short hair was coloured a pale beige blonde and her clothes were not the kind Felicity associated with a secretary. A bare midriff bulged over scruffy jeans, exposing a small silver ring which pierced her navel, and her skimpy lace blouse's once-fashionable ragged edges were crinkled and discoloured with brown spots of tea or coffee.

'Yeah, what do you want?' she said in an apparent attempt to be pleasant. A cup of weak cold coffee with blobs of congealed milk on the surface stood on the desk in front of her together with a half-eaten unsavoury-looking cheese sandwich, and a part-knitted jumper rested on top of some files. It was not an inspiring scene.

'I am here to see Mr West,' Felicity answered in a firm tone. 'I have an appointment at 2.30 pm.'

'Oh, yeah,' the girl said in an insolent voice. She looked out of the corner of green slanted eyes at a desk diary she retrieved from under a pile of letters, pulled it towards her with a languid hand and opened it with a studied reluctance. 'Ms Felicity Brown is it?' she drawled. Felicity nodded. 'I will ring through and tell him you are here.'

Not an auspicious start Felicity thought.

Richard West, a burly ex-policeman, broad shouldered and well over six feet in height, appeared at the door of his office.

'Come in,' he gushed. Work was short and he was pleased to have this client. She had not, so far, suggested that his fees were too high and tried to negotiate a cheaper rate which made a change from the stance taken by most of his clients. She was well dressed and he anticipated that he could probably charge her his top rate without her quibbling. He smoothed his fine greying hair back from a broad forehead. His eyes were round, deep boot brown, and his wide mouth appeared firm but generous. He smiled warmly at Felicity.

A strong man, tough and dependable, trustworthy too Felicity thought, or at least hoped he was but she realized that looks could be deceiving. She liked him although could not imagine why. The feeling was not reciprocated but he managed to present a friendly and dependable front to all his clients. His living depended on that. He indicated that she could sit in a comfortable looking armchair at the side of his desk and once she was seated he turned towards her and gave her his full attention.

Felicity relaxed, as he had intended she should, and against her better judgement found herself anxious to confide in this charming man and enlist his help. The grotty office and rude secretary were forgotten.

Felicity told him about her desire to trace Tom Hands. She said that his family had lived in London, where she too had lived with her parents until her mother was killed in a car crash. That much was true. She told him she had moved to Canada later but on returning to England a few months ago she remembered that she had a relative who had been evacuated to Russetshire during the war and she was anxious to find out whether he was still alive.

'Tom Hands, a little older than me, lovely chap, er ... distant cousin on my mother's side I think,' she lied. 'I do hope he is well.'

Easy enough case Richard thought. She is not telling the truth but I will work around that.

'Please tell me everything you know about the person you are trying to trace,' he pontificated and produced a notebook and pen with a confident businesslike flourish. He cast a quick glance at Felicity who appeared to be impressed by his manner. He had made a good start.

Felicity produced the photographs she had obtained from Marianne.

'I believe he was placed with foster parents in Enderly then later adopted,' she said, concern mounting in her voice and crocodile tears forming in the corner of her cold sly eyes.

'He may not want to meet you,' Richard warned. 'I will, however, do my best to help.' He estimated that he could charge double the fee that he had in mind earlier. 'There could be a lot of paperwork involved in this case, which may push up the fees,' he lied and when he told her, with some hesitation, how much it might cost she was not, to his intense surprise, in the least concerned.

'Please get on with your searches,' she said. 'I will look forward to the results.'

'I will contact you as soon as I have found out anything concrete,' he said.

Felicity's legs felt wobbly as she stood up and he took her hand in his. He moved closer than was necessary. Nice easy job he thought as he showed her out of his office and watched with interest the flush that had crept up her scraggy neck and face as she departed. Amusing really, he thought. Ah well, all in a day's work.

Felicity felt happier than she had for a long time. She hoped that Auntie's credit card would take care of Richard West's fees but she would have to check the bank balance with care. Tom Hands could be the last thorn in her side. She did not know how true that thought might prove to be. She was making progress – she had not yet decided what she would do should they meet but she did know she would enjoy getting rid of him and the sooner the better. Of course, he could be anywhere in the country, if indeed he was still alive, but a short holiday in order to meet him would not be amiss, depending, of course, if Richard West was able to track him down. She had faith in the man. Not bad looking, she thought . . . I wonder if he is married and if he has any money.

Richard West had left the police force under a cloud. It had been suggested that he had been involved in a local fencing racket. Nothing had been proved but his name had been blackened and he had resigned. To obtain an income he had opened the detective agency in Brinton. He had made a fair living over the past few years, following and reporting on cheating spouses and tracking a few people who had attempted to disappear. He was good at his job and to find Tom Hands, alive or dead, would not be much of a challenge. He rubbed his hands together with pleasure. Easy-peasy case this one; it would be money for old rope.

It did not take him long to discover that Tom Hands the evacuee who had lived with the Merryweathers had later been adopted by a respectable middle-class family. He had his contacts and a little bribery as usual produced some good results. Greed and avarice was the human failing he could play on with an expertise acquired over many years. He soon discovered that Tom Hands had changed his name and had been a successful academic in Oxford. He wondered if he might be worth more to him financially than the spiteful looking Felicity. He would bide his time and keep Felicity Brown waiting for answers.

He found out that Robert Thomas Barker had been living in Enderly for approximately ten years after a successful career as a history professor and since his retirement had been working as a gardener for Felicity Brown's aunt. The situation was interesting. Robert Barker was without doubt a man who was not short of a penny or two. He followed Robbie from what he thought was a safe distance for a few days, which was a mistake. Robbie became suspicious that someone was following him in Brinton and a strange man with thick-rimmed glasses and an odd pointed beard had observed him too closely for comfort on several occasions when he had been dining in the Green Man.

Robbie recalled Felicity's conversation with Marianne. Felicity was the cause of this problem. He decided to approach DI Peter Holmes and ask his opinion about the stalker. He didn't want to waste police time but there was something unsavoury about the whole business, though he knew he needed concrete evidence. He told DI Holmes about his childhood as an evacuee and his suspicions about Felicity Brown's motives for tracing Tom Hands. It could only be money and possible legacies in which Felicity was interested. She was already spending her aunt's money like water.

DI Holmes respected Robbie, he thought he was an intelligent man; he also had doubts about the unpleasant Felicity and the strange accidents that had befallen the Mace family who may also have been beneficiaries in Janet Lacey's will. He would make a few further enquiries. If, as he suspected, Felicity was using Richard West's detective agency it might not be long before she found out that Robbie was Tom Hands.

Robbie had stirred up his suspicions about Felicity Brown. His mind reverted to the day of Matthew Mace's so-called accident. A walker who had come forward when she read about the incident in the local paper told him that she had seen a woman in a

Barbour coat not far from the river that day but it had not been possible to identify her as Felicity, though he was suspicious that it was the wretched woman and that she had in some way been involved. In his opinion she was a dangerous individual.

'Be careful Robbie,' the detective said. 'The woman is an unknown quantity. Be careful. We suspect that Felicity Brown knows more about the deaths of Peter and Matthew Mace than she has so far admitted. We know Matthew Mace had a boyfriend, Timothy. There was some chat about it in the village shop and their liaison was not so private as they had imagined it to be. You probably already know about him. He was on the river bank on the day of the accident but declined to admit that he had been there to meet Matthew or admit that he had seen the woman in the green Barbour. We think that woman was Felicity but we have no proof.'

Robbie could not answer. He too thought Felicity was involved in Peter and Matthew's deaths. He would certainly be careful as the detective had suggested.

DI Holmes found Robbie's latest suspicions about Felicity very interesting. Human beings are greedy things, he thought. So many crimes he had dealt with had been committed in the pursuit of money. He continued to mull over some of the recent disturbing events in which he was convinced Felicity Brown had been involved.

DI Holmes did not trust Richard West. In his opinion he was a bent copper who would stop at nothing to line his own pockets and would not care whom he cheated to obtain money from clients. He knew he would charge Felicity as much money as he could get away with and would not conclude the case too quickly.

'I will keep an eye on Richard West, you may rest assured. It will be a pleasure,' DI Holmes had told Robbie before he left his office.

He had been in communication with the Canadian police and they had a few unresolved queries about Felicity Brown in the past and her fingerprints and details were on file. He thought once again about the death of Peter Mace. The blow to the side of the head was not consistent with a fall but more likely to be the result of a deliberate attempt to crush his skull with a stone to ensure his demise. The stone had been sent to the police forensic laboratories but unfortunately the one smudged fingerprint did not match those of Felicity Brown and there was no DNA. Robbie's visit had re-opened a can of worms.

In the meantime Felicity was getting impatient for news from Richard West. A few weeks had passed. It is about time he had some results, she groused to herself, and resolved to tackle him the next time she went into Brinton.

Following Robbie's visit, DI Holmes's assistant DS John Cross had taken to spending some evenings in the Green Man in order to watch the despicable Richard West. John wore jeans and an old jacket and claimed he was on an extended holiday in the area when asked if he was just visiting by the red-headed publican. Richard West did not know him, though he would have recognised DI Holmes. John enjoyed the beer and had a few good games of darts with the locals. Richard West, however, had found out what he needed to about Robbie. He was biding his time and had decided that there was no point in spending any more of his cash on beer in the pub.

Felicity tackled Richard West when she next went into Brinton. He was evasive and, as DI Homes had expected, said that he needed more time. He was making progress but would require some more cash to cover his expenses. A frustrated and annoyed Felicity paid up.

Richard West decided that he could keep the investigations going a little longer then arrange a meeting with Felicity. By that time he should have lined his pockets reasonably well for very little work.

Three weeks later he told her he had some interesting results for her. Felicity met Richard in his office. She was excited and agog with anticipation.

'I'm really looking forward to meeting my long-lost relative,' she said. Her face was unusually flushed and her fingers itched to pick up the papers Richard had displayed so tantalisingly in front of her on his desk.

'You have already met him,' Richard said, watching her reaction with undisguised interest. 'He changed his surname to Barker, his adoptive parents' name. His name is Robert Thomas Barker, Robbie to his friends, and he is working, as he has been for the past ten years, as your Aunt Janet's handyman.'

Felicity clutched the edge of the desk. She thought for a moment that she might faint but she soon recovered her wits.

'Robbie!' she almost screamed. 'I can't believe it. I will look forward to telling him.'

That was in fact the last thing she had in mind. She needed time to digest the information and then decide what to do.

She settled her bill with the detective, which she thought was far too large, but who was she to argue? She had discovered the whereabouts of Tom Hands. It was a shock. What on earth was Robbie trying to do? No wonder he looked familiar. She could not remember him clearly from their early meetings when she was very young but recalled that there was a photograph of him as a young boy that her aunt kept in a silver frame for a while in the lounge after Uncle James had left. The way he stood … his eyes … yes there was no doubt. She was certain her aunt did not know that she had employed the precious evacuee for so long. She would not tell her. She needed time to think about the situation. It was strange but intriguing.

Robbie met Felicity in the market place where he always parked the car when he took her shopping. She was laden with the usual groceries and bags indicating she had purchased even more new clothes. She was very quiet on the journey back to Primrose House. She knows, he thought. He smiled to himself and wondered what she would do next. It would be necessary to be on his guard. At least he had alerted DI Holmes to her unsavoury activities and that knowledge provided him with some comfort and reassurance.

Chapter 18

Ronald Brown

onald was intrigued to find that Primrose House was still so pretty. The strong red bricks contrasted with the grey stormy sky behind the building. The edges of some of the bricks showed grime and dirt that had collected on their surface over many years but this did not detract from the attractiveness of the building. He stood near the front gate under the shelter of a large bush that grew on one side where he could see but not be seen from the house. The old oak front door looked much the same, at least from his vantage point, fine grainy oak, though slightly scratched, and the trees planted by Janet many years ago were now tall and towered above the roof in some places, but strategically placed so that the lovely view across the fields to the river was not spoilt by drooping branches. Memories of things he thought were buried and forgotten began to intrude upon his thoughts.

Enderly itself had not been changed by large modern estates or new shops. The small post-war estate by the school looked neglected but the Green Man pub was well cared for and inviting. He made a bed and breakfast booking for one night in the pub, had a bar snack and looked forward to revisiting his old haunts. He made brief enquiries about Primrose House and Janet Lacey.

'She's still living there,' the red-headed publican told him. 'Are you a friend?'

'Oh, no, she was a friend of my father's many years ago.'

He was anxious not to draw attention to his interest in her and hoped he had not said too much. Ronald wanted to bide his time and consider with care how he would approach Janet. It had been a long time.

Holidays with Aunt Janet and Uncle James, and later briefly with Janet, had been a refuge for the quiet and introverted child after his mother had died and his father had been away from home most of the time. He hated Northumberland and the time he spent there with his father's aunt and uncle. They were old wrinklies, fussy and lacking in affection, far too ancient to understand his needs although he had understood that they were well meaning. Two young children must have been hard work for them. He could not wait to escape from them so he studied hard and eventually obtained a degree in dentistry, after which he emigrated to Australia as soon as he could make the arrangements. A new start in a new country was what he needed. Felicity was now remembered as an unfortunate relative, spiteful and lacking in conscience, a sister whom he did not want to see again as long as he lived. He received the odd postcard from her, views of mountains and bears, but, after a brief check to see if she, horror of horror, was anticipating visiting him and his family, relegated them to the dustbin. He sent her the occasional Christmas card and postcard and that was more than enough.

At the age of sixty-two he found himself a widower and alone in Melbourne, his only daughter having married and moved to Queensland. He set off on his travels after taking a well-earned retirement from his practice and after stops in Singapore and Paris eventually arrived in Russetshire. From there he planned to revisit Northumberland and his first home in London. There was no hurry and Australia and the retirement residence he planned to buy, possibly on the Whanregarwen Road in Alexandra, not too far from Melbourne, could wait. The incentive was not the same without his wife and soulmate of so many years. Primrose House was the first place that had roused a real spark of interest in him during his trip. He wondered if Aunt Janet would welcome him with open arms after so many years. She had been kind to him, unlike his Uncle James.

Ronald stepped gingerly along the brick path in front of Primrose House, which was uneven and flaking in places, invasive moss and weeds were wrecking havoc despite Robbie's intensive efforts. As Felicity had earlier, he noticed the new knocker and bell push. He tried them both after attempting to rehearse for a few moments in his mind what he would say to Janet if she answered the door.

Silence pervaded. He tried the bell once again. It appeared that nobody was coming to open the front door. It's quite likely that Aunt Janet is deaf, he cogitated as he walked round the side of the house to where he remembered the kitchen door had been years ago, with a small flight of rickety iron steps leading up to it. I'll try that, he thought, there was a light shining from a window on the side of the house, someone must be around. The steps and door to the kitchen were there, just the same as he recalled them.

He climbed the icy steps with care noting the frosty white crystals glittering on their edges. He knocked on the door but the only sound he could hear was the wind whistling through the bare branches of a nearby birch tree. The normally attractive and well cared for garden was deserted and cloaked with grey-white winter dullness. He tried the black iron latch that protruded from the kitchen door and discovered it lifted easily under his hand. Stepping into the kitchen on to the red polished tiles, just as he had as a small child, he called out 'Hullo,' several times but nobody came, causing him to glance with unease around the large old kitchen that looked much the same as it had in the past. The scrubbed pale pine kitchen table he remembered was in the centre of the room and a battered tin tray was placed in the middle of it. There were some tea cups, saucers and small plates on it together with what he imagined were sandwiches or cakes covered with a clean cloth. The smell of smoked salmon and egg sandwiches reached his nostrils. Hmm, Aunt Janet must be expecting someone to tea, he thought. He called out again to try and rouse Janet or a possible house maid, to no avail. He looked at the old Aga; memories of sitting on a wooden stool next to it when he was a small lonely child mourning for his mother came back with startling clarity. A picture of Felicity trying to force his hand and thin young arm on to the hot plate on the top of the stove in the hope that he would squeal like a pig going to the slaughter came into his mind. It was a sharp memory and so clear that it could have happened yesterday. More often than not he did squeal and he still had some scars on his arms to prove what had happened but had not told anyone how he got those, even his wife. She had asked him a few times but he had been too frightened and ashamed to tell anyone about the burns. There had been no doubt in his mind at the time it happened that Felicity would have thought of something more cruel with which to torment him if he had told anybody. He realized now that she had been jealous of her little brother, unhappy and restless, and had forced some of her misery upon him.

A cold voice calling out to Janet that tea would soon be ready cut across his reminiscing. Footsteps approached the kitchen. Oh God, a Canadian accent and a grating familiar voice like chalk being sharpened by a blunt tea knife reached out to him from the past – it could be Felicity – yes, he was sure it was. His heart was beating and bumping so fiercely in his chest that he was convinced it could be heard. What on earth could she be doing here? Sponging on Janet was the first thing that came to mind. He turned with unusual speed towards the back door and opened it but as he stepped out he collided with an elderly man. Instinctively his arm shot forward to fend off the newcomer. There was a sickening bouncing sound and final thud as the man fell down the steps and hit the ground. The stranger opened his eyes briefly and appeared stunned. Panic set in. The man was not dead, thank goodness, but Ronald would, quite out of character, have to make sure he remained unconscious for a while. He could not risk meeting Felicity or having the man describe him, at least not until he was well away from the scene. He carefully shut the kitchen door, crept as quietly as he could down the metal steps and picked up a large stone from the side of a bed that had been planted with wallflowers by Robbie ready for the spring. Without thinking he brought the stone down with some force on the side of the man's head. Not too hard he thought, at worst that would give him a bad headache. It should enable him to get away from Primrose House without being spotted by Felicity or recognised if the man gained consciousness too quickly. He was not wearing gloves. Oh God, fingerprints and DNA. He dipped the stone into a watering can that had been left at the side of the steps. That would deal with some of the problem anyway. He looked round the deserted garden, heaved a sigh of relief and made his way to the gate as fast as he could walk. The whole venture had been a mistake. He had forgotten what tumultuous emotions Felicity evoked in him as a child and could even now after so many years. At last he could admit that he hated her. It was a relief. She was a psychopath and he would like to get rid of her once and for all if the opportunity ever came his way, though he was not sure if he had enough courage to murder anyone. He was highly principled and it was alien to his naturally gentle nature. What had she done to him?

He scurried down the road to the Green Man and told the land-lord that he had decided not to stay the night after all. He swiftly placed his luggage into the boot of his hired car and without delay left Enderly and its associated memories behind him. He needed time to think and recover from the feelings of sheer blinding panic that had reared up when he heard his sister's voice. He turned the car northwards when he got on the motorway at Russhampton. Northumberland could be a good peaceful place for a while, but he would be back when he had recovered from the shock of the recent events at Primrose House. A clever man like he was should be able to plan a suitable revenge for the misery Felicity had inflicted upon him in the past. He had not thought about that for many years but bile now rose up and he felt an unpleasant burning in his chest which would not be easy to remove. His hate was beginning to override his commonsense.

The red-headed landlord was for a moment perplexed when Ronald cancelled his booking. He was sure he had seen the man somewhere before. That tapir like nose and the strange flecked blue eyes appeared familiar. Perhaps he resembled someone he knew. Oh well, he would probably remember later on. He shrugged his broad rippling shoulders and disappeared into the cellar to do some stocktaking before his busy evening began.

Chapter 19

A Bridge Evening

The bridge sessions in the Green Man at Enderly were becoming very popular. Some new members had joined the club and there were at least eight tables in play on Tuesday evenings. Overall they were a friendly bunch of people. Felicity and Marianne had a few arguments but were soon able resolve their difficulties. Felicity was far more interested in watching Robbie, or Tom Hands as she thought of him, and wondering how she was going to deal with him. He was a respected member of the club and her Aunt Janet needed his assistance in Primrose House. He drove her to the shops and was generally, she had to admit, useful. What was his game though, working incognito? There was no doubt in her mind that he did not need the money. He must be peculiar but not so odd that he would not take a good chunk of money if it was left to him in the old girl's will; nobody was that daft she told herself, or were they? She attempted to ignore any pleasant feelings she had towards him. She found her thoughts centring far too often round the enigma and she wondered too how much longer Janet would live. She estimated that she could not live more than another year or two. She would have to resolve the Tom Hands problem fairly soon though she had begun to wonder if Robbie's share of her aunt's money was large enough to worry about.

Jeremy Mace, shattered by the death of his son and father within such a short time, was admitted to Russhampton Hospital after suffering a stroke and was not expected to live more than a few days. Felicity anticipated with interest that there would soon be another funeral to attend. Jeremy was now unlikely to inherit any of Aunt Janet's money and that at least was, for her, a good result. That silly lazy old Jeremy has got his come-uppance, she told herself with satisfaction.

One evening at the bridge table a few days later she had to stop herself laughing out loud during a game when she thought about him and found her mind wandering. Marianne's puzzled and annoyed stare urged her to concentrate on the cards in her hands. Their opponents did not mind and were quick to take advantage. Felicity felt Marianne's warning foot touch hers. She instantly relaxed and knew she was being silly to be thinking about Jeremy's imminent demise and worrying about Robbie's name being on Auntie's will. She should be concentrating on her game of bridge which was more enjoyable and important than her daydreams about money; they could wait.

The next couple they played that evening were Patsy and John. Felicity had dubbed them the lovebirds and enjoyed watching their gauche efforts to communicate their obvious deep affection. Felicity experienced a genuine glimmer of friendship for the odd couple which was alien to her usually abrasive nature. Patsy and John were now regular bridge partners and Robbie had found a new partner, a young man he had first met in Little Brinton. At first Robbie had found him conceited and arrogant, but they played well together in spite of his earlier reservations.

Felicity found it difficult to understand why the skinny Patsy had not jumped at the chance of getting closer to John Elk. He obviously adored her but they rarely showed any physical close-ness, just the occasional linking of arms like old friends. She wondered if they would ever get round to tumbling into bed together and her mind deviated once again as she considered the possibilities. They reminded her of a couple of stick insects, clumsy and ungainly as they circled around each other.

Patsy too was wondering the same thing. She was perplexed and concerned about her strong feelings for John. Could she force herself to share a bed and have sex with any man? He was a perfect gentleman. The habit of repressing any natural sexual urges had been with her for a long time though her reserve was beginning to crack. Her feelings for the opposite sex had remained dormant for so long, making the stirring in her lower body that surged without warning when she looked at John Elk very difficult to control.

She squinted at John through her modern oval glasses with their expensive light titanium frames. Her face softened and she longed to stroke his vivid springy ginger hair, feel it curl round her fingers and touch his strong masculine chin. Could she do it? She sighed and he glanced at her with undisguised concern. If only that wretched boy in Germany had not hurt her, mentally and physically. She was an intelligent woman and knew that it was about time she came to terms with that horrific incident. She had wasted too many years fretting over that German boy, probably the best years of her life. She could have got married and had a family, then ... well she would not have met John. He was worth waiting for. 'Hartz Mountain God', she remembered she had labelled the German boy. He had blond hair and broad shoulders. She had fancied him and had been too easily led into the bushes on the last evening of the holiday. She still remembered the Brinton Comprehensive School Band and the German School Band playing together, the music loud and skilfully blending, German beer for the adults, sausages and mustard with bread rolls and lemonade for the young bandsmen and women. She had wanted him to make love to her, but instead he had raped her, brutally and painfully, then laughed at her with derision, leaving her sobbing and shattered, convinced that she could not be attractive to any man and her best course in life would be to steer clear of the male sex. It was a secret she had kept too long and she had allowed the memory to fester and ruin her life, until now.

'Time for a break,' the director announced in his crunchy old voice and the players who had finished their current game moved, like a thirsty herd of cattle jostling to be the first in the queue, towards a bar counter the landlord had strategically placed in a corner of the room where it would be easy for him or his staff to serve alcoholic drinks or coffee and biscuits according to the members' preferences. As if telepathic the red-headed landlord appeared exuding enthusiasm and charm, hoping the players would dip deep into their pockets and indulge in a few glasses of his more expensive liquors. He was not often lucky. Most of the bridge players were cautious with their money and in any case preferred coffee.

'There is a nice glass of wine, and a packet of crisps if you want one,' would form part of his regular patter. 'Come on folks, we have the best Russetshire handmade pork scratchings!' But his efforts made only a small dent on the desires and spending habits of the bridge club clientele. One week he had sent his most glamorous barmaid Betsy Ann to serve the bridge players. Betsy Ann was a bleached blonde who fluttered long false eyelashes and whose skimpy T-shirts exposed the tops of large breasts that looked like soft downy plumped-up pillows. Sales did not improve and in spite of some of the male bridge players gawping inanely at her bust they managed to ignore her come-hither comments like 'What can I do you for dear?' which interested most of his punters. He decided that she would be better employed behind the bar with some of his regular beer drinkers who were more appreciative of her charms.

Some of the members would leg it into the pub garden to smoke during the break, frowned on and muttered about by some of the older ladies, or just get a breath of fresh air and clear their heads in an effort not to get too irritated with a partner's poor play. It was never ever their fault, of course, when mistakes were made.

John Elk urged Patsy to put her coat on and go outside with him for a few minutes. He suggested that they could walk down the road a little way and get some air though all he really looked forward to was a moment or two alone with her.

They linked arms, a habit they had now accepted as the norm, went out of the back door of the pub and a short distance down the now deserted lane at the back.

'The cool evening air will do you good, Patsy,' he said looking at her pale face with concern. 'Are you feeling all right?

She turned her face towards his and caught her breath. To her surprise, and his, she placed her arms around his neck and tentatively kissed his lips.

John gasped momentarily then held her close.

'Oh, I thought that this day would never come, I didn't—'

She kissed him once again and they were soon in a close and breathtaking embrace. Patsy thought she would faint, she had been longing to kiss him for so long though she hadn't been able to admit that to herself. It was as if some curtain in her mind had been dragged back and light had flooded in. Her eyes softened and her usual sharp reactions subsided. She was, she realised with interest, almost acquiescent. It was a start. She had overcome one barrier but could she overcome another and get even closer to this man? Could she be the kind of warm loving woman he wanted? She was not quite sure but time alone would tell.

The colour had flooded back to her face and John beamed. They went back to the bridge room with renewed energy and the knowledge, although little had been said, that they were destined to be together, one way or another. He would bide his time and when he thought she was ready, he would ask her to be his wife.

Felicity lifted the glass of bubbly lemonade to her mouth and the gas whisked uncomfortably into her nostrils causing her to cough. Robbie was standing by her side and she glanced at him with an apologetic, or as near as she could get to that, expression on her face. He turned a slightly flushed face towards her. She scowled. Huh, looks as though he is going through the menopause, she thought uncharitably. Except that he is the wrong sex and a little old for that nonsense. Perhaps he is ill and might die, the crass thought lingered. Well, she could accept that. A spurt of selfish relief welled up like a hiss of gas from a volcano. It could save her a lot of trouble. Life in Enderly had become quite agreeable, she now had plenty of lolly, new clothes and a crafty, if somewhat tricky, old bird with whom to play a good game of bridge. Robbie was a useful chauffeur but chauffeurs and gardeners could be replaced. She didn't want to rock the boat at present and her devious mind, as usual, bolted ahead.

Robbie stared for a moment at Felicity and reflected on what an atrocious woman she was. His limbs ached and tiredness threatened to swallow him. The drugs he was taking for prostate cancer swamped him and made him feel very tired but he was not going to give Felicity the satisfaction that she craved. She had so far kept the information that he was Janet's evacuee to herself. No doubt she had some devious reason for that. He could live as long as Janet, possibly a good few years longer, and his mission now to protect her loomed even greater. Think positively, do not give in, had become his motto in recent months. Felicity was not going to win.

Chapter 20

Ronald's Second Visit

Ronald turned his small hired car into the new tarmac car park at the side of the Red Rooster in Little Brinton. He had made a bed-and-breakfast booking for two nights, which he hoped would be long enough for him to complete his business in Enderly, though if need be he could always stay another day or two. Northumberland had been blustery and unwelcoming and spending the Christmas break on his own had not been much fun. Chat during the evening with the grouchy publican, following some skilful probing, revealed that a local solicitor had fallen down some steps at the back of a house in Enderly and had died. Ronald felt a tightening of his neck muscles and struggled to avoid flinching.

'What happened, how exactly did that come about, was it an accident?'

'I don't know, the local police think foul play could have been involved but they haven't arrested anyone yet.'

So the old fart died. That was bad luck, or was it? He was surprised that he felt so little remorse. Oh well, they will have something more dramatic to deal with soon. He turned his head away from the landlord and tried to avoid displaying an expression of sheer joy on discovering this welcome news. The old boy will not be able to identify me now, praise be to God. He placed his hands together under the bar counter in a gesture of prayer and ordered a double whisky. Excitement and anticipation threatened to overwhelm him.

He had grown a short beard and a thick moustache during his

stay in Yorkshire and purchased some new spectacles with clumsy thick brown frames in the belief that he would not be recognised when he returned to the Green Man to do some last-minute research. There was no way he could hide his tapir-like nose, a legacy from his mother Anne, but he was convinced that his disguise was adequate.

An evening meal in the Green Man bar would be a good start. He sat at a small table in the dingiest corner and, after ordering his favourite cod and chips with mushy peas, which he smothered with tomato sauce, he sipped a pint of strong local cider and sat back to listen. He had taken the precaution of buying a copy of the *Everton Journal* so that he could, if need be, pretend he was reading and lift it up in front of his face. He did not want to meet Felicity. If she recognised him he would be robbed of all of his planning and pleasurable revenge. He was looking forward to rewarding her for past indignities. The time spent apart had not softened his feelings towards his sister but had served to fuel his hate.

Ronald soon discovered that a small bridge club met in the pub on Tuesdays. He remembered Felicity liked playing card games when she was a child, and mentioned that she was learning to play bridge in one of her brief letters from Canada shortly after she left England. There were some bridge results posted on a notice board by the bar and he decided to check later to see if her name was on the list. He looked round with interest as Robbie and Pat came into the pub and sat at the next table. Robbie looked familiar in a vague sort of way but, he could not remember where he could have seen him before. Old Pat he did not know but when he commenced chatting to his companion Ronald became alert and excited. Robbie had to attend the hospital in Russhampton the next day, his appointment apparently scheduled for the afternoon.

'I won't be able to go to Primrose House and do the tidying up in the garden as planned. Joyce Skillet has an afternoon off too but Felicity should be able to look after Janet and prepare the tea. I can't stand the woman but she does have her uses,' he said, an anxious note surfacing in his voice.

Pat grunted in agreement. 'Janet Lacey has been lucky to have you to keep an eye on her for so long,' he said with feeling. 'You're not so old as I am, I'm getting on for ninety. I'm so sorry that you have to struggle with prostate cancer.' His weak old eyes filled with tears. 'Have you told Mrs Lacey?'

'No, there's no point,' Robbie responded. 'She wouldn't remember for more than five minutes. I'm glad to have the job to keep me occupied. They tell me that the cancer is at present under control, indeed I hope to keep an eye on that vile niece for as long as necessary.'

Ronald was more than interested. He was in wholehearted agreement with Robbie's assessment of Felicity. Well, he wouldn't have to worry about her for much longer. The stage was set. Everything would be clear for his planned action the next day. What luck to discover that only dotty Aunt Janet and Felicity would be at home in the afternoon.

The next morning he ate a hearty breakfast that consisted of eggs and bacon, fried bread, mushrooms and good strong coffee in the Red Rooster dining room. The thought of the interesting day that stretched before him had stimulated his appetite. He filled up his hired car with petrol at a garage on the road from Little Brinton to Enderly. He would need a full tank early the next day when he made his departure from Little Brinton to Heathrow. He planned to stay in a hotel there for a short time and if possible catch an earlier flight back to Australia than the one he had originally booked. If his business went as planned he did not want to hang about too long, indeed he thought it would be sensible to collect his belongings from Little Brinton and depart that evening. He parked the little blue Peugoet in a small layby that bordered the tiny Enderly village green. There were two other cars there and he hoped that his would not be too memorable. It would be too bad if he was traced by anyone after he had completed his business.

The March winds whipped cold fingers round Ronald's stubby legs as he trudged up the rise to Primrose House. He had taken the precaution of buying a good thick Harris tweed suit in Northumberland; he wanted to look like an English gentleman even if he had acquired a slight Australian accent. He was glad of the thick trousers now. The surrounding area was deserted, it was not a good day for walking by the river or in the nearby fields and he looked with caution at the house. He couldn't see anyone peeping out of the windows in the front. He would risk walking round the side of the house and try the kitchen door once again. It was left unlocked, which was convenient, just as it had been when he was last in Enderly. It had been raining earlier in the day and the metal steps shone, their slippery glistening black treads gleaming in the weak winter sunshine. He mounted the steps with caution, holding on to the shaky rail that was placed on one side and wondered what would have happened if the old chap he had met last time had been able to grab it. The stone, pale yellow and Cotswold, which he had picked up to hit the side of the old boy's head, was missing. The only stones that he could see now exhibited grey mottled surfaces.

The kitchen door opened with some reluctance and creaked in a disconcerting manner as he lifted the latch. Jack, who was sitting by Janet's feet in the dining room, growled and barked once or twice, then there was silence. The dog had been soothed by Janet and told that nothing was wrong. Ronald heaved a sigh of relief.

The old Aga gave out its familiar comforting warmth and the thick rough pine kitchen table he remembered so well from his childhood was now covered with a wipe-clean checked red and green cloth which was no doubt Felicity's doing. Two fine china teacups and saucers and a plateful of rich Belgian chocolate biscuits covered with plastic film sat on a pretty floral tray. He couldn't smell any sandwiches but Felicity's favourites were prepared and waiting in the large old-fashioned fridge that chugged away in the corner of the room. He heard footsteps approaching the door which linked the kitchen with the hall. He held his breath. The door swung open and he confronted his sister.

'Who on earth ...' she uttered, surprise distorting her face. 'Who the bloody hell are you?'

'Don't you know me?' He shuffled slightly forwards. He gave her a welcoming smirk as the fingers of his right hand slid down into his trouser pocket to grip something he had placed there earlier.

'No, or is it? It can't be ...' She inched closer. 'Ronald?' She smiled as a warm welcoming expression lit up her face. Heavens ... after all those years apart. He was here, really here, her brother; the brother she had often thought about but who had shown so little interest in contacting her over the years. A warm glow spread across her chest and excitement caused her pale cheeks to achieve a soft pink blush. Her little brother ...

He positioned himself near to the Aga and looked at the hotplates. Childhood memories flooded back, vivid and unforgiving. He remembered sitting on a wooden stool warming himself and Felicity pressing his arm with force on to the hot surface of the Aga, laughing and warning him not to make a sound. He didn't. Bitter bile forced itself into his mouth as he remembered. Something snapped. His next movement was not one he had planned but he seized her by the arm, he was larger and stronger than her now, pulled up her sleeve and slammed her arm down on to the heated surface. She was too surprised to resist. A smell of burning flesh permeated the room. She, unlike the stoic little brother of their childhood, screeched 'Ooooh ... aaarrh ... you beast! Are you mad?' Fear and anxiety rushed through her body with such force that her lungs felt fit to burst. Jack barked furiously in the dining room but Janet was sound asleep, oblivious and unheeding. She was becoming deaf and there was nobody else who was able to come to Felicity's aid. After what seemed an eternity to the unfortunate Felicity, although it was only a minute, he swung her round and pulled a length of thick cord out of his pocket. His eyes were bright and manic and a small twisted smile curled round his mouth.

'This should fit neatly round your neck. Remember the time when you put a dog collar on mine and dragged me round on a lead? I couldn't have been more than four years old and the deep wheals on my neck took weeks to heal. Mum had not long died and nobody was interested in my troubles. Dad left us to fend for ourselves. Unfeeling bitch! What a rotten sister to have. I have never forgiven you.'

Felicity tried to back away but he held her in a vice-like grip. Panic and pain threatened to overcome her. Clutching her with strong determined fingers he looped the cord with a surprising swiftness around her wrinkled neck and pulled.

'Come on, doggy, doggy,' he drawled, 'see how you like it. You didn't mind doing that to me.'

Felicity started to choke and struck out violently with her arms but with little effect. Ronald laughed with glee. The cord round her neck was tightening and she knew she would not remain conscious for very long. What on earth had got into him!

Ronald dragged her to the back door which he opened, for a brief moment removing one wiry hand from her shoulders in order to push her towards it.

'Down the steps with you! Nice tumble should complete the job. Vile bitch!'

Ronald was enjoying himself. A rush of adrenalin urged him on and his hysterical laugh echoed round the room, loud and high-pitched, but only Felicity could hear it. He had waited a long time for this treat and had not realized how much the need for retribution and revenge had grown and festered within him over the years they had been apart. He relaxed for a moment and took a brief look at the steep slippery metal steps. He wanted to make sure her decent was swift, direct and effective.

'You are soon going to meet your maker!' he shrieked, a mad demonic note surfacing in his voice, then he emitted an eerie blood-curdling sound, shaking his head in a weird way from side to side, saliva frothing from his mouth like a rabid dog.

Felicity rallied and seized her chance. She struck out with a foot and as it met his shins Ronald lost his balance. He plunged down the steps dragging the unfortunate Felicity, reeling and spinning, with him. The pain from the bumps inflicted on him by the metal as he descended was excruciating. The last thing he saw was Felicity's shocked face just above his before his neck snapped and merciful oblivion overtook him. Fortunately for Felicity he loosened his grip on the cord just before he reached the ground and her fall was broken by his soft rotund body. She struggled for a moment or two in an attempt to loosen the rope that still threatened to choke her, almost succeeded, then fainted.

The sound of loud voices penetrated her consciousness. First a woman's voice, light and high, shrill with emotion.

'The ambulance is on the way, she is breathing. It would be better not move her, she might have injured her back.'

A man's voice, deep and calm, responded. 'I think the man is dead – there's not much we can do for him. He was probably an intruder.'

Some intruder, Felicity thought. A once dear brother she had not seen for so long. Her brother ... perhaps he had a good reason for wanting her to die but, oh ... her own brother, that quiet little boy she remembered so well. He was such a timid child, no spunk, and a gawky quiet teenager later, but in her way she had retained some affection for him, even if it was disturbed and bent. Communication had been sparse over the years but she could not have murdered him. No, never! Did she really hurt him as a child? She supposed she must have but could not remember the details with any degree of clarity. She did recall that they had been unhappy children.

She did not open her eyes and pain in her right leg threatened to traumatize her. She didn't want to discuss with anyone why her brother might have wanted to kill her. That could wait. She would say she had lost her memory until she had time to plan her answers and come to terms with the horror that had been inflicted upon her.

'The police are here,' the woman's voice continued, her more normal local tone becoming evident. 'It was lucky we came today, my day off too. I remembered that the milkman had not called as usual, I can't think why but thought I had better leave Mrs Lacey some fresh milk for her tea. There was not much left in the fridge yesterday and I didn't think that Felicity would notice until she prepared the tea. It was a good job I had my mobile with me.'

Joyce turned to her husband.

'There is not much hope of getting into Everton now for that meal, the police will want statements and goodness knows what!'

Felicity, who continued to keep her eyes closed, was moved

gently on to a stretcher and taken to Everton General Hospital. After the police had examined Ronald's body, and DI Holmes had arrived, it was moved to a local mortuary pending further enquiries, and DI Holmes thought that there would be many, especially as Felicity had a deep rope mark on her neck, a severe burn on her arm and was lucky to be alive.

Joyce and her husband stayed to reassure Janet and keep her company.

'Felicity will soon be home,' she told her with a confidence she did not feel. 'My daughter has gone to the hospital with her and will let us know.'

Joyce thought it would not be wise to mention the police to Janet but she knew they would want to question her to discover if she had heard anything unusual that afternoon. She was concerned that her elderly employer would be confused. With luck, she may be able to provide some clues to the afternoon's tragic events but Joyce doubted whether the poor soul would remember anything useful.

Chapter 21

A Change of Heart

DI Peter Holmes and DS John Cross considered their options and discussed the situation and the facts as far as they knew them. DI Holmes decided that he would go to Everton Hospital after checking the scene of the 'accident' or 'attempted murder' for clues, and if Felicity had recovered consciousness he could perhaps question her. Joyce Skillet was warned not to move anything in the kitchen and the room was checked for fingerprints and DNA. Burnt skin clung to one of the Aga plates and the odious smell lingered. DS Cross, a gentle but intuitive young detective, questioned Janet.

'Did you hear anything, Mrs Lacey?' he asked after he had explained, with the support of a concerned Joyce Skillet, that Felicity had surprised an intruder and had gone to the hospital to be 'checked out'.

'No', Janet said, 'at least I can't remember anything. Jack barked for a while but he is old now and imagines things, it was probably only Felicity rattling the tea cups. I patted him and told him to be quiet. I must have dozed off after that. I did wake up once, I thought I heard a scream but it is so difficult for me to distinguish between my dreams and reality now, you know … I am getting deaf, too.'

'That is all right Mrs Lacey,' he replied kindly. He was not going to get anywhere with this line of enquiry and he decided to let the old lady rest. Joyce hovered anxiously at the door.

'I'll get someone to stay with her,' she said. 'There is a reliable woman in the village who helps out occasionally. I'll telephone her.'

'That's a good idea,' he said. 'Someone should stay with her. She shouldn't be left on her own today, although the intruder is dead and won't be worrying her again in a hurry. However, that back door must be kept locked in future. Of course, this is a crime scene, and you must warn the woman if she comes not to move anything.'

'I will stay then,' Joyce said. 'I can ensure everything is left untouched.'

DI Holmes approached Felicity's hospital bed quietly. He had been warned that she was still very confused. Her right leg had twisted under her but was not broken. She was fortunate that her injuries had not been worse. There was, however, the possibility of some concussion.

'Mrs Brown,' Peter said, 'I would like to ask you a few questions about the intruder. It would help us if you could tell us anything you remember about the incident.'

Felicity hesitated. Her head ached despite the tablets she had swallowed to ease the throbbing. Her leg felt uncomfortable from the twisting inflicted upon it as she tumbled but understood that it was only badly bruised and her arm was still very painful as she had sustained a third degree burn.

She turned her head to look at the detective. Nice enough man, she thought, pretty astute, it's no good trying to fool him. He will find out about my brother soon enough. She decided to be honest with him and try to face the horror inflicted upon her.

'The intruder was my brother Ronald Brown,' she said in, what was for her, a soft quavering voice.

'I haven't seen him for many years, I thought he was in Australia, it was a complete surprise. I had no idea he felt so antagonistic towards me.'

What on earth did I do to deserve his hate, she thought, and really had no idea. Her face was pale and drawn. The young nurse who hovered at the door of Felicity's single room looked at her with concern.

'We have found his passport and other papers which were in his coat so have established his identity,' DI Holmes said. If you can think of anything that can help us further please tell me. We have yet to find out where he was staying and how long he has been in this country. There were no flight tickets in his wallet which is rather odd. We imagine he had booked a return flight.'

'Is he ...? Felicity found it hard to say 'dead'.

'Yes,' Di Holmes said. 'I am sorry.'

Felicity did not look too sorry, just relieved. She is a hard nut, the detective told himself but who could blame her under the circumstances with a brother intent on murder!

A doctor appeared at the door.

'Ms Brown needs to rest. Can you come back tomorrow? She has suffered a severe blow to the head and we need to obtain some X-rays now.'

The detective had no option but there was a lot he needed to ask this woman. He still did not trust her but in this instance she appeared to be innocent. She had fallen down the same steps as Peter Mace. Perhaps she was not the one who had pushed the solicitor after all, but he would keep an open mind about that.

DI Holmes made some enquiries in the Green Man but the landlord had no recollection of anyone who answered Ronald's description staying there. He did think the man may have had a meal in the pub the day before, but was not sure.

DS Cross was given the job of checking the local area to try and discover if a Ronald Brown had booked into a hotel or pub. He was fortunate to receive a call from the landlord of the Red Rooster in Little Brinton. He had heard something about the attempted murder on the local news and realised that Ronald Brown fitted the description of a man who had booked into his pub for two nights bed and breakfast. He had not returned that evening and his baggage was still in his room, but his hired car was not in the car park.

DS Cross visited the Red Rooster and checked out Ronald's room and luggage. His flight tickets were in his case. He had been in England since September. There were some details of a hotel in Northumberland where he had stayed over Christmas, and a leaflet about the Green Man in Enderly and a note in his diary concerning a booking the day Peter Mace died. There was a copy of a deed for a grave for Anne Brown who had been buried in

Roehampton Cemetery just after the Second World War together with a used District Line ticket from Earls Court to Wimbledon. His hire car was found in Enderly the next day.

In the light of the latest evidence it seemed likely that Felicity Brown was not after all responsible for the death of Peter Mace. Unbeknown to her, her brother had been in Enderly the day he died and knew how to get into Janet Lacey's house where he had stayed as a child. If he had been in the kitchen and was surprised by Felicity's approaching footsteps he could have rushed out of the back door and bumped into Peter Mace. It could have been an accident but the blow on the side of the man's head was ominous and pointed to murder. Forensics could now check the fingerprint found on the stone with Ronald Brown's.

The medical staff at the hospital decided to keep Felicity under observation for a few days. She continued to display symptoms of shock and was very quiet. She told DI Holmes once again that she had no idea that her brother Ronald was in the country and would have been pleased to see him if she had known. For once he believed her. She was fond of him she stressed, he was her little brother. Why he had attempted to kill her she had no idea, and she really believed that. She had not seen him for many years, or his family in Australia, though she believed his wife was now dead and his daughter had recently got married. She had never met her niece and they exchanged very few letters, probably only once a year at Christmas.

Why would Ronald want to injure or kill me? Felicity continued to ask herself. It did not make sense, she was family after all. She wondered again about Ronald's accusations and found it difficult to believe that she had been such an unkind sister. Although she had forgotten so many things about their childhood she accepted that she had a tempestuous nature when young. She had a lot of time to think whilst lying in the hospital bed. What a monster she must have been to provoke her own brother to inflict such revenge upon her. Was she any better now? She had been driven by lust for money since she had been living with her aunt. The attempt on her life was a wake-up call and although to change her nature would not be easy, perhaps even impossible, she knew she must try.

She thought back to the last time she had seen Ronald a few months before she left for Canada and her visit to Aunt Janet. She had travelled to Northumberland to say goodbye to him. He was eighteen years old, a spotty-faced youth dressed in an old green woollen sweater and drainpipe trousers that were frayed at the hems and markedly short on his straggly and fast growing limbs. They did not have much money, or really much else of value in life. He had looked at her through brown flecked thick-framed glasses that covered eyes so similar to her own. His fine fair hair had stood up in tufts on his head and had reminded her of an odd yellow mop. They had hugged briefly and she had actually felt a tugging at the heartstrings when she left him. They were the same flesh and blood she remembered and were parting for what would probably be a long time, even for good. If she had been unkind to him when they were young she expected that he would forgive her and, with her innate lack of conscience, had not realised until now how deeply her actions had affected him.

On the second morning of her stay in hospital Robbie arrived to see her. He walked towards her in his usual relaxed and reassuring way, bearing a large bunch of bright yellow roses tied with gold ribbon and a card from the Enderly bridge club members. He hesitated but Felicity, her face softer than he had ever seen it before, flashed a tremulous smile and beckoned him to sit on a chair next to her bed. She was touched to see the flowers and the card which had been signed by all the members of the club.

'How are you feeling now?' he asked, and hesitated before taking the proffered seat. He flashed an anxious glance at the still deep pink line on her neck.

'Oh, not too bad,' she answered in an attempt to make light of the situation. 'I can go back to Primrose House tomorrow.' She grimaced with pain. Her leg was giving her gip. 'Auntie has apparently missed me. Well, she told Joyce she has and Joyce was good enough to bring me a few things I needed earlier today.'

Robbie thought that perhaps her aunt really had missed her. Janet might be glad of the company, even if it was only that provided by a crass avaricious niece.

'Well, yes,' he said, 'I don't doubt it.' He blew his nose and smoothed his hair back from his face, a nervous gesture he often made. 'Can I get you anything? Fruit, squash ...?'

'No, but I would appreciate it if you would drive me home tomorrow. I don't want any nosy taxi driver coming to pick me up or the local press chasing me, if that can be avoided.'

'Of course,' Robbie said and gave her a puzzled look. She was trying to be pleasant.

'Robbie ... ' She hesitated. 'There is something I must tell you. I have discovered that you were Aunt Janet's evacuee Tom Hands.' She clutched the edges of the sheet and blanket that covered her bed so hard that her burnt arm caused her to flinch.

For a moment Robbie was speechless. He opened his mouth to say something but words failed him and he closed it once again with a snap. It was the last thing he expected her to tell him. What had happened to her? It appeared that she had turned over a new leaf. It must be the trauma of seeing her brother again after so many years and the fact that he had tried to kill her. He did not think that this change of heart would last!

'I know you are a good man,' she continued, 'and have your reasons to work incognito for so long as a handyman and gardener. I will keep your secret. Will you do something for me?'

Robbie was once again lost for words. There must be a catch. What was she up to now?

'Well, that depends ...' He rubbed his forehead with his right hand and hoped he was not going to experience a bad headache. He felt tense and feared the worst.

'Just watch over me too,' she almost whispered with a catch in her throat and to his embarrassment stretched out one arm and touched his face gently as though she wished to show him some affection. Her eyes were moist and appealing. His stomach turned somersaults as he struggled not to show his revulsion.

He woke up with a start the next day as the sun poked shafts of bright light through the curtains in his bedroom. His head ached and was made worse by the clanking ring of his phone. It was Felicity.

'See you soon,' she said in an unusually soft girlie voice. 'I'm ready to go home.'

'I'll be there in about half an hour,' he managed to stutter.

He showered, dressed and shaved as fast as he could, though he felt like a car being driven with the brakes on. He swallowed a cup of strong coffee and the caffeine filtered through him giving him a welcome lift. He filled a bowl half full of cornflakes, dowsed them with milk and a large teaspoonful of sugar, and then swallowed them far too quickly. He would no doubt have indigestion and did not look forward to driving Felicity back to Primrose House. 'God, that ghastly bloody woman', he muttered, but she had been unlucky and he felt a a twinge of conscience. His mouth felt dry as he reached for his medication, too many damned pills he thought, and forced them down with the remains of his coffee. He, the reluctant employee, begrudging and irritable, made his way to Primrose House to collect Janet's beloved old Rover car and drive it to Everton Hospital to pick up Felicity. Was she his destiny? Heaven forbid! It was a ludicrous thought.

DI Holmes checked Ronald's fingerprints with the one found on the stone that had dealt the death blow to Peter Mace. It matched perfectly. That was one case that had been solved but he was not so sure about the demise of Matthew Mace.

Ronald's daughter was informed of her father's death and his attempt to murder his sister. She had little to say and refused to come to England to attend his funeral although his entire estate in Australia had been left to her. Following an inquest Ronald was cremated and his ashes scattered, as he had requested in his will, over his mother Anne's grave in Roehampton Cemetery.

Felicity did attend his funeral and cremation in Everton. She asked Robbie to drive her to the church and stay with her throughout the brief service for support. Janet was not well and unable to attend; there were no friends to say any kind words about his life. Felicity clutched Robbie's arm and although he was sympathetic with her plight the whole affair was to him like a bad, almost surreal, dream.

Felicity would never forgive Ronald or forget the horror she felt in the kitchen on the day of his death, or the corpse she had identified later as her brother, cold and lifeless. The experience had been sobering and caused her to reflect carefully once again about her life. He had looked quite different from the brother she had known years ago; now old and flabby, a waxy white creature with deep wrinkles etched into his brow, but his tapir nose and strange long lobed ears marked him out as Anne's son. A birthmark, on his right shoulder, small and brown like an acorn, provided definite proof of his identity. She had shuddered when she first saw him, almost heaved and turned her head away from the body. She looked at the pale grey floor in an effort to regain control.

'Yes, it is my brother Ronald,' she had mumbled and the the scenario in Janet's kitchen returned to her mind with unwelcome speed. Ronald had gone and in circumstances she must now make an effort to forget. Time would heal her wounds. She felt lonely and vulnerable. Janet was what she called gaga, she herself was over sixty years old and she began to wonder if she too would, like Auntie, have to endure a bleak old age. Auntie's money had provided her with the physical comfort that she had craved for so long but was that enough? She thought more each day about Robbie. What a nice man he was; she was beginning to enjoy his company and looked forward to seeing his thin intelligent face and deep hazel eyes.

Robbie wondered if this flippant woman, who had no apparent kind heart or conscience and was apparently crippled with greed for money, had changed. He hoped for everyone's sake that she had, but he was suspicious. She was treating him with respect now like an old friend but he doubted whether she had a sincere bone in her body. He would continue to watch his back.

'Can you check the security arrangements in Primrose House, perhaps change the locks?' Felicity asked him. 'The windows appear secure but the habit of leaving the back door unlocked for you, the milkman and Joyce will have to change. You must all have new keys.'

'I will see to it as soon as possible,' he said. He had long thought that would be sensible but Janet had been so trusting

Panic now threatened to overwhelm Robbie, kicking him in the guts and hurtling through his brain with cynical intensity when he considered Felicity's now frequently simpering and too-familiar attitude towards him. There was one thought uppermost in his mind – get away from her before it is too late! He doubted, however, that he could. Fate was closing in on him.

Chapter 22

Reconciliations and a Second Wedding

Felicity slowly regained her strength and was relieved to return to Primrose House in spite of the ordeal she had endured in the kitchen. She vowed get rid of that foul Aga if she ever inherited the house. Because Ronald was no longer in the picture, it was gratifying that his share of the estate could one day belong to her. That was some consolation for the trauma he had inflicted upon her and recompense for the suffering she had endured at his hands but it was cold comfort. Thank goodness she had not seen anything in the will that suggested that Ronald's share of Auntie's inheritance would be passed down to his daughter. Tom Hands, or rather Robbie, had only been left a small sum and she was now of the opinion that such a paltry amount was not worth worrying about. She was becoming fond of the man and it did not seem so important to her now whether or not he inherited some money although the thought remained that he did not need it and it should in fairness come to her. Despite her efforts to find him using the slimy detective, she had changed her mind about getting rid of him. Indeed, she had come to think of him as a friend since her 'accident', as she preferred to remember it. The attempted murder by her little brother was something that chilled and terrified even the cool Felicity and she tried not to think about it, although the horror of that afternoon would haunt her for the rest of her life.

Robbie would have been appalled if he had known that she cared for him in any way. The fact that she had warmed towards him surprised her as much as it would amaze him. She could tell he was not well and she would like to look after him. A motherly longing to hug him overcame her whenever she thought about him. She needed his friendship and wondered if she could throw herself on his mercy and gain his sympathy, but she was not adept at that type of behaviour. She knew it would beneficial to consider her options with care.

Janet too had warmed towards Felicity. She had been company for the ailing old woman, if somewhat prickly and vacillating, and Janet, ensconced in her confused and disintegrating world, was pleased to have her companionship. She was aware of her niece's lust for money but that did not matter because money and the acquisition of worldly goods no longer interested Janet.

The bridge club members welcomed Felicity back when she returned to play with Marianne after a few weeks' rest. Some shook her by the hand and others, to her embarrassment, put their arms around her shoulders to reassure her. It was a new experience for the once socially shunned Felicity. Her status had changed after Ronald's attempt to murder her, most members having been provoked into feeling sincere sympathy for the victim, despite the fact that she had not been one of their most popular players. Felicity felt some embarrassment at first but soon began to bask in and enjoy the unaccustomed attention and became more relaxed than she had for a long time. 'Anything we can do?' 'You can rely on us ...' 'Ring me at anytime if you would like to talk to someone ...' were some of the phrases she got used to hearing. She had been cold shouldered and disliked all her life because of her restless and difficult behaviour and she was, to her surprise, touched to the centre of her being and experienced a happiness she had not known before at any time in her life.

Patsy Croft and John Elk fussed over her.

'Dear Felicity,' Patsy gushed uncharacteristically as her face softened with genuine sympathy. 'We are here for you and were so sorry to hear about your dreadful ordeal.' John and Patsy were becoming noticeably closer as a couple and Felicity thought that the wedding to which she hoped to be invited, together with some of the other Enderly and Little Brinton bridge players, might soon be forthcoming. She was looking forward to it. There would probably be a good spread laid on for the guests that day in Little Brinton and she would buy an attractive outfit for the occasion.

'Welcome back, Felicity,' Robbie had announced earlier with his club chairman's hat on. Old Pat too had squeezed Felicity's arm affectionately. Felicity glowed with happiness, akin to a feeling she had not felt since she was a small child being rocked in her mother's arms. The attention she had craved all her life was now given to her. She mellowed, at least for a while, and became increasingly reconciled with the prospect of Robbie inheriting some of her aunt's money as she felt her affection grow for the man each day.

A week later Patsy surprised John by suggesting that they might spend a weekend together in Devon. She had found details about a bridge weekend that was to be held in a good hotel in Teignmouth. She had discovered from other bridge players in Little Brinton that the bridge there was always well organised and the food excellent. She showed John the brochure.

'There are attractive red cliffs and quite a reasonable beach to walk on,' she said in a matter-of-fact tone. 'It's nice little town with quite good shops and a few interesting places nearby to visit. A well-organised bridge company called 'Aces High' is running it and they have a sound reputation. We can book separate rooms, of course,' she continued, her small eyes twinkling as a smile fluttered round her pale pink mouth which had softened and looked almost feminine since she had been going out with John. A flush crept across her cheeks and she brushed the hair back from her face with neat manicured hands; nails painted with care to match her lips, John noticed. 'It will be fun. A chance to improve our bridge partnership.'

John hoped that was not the only partnership that would improve. He was getting restless and longing to get closer to the love of his life. They were not young and he didn't want to waste too many years, or even months, pussyfooting around as he thought of it. He agreed with alacrity and two weeks later they set off together in John's old Ford, their smart new suitcases nudging each other in the boot.

The bridge was as good and well organised as Patsy had suggested it would be and the food in the hotel well up to their expectations. They played well together and did not argue about the conventions or mistakes in their play which was unusual. There was often some small blip they discussed heatedly at the end of an evening, but not this time. John's thoughts were centred on how he could get Patsy into bed, indeed he was getting quite obsessed with the idea. Bridge was a secondary consideration.

Patsy kissed him briefly on the lips at the door of her room after the second evening of play finished at about eleven o'clock. It was the kind of affectionate kiss a daughter might give her father.

'I'm tired and must get my beauty sleep,' she said. 'It's getting late.'

She yawned, lifted her glasses, and rubbed the corners of her eyes.

John's face drooped and Patsy's heart lurched. She turned towards him and reached out for his one of his hands and stroked his long sensitive fingers. What was she doing? She turned and took an abrupt step towards the door. No, she could not ... but, why not? The touch of the brief kiss on her lips lingered and tingled, she longed to get closer to him, and the smell of his enticing aftershave, mmm ... so masculine ... what was it?

John turned his back on her. His narrow shoulders drooped and his thin gangly arms hung disconsolately by his sides as he crept along the thick fawn carpet that graced the centre of the corridor stretching towards the stairs. The prospect of being alone in his single room on the next floor was not a welcome one.

'John, oh John,' a voice, soft and urgent, sounded behind him.

He looked round and Patsy, a bewildered and forlorn expression on her face, held out her thin arms to him. Her pale blue evening shawl had slipped off one shoulder exposing a round and tantalising stretch of pink skin he longed to kiss.

'Are you sure, quite sure?' he asked, his breath coming in rapid rasps. He could not believe his luck. He turned on his heel and moved towards her.

'Quite sure!'

The past was no longer relevant. She loved John, really loved and wanted him. She wanted him close to her. Stunning realisation swept over her and the shackles that had held her in check for so long dropped away like autumn leaves being swept along by the wind. She led him into her room and locked the door. The passion that they shared together in her narrow hotel bed made up for all the miserable years endured in limbo; it had been worth waiting for.

The first words John spoke in the morning were to ask her to marry him, and soon.

'Darling Patsy,' he said. 'I can't live without you.'

It sounds corny, she thought, but I agree with every word.

'I can't live without you either,' she replied with sincerity and fervour.

She reached out her arms to hold him closer. Love for a man was marvellous. What a fool she had been to waste so many years as a miserable old spinster.

They drove into Exeter in the morning and purchased an engagement ring, sapphires and diamonds, 'like your eyes,' John said. In his sight she was lovely and he was happier than he had ever been in his life. She was his soulmate, someone he had thought he would never find.

They anticipated that the Enderly and Little Brinton bridge club members would be surprised, but the majority of them, like Felicity, had been looking forward to Patsy and John's wedding for some time. Old Mr Croft thought it was the best news he had ever heard. He had thought at one time that his daughter was too shrew-like to ever attract a member of the opposite sex. He longed to see her marry and enjoy life and perhaps have a family of her own, like so many of her school friends in the village had earlier. He could even suffer that lady vicar in Little Brinton church if she married them. He had found her even worse than some of the previous lady vicars who had been relegated to judging the local produce sale each autumn. They did not know the difference between a carrot and a turnip, his vegetables were the best but they never seemed to realize it. They were an ignorant lot. The next year they were to have a male vicar. There is hope yet, he thought with chauvinistic abandon that would have infuriated his daughter.

Patsy had at last become reconciled to the horror of the rape as a schoolgirl that had haunted her for so long and could now move on with confidence with John. Mr Croft had known that something dreadful had happened to his daughter when she went on a school holiday in her teens but would never discover what had taken place. Patsy had not told anyone about her ordeal except John Elk who had provided her with the friendship, love, patience and understanding that she needed.

A date was soon set for the wedding. It was to be held in Little Brinton Church in April. Invitations had been sent to all the bridge club members, family and other friends of the bride and groom. Felicity urged Robbie to drive her into Brinton where she purchased an expensive fine pale blue wool suit and small head band to match, soft Italian shoes and a lavish leather and fabric bag. She had regained her spirits after Ronald's attempts to shorten her life and plenty of cash and new clothes were, as always, essential to her well-being.

She showed her purchases to an embarrassed Robbie and pressed him into an opinion regarding the suitability of her goods, about which he had no idea.

'Does the colour flatter me?' she asked, her small eyes opened as wide as possible with feigned innocence and undoubted affection.

Robbie coloured. 'I am no expert Felicity. Ask Joyce Skillet or your aunt.'

'I am not interested in what they think, only your opinion,' she retorted.

Robbie cringed. What was the woman playing at now? She fluttered her newly acquired false eyelashes and leaned closer to him. He backed away. God, was she flirting with him? He hoped not. The phrase 'disaster threatens' passed through his mind and he heard alarm bells clanging. An unpleasant and persistent ache had invaded his forehead.

Felicity's hair was now tinted a pale auburn and she was convinced it made her look at least ten years younger. She was pleased with her new look and surprised that Robbie was not more responsive. He must have noticed. What was the matter with the man!

The wedding day in early April turned out to be slightly cool, but dry. Little Brinton Church was crammed with close family, villagers and bridge club members, some having to stand in discomfort close to the cold grey stone walls because all the pews were full. Patsy, despite her once sharp tongue, had many loyal friends and work colleagues anxious to see her tie the knot. John Elk was liked too and his parents, sister Joan and her husband and three young children were excited and pleased that their once lonely son and brother, who had appeared to be a confirmed bachelor, was at last getting married.

Old Mr Croft was dressed in a smart suit which was a change from his usual scruffy old tweed trousers and jacket. He was hardly recognisable.

'This is a great day,' he repeated to all and sundry, beaming. 'I never thought this would happen, marvellous. I have a lovely daughter who deserves to be happy.' He thought back guiltily to the many times he had told himself how glad he would be to get rid of his miserable child, a child he wished to be happy and had no idea how to help, but that bad patch was now behind them.

Patsy wore a cream satin dress scattered with seed pearls. A band of orange blossom on her head held in place a short cream lace veil that had belonged to her mother. Her friend Jenny Saunders was matron of honour and small cousin Jack, a gangly difficult child, proved himself to be a reluctant pageboy. The congregation gasped with admiration when they saw Patsy. She had abandoned her glasses for contact lenses and her hair had been curled and cut to flatter her face. The loose-styled dress suited her slim angular body ensuring that a feminine and attractive woman floated down the aisle.

The ladies of the Village Hall Committee in Little Brinton had also made an effort to attend and the chairman Ned Windsor looked proud of his club secretary. He liked Patsy, a feisty girl after his own heart. He had no time for weak women. He sat next to Mrs Blunt whom he had considered to be an old battleaxe when he first moved into the village shortly after Jack Headley left for Scotland, but they were now becoming close friends. They were an odd couple. She was an upright pillar in the local community, strait-laced, honest and determined, and quite different from Ned who had a criminal record, although the villagers, with the exception of Mrs Blunt, did not realise that. He had told her about his past, how he was imprisoned for killing his wife in a drunken stupor and had shared a cell with the bridge club's first chairman Jack Headley. She appreciated his honesty she told him, and promptly set about helping him to become a respected Little Brinton villager. He went along with that; it suited him. Jack had no idea that Ned was now living in Little Brinton and would have been very surprised if he had. Mrs Blunt held Ned's arm possessively and he smiled with obvious warmth. Many of the villagers noticed that he had mellowed since they had become close friends, indeed they hoped that there might be another wedding in the near future. He could be a difficult man when he wanted to be as some of the Village Hall Committee ladies knew. Used to getting their own way, even they were wary when dealing with Ned.

Felicity leaned close to Robbie in their pew near the front. He felt the unwelcome warmth of her plump thighs against his. He edged away but she placed her hand on his arm with an almost possessive and restraining gesture.

'This is a happy day Robbie,' she whispered, shifting herself so that she almost touched his body with her right hip. 'It is lovely to have such good friends. We are lucky.'

Robbie was not too sure he liked the word 'we' and an icy feeling claimed him like a clamp. He smelt her latest expensive floral perfume and shuddered. It crept into his nostrils and he blew his nose fiercely in an attempt to get rid of it.

Felicity held his arm for support as they left the church and made their way to the Red Rooster for a meal. Robbie, like a pitiful canary trapped in a small cage who could not stretch its wings and fly away, submitted to her attentions. She made sure that they sat next to each other at the wedding feast. When they toasted the bride and groom with champagne she turned her face to him and whispered, 'I wonder who will be next?' Robbie vowed vehemently that it would not be him. He had no doubt now that she fancied him. He was old and ill and she was the last woman in the world he wanted around him. He had felt happier when he thought she wanted to get rid of him. If Janet died, well, Felicity may be mistress of Primrose House. His job would be done, the wretched woman would have what she wanted, she would lose interest in him and his first priority in any case would be to escape from her clutches. He relaxed. If necessary he would move from Enderly, though he did not want to. He only had a few more years to live which he wanted to share with Janet.

Chapter 23

Rosalie

The small child scurried down the lane to the pale grey stone cottage. She was looking forward with eager antici-pation to seeing her mother. She liked the village school and had made a lot of friends but her mother was the most important figure in her young life. It was 1943 and her father had been drafted into the navy. He was serving as an officer somewhere in the Atlantic Ocean, they did not know exactly where, and his visits home were few and far between. They were proud of him. He was engaged in protecting food convoys, food essential for the country to survive. Her mother had told her many times that her daddy was doing a wonderful job for them all.

The Yorkshire hills rolled green and brown behind her home and the large uneven field at the back of the cottage, which was separated from their small garden by a wire fence and a thick hawthorn hedge, contained sheep whose frolicking lambs in the spring never ceased to amuse her with their antics. She was a clever child, happy, vivacious and full of energy, who showed academic promise.

She threw open the small garden gate and skipped like a small elf along the gravel path to the old wooden front door that was framed with bright red roses. As she approached, her mother threw open the door and lifted her into her arms.

'I thought I heard you coming, darling.' There were tears on her cheeks, her eyes edged with what appeared to the child to be a strange red tinge from crying.

'Mummy, what is it?' Rosalie whispered, as her small frame tensed.

'It is Daddy, dearest, he is ...' She did not know how to continue.

A voice from behind her she recognised as Granny Barbara's called out, 'Now Mary, the child will not find it easy to understand, come here dear, let me explain.'

'No, Mother, that is up to me.'

Her mother lifted her up and sat on a kitchen chair, balancing her on her knees.

'We, I ... have a telegram ... Daddy will not be coming home. He was brave and has given his life for his country. We too must be brave and carry on as he would want us to.'

'The child cannot understand,' Granny Barbara interrupted.

'I do,' Rosalie said, her face pale and strained. The vision of her beloved father sinking below cold turbulent water drifted in front of her eyes and would stay with her to haunt her dreams for a long time.

'What? Why Mummy?' she stuttered.

Mary tried to explain what had happened. 'Daddy's ship was hit by a torpedo.'

Rosalie tried to make sense of her explanation.

Life changed for Rosalie and Mary. They continued to live in the cottage but Mary who had been working part-time in a library in a nearby town had to find a full-time job to earn enough money to keep them in reasonable comfort. Granny Barbara, a widow, rather elderly and crotchety at times, or so it seemed to the young child, moved into the cottage to help look after Rosalie.

Rosalie resented Barbara's old-fashioned rules. She was a large woman who exuded Victorian values, strict and forceful. She was kind but nagged incessantly. 'Eat up those greens,' Don't lean on the table,' Hurry up or you will be late for school,' and so on. Rosalie loved her mother but was determined to leave home as soon as she could. She wanted to be a teacher and worked hard to get good grades at school.

Rosalie grew into a slim and energetic young woman. She would brush her fine brown hair to make it shine. 'At least one hundred strokes each time,' Granny Barbara told her, and it repaid her by exuding glints of red that lit up the brown. She often looked at her hair in her old bedroom mirror and wondered about her colouring. Her eyes were grey-blue flecked with brown, more flecks in the left eye than the right and emphasized by fine arched eyebrows. She did not look like anyone else in her immediate family. Perhaps some ancient ancestors had passed their genes to her. Her skin was fair and clear and she had an intriguing dimple in her left cheek. She was pretty but her mouth was slightly big for her face which her small straight nose tended to emphasise.

When she was eighteen her mother told her she was adopted.

'We wanted you, always, darling and I will love you until the day I die. We could not have children of our own and a friend told us about you and how you needed a mother and father .'

Rosalie was stunned but knew what her mother had told her was true. Her mother was short and stocky with fine fair hair and green eyes. Motherly and lovely in Rosalie's eyes but not very academic. Her father she remembered as tall and slim with red hair and a freckled skin and during the short time he had remained in her life he had seemed dependable, kind and reliable. She had loved him. He played with her and took her for walks, read to her and encouraged her when she had tried to read at an early age. She missed him a great deal when he went to sea. She had always felt wanted and loved, what was adoption anyway? She had been fortunate but sometimes wondered about her biological mother. Did she resemble her? Why had she given her up for adoption? She would, she vowed, look for her in the future, and maybe her father, but first of all she had to consider her career.

After attending a teacher training college she worked in a primary school only three miles from her home, and was content. When she was twenty she married a colleague in the school and worked for a few years before the birth of her own daughter, when she became a housewife, happy to look after Liz, her only child, before returning to her teaching career when Liz was ten years old. Liz, like her mother, had brown hair with red glints, blue flecked eyes and high aristocratic eyebrows. She too became a teacher, got married and had one daughter named Ellie. Ellie, in a quite uncanny way, resembled her mother and grandmother. It was as though the fathers did not enter into the equation. As she watched Ellie growing up, Rosalie wondered again about her own real mother and father. Perhaps they all looked alike! Peas in a pod! She would like to know before she was too old but she had never felt a great urgency to search for the parents who had abandoned her. It was probably only curiosity now and she had been reluctant to start searching while her adoptive mother was still alive. She did not wish to hurt her by looking for her biological parents, who probably didn't care about her fate anyway and who were most likely dead. It was better to let sleeping dogs lie, she concluded and her earlier vow to find out about her roots became irrelevant.

Liz had been curious at times.

'Wouldn't you like to know where we get our odd eyes and other features from?' she asked her mother. 'Ellie looks just like us.'

Rosalie smiled wisely. 'It doesn't really matter, we are happy. If my parents gave me up for adoption there must have been a good reason.'

Liz shrugged. Perhaps her mother was right. She should leave well alone. She too was happy with her life, what did it matter?

'We'll try and trace them one day if it is really important to you,' Rosalie said but that day was postponed and tucked away in the back of her daughter's mind as it was in hers. She feared that she may not like what she would find.

However, tracing one's ancestors became fashionable, many of her friends had done just that, and Ellie began asking questions about her to which she could not provide answers. Rosalie thought that she could be opening a can of worms by searching for her absent blood relations after so long but she would do it for Ellie's sake. But before she could start her search she received a letter from a solicitor in Russetshire, a letter that would answer her questions about her biological mother and change her circumstances in a completely unexpected way.

Chapter 24

Two Funerals

Joyce became more concerned about Janet's health as the days passed. Her memory was getting worse and she was often short of breath.

'Who are you?' she had said to Joyce several times over the past few weeks, then after a few moments she recognized her housekeeper. Once she asked Joyce if she was her daughter.

'You have not got a daughter,' Joyce answered. Oh dear, the poor woman would soon have to go into a nursing home. She was imagining things; she no longer knew what was real.

'I have a daughter,' Janet insisted. 'She will come and see me soon, I know she will.'

Joyce discussed the situation with Robbie. She preferred to ignore Felicity. She would never feel happy about the woman who she still thought of as a money-grubbing parasite, but she had to admit that the greedy niece had been a useful companion for her aunt during the past few months.

They decided that her doctor would have to be consulted.

'I will see to that,' Felicity made clear to Joyce when the subject was broached. 'It is my place, I am family after all! I'll ask Dr Parker to visit her sometime soon. He should be able to make a reasonable assessment.'

Felicity too did not like the idea of Janet going into a home. She wanted to keep some control over life in Primrose House as long she could. She was comfortable and could manipulate the finances to suit herself. She also enjoyed the Enderly Bridge Club where she had made new friends and in particular Robbie, although he did not reciprocate her attention but she was too thick skinned to notice any reticence on his part.

Jeremy's drinking habits took a final toll on his health. He had seemed to recover for a short time from the stroke he had suffered after Matthew's death but a second and fatal stroke soon followed. Jeremy was cremated, as he had wished, and his ashes were scattered over the graves of his father and son. Janet was unaware that he no longer came to visit her at Primrose House. She did not miss him. Felicity did not consider it worth mentioning his death to Janet. 'There is no point in upsetting Auntie,' she had remarked solicitously to Joyce and inwardly heaved a sigh of relief.

Jeremy's funeral was sparsely attended. There were a few people he once knew, consisting of a couple of old clients and four friends, who mourned his passing. The wake had been arranged in haste by a second cousin named as a beneficiary in his will who hoped for a generous handout, but Jeremy had been an embarrassment to the business before it was sold and Matthew had kept the creditors at bay with promises of repayment in the near future. They now closed in like eager vultures and the Mace home and contents were quickly disposed of to pay the numerous outstanding debts. Felicity thought, with a smug smile, that the avaricious cousin would have little with which to line his pockets.

Jack was becoming difficult. He was often incontinent and Felicity considered giving him a dose of poison to solve the problem to her satisfaction but she did not want to upset Janet. What a ghastly animal he is, she thought and looked forward to burying him in the garden before he wrecked all the carpets, and that idea gained momentum as the days passed.

In early July the garden surrounding Primrose House was looking particularly attractive. Robbie's bedding plants promised to fill the area with vibrant colour and Janet had watched him work with a burst of interest from her comfortable chair in the lounge. The way he stood was so familiar.

'Joyce,' she said, with a rare flash of comprehension, 'I think my evacuee has come back to me. It is Tom in the garden and now I can rest in peace.'

Joyce was startled. 'I think she is rambling,' she muttered to herself. Things were getting serious. She must prompt Felicity to get the doctor for an assessment but doubtless that witch would postpone the visit as long as possible.

'What are we going to do, Robbie?' Joyce said to Robbie over a cup of coffee in the kitchen that morning. She told him what Janet had said and was surprised that he was so quiet.

'I am not sure,' he answered after a few moments during which he appeared deep in thought. 'We will have to ask Felicity.'

Janet knows, he thought, after all this time, but she will not remember for more than a few minutes. A deep feeling of sadness came over him. Perhaps he should have told her who he was long ago but he could not bring himself to stir up the past. He had kept an eye on her for a long time and he had, in his way, repaid her and her family for past kindnesses. He walked sadly down the road to his cottage contemplating the unwelcome and difficult situation. At least he had a cheese and onion sandwich, downed with a pint of cider, in the Green Man and a chat with old Pat to look forward to.

Felicity walked back from the village after visiting Marianne. They met at least once a week to discuss bridge, local gossip and anything else that took their fancy. She was looking forward to the lunch that she knew Joyce would have prepared and afterwards a nice nap on her bed. Janet seemed to sleep most of the day now and would not notice if she was missing for a while. In some strange way she thought she had become quite fond of the old bird and that realization surprised her. She must be getting soft. She would miss her comfortable life at Primrose House if Janet's will was not favourable. That was something of which she was sure.

Joyce prepared the lunch of a light salad and salmon flakes with fruit compote to follow which she anticipated Janet would enjoy. As she turned the handle of the dining room door she heard Jack whine; a pitiful sound emerged from his throat. He was sitting at Janet's feet and as Joyce approached he gave a warning growl as if protecting a precious bone. Joyce felt puzzled and placed the lunch tray down on the dining-room table with a thump.

Janet seemed to be asleep. A slight smile lingered around her generous mouth, her head rested on the soft pillow that she placed under her neck to support her worn bones. She looked peaceful. Joyce approached with caution whilst an increasing tightness in her chest threatened to restrict her breathing. Was she ... dead? Jack growled low and deep then whimpered.

At that moment Felicity returned and opened the front door.

'Hullo,' she called out. She wondered if Joyce had served up lunch yet, her mouth filling as usual with saliva.

'I'm back. I'm late so I'll have my lunch in the kitchen if that's all right Joyce? How is Auntie?'

Silence greeted her. She walked down the hall and noticed the dining-room door was open. Joyce was staring at Janet, ashen and shaken.

'She's dead,' she sobbed. 'Poor dear woman, the best employer I ever had.'

'I'll call the doctor,' Felicity said in a businesslike tone. She too had paled. She had not expected to feel such regret when Janet died, it was on the cards anyway, but she did. Whether it was for the possible loss of her comfortable existence in Primrose House or some genuine feeling for the old girl she was not sure. The thought that Janet's will would clarify her financial status gave her some comfort but meanwhile there was a lot to be done, including arranging a funeral. Adrenalin started to pump through her veins and she took charge; after all she told herself, she was the next of kin.

She consulted Robbie, something she would not have done a few months ago. He told her that he was willing to help in any way he could. Janet's doctor signed the death certificate which gave the cause of death as heart failure. He said that it was just old age and probably a blessing when one considered her deteriorating mental and physical health.

The local firm of solicitors who now held Janet's will were approached and they arranged to read it to the beneficiaries after the funeral. 'We have contacted all interested parties,' they told Felicity, 'and four o'clock that day will be all right for the reading.'

Felicity wondered why they made such a fuss about contacting the interested parties; they all lived locally now and there were no wretched Maces or Ronald Brown to consider. 'We must prepare the lounge for the reading,' she said to Joyce but thought she would leave the hard work to Joyce. Joyce arranged to have, with Felicity's approval, cold meats, salmon, salads and wine for the lunch after the funeral, to be consumed in the back room of the Green Man. All Janet's friends and acquaintances they knew of were invited. Felicity comforted herself with the knowledge that Auntie's estate would be paying the bills and hoped the solicitors would sort things out quickly. She was getting short of ready cash now, and looked forward to her inheritance though she realised that probate would take some time. She had placed some money into a local building society, a few pounds each week secreted from Auntie's account, thinking it would be a handy nest egg for this kind of situation, and hoped there would be enough to last until Auntie's financial affairs had been resolved.

The coffin she had chosen for her aunt and considered to be suitable for a wealthy widow was made of fine oak with gleaming brass adornments. It was draped lavishly with colourful flowers from well-wishers in the village together with individual wreaths from Felicity, Robbie and the Skillet family. Many of Janet's past pupils, now quite old themselves and some of whom were grand-parents, attended the service. The church, to Felicity's surprise, overflowed with people who wished to pay their last respects. Felicity wondered wryly from where they had all crawled. What a pity they did not visit the lonely old woman when she needed company, she thought, and almost spat with genuine derision.

Janet was buried in Enderly churchyard with her second husband John Lacey. He was not after all buried with his first wife, an idea he had abandoned a year after he married Janet. He had loved Janet passionately and the short time he had spent with Pam faded into insignificance although he never forgot her or the baby they lost. It had been a short happy marriage despite the loss of their child. They were after all, he had realized, just a youthful couple who had little experience of life. His feelings for Janet were very different, deep and enduring.

Felicity surveyed the mourners who had been invited to lunch in the Green Man after the funeral. The vicar, grey haired and stooping, old before his time; Joyce and her skinny bossy daughter; the wretched financial adviser in his pale grey city suit – he could have worn black she thought; Alan Wilkins, Auntie's solicitor, and his colleague; Robbie, and a few of the bridge club members whom Felicity had suggested might like to join them, for example, old Pat and one or two of the other members who had known Janet quite well in the past. It was a sober affair. Robbie's offer to say a few words about Janet's life was accepted and appreciated by Felicity who was anxious to get the whole affair over and return to Primrose House as quickly as possible. She may soon own Primrose House she ruminated and looked forward to the will reading but she could not lose a vague feeling of unease that something might go wrong. I have just enough time to have a nap on the bed before the vultures arrive she thought. Joyce had already set out the cups and saucers on a table in the lounge and prepared the teatime sandwiches. Felicity was looking forward to those. Her appetite had not been dented and the possibility that she may in the near future own Primrose House and the bulk of Janet's estate continued to fill her thoughts, indeed she could think of nothing else. She hoped that she would soon be a very wealthy woman!

Chapter 25

The Will Reading

At a quarter to four the young female solicitor Felicity had met once before and her older colleague, Mr Alan Wilkins, tall, arrogant and grey haired, the epitome of the success-ful solicitor, suave and carefully groomed, arrived to read Janet Lacey's will. The couple hung their expensive dark wool over-coats on the antique mahogany hallstand that stood just inside the front door and were directed by Joyce into the lounge where they lifted their documents out of elegant leather briefcases and placed them with businesslike precision on a small table that had been put at one end of the room for their use.

The antique dining chairs had been pressed into service and Felicity eyed them with pleasure. The thought that the Mace family would not now get those was a satisfying one.

Robbie, Joyce, the vicar, local headmistress Anne Robinson, together with Felicity, sat down on chairs arranged in a half circle in front of the table. Felicity glowed. Thank goodness there was no longer the Mace family or her brother Ronald to come between her and Auntie's fortune. It looked promising. There were, however, three empty chairs which Felicity thought was strange. Joyce must have made a mistake when she arranged the room earlier.

Mr Wilkins fidgeted in his chair.

'We are still waiting for three other people,' he announced in a booming voice. 'They should have been here by now but their train may have been delayed, although I understood it left on time. Unfortunately they were unable to join us for the funeral.'

Felicity started and moved closer to the edge of her chair, her fingers clutching the soft striped velvet material with unease. Three more people! Who on earth could they be?

The doorbell emitted its strange electronic pinging.

'I'll go,' Joyce offered.

She returned a few minutes later with three women. One looked as though she was in her early seventies, the second her fifties and the third in her late teens. The two older women were smartly dressed in black and the young girl in cream and brown. After shaking hands with Mr Wilkins and exchanging a few brief words of greeting, they took the three vacant seats, shuffled uncomfortably, and wore serious expressions. The youngest looked round the room with undisguised curiosity which irritated Felicity. Who on earth are they? she screamed inwardly. Her question was answered by Alan Wilkins.

'Good, now to get down to business,' he said in his strong deep voice. 'I think you all know each other but may I introduce Mrs Rosalie Butterfield, her daughter Liz Jeffries and granddaughter Ellie Jeffries whom you have not met before. They have travelled from Yorkshire to be with us today and unfortunately could not join us for the funeral this morning. They are here now so we are able to read the will.'

He adjusted his expensive titanium-framed glasses that had slipped down his nose and cleared his throat with a loud guffaw. Felicity froze in her seat. Who were these interlopers? She turned her head to obtain a better look at them. Her heart missed a beat. She had seen them somewhere before. Rosalie's hair was white but her daughter's, though sprinkled with grey, still remained dark with a spattering of vibrant red which shone in the afternoon light that filtered in from a nearby window. Ellie had long dark hair, also speckled with red. Their eyes were blue with odd flecks and crowned with high aristocratic eyebrows. Three peas in a pod Felicity thought. Where had she seen those strange looped eyebrows before? She was mystified.

Mr Wilkins rustled the papers in front of him and pushed his glasses higher up on his nose.

'I will begin,' he pontificated, a haughty authoritative edge creeping in to his voice. 'There are a few small bequests.' He outlined them quickly. It seemed that the local church, Enderly primary school and Tom Hands were to receive £5,000 each. Her good housekeeper Joyce Skillet, niece Felicity Brown and nephew Ronald Brown were left £10,000 each. There was no mention of the financial adviser which pleased Felicity. £30,000 and a set of antique dining-room chairs were left to the Mace family but now that they had died their share would revert to the bulk of the estate as would Ronald Brown's share. Everything else after funeral expenses had been paid and Primrose House and the contents sold, together with Mrs Lacey's numerous investments, was left to the main beneficiary Mrs Rosalie Butterfield.

Felicity gasped and clenched her hands. Her knuckles became deadly white, almost blue, as was her face, as she assimilated this bombshell. She listened with disbelief and shock – it felt like icy water was trickling down her back. It was a different will, not the one she had found in Auntie's desk drawer and the wretched Mace family had not told her, despite all her efforts. They were crafty, cunning brutes!

Alan Wilkins continued in a confident monotonous tone. 'The remainder, that is the bulk of her estate, is expected to be in the region of eight million pounds after inheritance tax has been paid – the exact figure can of course only be estimated today.'

There was a stunned silence. Joyce looked at Rosalie. Oh yes, she was like Janet, there was no doubt she was her daughter, and Liz her granddaughter and Ellie her great-granddaughter. What an incredible secret she had kept all these years. An illegitimate baby she must have given birth to before going to teacher training college.

'The bitch,' Felicity stammered. Even Uncle James had been fooled. Innocent Janet Merryweather my foot! The old bag had known all along. She used me! The fact that she had sponged on her aunt did not enter into the equation, she was justified in helping herself to some of her money but to be cheated like this! She started to laugh in a hysterical manner and tears ran down her cheeks. She struggled and made an effort to stop but could not. 'Innocent Janet Lacey,' she uttered in a loud broken voice when she

Je

had regained some measure of control and all heads turned in her direction, 'whore supreme!' There was a further pregnant silence. A few feet shuffled uncomfortably and even Mr Wilkins, usually in command of most situations, looked shocked. There were sometimes difficulties when wills were read, and he had experienced a number in his time, but this promised to be what he thought of as 'a real humdinger'. Sweat formed on his brow and he made a desperate effort to grope in his pocket for a handkerchief.

Joyce realised with a start that Rosalie's eyes and eyebrows were uncannily like those of Peter Mace. She ignored Felicity's outburst and moved to have a closer look at Rosalie as soon as she was able. There was no doubt about it. She almost laughed out loud, bubbling squeaks of joy threatening to burst out of her chest and mouth. She gulped in a desperate attempt to control her emotions. My God, she thought, there is some justice in this world. That greedy avaricious niece has got her just dessert.

Felicity felt numb, her hands shook and her breath threatened to catch in her throat and choke her. Her eyes glittered maliciously and if looks could have killed, the solicitor and his assistant would have been dead or at the very least writhing in agony on the floor.

'I have a letter for you from your mother,' Mr Wilkins said to Rosalie when he had regained his composure. 'She wanted to explain why she gave you up for adoption so long ago and hoped you would forgive her.'

Rosalie had been silent and then spoke in a voice, clear and with a modulated tone exactly like her mother's. 'Thank you.'

She could not think of anything else to say. She was amazed. She had been asked to attend the will reading because she was a beneficiary but had not expected anything like this. Perhaps the letter would blow away some of the cobwebs of mystery that had surrounded her since she was a young child but she had always been happy and that to her was the most important thing. She had enough money to live on – no great worldly wealth but she was surrounded by a loving family and had enjoyed a satisfying teaching career. Janet's money would open new doors, perhaps travel and freedom from financial concerns, or would it? Money was often the root of evil and begging letters, not always justified, or greedy people grasping and hoping for a share of the cake, could be attracted and make themselves a nuisance. She was a strong woman, however, intelligent and rational like her biological mother and would handle the situation with her inborn common sense.

Janet would have been proud of the daughter she had longed to see for so long. The secret had been buried deep within her being until John had died. She had then thought about the child she had given up so long ago against her will, her family having been convinced that keeping the baby would have ruined her young life. James almost did that anyway she told herself, and John too had denied her the child she longed for though he had his reasons and she suspected he may have regretted their not having a child when it was too late.

She had made some discreet enquiries in 1990 and discovered that Rosalie was happy and had her own family around her. She wrote a new will, that was the least she could do, but could not bring herself to contact her daughter. The shame that had surrounded her as a schoolgirl when she gave birth to an illegitimate child still lingered with her. It was difficult to erase even though she knew that the shame would not be valid if she had been born later in the century. Her aunt in Yorkshire had written to her once or twice with some brief news about her child in the early days and sent her a photograph of the baby but after her aunt died so did the information about the little girl. Her family thought it was just as well and the whole sad episode should be forgotten. She had found out in 1990 that she had a granddaughter and a great-granddaughter whom she longed to see but realized that their existence was a secret she would take to her grave. She had deceived James and John and felt an almost crippling guilt.

'Darling Janet,' she recalled her mother saying. 'Wipe your memory clean. Get on with your life. You are a clever girl. Get married and have a new family. We must just hope your daughter, my granddaughter, will live a happy full life with her adoptive parents. Aunt Betsy tells me they are lovely people. We have done the right thing. The Mace family would not have allowed you to marry their precious middle-class son. In their eyes, because your father has been a farmworker all his life, we are yokels and turnip chompers! They will never acknowledge the baby.'

'Peter wants it and wants me Mum,' she had protested but knew that Peter was weak and would soon be overruled. His father had been adamant that he should study to be a solicitor and join the family firm. She had retained Peter's friendship but the baby was never mentioned again after the adoption. It was though she had never existed.

After the will reading the group of beneficiaries remained silent for a few moments. Robbie looked at Felicity whose hysterical outburst had stopped and hoped she was not going to faint; she looked as though she might. Her face was strained and ashen, blue smudges were deepening beneath her eyes and she shook and twitched in a strange manner. Robbie, like Joyce, could not prevent feeling joy when he thought about the irony of the situation although at the same time he felt a sadness for Janet who had longed to have another child and had been denied that pleasure. He guessed she must have kept in touch with someone in Yorkshire to receive news of her daughter. What a slap in the face it would have been for the beastly James! It was a pity he could not be told that news!

He too almost laughed out loud. 'Ironical, oh, really ironical,' he muttered. Felicity had been convinced that the bulk of the estate was to be left to her. She must have found an earlier will which wouldn't have mentioned Janet's daughter, the secret child born out of wedlock. Robbie guessed the child could not be acknowledged until John Lacey had died. Janet could not have told even him about the child; what a heavy burden she had carried for so long. The Mace family, or at least Jeremy and Matthew, must have known about the new will, drawn up in 1990, but they kept her secret well. He wondered if Jeremy had realised that Rosalie was also Peter's daughter, but did not think so. That taboo knowledge had been buried with care for far too long. Rosalie's eyebrows and eyes were exactly like Peter Mace's. He, like Joyce Skillet, had seen the resemblance to Peter as well as to Janet shortly after she walked into the room. Those eyebrows, odd flecked eyes and the speckled red hair told their own story. If Peter had known about the contents of the new will he would have been happy to discover that his daughter would inherit the Lacey fortune but he doubted that Jeremy would have been told that he had a half sister, and there was the question of client confidentiality. The Mace family were all dead anyway so what did it matter!

'Poetic justice … oh yes,' Robbie muttered under his breath and like Joyce struggled to contain his mirth.

Robbie continued to ponder on the situation. He had always realized that Peter was fond of Janet and it was obvious that Janet did not return his feelings though she still valued his friendship. He imagined that any romantic feelings for the man would have been killed when he did not support her and her baby. She was proud and independent and in his view far too good for the weak and snobbish Peter Mace. It was, he thought, surprising that they had remained such good friends for so many years, but he supposed there had been a bond created by the child even if it was not spoken about.

Poor Janet, what crippling fear young women must have had in the nineteen thirties and forties if they had a child out of wedlock. Shame, not joy, was heaped upon them and many unfortunate young women ended up in institutions for the rest of their lives. Janet had been lucky that she had contacts in Yorkshire who looked after her when she was pregnant and arranged for the child to be adopted. Janet had probably sworn to her family that she would never mention the baby again and had kept that promise until after her second husband had died. It must have been a dreadful millstone for such a kind and generous woman; she had not deserved that. He appreciated that Alicia Merryweather thought she was doing her best to support her daughter even if it had been misguided and moulded by the narrow-minded attitude of the majority of people in the nineteen thirties. The Maces were a middle-class professional family and marriage for their son would not be appropriate until he had established himself as a solicitor in the family business and was in a position to support a wife, and certainly not at any time to the daughter of a local farm labourer. The fact that they had a granddaughter would have been immaterial. There was plenty of time for Peter to father a family in the future.

Alan Wilkins looked at Rosalie and her family. He liked what he saw. Felicity Brown gave him the creeps, indeed 'cow' was a word that came to mind when he first met her. He hoped she was not going to be too much of a damned nuisance.

Anne Robinson too had no doubt that Rosalie was Janet's daughter. A picture of Janet taken on the day she retired from the local school was still hanging in the staffroom. The likeness between Janet and Rosalie was incredible; the only difference between the two was the colour of the eyes and the fine arched eyebrows. Where had she seen those before? She would remember later.

'Oh ... oh!' Felicity suddenly screamed, shattering the strange silence that had settled on the beneficiaries. 'Ahhhh! ... This cannot be right, I am her true heir!'

Joyce and Robbie rushed forward as if to help her but more in fear of what she would do next. Rosalie and her family looked pained and shaken. The solicitor and other beneficiaries were again stunned into silence. A puzzled Rosalie stepped forward as if to help Felicity but was restrained by Alan Wilkins.

'Leave her,' he said. 'Mrs Skillet and Robbie will assist her.'

The vicar, in an attempt to control what he anticipated could turn into a nasty situation, took Robbie to one side, tugging firmly at his arm until he went with him.

'Can you take her back to your cottage until she calms down?' he whispered. 'She will not be able to stay here, except to pack her bags. The sooner the poor woman leaves this house the better,' he continued doffing his forceful 'do-gooder' cap which had in the past so often annoyed his daughter, but a stance that was difficult to resist. Irritating as he appeared to some people he had a charisma and strength of personality that was difficult to ignore. He was used to getting his own way.

Robbie was overtaken with a feeling of horror and despair but found himself, against his better judgement, agreeing with the man, though he would hardly have described Felicity as a poor woman. He shuddered when he thought of the turmoil that was so evident on the surface and wondered what lurked beneath her hippo-like skin. She was like a volcano that had erupted once and would soon do so again, spilling hot and spiteful lava on everything and everybody around her.

'Yes, of course vicar, she can stay in my spare room ... er, that is, until other arrangements can be made.'

Did he really say that? Was he mad? he asked himself and shuddered involuntarily. He could barely keep his hands from shaking, he felt queasy and the inevitable headache started with a slow persistent throbbing above his temples. Felicity Brown in his dear little cottage! But it would not, must not, be for long he swore. The vicar had inflicted a horrible blow on him and he, poor fool that he was, had succumbed in a weak moment.

Robbie moved with reluctance towards Felicity who was sobbing with noisy rasps and being comforted by Joyce, who was struggling to keep a look of triumph off her face. He gazed at her, his eyes intent and steady in order to mask the distaste that threatened to show itself and distort his usual gentle features. The feeling that someone had pushed a cork down his throat and that it was pressing on his voice box increased but his voice eventually emerged in the form of a hoarse whisper.

'It is all right Felicity ... er ... you can come home with me.'

He placed a feeble arm nervously around her shoulders in an attempt to lead her away. She uttered a loud eerie sob, then leaned on him and emitted what sounded like a sigh of relief.

'Dear Robbie,' she mumbled as a feeling of doom threatened to engulf him.

The rest of the party, overcome with embarrassment, removed themselves with undue haste to the dining room. Conversation was stilted and there was a general curiosity to observe Janet's daughter and grandchildren interspersed with a number of genuine but feeble attempts to make them feel welcome. The vicar and Anne Robinson said a few complimentary and carefully chosen words about Janet. The majority of the guests had not had their appetites dented by the extraordinary events at the will reading and ate their sandwiches and drank their tea with obvious enjoyment.

Alan Wilkins suggested that Rosalie and her family should return to his office with him and they would discuss the will and its consequences further in more relaxed surroundings.

'I am so sorry for the unpleasantness at the will reading,' he mumbled. 'It was most unexpected.'

'That was not your fault,' Rosalie answered in a firm and confident voice.

She had booked rooms for her family in a hotel in Everton for a few days, something Alan Wilkins had earlier suggested, and now, although their spirits were dampened by the unexpected avaricious niece, they looked forward to exploring the area and discovering more about Janet. Felicity was an unhappy thorn in their side but not one of their making.

Robbie had made an effort to calm Felicity as well as he was able.

'Come on,' he said in a low soothing tone. 'I'll fetch my car. We 'll soon be out of here and you can relax in my cottage for a while.' Would he ever relax again? he wondered.

'Oh, yes, dear Robbie,' Felicity stuttered. 'Joyce will help me pack a case, I won't stay in this dreadful place a moment longer.'

She looked at Robbie with an expression of affection and reached out an arm to him for support. His heart sank and he was left with the uncomfortable feeling that it would soon rest with clumsy abandon in his boots, never to return to its rightful place. He must make sure she didn't stay in his home too long and his usually alert mind became cluttered with cunning half-formed plans on ways to get rid of unwanted guests. What an idiot he must have been to get himself into this mess. It was a pity that self-righteous vicar did not invite her to stay in his home; the foolish man was too free with his suggestions that other people should help. What horrors did the future hold for him now?

Chapter 26

The Guest

Felicity, with Joyce's help, packed two large suitcases with clothes and overnight essentials. She promised to return the next day to collect the rest of her things. Joyce had been asked by the solicitor to stay on as housekeeper in order to keep Primrose House tidy and help sort out Janet's personal possessions, and he also asked Robbie to continue to tend the garden until the house was sold. Some of the furniture and paintings would be valued professionally and removed to a safe location until a sale could be arranged.

Felicity carried her cases down the stairs and into the hall, the hall that she had stupidly thought would soon belong to her. She sat on the bottom step for a moment in disbelief. What an idiot she had been. She was leaving Primrose House, her home, forced out by those interlopers.

Robbie appeared in the doorway and collected her cases. He put them in the boot of his car and returned to assist a still shattered Felicity to the passenger seat because she claimed that her legs felt weak and she found it difficult to walk. As the car moved away she opened her mouth wide and uttered a pitiful ear-splitting howl like a wolf who had lost its mate. Robbie's blood ran cold and he shivered.

'Interlopers!' she shouted. 'What right has that woman and her brood to take my house?'

Robbie remained silent. It seemed the best option. What he had seen so far of Rosalie he had liked. She reminded him of Alicia Merryweather.

He parked the car in front of his old oak studded front door and opened the passenger door to assist Felicity. She stepped out into the bright afternoon sunlight at the front of the house where they were greeted by pots of vivid red geraniums that had been placed each side of the door. Felicity's spirits started to lift. An iron boot scraper, ancient and reassuring, was placed to one side of the door. A door knocker in the shape of a stag's head was quite mundane but the ordinary little black and white Russetshire cottage with its dark oak wooden window sills appeared to welcome her. The small front garden was crammed full of brightly coloured scented flowers and had been edged with pretty black iron railings very like those that had been removed from Robbie's London home when he was a child and which he was told were to be melted down for the war effort.

'Dear Robbie,' she said in an almost calm voice, 'it is so good of you to take me in, I won't be any trouble. It will only be until I can find somewhere of my own.'

As he opened the front door and led her into the sitting room Robbie hoped that would be very soon.

'Sit down on the settee and rest,' he mumbled solicitously, and turned to lug her cases into the cottage.

'I'll put your luggage into the spare bedroom,' he said, his arms aching with the weight of the damned things. He really should not be lifting them he told himself. He was feeling tired all too often these days, in fact he would be glad to give up the gardening job at Primrose House. He had worked there far too long.

Felicity did not answer. She was busy looking with a burning curiosity around the spacious lounge. She sank into the luxurious thick cushions on the large three-seater settee and felt comfortable and immediately at home. She eyed the walls, neatly white-washed brick, and the large wood burner in the hearth. That should be cosy in the winter, she told herself with a spurt of interest. Antique brass firedogs rested in the fireplace and a shiny brass-topped box containing logs was placed strategically on one side. The hearth was composed of warm red quarry tiles. The longest wall in the lounge was covered with oak shelves and these were crammed with academic books. Oh goodness, she thought, a clever man, I have a lot to learn about him. She gazed at the pictures that hung on the walls. They are almost as fine as Aunt Janet's, she surmised, if not better. There were some elaborate hunting scenes painted in delicate watercolours and a couple of old oil paintings, one of cattle, huddled together waiting to be milked, in a farmyard and another of a black and white border collie with her pups. There was an original oil painting of Robbie's dog Nap who had died two years previously. Delicate china filled a fine mahogany display cupboard, Coalport figurines and other fine ceramics were in abundance. She moved closer to get a better look. What a good collection, much better than Auntie's, he obviously knew more about such things although she had understood that the Lacey family had been keen collectors. What an odd print though on one wall … pearly kings and queens, what a strange choice. She liked it. It reminded her of her early childhood in London.

'Would you like to see your room?' Robbie's voice interrupted her thoughts.

'Love to,' she said pertly.

That didn't take long, Robbie thought. She seems to have recovered from her shock and tantrums. What can be going through her disturbed mind now?

Felicity looked with care at the small bedroom. Old oak beams straddled the ceiling and there was a tiny window with pretty flowered curtains through which she could see the neat garden, enclosed and private, behind the cottage.

'Oh hell, blue walls,' she muttered under her breath. Well that could be changed. Beggars cannot be choosers. I may not be here long flitted through her mind and … well … I might manage to settle in here for a while. Oh, the bed is not bad, quite comfortable – she stretched out a hand to feel the firmness of the mattress – though there is hardly room for all my new clothes in this room. One fitted wardrobe will never accommodate the collection of gladrags I've bought with Auntie's money. She smirked. Ah, there is room for another in the corner. I could offer to cook him a meal sometimes, hmm, I could make myself indispensable. I'll need somewhere to stay until I get my £10,000 and that pittance won't get me far in the property market. Her mind raced ahead, things may not be too bad after all. What a nice little cottage it was.

'Make yourself at home,' Robbie forced himself to say, hoping that she would not take that suggestion too literally though he feared she would need little encouragement. 'I'll get us a cup of tea and some biscuits.' Felicity perked up at the suggestion of food.

'I'll help,' she responded with alacrity.

She moved swiftly, her legs carrying her with determination towards the kitchen in which she found, to her satisfaction, nice new units of solid oak and a large range cooker. Oh, this is quite modern, she thought. I like it. She noted the smart new washing machine and dryer. Her mind went back briefly to some of the old equipment she had struggled with in her youth. There was none of that old rubbish here, thank goodness.

She soon found the biscuit tin and an expensive attractive Worcestershire plate which she loaded with Robbie's precious favourite chocolate biscuits. He normally rationed himself to one or two a day.

She carried them into the lounge and placed the plate on the coffee table, munching one as she went, sticky chocolate crumbs dropping down on to the kitchen floor Robbie's cleaning lady had mopped earlier in the day. Robbie carried in two steaming mugs of Indian tea. Lovely, she thought, not that Earl Grey rubbish.

They sat down together on the settee to enjoy their tea and biscuits. A strained silence cloaked them at first but was ignored by Felicity who was too busy crunching Robbie's biscuits to care. They disappeared down her throat with amazing speed. She hesitated. What am I doing? I'm being selfish, she thought and felt a glimmer of remorse, alien to her nature, and a slight cold sweat on her brow. She showed unusual self control by refusing a further biscuit.

Robbie on the other hand felt uncomfortable. Oh hell, he thought, is this the pattern of things to come? He was tired because he had missed his afternoon nap. His illness was under control with medication but he was now exhausted.

Felicity looked slyly at Robbie out of the corners of her eyes which she could turn oddly to one side whilst keeping the main part of her face facing forward. Grey hair curled over Robbie's ears and his fine gold-rimmed glasses made his deep hazel eyes look larger than they actually were. She warmed towards him, her recent shock forgotten for a short while. What a nice man, I wish I had met him a long time ago. He would have suited me I think. An intelligent man who probably has more money than some of those losers I lived with. He looks tired. She surprised herself once again with that solicitous thought. I must try and help him.

'I could cook us supper,' she offered throwing him a gracious smile. 'To return your kindness, I really would love to.'

I bet she would, Robbie almost said out loud, greedy wretch.

'I have no food in the fridge for supper,' he retorted with an unusual brusqueness, 'and precious few saucepans in the kitchen. I usually go to the pub for my evening meal. You are welcome to join me.'

A surprised Felicity agreed but determined that she would soon change that habit. He didn't know what was coming. She would alter his life for the better and he would not be able to manage without her. It would not be too hard to get her feet under his table, at least she did not think it would be. She had not reckoned with Robbie's stubborn independent resolve and should have known better but even if she had she would have been determined to try. It would suit her to remain in his cottage for a while at least, possibly long term if that could be arranged and they didn't bicker too much. That might prove to be tedious. The alternative was to rent a room from Marianne but her home was so cluttered and untidy the thought was soon abandoned. This cottage was the better option.

The next afternoon Felicity packed the rest of her belongings that remained in Primrose House. She stripped the bathroom cupboards of bath oils, shampoos and soaps. Janet always kept good stocks. Her rage welled up again when she returned to her old room. It was so unfair. She looked across the garden and fields to the familiar river view and her eyes filled with hot angry tears but that did not prevent her filling the six new cases that she had pressed Robbie to help her buy in Everton that morning. She added some oddments that she thought nobody would notice were missing, including the finely engraved silver-backed hair-brushes and a quaint tiny antique mirror that had stood on her dressing table that now belonged to Janet's estate. She crept into Janet's bedroom and opened the unlocked drawers of the dressing table. There was a row of cheap pearls in one. That rotten daughter can keep that rubbish, she thought. In another there were a few old photographs. She turned them over and looked at them with a scathing expression. There was one of Janet and John on their wedding day and another of a baby. She looked closely at the baby's face. It was her, Rosalie or whatever her name was. The eyebrows were arched even then. Her aunt had kept that photograph all those years, hidden and secret. A sweet face overall she had to admit but her hands shook and she longed to tear it into tiny pieces. She placed it back into the drawer with an effort that was quite alien to her tempestuous nature. No doubt the daughter would want it. She hoped the woman would appreciate how lucky she was.

Joyce called out at that moment.

'Can I help, Felicity?'

'No,' she said hastily, 'all done and ready to go, though I suppose I will need help lugging these cases down the stairs.'

Joyce and Robbie assisted her as best they could. The cases were heavy with her bounty but Joyce was so glad to see the back of the woman she almost shouted with joy and ignored her aching arms. Poor old Robbie stuck with that lecherous wretch! Not for too long, she prayed.

Robbie was not so sure. He did not know how long she planned to stay with him but he resolved to be firm. He would make an effort to find her somewhere else to stay, and soon.

Felicity stacked her cases of clothes against a wall in her new bedroom.

'Hmm. It is almost like home,' she muttered. 'I'll soon have everything shipshape.'

She lifted the solid silver hair brushes and mirror out of a case and spread them out on the small dressing table. She had left behind the pink plastic set she had brought with her from Canada. It was a fair exchange, she decided. On one of the silver-backed brushes a small clump of Felicity's tinted blonde hair had stuck to the bristles on one side as though stamping her owner-ship firmly upon it. Nobody but Joyce will notice those brushes and mirror are missing and she will be so glad to see the back of me that she will not care Felicity guessed, and made a small grimace of satisfaction. 'They would not fetch much in an auction,' she muttered in an attempt to justify her actions. She powdered her nose and put a smear of shimmering Italian rose pink lipstick on her mouth, filling the top lip in first and then squeezing her mouth together to even the colour out on her top and bottom lips. It was more efficient that way she maintained. Then she brushed her hair with one of the silver-backed brushes and smiled again, looking at herself with sharp critical eyes. I'm not too bad for my age, not too wrinkled, I could be worse but it is a pity about that nose. She sprayed expensive French perfume behind her ears and began to feel at ease. She looked at her neat ruby and diamond earrings with pleasure. She had had her ears pierced in Brinton not long after she moved into Primrose House and had purchased several sets of earrings with Auntie's credit card, good quality of course, with gold settings and real stones. Only the best for Janet's heiress she had told herself at the time but that pleasant dream had now cracked and disintegrated like the old pink hand mirror she had left in Primrose House.

It will soon be time for another cup of tea she told herself, and after that I'll have a nice nap on this comfy bed before a good evening meal in the pub, followed by a game of bridge. She smiled. She was a match for Robbie. He would not find it easy to get rid of her. She could be on to a good thing. She would certainly try to make the best of things.

Mrs Connolly, Robbie's cleaning lady who came in to tidy up for him twice a week, turned up the next morning and eyed the new resident with some distaste.

''Ow long is she staying Mr Barker? I can't get into the spare room, it's crammed full of cases and other rubbish. I can't clean it.'

Robbie squared his shoulders and braced himself.

'Not long,' he said, hoping that was the case but fearing the worst. 'Just until Mrs Brown can find somewhere suitable to stay.'

'Well, I needs to get on, lot to do in a short time. I 'ope she's not going to get in my way.' She grabbed a mop and some dusters from the hall cupboard and, sniffing loudly, made an effort to get on with her chores.

The days slipped by and Felicity made herself comfortable.

'Have you made any plans yet Felicity?' Robbie ventured at the end of the first week. His voice sounded dead. Hope for a swift departure of his unwanted guest was fast fading.

'No, Robbie, I cannot find anywhere. Marianne does not want to let me have a room.' She had not asked her and did not intend to.

Felicity turned her face towards him, her small eyes expanding with fear for the future, mirroring his own. He wondered if he was verging on madness. It was a like a nightmare from which he hoped he would be able to wake up soon and she would be gone. His spirits at times rose for a second or two then plummeted once again. He was kidding himself. She was digging in for the long haul. He found himself waking up in the middle of the night tossing and turning in his bed whilst a deep feeling of disquiet gripped his body ensuring restful sleep was impossible. His mouth felt dry most mornings when he woke up and his neck stiff with tension as he gazed around his comfortable masculine bedroom that he had chosen with such care when he first moved in. There were antique pine cupboards and a dressing table to match with cream bedcovers and curtains, plain and simple. He had had a new shower cubicle installed in one corner, now proving to be quite a boon as he was able to leave Felicity to use the bathroom, which she soon made her own and cluttered with bottles of scented bath foam and various creams and soaps which were alien to him and quite objectionable. Thick green fluffy bath towels were crammed onto his recently installed chrome heated bath rail and a luxurious towelling bathrobe, also green, hung with dogged prominence on the hook on the bathroom door.

After several weeks they settled into an uneasy routine. They had most of their meals, paid for by Robbie, in the Green Man, and if they did not play bridge would return to the cottage and sip a cherry liquor or make a cup of coffee and chat, or rather Felicity babbled on and he more often than not just listened. They discovered that their London background was similar and an uneasy truce settled upon them. Robbie's home that had been bombed in the war was only two streets away from the house that Anne and Richard had moved into when they had first married. An odd companionship started to develop. Some afternoons when it was sunny they would sit out in Robbie's small garden and sip a cup of fine Indian tea. There were no sandwiches but Felicity decided that she did not miss them. Her waistline was trimmer and she felt healthier. Robbie began to relax and his sleep patterns improved. Acceptance of a no-win situation settled upon him.

He woke up one morning a month after she had moved in to discover that the smell of fresh toast and coffee was filling the cottage. The small pine table in the kitchen diner had been set for two. He smelled the hard-boiled eggs, just the way he liked them; his daily newspaper was folded carefully and placed next to his plate. Until that day they had helped themselves to breakfast and tried to ignore each other in the mornings.

'I must pull my weight.' Felicity hesitated. 'I'll get the breakfast for us in future Robbie, it will be much more companionable.' She looked at him and waited.

'Well, yes ... well ... um, good idea,' he stammered.

He felt like a fly caught in a spider's web but admitted to himself that it was good to be waited on for a change.

Breakfast together became the norm and conversation became easier. They discussed the latest news from the bridge club and various village activities, for example the local fete and the possible fate of Enderly Post Office which had been under threat of closure for some time.

Felicity was looking more refreshed and relaxed. She dressed carefully in neat navy or black trousers and fine pastel-coloured jumpers most days. The strain of moving from Primrose House had, it seemed, almost disappeared. They did not mention Janet or her daughter. It was as though the whole affair had been brushed under a carpet and although Robbie continued to make plans to get rid of Felicity as the days passed his ideas became nebulous.

Robbie had installed a fairly large fish pond in one corner of the garden shortly after he moved in to his cottage. He had planted a lilac tree a short distance from the pond and the bright purple blooms in the springtime reminded him of his early childhood in London. Several cherished goldfish shimmered in the pool and, unlike his one pet when he was a child, enjoyed space and numerous pond plants to shelter under. The fish grew large, multiplied, were well fed and admired by visitors. A metal heron was placed on guard at one side of the pond in an effort to deter predators and wire netting fixed with care over the top. Robbie sometimes closed his eyes and attempted to visualise the small backyard, the Anderson shelter and the minute fish pond with his one small pet fish swimming manically round and round. One day in an unguarded moment he told Felicity about the London fish pond. He expected that she would scoff but to his surprise her face expressed genuine interest and she smiled in a way that was almost sympathetic.

'I like fish,' she said. 'I always wanted some when I was a child, but I was not allowed to keep any. My mother hated them. I enjoy watching these, it is quite soothing.'

A few weeks after moving in to Robbie's cottage she bought some good quality Indian tea and several packets of Robbie's favourite biscuits, using some of her savings, and offered to pay for some of their bar meals. Robbie felt wary about her motives.

Primrose House was put up for sale. Felicity was not so disturbed about the prospect of strangers living there as Robbie had expected.

'Good,' she had said. 'I will soon get my £10,000. Things are moving. I will be able to pay my way then.'

Pay her way, Robbie thought. That can only mean one thing, she means to stay here for some time. His mind once again became embroiled in turmoil. He must think of a way to solve the problem and soon. As a confirmed bachelor he had grown to value his own company. There was no place for any female who wished to organize and meddle in his life. At least that was what he told himself but he was in fact beginning to have doubts. He was developing a taste for being waited upon at breakfast and teatime.

Felicity continued to be impressed when she looked at Robbie's academic books that were crammed into the bookshelves, hundreds of them pushed close together. She lifted one or two down when Robbie had gone out one day to visit old Pat who had not been well, and perused them with genuine interest. Some he had written; Professor Robert Barker was printed clearly on the covers. She felt in awe. She had obtained very few paper qualifications except those for typing and cookery. Her restless and turbulent nature as a child had not allowed her to follow any academic course of study. She had once thought that in some ways she was quite clever but self-doubts and sobering truths had lately crept into her mind. Ronald's attempt to kill her had been a shattering experience. She had been an awful person, she now understood. She had knifed that boyfriend in Canada, though she consoled herself that act had been one of self-defence, drifted from one job to another and eventually let Matthew Mace die. Yes, she could have helped him, and a glimmer of conscience and remorse pierced her once tough hide. She told herself there was no way she could have saved him, after all she could not swim. But the fact remained that she could have gone to seek help. She vowed to mend her ways and try to make up for some of the evil she had strewn around in the past. Robbie, dear Robbie, would be the first beneficiary. What a kind man he was and he deserved some pampering. He had worked as a humble handyman in order to look after Aunt Janet, even if, as she strongly believed, his motives had been misplaced, and now he himself needed care. She would look after him. It would be a pleasure and her mission in life. A new set of dreams took over.

Chapter 27

Settling In

The weeks continued to slip by and turned into months. Felicity made excuses when the subject of finding accommodation of her own was broached. Robbie did not bring the subject up so often but continued to be concerned about her obvious reluctance to leave his cottage. She was procrastinating and he was weak and lazy, he told himself. Yes, he was far too weak. That interfering vicar had a lot to answer for.

'Marianne would have me, she has offered,' Felicity lied, 'but her spare room is so small, there is not enough room for all my belongings.'

She persuaded Robbie to allow her to cook their evening meal at least twice a week.

'It's much cheaper than those meals in the pub,' she said. 'There is nothing like home-made food, Robbie. The fried food in the pub is too greasy. I have a lovely Italian lasagne recipe, really authentic, which I made for Roberto in Canada,' and he had to admit that she was right, she was a good cook. Felicity was aware that he still liked to meet Old Pat and a few other acquaintances in the pub and chat over a pint of his favourite cider, but convinced herself that he would soon prefer her company. They were after all only a group of scruffy old yokels who had little in common with the academic Robbie. She was reading a few of his books and expanding her knowledge. She told herself that she would soon develop into a suitable companion for the clever man.

Enderly Bridge Club continued to flourish and Patsy and John Elk were the epitome of the happy couple.

'It is nice to see such a well-matched pair,' Felicity said to Robbie. 'They are perfect together and suit each other so well. It's good to have such pleasant companionship, I miss the closeness I enjoyed with Roberto and our many friends in Canada.' She did not in any way miss Roberto or any friends in Canada but hoped to press Robbie into admitting that he enjoyed her company and needed her. Her wheedling was still falling upon barren ground but she was determined to win and would not stop until she got her own way. She was not aware of the tension and conflicting emotions that plagued him.

He would miss me if I left now, she told herself.

An opportunity presented itself a few months after John and Patsy were married. John Elk called at Robbie's cottage one evening. He looked very sheepish and nervous. He looked down at his hands and large clumsy feet and stuttered.

'Patsy is going to have a baby ... er ... we thought it was too late, we're no longer young, but it's just been confirmed.'

'Congratulations,' Robbie said, beaming. 'I am really happy for you both.'

'It does mean,' John continued, one side of his face twitching nervously, 'that she wants to give up the post of secretary of the Enderly club, as soon as possible, after all she did say that she would only do it for one year. She has not felt too well and we don't want to take any chances. She will be an older mother, you know.'

'Of course, I'll ask around,' Robbie replied, his heart sinking. Good secretaries were hard to find; the job could prove more onerous than many members realised. A person would have to be keen to take undertake the position.

'She'd also like to play with me in Little Brinton club, if you wouldn't mind. She would try and find you another partner ...'

Felicity had been listening. She had been pottering in the kitchen, feigning tact whilst preparing some coffee and sandwiches for the visitor. She emerged quickly.

'I couldn't help overhearing,' she said. 'Robbie could play with me. I'd love to join Little Brinton Bridge Club.'

Robbie was so alarmed that he couldn't speak for a moment but John Elk responded with alacrity.

'That would be marvellous,' he said. 'Would that be all right with you Robbie?'

Robbie blanched. He felt stiff and cold and gave them a quelling look but neither noticed. They were too busy congratulating themselves on the solution which would suit them both.

'Oh, well … if you are sure Felicity …'

'Wonderful,' Felicity gushed. 'It's so satisfying to be able to help my good friends. Robbie and I will play well together. It will be a really good partnership.' She placed an arm with a possessive gesture around Robbie's shoulders. He cringed as she gave him an affectionate squeeze. He bit back a rejoinder and remained silent. She didn't notice that his bearing was stiff, almost rigid.

'I don't doubt it,' he mumbled.

She reached into Robbie's bureau drawer for some convention cards. 'Now tell me what you play,' she continued with obvious mounting excitement.

He was caught in her net. This really was the final straw - the nail in his coffin! Resentment reared its ugly head and he found it difficult to speak.

She was right, she told herself. What a wonderful opportunity. We are both experienced players. We will grow closer and be able to put any past misunderstandings behind us. She was like an excited child.

'I would be happy to be Secretary of Enderly Bridge Club too,' she continued. 'I would like to help you in any way I can, dear Robbie. You've been so kind to me, taking me in when my inheritance went against me and letting me make my home in your lovely little cottage.'

I am trapped he thought. He no longer had the strength to fight. The woman will never leave now unless I lift her up bodily and shove her outside onto the pavement with her bulging cases of clothes and lock the door after her, but I no longer have the willpower or strength to do that.

Following his meeting with Alistair Anderson Robbie had promised himself that he would read some books about Attention Deficit Disorder and at long last he made the effort to scan the internet for information about the latest theories and ideas about ADD. It was something about which he, together with many other people, knew little. He began to understand Felicity's unpredictable behaviour through reading extensively on the subject but still had no clear idea how he could help her or perhaps himself. It did seem to him that she might suffer from the condition, though he realized that he was not qualified to decide that with certainty. ADD was hereditary, he read, and, although a professional opinion was desirable, he doubted whether she would agree to visit a psychiatrist and he did not want to suggest that she should. Felicity appeared to be happier than when he first met her; indeed she did not appear to be the same person. He concluded that it was probably best now to let sleeping dogs lie. He was surprised that she had been able to play bridge so well. The game needed concentration, which in many aspects Felicity had demonstrated was for her limited, but it was a competitive game and no doubt enabled her to use a little of her excess energy to her advantage. Some understanding on his part was, however, a start. It could make living with her more tolerable. He regretted not reading more about ADD before though was intelligent enough to realise that a little knowledge, especially of amateur psychology, was often a dangerous thing and his interpretation of her condition required caution.

Felicity rearranged some of the cottage furniture, though she was careful to make the changes without haste, and the cottage began to acquire a feminine touch which Robbie had to admit he liked. He longed for a peaceful life and, although he found it difficult to admit, he discovered that he was beginning to enjoy having her around. He thought, in the same way that Janet had, that she was quite reasonable company, perhaps better than none, although he had been happy on his own and he found it difficult to acknowledge that his dependency upon her was deepening. She not only made his breakfast and tea and cooked the odd evening meal but also cleared away the crockery, and washed up or filled his dishwasher with an expert hand. He acknowledged that they had both changed their attitude towards each other. Even Mrs Connolly had come to accept her and acknowledged that Felicity had made her cleaning job easier. Robbie feared that Felicity now had her eye on his money but that was currently willed in a way that would surprise her even more than Janet's will.

'She's not a bad woman that one,' Mrs Connolly pronounced after Felicity had been in the cottage for a few months. 'Is she here for the long haul, Mr Barker?'

'I'm not sure,' Robbie stuttered, amazed at Mrs Connolly's acceptance of Felicity. She was more often than not choosy and difficult with regard to the people she liked.

Felicity could not understand why she felt so protective towards Robbie, the man she had tried to hunt down when she was looking for Tom Hands in what she now acknowledged was a futile effort to eliminate him from Auntie's will. His share of the legacy was small anyway. It had been foolish. She had for the first time in her life grown fond of someone. She had depended on Roberto when she was down on her luck in Canada but it was not quite the same thing. Felicity became aware that something had happened to change her personality when her brother had tried to murder her. The result was that she had made an effort to change and although that was difficult she felt that she was making some progress. She still had no conscience about the fact that she had used Janet's credit card with indiscriminate abandon; in her view her actions were justifiable at the time and were now entrenched in the past. She had a capacity for forgetting things that were unpleasant, burying them in her subconscious, a habit developed over many years, and she did not think about them again unless absolutely essential. She tried to convince herself that her brother had exaggerated her bad behaviour. The revelations, however, still surfaced in a few unguarded moments and were tinged with a fresh element of surprise and disbelief. She remembered what she wanted to, for example the few happy moments they had shared as very young children before their mother died. When he told her that she had been so cruel to him it had been devastating and she told herself that he was mentally unstable and was not responsible for his actions, though she knew in her heart that what he had said held elements of unpalatable truth.

Felicity partnered Robbie in Little Brinton Bridge Club and to his surprise they played together without any friction.

'We suit each other very well, came top two weeks running,' she said with pride after they had played together several times.

'Well, yes ...' Robbie agreed with some hesitation. He could hardly believe it but he was actually enjoying playing with the woman. He even agreed to enter some County competitions with her. Was he getting weak in the head?

Robbie's health was deteriorating and he found himself to his chagrin depending even more on Felicity. She was delighted to run round him and attend to his needs. She fussed over him and he, against his better judgement, found himself warming towards her. He was surprised to discover that she was reading his books with such eagerness and noted that her conversation skills had improved. The timbre and pitch of her voice began to soften and to his relief the odd strident Canadian accent, which he had at one time found grating, had mellowed, too.

Joyce Skillet called to see him and ask about his health.

'I really miss Mrs Lacey,' she told him. 'Primrose House has been sold and Rosalie Butterfield has returned to Yorkshire. She's a lovely woman, how Mrs Lacey would have enjoyed having her with her, and her granddaughter and great granddaughter. What a tragedy that they couldn't have got together earlier. I helped to sort out the furniture and other goods, which are all now sold. The new owners should move in soon. They're a nice family from Hampshire and should fit easily into village life.'

She'd realized that a few things were missing, for example the silver-backed brushes, but decided not to mention them.

'I miss Janet Lacey too,' Robbie admitted. 'I was her mother's evacuee, I never told her, of course, but I think she guessed at the end.' Robbie told her how he had first met Alicia Merryweather. She did not seem surprised and he wondered how much she already knew or had guessed.

Joyce was taken aback, however, when a meek Felicity brought in the tea. It was good quality Indian tea and scones with her own home-made strawberry jam and fresh cream.

Felicity set the tray on a small dining table and waited on the guest as though she was royalty. For a moment Joyce could not speak. Had the woman changed that much? She was suspicious. The thought that she was interested in inheriting Robbie's money occurred to her.

Nine months after Felicity had moved in with Robbie Marianne paid them a visit. 'I have a proposition for Felicity,' she announced, thinking Robbie, as well as Felicity, would be delighted. 'I have been left a little money by an old relative from London I didn't know still existed. Not a lot but enough to enable me to renovate my cottage. I can afford to install a new bathroom next to the spare bedroom on the first floor, a second bedroom there could be turned into a sitting room and I can then let it. I would let it for a very reasonable rent to a friend like you Felicity, would you be interested? I would love to have your company.'

Felicity remained silent. It was the last thing she wanted to hear. Robbie too was quiet. He had longed for this moment but now was experiencing a feeling of reluctance.

'I'm ... I'm not ... sure ...' Felicity said, taken aback. Her hands shook and a nerve twitched on the side of her face. She was lost for words. 'I would ... er ... like to think about it.'

'Of course, dear,' Marianne responded. She was puzzled. She had expected both Felicity and Robbie to jump with delight at the prospect.

'I'm well settled here now,' Felicity bumbled on. 'Robbie is not well and I'm looking after him. It suits us both.'

To Robbie's surprise he found himself mentally agreeing. He would miss her, the woman he had at one time disliked with intense fervour. He had found her morals and greed abhorrent. What had occurred that was prompting him to consider asking her to stay? She had become an important part of his life, he admitted to himself with some trepidation. The woman he had considered ignorant and repulsive had proved to be a good companion. Indeed he now depended on her. She was his partner and not just in the bridge room. He had been surprised when she had read some of his books and others from the county library. She was far more intelligent than he had imagined. They had discussed her views about some of his books and she had shown surprising insight. Until that time he had considered her to be quite clueless. Although he realised that she had some difficulty in concentrating she was very much more relaxed and happier than she had been when they first met. Her improved peace of mind had allowed her to sustain her enjoyment of reading. They had a common background, they were both children brought up in London for a few of their formative years and they would chat about those days and share memories. His mind rambled on ... he no longer wanted her to leave. He still had grave doubts about the part she had played in the death of Matthew Mace, or the accident that it most likely was, but was willing to forget that now. It was no longer important. Were his principles slipping? Life was now too short, yes that was the explanation. He felt uncomfortable and broke out into a slight sweat as he thought about Matthew's death.

'Felicity, you must do what you think best,' he stammered after a few pregnant moments.

Marianne looked embarrassed. She stood up, stiff and awkward, tucked her voluminous handbag under her arm with a flourish and took several swift, almost eager, steps toward the lounge door. She glanced at Robbie and Felicity over her shoulder and a puzzled frown appeared on her wrinkled forehead. It was unbelievable.

'Well, I'll be going. Let me know, Felicity. There's no hurry. I'll let myself out.'

She left with a bewildered expression on her face. She had expected Felicity to jump at the chance to live with her. Robbie, she thought, would be overjoyed to lose the uninvited guest that had been foisted upon him by the vicar, a guest that she thought must have outstayed her welcome several times over. His hesitation and reluctant stance was incredible to her.

'Robbie,' Felicity said, 'I really do want to stay. I'm happy here but it is your cottage and you have been very good to me. I know that I have behaved badly in the past, with Auntie and Ronald. Could you forgive me and let me stay with you?'

She looked at him with an earnestness and sincerity he would not at one time have believed her capable of. He felt himself soften and warm towards her.

'I will think about it,' Robbie replied, relief flooding through him. 'Let us both sleep on it for a day or two.' He did not want to appear too eager. He did want a day or two to think further about the situation because he felt that would be the sensible thing to do, but he knew the answer already. Perhaps he was being a fool. Could she really have changed so much? He would have to take a chance on that if he let her stay. Did a leopard ever change its spots? Money was the crux here. John Lacey had, he now understood, known what was the most important thing in life – love and affection, companionship and warmth, not wealth. The majority of people were driven by greed and lust for money and he would, until recently, have classified Felicity as one of them. Having her around did of course make his life more comfortable and that was something he would not have thought possible when she first moved into his cottage. Her morals had been lax; she had spent Janet's money on clothes and frippery without a second thought, but Janet had not been very concerned about that so why should he? Janet too, he guessed, had come to see that worldly goods were of little real value when John had died and she was struggling with old age. She had not protested when Felicity had spent so much of her money. Although she had started to suffer from Alzheimer's disease she must have realised what her niece was doing and made a conscious decision not to object. Felicity had tried to eliminate some of the other contenders for Janet Lacey's worldly goods but had not it seemed actually committed the murder of Peter Mace, though at one time he believed she had! He would always be suspicious about the circumstances surrounding Matthew's unfortunate drowning but she was needed, yes he needed her, she must stay now because he could not imagine what life would be without her. He concluded that she was a dreamer and that her lust for money and some of her silly schemes to eliminate the beneficiaries of her Aunt's will had been little more than figments of an overactive imagination. It was what he now wanted to believe and his study of ADD confirmed that belief.

He was a sick man and knew he would be glad of her help as his health deteriorated. Perhaps he was being selfish. He would change his will to ensure that she could live in the cottage for the rest of her life if he died before her, which was likely, if that was what she wanted, and he guessed with his usual astuteness that she would jump at the chance. It would be his way of paying her back for companionship and care.

During the next few days Felicity became withdrawn and worried. Would Robbie want her to leave? She found tears welling in her eyes when she least expected it and moped round the cottage like a lost being. She found sleep impossible and longed for him to tell her she could stay. She believed that they had become friends and she had not had much experience of true friendship in her life. She didn't want to marry him and money was no longer important – that amazed her – but she did want his companionship.

She did not have to wait long.

Robbie set some ground rules. They would just be friends.

'I am too old and don't want another wife or girlfriend,' he made quite clear. 'I enjoy your company, something I did not think at one time that I would, Felicity.'

'Dear Robbie, I enjoy being with you too. We will be able to help each other,' she said in a contrite tone.

'A trial period only, you must understand,' he urged as he mopped the sweat off his brow. What had he taken on? He wanted to keep her with him but a feeling that he was being foolish was hard to dispel.

That Robbie had invited Felicity to stay on in his cottage soon became common knowledge and astounded most of their friends and acquaintances, Joyce Skillet among them.

'It won't last,' she pronounced to her family and close friends, but even she had to admit as the months passed that it seemed as though it might and indeed the arrangement was proving to be, as far as any of their acquaintances could tell, successful.

Chapter 28

June 2008

Felicity placed a wreath of scented white lilies on the grave of Robbie Thomas Barker. He was buried as he wished in Enderly churchyard next to Janet Lacey and her parents. He had arranged to have his plot many years earlier.

A distraught and shocked Felicity made the funeral arrangements. Robbie had drawn up a list of old colleagues and friends he wished to attend his funeral and left instructions about the hymns and music he wanted. He had told Felicity about his wishes some time earlier. At first she had not wanted to listen because she could not bear the thought of life without Robbie.

'You will live a long time yet Robbie,' she insisted when he broached the subject of his death. 'You must not leave me, we need each other. I really do not want to think about it.'

Robbie sighed. 'All right, we won't discuss that at present.' If she was happy to bury her head in the sand, so be it. He would ensure she was cared for after his death. That they had come to depend upon each other was something he would not have believed possible.

Felicity knew that sooner or later his illness would take over and she had to admit he was right to express his wishes and promised to carry out his instructions should he die before her.

His death was sudden. Robbie died from heart failure, peacefully, when sitting one evening companionably in his favourite armchair next to Felicity. They had eased themselves into the habit of quietly sitting in the lounge together and reading after supper if they did not go to the Green Man or one of the bridge clubs. The cancer that he thought might claim his life in a few years' time was not after all the culprit and that could have been a blessing.

The funeral in Enderly church was well attended. Robbie was a popular and respected resident of the village and the Enderly and Little Brinton bridge clubs. John Elk, one of his old colleagues from Oxford and the vicar had addressed the congregation in the church and outlined the life and virtues that pertained to Robbie. Many of the villagers were surprised to hear that Robbie had lived in Enderly as an evacuee and had been a revered college professor. Gasps of amazement were heard as this information was relayed to the congregation.

Refreshments had been arranged for the mourners in the Green Man after the service and many of his friends were invited by Felicity to attend. The room at the back of the pub where they normally played bridge had been set aside for the meal and was packed with the friends, villagers and old colleagues who wished to pay their last respects.

'He was a lovely man,' the vicar said to Felicity as he sipped a glass of good white wine and piled his plate with sandwiches and other delicacies. 'We have been privileged to know him.'

He hoped that Robbie would leave some money to the church. They certainly needed it.

Felicity for once in her life could not think of anything to say. She was stunned and silent as though a mute button on a television control pad had been pressed and her voice had disappeared. She had lost the only man she had ever really cared for, and more importantly come to respect, something she would not have believed possible when she first came to Primrose House in 2004. She was not hungry, indeed her stomach churned with rebellion as she mingled in a trance-like state with the guests. Her voice later returned and emerged as no more than a husky whisper. She thought she gave the right answers when spoken to but was not sure.

Joyce held her arm at one point. She was concerned that Felicity would faint before the meal had been eaten and the guests had departed. She had never liked the woman but felt sorry for her now and an admiration for Felicity was surfacing against her natural instincts and common sense. She could not explain the latter.

'If there is anything I can do . . .' she said, '. . . just phone me or come round and see me at any time.' She, like Robbie, was surprised that she could offer friendship to Felicity but she did now believe that the woman had changed. Without any doubt Felicity was a much more pleasant individual than she had been in the past.

Several of Robbie's old friends from Oxford whom Felicity had never met attended the funeral. A reporter, nosy and brash, pushed himself into the mourning group. He was anxious to obtain a good write-up on the brilliant professor who had abandoned his academic life in Oxford to work as a handyman in Enderly. The once tough and turbulent Felicity continued to be subdued. She hoped they would soon all go away and leave her in peace. Her head ached and her face was white and drawn.

A strange thin elderly woman wearing a smart black suit edged nearer to her. 'I am Julie Barker,' she said, peering at Felicity as though she was observing something that had been dragged out of the gutter. She fidgeted with her expensive slanted glasses, from which artificial diamonds glittered at the hinges, and clutched her large ostentatious black and silver leather bag closer to her side with a movement that suggested that Felicity should not touch it. Felicity felt like a leper. She could not remember sending an invitation to the funeral to a Julie Barker. The solicitor must have invited her. She had made a list of names in an effort to estimate the numbers for the catering but ... she sighed. It was all too much.

'Should I know you?' Felicity muttered.

'I am Robbie's ex-wife my dear, divorced, but I wanted to pay my last respects.' Her eyes roved over Felicity with an unpleasant sharpness.

The dislike was mutual. Felicity woke up. What was this woman's game? She was after his money and the cottage. The will was to be read later that day. This vile woman must have been summoned by Mr Wilkins. She hoped Robbie had not been stupid enough to leave the bitch any of his hard-earned money. She was without any doubt a leech. That she had once craved her aunt's fortune did not enter into the equation. This was quite different.

'Really,' Felicity said, her voice gaining strength. 'Robbie has not mentioned you to me. He did say he was married a long time ago but that the marriage was short and disastrous. Divorce was a blessing.'

She looked innocently at the odious Julie Barker whose face was now flushed and unpleasant.

'We were once very happy,' she retorted, spite spiralling in her thin upper-class voice. 'We were just too young to know our own minds.' She turned her back on Felicity, patted her brassy dyed hair with a well manicured hand, and moved away to help herself to the delicious salmon delicacies on a nearby plate together with another glass of fine white wine.

The proprietor of the Green Man had excelled himself; the spread for the guests and the drinks were the best he could produce. Nothing was too good for Robbie's wake. He was going to miss him as a customer in the pub and in his role of chairman overseeing the bridge club. Producing a good meal in his honour was the least he could do.

Julie Barker strutted over to some of Robbie's old colleagues.

'I am Robbie's ex-wife,' she announced in loud tones to ensure Felicity would hear.

They were taken aback but not impressed which pleased Felicity. It gave her the courage to mingle and make herself known to these strangers. After all, she had been his close companion for the last two years and they had, although it had taken a little while to achieve, been happy. She was told by one Oxford don that Robbie had written to him and told him about her and how much he was enjoying the company of his new woman partner. Felicity was intrigued and the pain of losing him eased a little. Robbie had in the end appreciated her company and that was wonderful.

Mr Wilkins and his young assistant were due to arrive at the cottage at 3.30 p.m. to read the will. There were only a few people summoned by Mr Wilkins and they were keen to hear the contents. The vicar's daughter, the once-gormless Lily, had attended Robbie's funeral and made a point of commiserating with Felicity. She had telephoned Felicity the week before as soon as she heard about Robbie's death.

'I have left home now,' she said, a catch in her usually steady voice, 'and I've almost completed a catering course in Russhampton where I've lived for the past two years. I specialized in bakery and hope to set up in business for myself soon. My aunt has left me a small legacy which will enable me to buy a small tea shop in Russhampton. I would like to help you with the funeral catering,' the girl continued. 'I'll make some biscuits and cakes for the guests at the will reading, that is, if you would like that. It will be my contribution. Mr Barker was always so kind to me. I realize that the main lunch will be held in the Green Man.'

Felicity was surprised. She hoped that her acceptance of the offer would not prove to be a mistake when she thought back to the plain and quiet little girl who had come to help in Primrose House. She was, however, intrigued to see how much Lily had changed when she met her a few days before the funeral to discuss the offer further. Lily looked quite presentable and efficient. She was dressed in a pale blue well-cut suit with smart matching accessories and Felicity accepted her offer with a pleasant smile.

'Thank you so much,' she said. That will be a great help,' and meant it. She was going to provide the tea herself but it was a relief to have the work done for her.

It should not be too much of a disaster, Felicity thought when Lily arrived to make preparations just before the will reading. A whiff of light floral perfume assailed her nostrils. Hmm … lovely scent she thought. She looked at Lily again. The girl's spots had gone leaving a fair flawless skin. Her hair, tinted a deeper shade of blonde than Felicity remembered, was twisted with skill into a neat knot on the top of her head. Her make-up was light and unobtrusive with lips outlined in pale pink lipstick and eyebrows plucked and neatly etched with a dark brown pencil. She wore a plain black dress, suitable for the occasion, and had tied a neat little lace apron around her waist that emphasized her stunning figure. She had expected the girl to rebel once she had left home after years of repression by a domineering father. Felicity was impressed to see that the refreshments, small cakes and home-made biscuits, were displayed in an attractive manner and there was a choice of teas.

Felicity was amused. Lily was no fool and without doubt not the gormless creature she had once dubbed her. She had acted as the meek little vicar's daughter; a good performance Felicity now appreciated, and was today acting the part of the efficient caterer, which indeed she was, and making an excellent job of that role. She would be successful in the business world. Lily's large blue eyes sheltered under lashes that were carefully groomed and lengthened and, as in the past, gave very little information away about their wily owner.

Felicity was anxious to know what Robbie's will contained but she was nowhere as concerned as she had been when Janet had died. She did not expect much. Her hands felt sweaty and she was aching in unexpected places with sheer exhaustion. She would be glad when the day had come to an end though then she would have to think what she was going to do in the future. She wondered in a vague way if Marianne still had a spare room but she didn't think so.

The beneficiaries of the will were soon seated in anticipation in Robbie's lounge. Julie Barker was one of the first to arrive and Felicity gave her a scathing look. Still here, she must be getting something, she thought. A young anxious woman arrived a few minutes later and sat next to her. Who on earth is that scruffy creature? Felicity wondered. A skinny woman with large wild anxious eyes, tangled blonde hair and jeans that emitted a strong smell of dogs, ugh! Joyce Skillet too, well that was to be expected, and John Elk. The vicar … 'Huh, I hope he doesn't get much for that church, some of those repairs he has in mind would be a waste of money,' she muttered to herself. Mr Wilkins and his assistant arrived and sat on slim ladder-backed chairs next to the small antique mahogany table Felicity had placed ready for them, and spread out their papers with care. Lily had covered the refreshments, which were set out on a table in one corner of the room, with an elegant white embroidered cloth. The old grandfather clock that Robbie had loved and had pride of place in a corner of the lounge struck a resounding chime for half past the hour as a feeling of anticipation filled the room.

Mr Wilkins cleared his throat. A hush descended as he outlined the will. There were several small bequests: £5000 to Joyce Skillet, which produced a gasp of surprise from her, £3000 to the church fund for new bells, which prompted Felicity to emit an irritable cough and Lily to fetch her a glass of water, holding up the proceedings for a few minutes. Mr Wilkins then continued, '£2000 to Enderly Bridge Club to buy new equipment and £2000 for his good friends Patsy and John Elk to be used in any way they wish for their new baby.' Felicity smiled. Pity he had not left the £3000 to John and Patsy as well as the £2000. She did not like clanging church bells. They were noisy things. '£10,000 to Julie Barker provided she has not remarried.' Robbie guessed she would not. She was promiscuous and enjoyed her freedom too much to be tied down by a further marriage or a family. She had deserted Robbie for another man a few months after their marriage and he had as a result divorced her. There was no money available to give her at that time and in any case he had then felt that she did not deserve any. However, he indicated in his will that he realised in recent years that they had married when they were both far too young to know what they wanted and a small legacy might be of use in her old age. This had been added to his will during a weak moment of conscience. He considered that he owed her that much because he later understood that he was a confirmed bachelor at heart and should not have married the wretched woman in the first place. The money left to Julie Barker was what she thought of as 'a godsend' but she was too proud and arrogant to admit to anyone how much she needed it, as Robbie had known she would be. She sank back into one of Robbie's armchairs with a triumphant smirk upon her face. Felicity looked at her with disdain and thought that a good slap would not be amiss and far more appropriate than £10,000. What a dreadful woman. I'm not surprised she didn't get married again, she thought, I can't imagine anyone wanting to live with that arrogant tart.

Robbie had arranged to make the cottage available for Felicity Brown to live in for as long as she wished. He had also altered his will to leave her a portion of his numerous investments, to be managed by his financial adviser, which would yield £20,000 a year, also only for as long as she lived. If she died the investments and cottage would revert to the main beneficiary, the Collie Rescue Centre in Everton. The remainder, indeed the bulk of his numerous investments, he had left to them and that amounted to approximately three million pounds. He had obtained his dog Nap from this Centre when he had first moved to Enderly from Oxford and he admired the work that was done there and had, Mr Wilkins explained, until Felicity had proved to be a good companion during the last couple of years, willed the whole of his estate to the Centre. Their representative Miss Eleanor Evans, the thin blonde who reeked of dogs, was startled then beamed widely. She had not expected more than a small donation to the rescue centre.

'We will discuss the details later Miss Evans,' the solicitor said. All heads turned to look at the unkempt young woman.

Felicity was astounded. She was at first oddly subdued then a feeling of elation caught up with her. Bother Miss Evans. She could stay in the cottage she had come to love. There would be no Robbie to keep her company but she understood that many of his books and paintings would remain in place, together with the furnishings, for as long as she lived there and would remind her of him. It would be as though, in some ways, he was still there with her. She would look after it all for him as he wished. That would be her mission for the rest of her life. He requested that the books should go to one of his Oxford University colleagues when Felicity no longer wished to live in the cottage and the paintings and other furnishings would then be sold, together with the cottage.

Robbie had guessed with his usual fine insight that Felicity would continue to read and benefit from his vast collection of books, as she had been doing for the past two years. It had taken him a long time, and a fair amount of study, to understand Felicity's difficulties. He had been gratified that he may have helped a difficult and disturbed individual to come to terms with her inner demons and develop into a more relaxed and balanced person. Although he was not a professional trained to assist hyperactive people he did believe he had come to understand her. From his reading he had concluded that a little ADD could be observed in many people. Indeed, he could see some of it in himself and that had prompted him, together with Alistair Anderson's remarks, to sympathise with his troubled guest. He realized that many people would dismiss the whole idea of ADD as pure fantasy but his experience with Felicity had prompted him to consider it seriously. After a while Felicity had been able to enjoy books without tossing them to one side when only halfway through reading them, and make friends with greater ease. She had shown him genuine affection which she had been incapable of when he first met her. The fact that she was a good bridge player and cook had astonished him. He had discovered that she was a complex individual, full of interest and never dull.

When the other beneficiaries had left Felicity went into the garden and sat by the pond watching the goldfish, their golden scales glinting and flashing in the early evening sunlight as they darted and flitted near the surface of the water. Dear Robbie, she thought, how you loved those fish. I will feed them and look after them for you. She sprinkled some food over the surface and leaned back in one of the new plush garden chairs she had urged Robbie to buy. He had been more generous than she had imagined possible. Tears formed in the corner of her eyes and trickled slowly down her face. She pondered further over his will. She had walked a long and twisted path to get to this stage in her life. She realized with a new and unexpected insight that she was a turbulent and difficult woman and had been lucky to find some peace, security and, what was more important, the understanding of a kind and generous man, which was more than she deserved. This had helped her to achieve some inner peace. She had lived with an internal restlessness for most of her life, something that could only be soothed by challenges. Her obsession with Aunt Janet's money and even competitive bridge provided some outlet for the head of steam that often built up within her. Her mind would become focused on one thing, one goal, at one time and she had not been above violating normal rules of behaviour if that suited her. She now felt a twinge of conscience when she thought about some aspects of her stormy past. Robbie's friendship had boosted her once fragile self-esteem.

She smiled to herself as she cogitated and with genuine tenderness felt the small silver cross on its slender chain that encircled her neck, a family heirloom she understood, and given to her some months before by Robbie.

'Take care of it for me,' he had said. 'It once belonged to my mother and her mother before that.'

He had put it around her neck for her and done up the clasp with trembling fingers.

'I will cherish it,' she said with genuine feeling, and she did. She wore it every day. It was her most prized possession.

She did, however, continue to ponder on Robbie's will. I wonder what that Collie Rescue Centre will do with all that money? she thought. Do they really need it? Robbie was the most generous and sweet man but that legacy did not make sense, at least not to her. She was convinced that there must be a better way to employ his capital than housing and feeding a few mangy dogs. She doubted whether there was anything that could be done to reverse that part of his will, in any case that was what the dear man wanted, but it was a very interesting thought, after all she had become his partner during the last part of his life; surely she was more important. He had come to care enough for her to see that she was provided for. Well ... she would perhaps explore the possibilities. In any case she could, in her usual way, dream about it. She guessed that Robbie knew she would. She laughed out loud. She realized too that towards the end of his life he had accepted her for the person she was and given her true understanding and she appreciated that there is no act between two human beings that requires greater skill.

The only things that she had been able to concentrate on in the past were typing, cooking and bridge. Organizing her life had always been difficult; many activities left her irritated and bored but thanks to Robbie she was now managing well. He was the first person during the whole of her life who had been able to help her and she was grateful. The sad little evacuee Tom Hands and the unwanted and misunderstood Felicity Brown, once they had overcome their initial dislike and suspicions, had ultimately formed a mutually beneficial partnership, the composition of which very few of their friends and acquaintances would ever comprehend.

Felicity discovered that she could relax at last. She would miss Robbie with a depth of feeling she had not known was possible but knew she had good times to look forward to and intended to make the most of the comfort Robbie had bestowed upon her. She no longer looked young; her tapir nose appeared more pronounced than it ever had but she was not too concerned about that. Romance was no longer on her agenda. She had looked that day in the mirror in her bedroom at the strong streaks of grey that cloaked her hair, which were becoming more difficult to cover for any length of time with colour rinses; the crows feet at the corners of her eyes stood out like fine bunches of grape stalks whilst her thinning mouth had become streaky and crinkled but her once greedy and hard-looking blue eyes had softened. Her face had become what could be described by many people as appealing.

A few months later a retired widower by the name of Jack Headley purchased the small cottage next door to Felicity. She heard that he had been living near his sister in Scotland for the past few years but was a native of Russetshire. She heard too that he had lived in Little Brinton for a while and was the first chairman of the Little Brinton Bridge Club but had left the area under a cloud after being wrongly convicted of murder. She understood that nobody expected him to return to Russetshire and his return was the subject of some gossip in the local bridge clubs. A few weeks after he moved in Jack asked Felicity to play with him in the Enderly club. She hesitated for a while before accepting. She was aware that he liked her and was curious to find out more about him. She wondered what his plans were. He would never take Robbie's place as a friend but might be a useful bridge partner and some masculine company if she needed it. Well … he was not bad looking, rather conceited and not her type; she was far too old for him anyway. She was intrigued. There must be a strong reason for his return to Russetshire after the murder scandal even if he was an innocent victim. She had heard a rumour that the real culprit, Jack Headley's brother-in-law George Berry, had been arrested and was to stand trial for that murder and other heinous crimes in South Africa. She surmised that Jack must think that he was now free of any suspicions in the minds of the locals in Little Brinton and that thought had provided him with the courage he needed to return to the area. Knowing the locals as she did, Felicity considered him to be foolish but it would be interesting to find out how much money, if any, he had tucked away. That was, of course, purely academic. She laughed and her spirits lifted as a plan began to form in her mind and her fertile imagination, as so often in the past, took flight. It was good to have something like that to think about again.

List of Characters

Alistair Anderson	Son of James Anderson and Judith
James Anderson	Janet's first husband
Aunt Dolly and Uncle Bert	Richard Brown's elderly aunt and uncle
Julie Barker	Ex-wife of Robbie Barker
George Berry	Brother of Jack Headley's dead wife
Mrs Blunt	Little Brinton shopkeeper
Bob	Richard Brown's Canadian friend and Felicity's employer
Anne Brown	James Anderson's sister; mother of Felicity Brown
Felicity Brown	Janet's niece; daughter of Anne and Richard Brown
Richard Brown	Father of Felicity and Ronald
Ronald Brown	Son of Anne and Richard; Felicity's brother
Mrs Betty Bumble	Boutique owner, Brinton
Mary Butterfield	Rosalie's mother
Rosalie Butterfield	Daughter of Mary Butterfield
Timothy Carter	Solicitor's clerk
Mrs Connolly	Robbie Barker's cleaning lady
Mrs Crabb	Local Authority employee
Patsy Croft	Bridge club secretary

DS John Cross	Detective, assistant to DI Peter Holmes
Karl Davies	Murdered South African jockey
John Elk	Bridge player
Eleanor Evans	Dog Rescue Centre representative
Pat Field	Elderly Enderly resident and bridge player
Marianne Fright	Felicity's bridge-playing friend
Ruth Hands	Tom Hands' mother
Robert Hands	Tom Hands' father
Tom Hands/Robbie Barker	Evacuee Tom Hands, later known as Robbie Barker
Jack Headley	First chairman and founder of Little Brinton Bridge Club
DI Peter Holmes	Local detective
Liz Jeffries	Granddaughter of Mary Butterfield
Ellie Jeffries	Great granddaughter of Mary Butterfield
Johnny	Anne's wartime Canadian boyfriend
Lily Jones	Daughter of Enderly vicar
Judith	Mother of Alistair Anderson
Jack Lacey	Entrepreneur father of John Lacey
John Lacey	Academic son of Jack Lacey
Pamela Lacey	John Lacey's first wife
Jeremy Mace	Solicitor son of Peter Mace
Matthew Mace	Peter Mace's grandson
Peter Mace	Janet Lacey's old friend and solicitor
Alicia Merryweather	Mother of Janet and host to evacuee Tom Hands
Janet Merryweather	Daughter of Alicia and Will, wife of James Anderson and later John Lacey

Will Merryweather	Husband of Alicia and father of Janet
Helen Moore	Pattie Moore's daughter, works for Janet's financial adviser
Pattie Moore	Felicity's friend
John Peters	Alistair Anderson's stepfather
Anne Robinson	Enderly School headmistress
Roderick	Red-headed publican, the Green Man, Enderly
Roberto	Felicity's Canadian partner
Joyce Skillet	Janet Lacey's housekeeper
Tim	Grouchy landlord of the Red Rooster, Little Brinton
Richard West	Shady private detective
Alan Wilkins	Solicitor
Ned Windsor	Chairman of Little Brinton Bridge Club

Lightning Source UK Ltd.
Milton Keynes UK
12 October 2009

144837UK00001B/38/P

9 780956 341907